For my new
friend Jo'u
life is good
you don't wear
L.D. Sledge

DAWN'S REVENGE

L.D. Sledge

Cover Photo provided by Ville Nikula
ISBN-10: 1463720092
EAN-13: 9781463720094

To Jake, who will live forever in my heart.

Praises and Reviews for Dawn's Revenge

"Your *Dawn's Revenge* is a true thriller that kept me intrigued and captivated. I particularly enjoyed the local color in your settings and characters. I found my senses savoring typical New Orleans scenes and colorful Louisiana characters given vivid life by your superior descriptive powers. Your keen knowledge of the New Orleans legal and political system was obvious in your creative yet bizarre manipulation of the system's characters. The reader is so drawn into the powerful plot that he is relieved to realize that life has sheltered him from such heinous realities that are deeply disturbing. What a refreshing surprise to, at last, see an accurate portrayal of a true Cajun character. Nookie Naquin will win hearts.
Edwin W. Edwards, Four Term Governor of Louisiana.

"I raced through this book. It is a wonder that Sledge can document the existence of the seamy side of life while maintaining our hope for a better way. His description of New Orleans, the Cajun culture, swamps and bayous, and a few Louisiana politicians are not to be missed. Fact is often stranger than fiction. Truly, a fantastic read."
Buddy Roemer, Governor of Louisiana

"The exotic streets of New Orleans' French Quarter and the mysterious swamps of south Louisiana have attracted writers from Longfellow to Anne Rice, Faulkner to James Lee Burke. They provide the setting for a thriller by Baton Rouge attorney Sledge, who doesn't write like a guy who has a day job. It is a gripping, fast moving tale about Jack Chandler, an under-achieving French Quarter lawyer who takes on the corrupt power structure to uncover a ring of child molesters. Jack is running for his life during a massive hurricane. (written in 1993 with an accurate prediction of Katrina complete with breaking the levees) He is in love with a bright, beautiful woman, Dr. Victoria Keens-Dennison, whose heritage encompasses Trinidad and Casablanca, with "Moorish features and emerald eyes", but she is black, and he hesitates to cross the line. The story may be fictional, but the kind of description in this book is by a man who knows his territory and presents it realistically, warts and all. Such honesty alone is worth the price of the book."
Smiley Anders, Baton Rouge Advocate Staff Writer

"What do you get when you mix murder with magnolias, Cajuns and corrupt police officers, a dead body and the bayous of South Louisiana? You get one thrilling novel by Baton Rouge lawyer and Louisiana native, L. D. Sledge. It reads much like a hard-boiled detective novel with Sledge providing the requisite bad guys, chase scenes, overactive libidos and a simmering inter-racial love interest. Some of his finest writing is found in the subplot describing the romantic entanglements between Jack and Victoria, the Tulane pathologist. Sledge's use of inner monologues about Jack's feeling of inadequacy and uncertainty about Victoria are short, thoughtful and sometimes hilarious."
Kevin Cuccia, Shreveport Times Writer

"This book is provocative. Sledge explores all the taboos which are more times than not swept under the carpet. Subjects such as child molestation, interracial relationships, and corruption in the political, justice and social welfare systems.
The Gonzales Weekly

"L D Sledge, prominent attorney-turned-author, lived and worked in the New Orleans French Quarter before establishing a 43 year private practice in Baton Rouge. Validity of his fictional thriller demonstrates keen observations by a rampant imagination penned by a true wordsmith. The bizarre modus operandi of his plot hits so close to real life headlines that the author leaves little doubt of a certain first-hand knowledge of the Quarter's darker edges. A parallel plot of biracial romance adds to the exotic titillation, seducing the reader at every bend of the bayou and stalk on the wild side. Be prepared to experience residual sensory overload that will linger with longing much like the adrenaline rush of skiing a perfect powder black-diamond slope. The mental exhilaration is worth a visit to your local bookstore.
Penny Meaux, Writer for Baker Observer

"The first thing you need to be a writer is the ability to write well. L.D. proves that hands down in *Dawn's Revenge.* His writing style is clear while at the same time very descriptive. The second thing is a good story. *Dawn's Revenge* will satisfy your quest for a really interesting tale. He puts a lot of himself into the yarn. Jack is one of those guys in a cramped little office who has trouble paying the light bill much of the time, but he likes to do the right thing in the name of his profession. It gets him into a lot of trouble in 308 pages of intrigue, swamps, snakes and bad guys. And, oh yes, there's a love angle too. A love angle that gets into that controversial area called crossing the racial line. Here's Jack falling for a beautiful woman with Trinidad and Casablanca as a heritage. This may not play too well in Des Moines, but it makes a really interesting part of LD's story."
Lou Major, Editor, Bogalusa Daily News

_____

From Amazon:

5.0 out of 5 stars *Dawn's Revenge* **is the most captivating book I have ever read.**
By A Customer

I was working in a Houma, Louisiana bookstore and Mr. L.D. Sledge was invited for an author signing. To prepare for the day I read the summary of *Dawn's Revenge*. As a native of Louisiana, I found it quite intriguing. Being an avid reader, I purchased the book and had it autographed. This was one of the wisest things I have ever done. I have found what I believe to be one of the best Louisiana authors in a long time. Mr. Sledge describes southern Louisiana flawlessly; the humid summers, the voodoo culture, the corrupt politics, even the lifestyle of the Vieux Carre'. *Dawn's*

Revenge has definitely become my favorite novel. I have not been as enchanted with or satisfied by a selection since I completed this book. Mr. Sledge I am anxiously awaiting your next release.
Avid Reader

We've got four little kids so I don't have a lot of extra time. But I'm making time to read *Dawn's Revenge* because once I started I couldn't stop. There's a bit of everything: murder, love, action/suspense, foul weather and the intriguing city of New Orleans. I'm half way through now and find myself looking forward to the little bit of time I have before going to sleep so I can pick it up again. Can't wait for L.D. Sledge's next book too!
Literati in London

I was hooked from the first page. This book is filled with suspense. Originally from New Orleans I could see everyplace described clearly as I read. This book is a definite must read.
Barbara the Book Babe

"Dawn's Revenge was recommended to me as a "good read." It was all that and more. A fast paced story in N'Orleans, with totally believable characters, and a gritty environment that makes this book a page turner with a very surprising end. Warmly Recommended.
Stu Sjouwerman, Clearwater, Florida.

"Gripping stuff. Couldn't put it down."
Ken Klaebe, Sidney, Australia

I was interested in this novel for two reasons. One, I'm a Sledge originally from Louisiana and two, I had just returned from New Orleans when the book was published, I was delighted to find out that the author will give the name of Sledge a good turn. He wrote a captivating, engrossing mystery. After having been in New Orleans in July, I could feel the heat in the streets there as he described it. It was a pleasure to read a story with interesting characters and scenarios. I hope he writes another soon.
Elizabeth J. Sledge, Oak Harbor, Washington.

I don't read a lot and usually if a book does not grab me from the get-go, it's gone and forgotten. With *Dawn's Revenge* I could not put the book down. I actually felt somewhat despondent when it ended. The story was gripping. The setting made me want to go to Louisiana and stay there – the author's love for the land shines through and is infectious. The way Dawn was actually revenged, brilliant, absolutely brilliant. And the main character, you can't help actually being right there with him. I would recommend this book to anyone. Actually, writing this review, rekindled my passion

for it. I think that now I have to go back and read it again!
Carolina Terzi, Sunland CA

I read *Dawns Revenge* several years ago and I was stuck by the idea that Sledge lived a wild and exciting life and knows the underbelly of the New Orleans culture like the back of his hands and can express it in vivid detail. He has a deep understanding of humans and can bring up things hidden for all to see. It was fascinating to get an inside view of Cajun culture and experience a terrifying storm as well. This book is a page turner and will keep you up late.
Ron Kessinger, Artist and Designer, Denver, Colorado

~

Read Other Books by L D Sledge

At the end of this book, read chapters from two other novels by this author.

Command Influence is a courtroom thriller, a fictionalized account of an actual military courtmartial defended and won by L D Sledge while he served as a Captain in the Judge Advocate General (JAG), U.S. Army in the early sixties.

Nimrod's Peril is a literate adult fantasy of a young Wanderer on a huge planet that is mostly unexplored. His beautiful human size-mouse traveling companion is kidnapped and he is on a quest to rescue her.

Other published works:

No Fail Hiring, Your Ultimate Guide to Attracting and Recruiting Top Players In a Troubled Economy, co-written with Patrick Valtin, international management consultant, on the problems and solutions to hiring employees in the United States.

Riches to Rags, Why Celebrities and Pro-Athletes go Broke and How to Avoid it. Originally ghost written for Dr. Ernest Pecoraro. An easy to read and apply manual on money management that should be in every high school curriculum-for everyone but designed for celebs and pro-athletes.

DAWN'S REVENGE

A PROSE POEM TO NEW ORLEANS

The people of New Orleans with French, Spanish, Indian, and Black legacies mixed in a tumble of cultures often live cheek by jowl on tight, narrow streets. Their very breath is a living fusion of their history, their blood the blood of pirates, prisoners, pilgrims, adventurers, mercenaries, scoundrels, speculators, royalty and slaves. Within their breasts beats the hearts of all their forebears, the past barely concealed beneath the surface of present memory, and it can be felt in the scorching summer day, the sultry nights and in the cool mists and fogs that hang low on the back ways and hard against the levee at daybreak. It can be heard in the cacophony of the streets, the midnight bark of dogs, the crow of roosters, and the sounds from the river. The people are at one with all this and the fragrance of night blooming jasmine, tastes and smells of coffee and chicory, red beans and rice, sauce piquante and cold beer, crawfish and gumbo. The stilled passions of the ages sleep, sated with the fatness of the present. But it is an uneasy sleep. Everyone there feels it, knows it, and embraces the togetherness of their past and present as a blessing.

Chapter 1

DAY ONE

The tired whore counted out four hundred dollars in tens and twenties and laid them on the desk. She sat back and said, "That's all I got right now."

Jack Chandler looked at the stack of rumpled bills for a moment and raised his eyes to his client. "You can pay the other hundred later, Queenie," ruefully thinking any other lawyer would charge three times that to defend her on the petty theft charge. He looked at his watch. It was after midnight.

She stood regally and smoothed her dress as she looked down at Jack. "Sorry I bothered you so late. I had a lengthy engagement. I'll have the rest tomorrow."

"You're good for it," he said, walking her to the door. She always paid and always came back.

Jack retrieved her umbrella from the hat tree in the hall. "It's pouring out there. Will you be okay? Let me call a taxi."

Queenie turned fully around and faced Jack. She grasped his hand in her long, cool fingers and looked him straight in the eye. She broke into a smile that Jack knew was the real paycheck for helping people like this.

"Thanks for the thought, honey," she said. "Queenie's always fine. You know, you don't charge enough. That's why you ain't rich. See you tomorrow."

Shaking his head at the grim truth of her observation, Jack watched her unfurl the umbrella and step into the deluge that made a river out of Royal Street. He returned to his desk, slumped into his chair, and took a deep drag from the cigarette he had left steaming in the ash tray.

The phone rang.

"Not another one," he groaned.

It kept ringing until he wearily answered. He immediately became alert when he heard his housekeeper's frantic voice.

"Lawyer Jack," she wailed, "they killed her! She didn't commit suicide. I swear to God she didn't. They killed her!"

"Hang on, Estelle," Jack interrupted, "Who are you talkin' about? Who killed who?"

Estelle choked down her racking sobs and gasped, "My baby. Dawn Marie. She's dead! They killed her! Oh my God! Oh my God!"

"Who killed her, Estelle?"

"I don't know. They just called and said she was down at Charity Morgue—to come identify her. Oh my lord!"

"What did they say? What happened?"

"They said she was arrested for shopliftin' down by Holmes's Department Store, and they put her into Juvenile Detention and she killed herself. She ain't done no such thing, lawyer Jack. Oh, Lordy, Lordy!"

Fighting the impulse to be pulled into Estelle's torrential emotion, Jack asked, "When're you goin' to Charity?"

"Me'n Martin, we goin' right now. I ain't waitin' another minute."

"You ain't goin' without me. Come by here first," Jack ordered, frowning into the phone. "I'll go with you, okay?"

"Anything you say, Lawyer Jack. I don't know what I'm gonna do. She's my only baby."

"Estelle, listen to me. Pick me up on the way, you hear?"

"Yessir, Lawyer Jack. We'll be there."

Jack hung up and stubbed out the smoldering butt that had burned too short to hold. Pressing the heels of his hands against his eyes didn't relieve the pressure swelling in there. He let out a long sigh. The call from his housekeeper echoed in his head as he stared numbly at the midnight rain beating against the windows of his French Quarter law office.

It was one in the morning and he was going to the morgue.

Jack slugged down the rest of the warm Dixie beer and tossed the empty can into a trash can across the room. Estelle had cleaned just that morning and it was a mess again. Books and papers were scattered on the chairs and tables. Another late night researching and drafting documents. He wasn't about to pick up until morning.

After locking the door behind him, his steps echoed in the wide hallway of the Marquis de Mandeville Apartments. He walked toward a long, winding staircase, lighted at the foot by a dim bulb in an elaborate sconce.

On the second floor, a hallway switched back to lead to his apartment directly above his office. The tall sliding doors rumbled open smoothly, revealing a one bedroom apartment with bath, sitting room, fireplace, kitchenette, and balcony with Spanish wrought-iron grillwork overlooking the narrow French Quarter street below.

Jack splashed water in his face at the bathroom sink and looked in the mirror. His cold gray eyes beheld a trim, well-built young man of thirty with a two day stubble and dark hair pulled straight back and tied in a short pony tail.

He went straight to the refrigerator and regarded the extent of his larder. Other than two six-packs of Dixie, there was a well-whittled ham, an almost empty jar of Miracle Whip, wilted lettuce, mustard, peanut butter, apple jelly, eggs and some T.V. dinners in the freezer compartment. Assorted boxes of old Chinese, Italian and Mexican take-outs were scattered throughout in various stages of decomposition. Everything needed for adventures in bachelor dining.

Jack popped the top of a cold Dixie and went through the sliding glass doors onto a wide, vine covered gallery overlooking Royal Street. The roof over the balcony leaked. He pulled a chair from beneath the drip to a dry spot and sat heavily. After taking a sip, he shook out a Picayune cigarette and lit it with an old Zippo.

As he thought of Dawn, he flashed back to having seen her just that morning as he entered his office. He was greeted by two cheery voices. "Hi lawyer jack!"

He remembered smiling when he realized Estelle, his housekeeper and her daughter, Dawn, were cleaning his office this morning.

Dawn was in her jeans and T shirt, and Jack felt his gut tighten at the raw promise of this young girl. He cursed himself for the reaction. *Dirty old man,* he thought. *But great godamighty is that a fine innocent young thing.*

"No school today, Dawn?"

"Teacher's meeting. So I'm helping mama clean."

"That's cool. What's that?" He pointed at some movement in her backpack sitting on a chair.

"Oh," said Dawn, "that's Gris Gris."

A black kitten with bright yellow eyes poked its head out of the opening at its name and mewed at Dawn. When she picked it up she was nuzzled and nibbled energetically by the kitten. Dawn glowed, holding it close.

At that instant, the sun broke through the clouds, with Dawn silhouetted before the tall many paned windows facing the street. The prismed hand blown and beveled glass imparted a halo of rainbowed light that seemed to surround her, and Jack fancied a joyful warmth radiating from her that enveloped him. *Wow,* he thought, *your imagination is working overtime this morning.*

He returned to present time and shook his head at the awful thought of that beautiful young girl lying cold in the morgue, and what really had happened.

Traffic had almost slowed to a stop because of the heavy rain. At one in the morning, the Quarter streets would normally be jammed with tourists, drunk conventioneers, whores, pimps, glassy-eyed hippies, queers, and sailors from the merchant ships docked just behind the levee. Tonight it was impossible to go out without getting drenched.

The sky would occasionally crackle in a blaze of sizzling lightning, followed by an ear-splitting blast that rattled an empty Dixie can sitting on the little marble-topped table. The night embraced Jack in a warm, damp caress, possessing a strange expectant feeling; that quiet intimation that something was about to happen. He tried to relax and sucked in the soft, lulling aphrodisia of the New Orleans midnight, glad he was alone.

An old pickup honked beneath his balcony just as he finished the second Dixie. He flipped the cigarette over the railing, grabbed a raincoat and hustled downstairs, dreading what he was about to confront.

Estelle stared bleakly through the rain streaked pickup window. The door swung open and Jack darted through the deluge and slid in alongside of her.

Estelle had on her going-to-church clothes. She wore a dress of white satin that emphasized, rather than down-played her rotund figure, a white pillbox hat, white patent leather pumps, and gripped a small beaded purse in a white-gloved hand. Jack hardly recognized her. Her usual attire was the nondescript dress of cleaning women. She was quite pretty after all, done up like that, but her eyes were red, and she was trembling.

Gripping her left hand was a light-skinned man with cold green eyes and a pencil-thin, precisely trimmed moustache. The muscles of this huge man were barely concealed beneath his shiny black suit with its white tie.

Not knowing the proper attire to visit a dead daughter, they did the best they could.

The man was Martin Delacroix, Estelle's husband and Dawn's father, a longshoreman who worked the wharves on the New Orleans side of the river. Martin's cold glare attempted to hide the underlying suppressed grief raging beneath like a torrential subterranean river. Estelle appeared to be wrung dry.

They drove slowly through the downpour, as Martin reiterated what Estelle had briefly explained on the phone earlier, except he went into more detail.

The officer said Dawn Marie hanged herself in the cell with a sheet she had torn into strips. Estelle shook her head in disbelief. "She's my only baby," she said from time to time.

Dawn was the center of their lives. The horror of her death was more than appalling because of where she died and the chosen method. Their suspicions of a darker truth lent an element of outrage crying for an answer. It was all too unlikely.

The facts presented were so improbable that Jack knew they were thinking it was all a hideous dream that would surely end soon and they would wake to find Dawn Marie living and laughing with them again.

The image of Dawn Marie sprang into his mind: sixteen, cafe-au-lait complexion and soft almond eyes that would stagger a man. She wasn't the type to steal anything, or to take her own life—that Jack knew for sure. He had always thought of her as a seductively innocent little girl with the body of a woman. Now she was dead, and he was going to have to see her corpse. That somewhat mysterious womanchild's untimely death echoed her name: Dawn. She had been snuffed out in the dawn of her life.

Estelle had cleaned Jack's office and apartment for three years and had come to confide in him. She turned to him and said, "This ain't happenin' is it? You know my Dawn Marie, Lawyer Jack, she real special. She ain't jes my chile. No, sir. You see, she. . ."

Estelle sucked in her next words as Martin gently touched her trembling arm. He seemed to caution her against speaking further. Jack was puzzled at this knowing exchange that lapsed Dawn Marie's parents into an unknown abyss of secrecy. Jack respected their intimacy, but had that gut level feeling that Estelle had considered revealing some mysterious knowledge to him before Martin intervened. It may have been nothing more than the invisible barrier that existed between black and white, regardless of their closeness, and Jack respected that.

Jack said nothing, but hugged her and watched as she gripped the illusive and tentative edges of sanity. He could see her scouring the outer reaches of her mind for some vestige of hope that all of this was unreal.

Jack fought his impulse to be drawn into their gut wrenching anguish. He wished he wasn't so damned empathetic, feeling other people's emotions so strongly. Of all the people in the world, they had chosen him to walk them through the nightmare labyrinth of their despair. And he didn't know what the hell to do about it.

Since law school, Jack's last five years scratching out a living handling everything that came through the door gave him nothing to provide counsel for what he was about to face.

He could go with them, they would identify the body, and the ordeal would play itself out in time. Estelle and Martin would somehow adjust to this horrible loss. He could simply do some hand patting and that would be that.

They drove up Rampart to Canal and then over to Tulane Avenue. Charity Hospital, sitting alongside Tulane and L.S.U. medical schools, is a two block long, 16-story mountain of cement and mortar built in the thirties by Huey Long, legendary governor of Louisiana.

They parked on the street near the emergency room entrance.

Martin took an umbrella from behind the seat and held it over Jack and Estelle's head as the three splashed over the flooded sidewalk to the overhang at the rear door to the hospital.

The grimy halls were filled with patients. Some still bled from knife fights, sitting apathetically beside expectant mothers, accident victims, and every kind of infirmity that needed hurried care. But care didn't hurry at Charity. No cheer, no smiles, and the mood reeked of fear and death at the best of times.

The emergency room at Charity was a crucible of experience for new interns and resident physicians who wanted to see, in one large dose of hands on, every conceivable kind of physical problem man could have.

Jack steeled himself and led the miserable pair through the lines of pathetic, ailing humanity.

An orderly pointed down a dim hallway to a large smudged and scarred elevator door. The slow descent took them to the basement and an even more dimly lit corridor.

Estelle went rigid, and began to mumble incoherently. Martin, tall and massive alongside the diminutive but rotund Estelle, seemed to try to cover her, to block the horror tearing at her, whispering words of assurance that she didn't hear. Their steps rang hollow against the dead gray walls as they walked slowly toward what waited beyond the large metal door at the end of the hall.

A morose, sallow-faced orderly in a gray smock turned to face them. The little man raised his thin eyebrows questioningly at the three who had the temerity to, unbidden, trespass into his silent world of formaldehyde, chrome and cold clay.

"Estelle Delacroix to make an identification," Jack said, assuming a voice and stern expression that worked on people like this. Jack pulled himself up to his nearly six feet and looked the little gnome of a man straight into his watery eyes and added coldly, "now!"

The orderly stooped slightly and lowered his head, looking sidelong at Jack as if he was about to be struck. Jack thought of Igor, Dr. Frankenstein's assistant, the hunchback with the bulging eye.

"Well?" Jack said impatiently.

"Dr. Sanchez," the gnome said quietly, pointing to an open door just a few feet from where they stood.

Jack led his little group through the door to a small windowless office. An immense, florid-faced man sat behind a desk. The man's small black eyes lifted from a magazine and beheld his midnight visitors. The little plastic plate on his desk read, "Ramon Sanchez, M.D., Deputy Coroner."

"Dr. Sanchez?" Jack asked. "Estelle Delacroix was called to make identification?"

The man peered at a stained appointment calendar and nodded. He rose from his chair and, saying nothing, walked toward the trio standing in the door as if he were going to walk through them. He was as tall as Martin and owned the kind of gut that bulged below the belt.

Sanchez brushed past them and opened the large metal door into a refrigerated room with banks of pull out drawer compartments. They all knew what was in those drawers.

Estelle began to shake and moan, and Martin tried to soothe her. He spoke in low tones saying, "Now, it's okay, baby. It's gonna be okay. We'll be through all this here in jus' a minute, Mama."

Dr. Sanchez headed straight to a drawer and pulled it open with no hesitation or fanfare. His little pig eyes turned coldly to Estelle as she viewed the sheet-covered form lying on the cold tray before her.

Sanchez pulled the cover back and Estelle shrieked and fainted dead away in Martin's arms. Martin's eyes protruded at the sight of his daughter lying there, her creamy complexion now a waxy yellow, long ebony hair resting on her naked shoulder.

Dawn Marie's death and the sight of her mortal remains were enough to paralyze a parent into stupefaction, but the thing of alarm was the expression frozen on her delicate features. And her once beautiful full lips were swollen and cracked—like they had been bruised.

Martin struggled to hold Estelle's dead weight up while he and Jack stared at the body.

The deputy coroner's eyes never left the faces of the two men who gaped in revulsion at what the little body before them suggested. Sanchez had a hooded look, watching revelations develop on Jack's face.

"As you can gather, this is Dawn Marie Delacroix, and Martin here is her father," Jack said.

Martin nodded slowly, deadpan as tears washed his cheeks.

"How did she die?" Jack asked.

"Suicide."

"How?"

"Hanging. Used a sheet."

"Is that your conclusion or the medical examiner?"

Sanchez recoiled at Jack's suggestion that the head coroner's opinion of the cause of death may possess a flaw. "It is the opinion of Dr. Marriot, Orleans Parish Coroner."

Jack fumbled with his next decision and, gritting his teeth, said, "Okay, let's see the rest."

"What do you mean?" Sanchez snarled.

"I want to see the rest of the body," Jack ordered, staring Sanchez directly in the eye.

Sanchez began pushing the drawer shut, saying, "You've seen enough."

Jack grasped the sheet and swept it back before Sanchez could stop him.

The trim, naked body of Dawn Marie lay before them. Martin and Jack sucked in their breath at what they saw. The skin between her thighs and her groin was raw and bruised. There were scrapes and scratches on her abdomen and dried blood caked and smeared her belly and mons pubis. Abrasions on her wrists and ankles suggested that they had been bound. A thick blackish smear of dried blood had collected around an inch long penetrating wound directly between her breasts.

Jack suppressed his rage. If Martin had not been holding Estelle's heavy body, he probably would have attacked Sanchez just to vent his rage at anyone near.

She was murdered, Jack thought, *and what can I do about it?*

Jack tried to keep the mounting fury from his voice. "Well, let me tell you, Dr. Sanchez, what I see here demands an inquest and autopsy. I'm going to petition for an inquest, a thorough autopsy with retained pathologists when it's conducted. I'm officially asking that this body not be touched until every test known to modern pathology be conducted, fairly, and in keeping with accepted standards."

Sanchez snapped the cover back over Dawn's body then slammed the drawer back into the wall. He said nothing and stormed back through the morgue. Martin struggled with Estelle, who was reviving in his arms.

Sanchez was talking to someone on the phone when Jack opened the closed door. Sanchez snarled, "Do you know how to knock?"

"Sanchez," Jack glared back, "I'm goin' to the district judge when I leave here and get a court order to keep anyone from doing anything with her until we can get some independent people to double check. I'm gonna get a restraining order to stop you from doing anything with her. If you so much as open that drawer again before we get some people over here I'll call the D.A. and the U.S. Attorney so fast it'll make your fat head swim. I guarantee the Sheriff and the TV boys are gonna find it damn interesting."

Sanchez watched Jacks agitation indifferently, all the while holding the phone open so the party at the other end could hear everything Jack said.

Jack spun out of the room and caught up with Martin and Estelle. His head reeled with what he had seen and what he had to do. Martin's face was drawn into a pinched mask of despair and Estelle clung to him as they stumbled blindly away from the unacceptable truth lying cold in the box behind them.

"I'm gonna do something about this," Jack said quietly with grim determination. "Too late tonight. Gotta stop 'em from doin' anything more."

Jack removed his shirt and pants and threw them on the furniture as he walked through the apartment.

In the bedroom, bookshelves reaching toward the high ceiling sagged with a wild variety of books ranging from music, art, history and science fiction to calculus, poker, whisky distilling and street fighting. Several landscape oils Jack had painted hung about the room in a haphazard fashion, and a guitar leaned against a table on which were scattered attempts at writing poetry and short stories. A set of well-used barbells and dumbbells were in the corner.

As tired as he was, Jack's eyes narrowed in a satisfied smile as he briefly took inventory of his small arsenal. A sawed off pump shotgun leaned against the wall by the bed, a snub-nosed .38 revolver hung from the bedpost in a shoulder holster, and a .32 automatic was tucked in a backpack hanging over the chair. Three rifles of varying calibers stood behind his hanging clothes in the closet, with a secret hidden closet within that hid his prize weapons. To round out his edged weapons armory, a razor sharp bowie knife in a scabbard hung from the closet doorknob; an epee', a civil war saber, and a pirate cutlass lay in a gun rack hanging on the wall.

Jack was ready. As a matter of fact, he secretly wished an opportunity would present itself to use what these weapons were created for.

Deep in the core of Jack's psyche slumbered an artist without an art, a diamond that probably would never get polished. His fires were well banked, but were easily kindled, depending on the stimuli. Once, a lady visitor beheld the jumble of art, books, and weapons. She asked him what he thought himself to be. He said, after a moments consideration, "Poet, lover, swordsman—barbarian."

He pressed a button on the air conditioner and the wall shook for a moment before the old unit settled into its job of pumping out cool air into the stuffy bedroom. The sheets were cool; he tried to read but his eyes kept closing.

In the middle of the night, Jack sat up in bed, trembling, drenched in sweat. After a few moments, he gained control of his quaking body and realized where he was.

He had survived it again. The interminable chase had haunted his dreams since he was a child. The same vast glacial spaces, the same icy rivers cutting through deep evergreen forests emptying into turquoise lakes, and the same faceless pursuer. Why was he running? What was it about whatever, or whoever, it was behind him that challenged his very soul? He could never escape, nor could he turn to confront whatever followed just beyond the last turn. Yet he felt the distance narrowing between them. *What could that mean? Probably nothing. Nothing at all.*

Jack laid back down and allowed his pulse to calm, trying to convince himself for the thousandth time that the dream was not real. It was always so real. *Is this real—this life—this room? Could it all be illusion? What was real? The damned dream seemed real enough,* he thought as he dozed back off to sleep.

Just before daybreak, the great bells of the St. Louis Cathedral tolled the hour. He awoke, fuzzily remembered what he had to do, and frowned.

The bathroom mirror was unkind. His hair fell over his face and his eyes were bloodshot. Jack scowled at the image, feeling just like he looked. Then he went out on the balcony and looked at the gray light of dawn laboring to illuminate the Quarter. The rain had stopped. There was no wind, only the steady movement of dead gray clouds scudding from the south. The air felt odd. *Barometric pressure is dropping,* he thought.

A strange dread seemed to fill the morning. "Must be the storm," he said aloud.

Jack turned on the T.V. Overnight the tropical depression had developed into a hurricane named Aurora and was headed north. Spawned in the Atlantic, it moved westward and gained momentum, chewing its way up the Florida Gulf Coast. The storm was predicted to move inland somewhere along the Florida panhandle.

Jump-started by two large mugs of scalding coffee and chicory, followed by thirty minutes of calisthenics, weights, and a cold shower, Jack felt that he could face what the day had to offer.

The strange feeling didn't leave. *Hum,* Jack thought, *it must be this Aurora. What the hell! Hurricane time is party time around here. Everybody takes off and has a good time.* Jack wrinkled his brow and waited for the conclusion to allay his uneasy feeling.

It didn't.

Chapter 2

DAY TWO

Knowing it was too early to reach anybody, Jack decided a walk might shake the strange feeling he was experiencing. He pulled on a pair of jeans, T-shirt and sneakers, then headed down Royal Street.

The streets were wet and the Quarter slowly woke to an overcast, muggy day. The air was oppressively still. There was little movement so early in the day, and Jack's spirits lifted as he briskly walked over the uneven, broken sidewalks, allowing the streets to work their spell.

All day the rays of the swollen summer sun licks the Quarter like a mother dog licks her puppies, and the steamy breath of the river fuses with the flatulence of the primeval ooze snoring just below the broken pavements. In the evening, after these elementals punch out following a hard day's work at suffocating the city, the residents sit on their stoops or balconies and talk, laugh, drink, and fan the steeping day into steeping night.

Behind those closed, cypress casement shutters, denizens of the Quarter live their lives as private as hermits in the north woods. Jack never considered living anywhere else, where everyone's conduct had to meet certain "normal" standards. He was as normal as any man, but he wouldn't abide anyone telling him how he should live. Yet he didn't have the thoroughbred New Orleanean viewpoint that there were only two places in the world: New Orleans and some place totally ridiculous.

He smiled at the Quarter's pungent fragrance, feeling a deep affinity for its deliberate refusal to join the twentieth century and move in the stream of time. It's probably as close to Paris as I'm gonna get, he thought.

Jack stopped at the French Market along Decatur, where the vendors were restocking their stalls with exotic fruits and vegetables. A bouquet of bananas, turnips, potatoes, mangoes, huge garlands of garlic, pineapples and cantaloupes blended with the smells of the river just behind the levee.

The big ferry, carrying automobile traffic across the river, blew its sonorous steam whistle, and the ponderous bells of the Saint Louis Cathedral chimed the hour.

Jack realized he was smiling, and the pictures etched in his mind from the night before seemed less horrible.

An ancient bearded man of obvious Latino descent sat intently on a crate, watching Jack poke among the ripe fruit.

Jack looked up as the man muttered, "Rompe la Aurora."

"What's that you say?" he asked.

"Rompe la Aurora," the man repeated.

"I don't understand. What does that mean?"

"De Dawn, she breaks," the little man explained, as if he was an oracle uttering some implacable truth.

They looked at each other for a moment and Jack felt a faint chill. *Dawn. Aurora.* Drawing on his vague recollection of college Spanish, Jack remembered that *aurora* is the Spanish word for *dawn.*

Hurricane Aurora. Hurricane Dawn. Somehow he felt as though the old man was trying to make a connection between the hurricane and Dawn's murder.

"Yeah, she's comin' alright," Jack muttered back. The strange feeling clung on as he confirmed to himself that it was just coincidence.

He bought a ripe mango, a half pound of fat figs, and two plantains he planned to fry in butter. After poking around for nearly an hour, he returned to his apartment. He walked out onto his balcony and peeled and ate the mango as he fretted about the challenge he faced. It was just after eight.

Maybe I can catch Fred Campbell at home in Baton Rouge. *He'll call the D.A. or the Attorney General and put a freeze on this 'till I get an investigation started,* he thought.

Campbell, a family friend from home, had served as executive counsel for the last governor and was a political animal who not only knew every politician of any consequence in the state, he also knew something "on" them as well. He understood, lived and breathed politics. He was one of the good-old-boy crowd who could do wonders with a phone call. But he measured his every act by how many "green stamps," as he put it, that it would cost him to do something. He had lots of green stamps, but he hoarded them and made sure he got mileage out of everything he did for someone before he did it.

A consummate networker, Campbell was a local power broker. He wouldn't take a client unless it was a referral, and then he wouldn't charge a fee, but simply did his job and billed a favor. It paid off, for Campbell lived better than anyone Jack knew.

In a moment, Jack had Campbell on the phone. He explained the situation—that he needed the coroner to hold up any autopsy or tests until he had secured independent testing.

Campbell heard Jack out, and said in his exaggerated country drawl used to disarm the unwary, "What the hell is it to yew, Jack? Do these people have money? What can yew git out of it?"

"Damfino, Fred," Jack protested. It's one of those things, you know, that you gotta do. I may not get a damned thing, but something's gotta be done."

W'aal, Jack, yew know how it is, son. Yew ain't got nothin' to trade and ah can't use up that many green stamps fer free. Ah could call Delahoussie, the D.A., an' ah don't know fer shore, but don't s'pect he'd do nothin' for nothin' neither, if yew ketch mah drift."

"You mean you ain't gonna help me?" Jack asked, his eyes wide in disbelief.

"Jack, yew been around. Fer them to set up an inquiry like that, there must be some kind of a serious thang."

"It is serious, Fred. I know this: she was murdered, and they can cover it up by not conducting an autopsy with proper tests. They could mess it all up and that'd be the end of it."

"Ah can't hep yew, Jack. Sorry."

Jack heard the click at the other end of the line, and then a dial tone as he stared at the phone in his hand.

"That son-of-a-bitch," Jack said between his teeth. "Merdido! Squeeze! Always squeeze! You'd think we were in Mexico, or Morocco the way things get done around here with payola!"

Jack slumped in his chair. He already had his Picayune going. After staring intently at the computer monitor for a full minute, he attacked the keyboard in a frenzy of typing and didn't stop until the screen was filled. He pulled some books down and copied some phrases and paragraphs, and when it was done, the printer fed out a copy on a legal sized page. He grunted approvingly at the product.

"Temporary Restraining Order, Injunction, Protective Order." "Gotta show immediate irreparable harm or it won't be issued," Jack murmured, nodding as he re-read the words.

He found Judge Joseph Mahoney's home phone in the directory and dialed the number.

"Mahoney," came a voice at the other end of the line.

"Judge. Jack Chandler here. I hate to bother you so early, but I have a serious situation and it can't wait."

There was a pause, and the voice asked, "What's da problem?"

Jack had been holding his breath, waiting for the judge to scold him for calling on his day off. He suppressed a sigh of relief that there was no resentment in the question. Most judges didn't like to be called at home and usually let you know quickly that anything can wait.

Jack related the situation and again there was a pause while the judge thought about it. The clear New Orleans-cum-Bronx accent said: "Alright, c'mon over. You know wheah my house is at?"

"I can find it, Judge; it's in the Garden District somewhere off St. Charles, I believe?"

"Yeah, Peniston. You'll know it by my garden inna front. I was supposed to meet Al Hirt at his camp on the Northshore this afternoon—specks been runnin' good in the Rigolets—but looks like da goddam storm gonna screw it up. I ain't goin' nowheah. Bring ya papers and let's see what ya got.

"You got it Judge," Jack nearly shouted. "I'm goin' by their place for their signatures. I'm leavin' now."

Jack called Estelle and Martin and asked them to meet him outside their house to sign the papers. In fifteen minutes, he found them waiting in the front of a well-kept little shotgun house with shuttered windows. He explained what he was trying to do and they signed. He left them standing on the sidewalk with hopelessness stamped on their faces as he drove away.

Damn! Jack said to himself. *I just gotta help 'em.*

Jack admired this judge. Mahoney was the courthouse maverick. He had been elected to the criminal court bench over heavy opposition from the old line courthouse gang, which usually called the shots in politics in the parish. Mahoney waved the bloody flag of individual rights, showing a vast T.V. audience the corporate and moneyed hegemony had always run roughshod over the worker and individual. For the first time in the area's history, the people anointed a judge who flung himself wildly into the election melee and didn't give a damn about personal or financial consequences. And he had won.

Jack hoped maybe, just maybe, he could get the restraining order to stop any further interference with an investigation he would initiate. This was Mahoney's cup of tea: to create effects on the power structure for the working classes.

Jack unfolded his wrinkled city map. The judge lived in the Garden district, an area beyond Canal and south of the Quarter.

He drove into the Garden District. Street cars clanged and rattled down the middle of St. Charles Avenue through a tunnel of live oaks. Mammoth, elaborate, turn of the century homes stood haughtily side-by-side, bordering the boulevard for miles.

Traffic was light, and drivers didn't seem to be going places in such a hurry. The electric trolley car rattled down the median, clanging its bell. The windows were open, and passengers rocked back and forth in the rolling rhythm with their elbows on the windows-sills, hair blowing in the damp wind.

Jack turned south on Peniston and drove toward the river. He found the address and pulled over at a white frame, gingerbread house built on high piers with room for parking beneath.

As soon as the latch clicked on the white picket gate, he felt he had stepped through a time warp into a garden wonderland. Ever-ready to be swept away on the gossamer wings of sensation, Jack came to a rapt standstill, absorbing the hushed essence of the garden. He smiled. *This is my bonus for puttin' up with the rest of the crap life dishes out.*

The air was candied with the spicy aromas of jessamine and sweet olive. The trellised path to the front door dripped with clusters of violet bougainvillea. Radiant hibiscus blossoms, ginger lily, lantana, and cascading blue plumbago flowers set among thick ferns nearly overloaded Jack's senses. He felt muscles and nerves, that he didn't even know were tense, relax. He floated through the raised planters overflowing with fragrant herbs, mint and sweet basil.

Iridescent hummingbirds darted among the flowers. To fill out the sensual little space was the warbling of a mockingbird, the chirping of many bright red cardinals and the screeching of blue jays. Somewhere a mourning dove cooed. Jack wanted to sit down beneath an arbor and not think of anything.

He walked up the wooden steps to a high veranda that encircled the entire house. Hanging baskets of dripping ferns and blooming bougainvillea of all colors swung from the top edge of the porch.

Jack punched the door bell alongside an ornate stained glass door and, in a moment, steps could be heard from the other side. The door swung open and a small, bright-eyed man thrust his face forward.

"Yeah?"

Chapter 3

"Judge Mahoney, I just called about the order?"

"Oh yeah, c'mon in," the little man said, reaching for the papers Jack carried. He turned and signaled Jack to follow him down the hall.

As the judge led the way, Jack noticed how diminutive—even tiny—this man was. On the bench or behind his desk, which was the only way Jack had ever seen him, he had appeared to be much larger and imposing. Nonetheless, Mahoney walked with a certain tread, and Jack got the impression that regardless of his size, he could trample anyone into the ground.

Jack Mahoney's ancestors had migrated from the northeast at the turn of the century when the garment industry was big in New Orleans. He was "Black Irish," richly bearing the mark his nationality: cream complexion with cold black hair and blue eyes. His mercurial personality was also characteristic—given to quick temper and readiness for combat that would melt away to a song in a wink, and wit that could charm or impale.

Mahoney took a pair of reading glasses from a table in his study and snugged them on his nose. "Let's see whatcha got."

He scanned the papers for a moment and, without hesitation, scratched an illegible signature across the line at the bottom of the page above his typed name. He started to hand the papers back to Jack, as if his business was done, then paused, raising his sharp eyes to search Jack's face.

"You know whatcha doin', Son?"

"No sir, but I gotta do somethin'."

"Yeah. Know whatcha mean. Done plenty stupid things myself. And this," he said, shaking the papers, "gonna raise a stink."

17

"Whatever, Judge. I saw that little girl's body lying in that box and I knew somethin' was wrong. If I'm right, there's nothin' wrong with what I'm doin'. I'm not sure what I *am* gonna do, but I'm willin' to kick some ass."

Mahoney's eyelids crinkled at the thought and he chuckled softly, nodding as he led Jack out onto the porch.

The Judge extended his hand and said, "Good luck, Son. If I can help you, call me. You know, down at the courthouse they think of me as a rebel. If they think it's somethin' I want, they gonna try to stop it. But I got stayin' power, and they gonna be surprised. You're takin' on the establishment with this, you know; you spittin' in they eye. All I can say is—go ahead on."

"You took 'em on didn't you, Judge?"

The judge nodded. "I been a lawyer out there inna trenches. Bastids like you, and me, never had no regular paycheck like the corporation and bank lawyers up in One Shell Square. The Bar Association belongs to the fat cats inna big firms. Most judges been D.A.'s are in some political or big company hog-trough and ain't never worried about the light bill in their silk stockin' lives. I'm their judge too, and I give 'em a fair shake, but I know how it is with you poor son-of-a-bitches grubbin' out a livin' helpin' the little man."

"That makes you dangerous, Judge," Jack said as they walked down the steps.

Mahoney grinned, slapped Jack on the back and said, "Like my garden?"

"I'd like to sit in that swing under the trellis for the rest of the day, Your Honor."

"Yeah. That's what a garden s'posed to do, huh?"

The two men walked down the steps and stood quietly in the center of the garden, breathing its breath.

"There ain't but a few things on this earth to admire or work for," Mahoney said quietly. "One's beautiful things, an' the other's other's truth, even if it means riskin' your life for it."

Jack was six inches taller than Mahoney, but he knew this little man would stand in the path of a charging rhino for either. *I have to find beauty for myself, and truth finds and tests me daily. So, what else is new?*

Jack held Mahoney's gaze as they shook hands and then he walked to the gate. He turned and grinned, waving the signed papers as he stepped onto the sidewalk. When Jack reached his car, the judge was bending to pluck a renegade leaf or to uproot up an interloping weed.

Jack sped back down St. Charles and was soon at Charity Hospital. His mood was almost gleeful as he strode down the hall toward the morgue. Three men stood in conversation outside Sanchez' office as Jack burst in and headed toward them with no uncertainty in his step.

Sanchez was the only one Jack recognized. "Dr. Sanchez, true to my promise this morning," Jack said, waving his papers, "I have a restraining order and injunction stopping anyone from doing anything with Dawn Marie Delacroix's body."

The three glanced at each other knowingly and stood quietly, leaving Jack to make the next move.

The coiffure salt and pepper hair, tennis shoes, white shorts, knit shirt, and cool eyes of the man in the middle spoke of old New Orleans urbanity and country club.

"My name is Jack Chandler." Jack said, extending his hand. "Attorney for the Delacroix family."

There was a long pause, with Jack holding his hand out for the expected handshake.

"Dr. Charles Marriot, Coroner," the man replied, a flicker of disdainful amusement passing over his face. He didn't offer to take Jack's hand.

A potgutted Major of the Orleans Parish Sheriff department flanked the coroner on the right. Jack handed the papers to Dr. Marriot, who examined them briefly and gave a low chuckle as he handed them to the deputy. The deputy flipped through the documents and dropped them on the floor.

The three men laughed at Jack's befuddlement. Jack said, "Those are official legal documents," he said, retrieving them from the floor.

"I'm sorry, young man," Marriot said, "Do you think that handing me these papers constitutes proper service of process? Shouldn't it be served through the Sheriff? I can't accept these, as you are obviously not qualified to serve them."

"Of course I know it is not official service. I am showing you that I have an order that will be served. I am taking them to the sheriff's office first thing Monday morning."

The coroner and deputy laughed.

Jack's stark face betrayed his sudden realization that the coroner was right. He looked and felt as if he had been struck in the gut. His strutting confidence fled and he felt naked and vulnerable before the three men whose faces were as cold as the tenants in the room beyond the steel door. *Of course! The sheriff's office runs Juvenile Detention, where Dawn Marie died! And here is a high-ranking Sheriff's deputy. What is he doing here?*

"Have you moved her?" Jack asked, starting to push through to the morgue door.

The big-bellied sheriff deputy, whose nametag identified him as Parker, stepped in front of Jack and said, in a heavy lower ninth ward accent, "You ain't goin' nowhere, counselor!"

"I got a court order," Jack protested.

"You ain't got no search warrant, and that paper ain't worth shit. A shariff's gotta serve it an' you ain't no shariff."

"Well, I'm gonna stop you from disposin' of that body!"

Poking Jack in the chest with a stubby finger, Parker said, "If ya know what's good for ya, ya better get ya ass outta here before I press charges for disturbin' the peace and comin' in here molestin' the corpses. Yeah, that'd make a good charge against somebody like you. That shit wouldn't never rub off if ya got charged with that. Ha Ha! Git out before I throw ya out!"

Jack ran out of things to say, confronting the hostility flowing at him like the heat from a blast furnace.

They're are gonna move her. They could even say that the Estelle and Martin were mistaken, and slide in another body that was similar, and do anything at all and get by with it. They can just lose it somewhere in these hospital complexes of the Charity Hospital, LSU and Tulane Medical School; incinerate it and it will be gone forever.

Jack turned around and walked to the door. There was nothing he could say. He had been so cocksure of himself when he walked in waving that paper, and they had told him to wipe his butt with it. They were right, all papers must be served by the sheriff's office, but he had thought a judge's order, even unserved, would have some effect. The sheriff's department is involved, and they could lose the papers, or not even find the coroner to serve him. He was screwed!

The sheriff in Orleans parish was a plenipotentiary power with a fiefdom all his own. Anyone Mahoney would appoint to serve the papers, in case the sheriff couldn't or wouldn't, could find himself arrested for any assortment of crimes. Who had the balls to do it in the first place? Jack's mind raced over the limited possibilities, each of which was immediately eliminated as unworkable.

Jack opened the door to leave the room and Parker said, his gravelly voice full of venom, "Forget it counselor, if you smart."

Jack slowed, and just as he closed the door behind him, he heard Parker shout, "They got a tray in here for you."

The door shut behind Jack and he stood in the strangely still air. His gut wrenched in anger, instantly descending through fear to a gut-sucking apathy, and drove home slowly, gnawing on his exasperation, feeling as dark as the lowering clouds scudding from the south.

Maybe a beer'll help. He locked the door to his old Ford. *I need to get some advice somewhere.* As he passed his office door, he noticed a small scrap of paper wedged in the crack by the knob. It was a crudely drawn sketch of a tombstone, with his name scrawled across the marker.

Jack slowly wadded the scrap of paper into a ball and a chill ran down his spine.

As he stepped outside of the building and looked up and down the street, Jack noticed there was little traffic on narrow "Rue Royal"; only a few brave tourists were out before the weather shut everything down. No suspicious characters lurked about.

Now what? Maybe it's a joke. Maybe somebody's waiting upstairs for me. What the have I got myself into?

He slowly walked up the steps, pausing every few moments to make sure nobody was hiding around a corner. *For a man who owns an arsenal, I don't even have a pocket knife on me.* His heart pounded as he slid open the door to his apartment.

He looked in. Nothing was obviously amiss.

It was totally quiet. Only the sounds of the street. With false confidence, he shouted through the open door, "If somebody's in here, I'm comin' in and I got my .38 with hollow points and I'm itchin' to pull the trigger."

Jack eased through the door, his nerves tight wire, and slowly stepped into the bedroom, which was the only room other than the little bath where someone could be hiding. He grabbed the sawed off shotgun and immediately felt better. He noisily pumped a shell into the barrel and poked it at the clothes in the closet, then pushed open the door to the little bath with the gun barrel.

Jack was wrung out by the time he found himself alone in the apartment. He locked the door and decided that a beer wasn't the answer. A straight slug from the fifth of Jack Daniels he took from the kitchen cabinet helped.

"I ain't no hero, that's for sure," Jack breathed out loud after his pulse calmed and he'd had a couple of pulls on from the fifth. He sat on the porch for a long while worrying.

I gotta do somethin'. I can't just sit on my ass. This is a big deal and I'm up to my eyeballs in it, whether I like it or not. Somebody thinks I know more than I know, and they might move. They'll move if I don't. But again, maybe they won't if I don't. But if I drop it, could I ever look at Estelle in the eye again? Could I look at myself in the mirror again? But what can I do? Jack slumped in the chair, his eyes pinched shut and his lips drawn into a thin grimace.

It was past noon. He slapped together two ham sandwiches and ate them with a glass of cold milk on the balcony while watching the low, darkening clouds race overhead. The rain had stopped, leaving an odd, expectant mugginess in the air.

The T.V. was full of news about the hurricane. Aurora was stalled in the Gulf, picking up speed all the while. There were speculations about where it would make landfall. A hurricane watch was in effect from the Florida panhandle to Corpus Christi. When a blow the size of Aurora slammed the land, everybody usually took cover and secured everything that could be blown away. The French Quarter residents simply had to close their cypress shutters.

Usually, the power went down and it was a time of partying because there was nothing else to do. They talked, drank and played Bourre', a French card game with elements of bridge and poker, by lantern light. Jack's experience with storms had only involved trees and limbs blown down and maybe some minor flooding and damage to the landscape, so he wasn't worried. The residents of the apartment complex would be partying, and he would too, after he had figured out what to do about Dawn Marie.

He called several lawyer friends, but could reach nobody. Jack gave up after unavailing attempts at reaching any of the other friends he could rely on for advice and help. Maybe the guys who lived in the other apartments would be around the pool in the back.

The Marquis de Mandeville had once been several homes built side by side with common walls. They were consolidated into an apartment complex of twenty units, with the residents sharing common areas. There were many similar apartment complexes in the Quarter, all with secluded courtyard gardens that would never be suspected from the street. The residents lived their own private lives and minded their own business. In keeping with what could be expected from those electing to live in the Quarter, they were often eccentric individuals whose nonconformity added to the uniqueness of the area.

The Quarter was first called the Vieux Carre', or old square, and was settled by Jean Baptiste de Bienville. Situated hard by the Mississippi river, it is bounded by Canal, Rampart, Esplanade and Decatur streets. The majestic homes of the French and Spanish settlers and nobility eventually grew together to form solid blocks of residences over the years, separated by what was known legally as "party" walls. Tourists seldom see past the shuttered windows and doors of these labyrinthine buildings.

Jack went down the circular stair and through a long hall with doors to apartments to the right and left. An arched portal opened onto a plush courtyard surrounding a small azure swimming pool.

Two and three stories of apartments with balconies hung over the courtyard. Those alongside the pool and behind it were called "slave quarters," once housing slaves who served the original owners. The slave quarters were small shuttered two-story houses with ivy and figvine matted to the white stucco walls. Date palms hovered over the courtyard, and along the walls were ferns and lush, huge leaved banana trees bearing green finger-sized fruit hanging in clusters. The air was saturated with sweet olive and ginger lily.

Jack often dropped into one of the chaise lounges by the poolside and always was restored in minutes. It was a Lourdes for the mind and soul.

A Billy Joel album played; several men and three women lounged around the pool, drinking and talking.

"It's Jack," drawled someone and several other voices chimed in. "Jack, party time!"

The party had already started.

Draped on a chaise was a lean, laconic lioness in a string bikini; her dark ginger skin glistened from a recent swim. She turned her blue-green eyes on Jack and he got the jolt to his viscera he always felt when she looked at him, especially when she wore that bikini which fully displayed her tiny waist, tight, high-rising behind, and that glorious mons pubis that drove him crazy. Her eyes sparkled as he sank into a chair next to her. As usual, she had one of her muscle men in tow, and that bothered Jack much more than he cared to admit.

She was Dr. Victoria Keens-Dennison of the Pathology Department at Tulane Medical Center. Once Jack was at her office and found, in next room, shelves packed from floor to ceiling with plastic bags filled with every kind of body part. It gave him the creeps.

He sat heavily into a chair next to her and she handed him a bottle of Dixie.

Vic held up her beer and said, in her soft British-Caribbean patois, "This storm, it is to be a big one. We can party for days!"

Jack nodded and tapped his bottle to Vic's in a salute to the hurricane. He tried not to notice her slender wrist draped across the hairy, upper thigh of the muscle bound creep with her. She watched Jack's discomfort and smiled.

Vic's father, an English native of Trinidad and noted neurosurgeon, had met her mother, a nurse in a Casablanca hospital, when he was an intern. They fell in love and he stayed long enough to marry her and take her back to Port-au-Spain with him. Vic had her mother's dark, exotic, Moorish features and emerald eyes that came from her father's side. Those eyes set in that light burgundy face with the chiseled aquiline nose and pouty lips were enough to paralyze a man, and Jack was catatonic.

Jack's breath caught in his throat each time he saw Vic, yet he dared not cross the line and initiate anything, regardless of how beautiful and appealing she was, for she was unequivocally black, and that was verboten. But underlying it all, Jack believed she probably wouldn't have him in the first place. She was a class act, and he knew his place as a transplanted red-neck from the hills of northern Louisiana. The real truth was he didn't feel worthy of such a fantastic creature as Vic. Jack spoke to the rest of the group. There was Lloyd Murchison, a professor at Tulane Law School, who was a loose, rangy red haired boy from the Delta country around Greenville, Mississippi; Ernie Hotchkiss, an out of the closet (if he'd ever been in it) homosexual psychiatrist with the Orleans Parish Mental Health unit, whose slave quarter apartment overlooked the pool; Ellen Crump, an old maid airline stewardess approaching burnout; and Archie and Ann Lambert, who could truly be called an odd couple. Archie was an artist who painted portraits around Jackson square during the day and played the trumpet at the Paddock Lounge on Bourbon Street at night. Ann was a cool, bean-counting CPA with a national accounting firm.

Archie continually complained about Ann's idea of a good sex life, regulating him to a routine interaction once weekly. And according to Archie, even then she wasn't very interested. He bitched to everyone about having to beat off to handle his needs. Some sense of personal ethics or inhibition kept him from supplementing, as there was abundant opportunity for a handsome, long haired, artist-musician in the French Quarter. He was miserable, and obviously had it on his mind all of the time. She tossed her pretty little brunette head, telling him it was splitsville if he fucked around on her, and somehow that kept him within the traces.

Jack was glad Ernie lived in the back, away from him. Ernie had his gay friends over for parties on a regular basis. Some looked like fine women with big tits and all. That disturbed Jack considerably, and not just because of what they probably were doing in there. It made him very uneasy, and Ernie's effeminate ways and lisp were totally disgusting.

Ellen was away most of the time. It was rumored she had a thing going with the owner of the apartment complex, a psychiatrist who visited her from time to time. It was also rumored that he had a fetish for shoes, and since he had a master key to all of the apartments, Jack checked his own shoes from time to time. Once he even made chalk outlines around his shoes in his closet, suspicious that the weirdo may do something bizarre to his footwear.

They talked about Aurora, where it would make landfall, comparing this one to others they had experienced or knew about, and their conclusion was that New Orleans would probably feel the effects of it wherever it hit.

"Jackie," Ernie lisped, "you are unusually quiet today. Anything wrong?"

It galled Jack for Ernie to talk like that to him. The more Jack withdrew, the more aggressive Ernie would become, obviously getting a perverse pleasure out of making Jack uneasy.

Vic made sure that Jack was watching, and placed her hand on the upper thigh of Mr. America. She pushed herself up and leaned over toward Jack, allowing her cleavage to display its generous self to his resistant gaze.

"What is it Jack? This is going to be a great holiday, and you seem down."

Jack explained to the group what was going on, and that he had a delimma about how to proceed. He knew that he should be doing something other than sitting around, for he surely wasn't enjoying it with all of this preying on his mind. Besides that, seeing Vic with this big bastard gave him a feeling that approached grief, and he certainly wouldn't reveal that!

Ernie became very still, sucked on his pink Sherman, then blew a smoke ring—doing strange things with his lips in the process. "Drop it, Jack," he said. "They mean nothing to you. No money. And there is danger. What in heaven's name could prompt you to do this for nothing?" He reached out to touch Jack's hand with the tips of his soft fingers. Jack drew his hand back.

Ernie shrugged affectedly, doing another smoke ring at Jack.

"Yeah, no margin of profit I can see," Ann the CPA said, laughing.

Vic took it more seriously, seeing Jack's evident distress. Her look softened. "Look, Jack, if you get in the bind, I know Jester McConothy. He's known in international circles as a top forensic pathologist; his office is in Mobile. He gives not one damn about politics and takes on cases like this—usually free. He would require state of the art chemical and toxicity testing at the best path labs in the country. I would even sit in, free of charge, if you want."

"That would be a great help," Jack said, brightening. "Gotta slow 'em down somehow. That's my problem right now. They've probably already moved the body."

"If that's the case," Lloyd said in his old south delta drawl, "you're gonna have to get an injunction from the State Attorney General. You gotta convince the State to take jurisdiction to ovahride the local authorities. Maybe even go Federal."

Ernie leaned back, sipping his little pink drink. "Do you know anything about this other than what you have said?" Ernie asked, appearing casually interested.

"No. Just that Dawn was murdered. I know that. And probably raped. I gotta find out just what's goin' on. Somethin's bad wrong here."

"Hum," Ernie said, his eyes narrowing to slits.

"Don't forget what I said," Vic said. "We can put a team together quickly. You need to find a way to stop tissue destruction."

"And ah would be willin' to help with any legal research you would need," Lloyd drawled, the dollar signs showing in the little thought bubble appearing above his head, "as long as ah can stay out of the limelight. You know how it is."

"Yeah," Jack said, half smiling, "and out of the line of fire?"

"W'aal," Lloyd snorted and shrugged, caught in the act of trying to horn in without taking any risks, "ah did offah."

The subject changed back to the weather and a myriad of other things as this group of diverse individuals would discuss. Jack realized that it was mid-afternoon. He excused himself, thanked them all for their input and offers of assistance, and left reluctantly, resisting the intrusive thought that he may not be able to return to this little safe harbor in one piece.

As Jack walked under the archway separating the pool from the hall, he turned and Vic's eyes were trained on him. He felt a rush of heat as their eyes met. He imagined an electric sizzle and could hardly catch his breath. She smiled slightly, lifting her hand in a small wave.

Jack waved back and quickly turned to walk down the hall, his heart beating like a tom tom.

Chapter 4

Jack slid the massive doors closed behind him. The tension and lack of sleep was making his thinking fuzzy. Maybe if he sat on the sofa and chilled out for a few minutes he could get a grip and work out a sane solution. He closed his eyes and instantly dropped off to sleep.

It seemed like the droning of a worrisome mosquito at first, then it was a phone ringing in the distance. He realized the phone, on the table nearby, had been ringing for some time. It continued ringing while he cursed the intrusion and finally gave in and answered.

It was Martin Delacroix. "Lawyer Jack, I got somebody here you need to talk to."

Martin's voice was strained, as could be expected, but there was an underlying tone of contained animosity. Jack felt anger was healthier than the morbid apathy and grief that possesses the bereaved.

"Who is it Martin, and what's it about?"

"I been around this town a long time, and there been lots of children put in that place. This here boy been in juvenile detention, and he got somethin' to say. Can you come over now?"

"Sure Martin. I'll be right there."

He picked up a micro-cassette recorder, his camcorder and a legal pad, then opened the door to his office and started to leave the building.

Vic stood in the doorway in black leotards that seemed to be painted on.

Jack's eyes raced over her and again couldn't find his tongue.

"Where do you think you're going in such a hurry?"

Gathering his wits, Jack explained where he was going and why.

"I'm off today. Could you stand some company?"

This was unbelievable. Jack stammered, "Uh, well, I guess." Then Jack felt a wave of resentment and said, his lips tightening as he said, "Where's Mr. America?"

Vic laughed. "Sent him home."

The answer only partially handled Jack's feeling about Vic's muscle-bound friend by the pool, but he couldn't help wondering what she and the big ape had been doing after he had gone to sleep, and what their relationship really was.

Stifling his jealousy, he thought about the danger and said quickly, "wait, this can be dangerous. I didn't tell you about the note I found in my door."

She raised her eyebrows and Jack told her about the note with the picture of the tombstone.

"That means you really need some company. I can whip your ass in Judo, so I can help if you are in a spot. So don't give me any backtalk, I'm going with you. I'll be back in a moment."

This woman is in your face. I love it.

Vic ran down the hall to her apartment and in just a few minutes returned wearing a conservative skirt and blouse. "Have to show them respect," she said, leading Jack out of the front door.

The air was thick and oppressive. Although it was mid afternoon, the light was failing. There was a yellowing grayness in the atmosphere that stole the color from everything else. Gusts of humid wind blew from the river, carrying the smells of mud, fish, and decay.

"Jack, let's bring some food. Estelle won't be up to cooking," Vic said. They stopped at the French Market. There was little traffic and he was able to park alongside the fruit stalls.

They bought a big bag of assorted fruit, including a large late watermelon. Then he went to the Central Grocery across Decatur and had them build immense Italian Muffelleto filled with salami, baloney, ham, olives, and Italian dressing, and two dripping roast Po-boy sandwiches. After he put these in the car, he trotted to the Cafe Du Monde, an open air coffee house that made New Orleans' square doughnuts called beignets blanketed with powdered sugar. Taking a large bag of the hot beignets and two quarts of muscular chicory coffee, they drove through nearly vacant streets to Estelle's.

When they walked into the neat little bungalow with the many bags of food, Estelle burst into tears. Martin, a mountain of a man, hugged Jack unexpectedly, for the color line, while blurred, still existed. Kindness couldn't be legislated.

A waif-like teenage black boy helped Jack and Martin bring the bags in, and then he stood back while the little banquet was spread on a small kitchen table covered with a checkered tablecloth. He could be twelve or thirteen, with delicate features, almost pretty, Jack thought. His eyes darted at every sound.

Martin and Estelle launched into the sandwiches and coffee, seemingly forgetting for the moment about the tragedy that had occurred in their lives. The lad nibbled on a biegnet. Vic sat near Estelle while Jack turned to the boy. Vic sat in a corner as unobtrusively as she could, with the camcorder.

Jack asked, "What's your name, Son?"

"James."

"James what?"

"James Morris."

"How old are you?"

"Sixteen."

"Where do you live, James?"

"In the projects."

"Desire Projects?"

Nod.

"Live with your folks?"

"Ain't got no mama," Martin interjected. "Old man run off. Live with his auntee." The projects were public housing, consisting of row upon row of two story brick apartments conceived as slum clearance and decent housing, they had turned into a breeding ground for crime and terror. *This little boy must be a leaf in the wind down there.* He looked too frail to protect himself from the gangs and brutality spawning in those dark buildings. It was a training ground for survival, if that life could be called survival. It looked as if this little boy's spirit had been drained from him. He wouldn't be one of the survivors.

Jack moved close to the boy and sat next to him quietly. At Jack's touch, the boy tensed and pulled away. He reminded Jack of a frightened fawn, tensed to dart away, to hide.

"What happened, James?" Jack asked quietly.

The boy hesitated, breathing shallow, gripping the edge of the chair with his thin fingers.

"Go on," Martin said to the boy, "This man gonna help you, and maybe when he through, won't nobody else get hurt down at that place. Go on now, tell him."

After more hesitation, Jack asked, "Were you in juvenile detention, James?"

Nod.

"What for?"

James relaxed and almost smiled as he said, "Stole some things."

"What did you steal?" Jack asked, grinning back, and finally the little boy broke into a smile as if he had actually accomplished something because he had taken what he wanted.

"Toys and things from Walgreens drugstore an' cigarettes."

"Did you ever get away with it before you got caught?"

"Uh huh," he grinned, nodding.

"What happened when you got caught?"

James stopped smiling and seemed to retreat within himself.

No answer forthcoming, Jack said gently, "You were in J.D.; tell me what happened there. I need to know, you can tell me, it's okay."

James began to tremble and burst into body wracking sobs so violent that Jack thought he might have a seizure. Martin gently cradled the wailing child in his great arms and rocked him as he would an infant, letting the boy cry it out. It took a long time.

Finally, James snuffled and rubbed his nose on Martin's shirt.

"Fucked me!" He howled and began to cry again, but this time there was anger in it.

"Who did?"

"Guards, and that big 'un, the head man. He did all the boys an' the girls hisself. He went first."

He moaned and sobbed again, then finally gained control.

"Who was the head man?"

"Leroy, Leroy Destrehan, the head man, and then he cut them other guards loose and let 'em do what they wanted. The worst 'un was that old jelly-belly. He like to whup up on you."

"Who else was there when they did it?"

"Weren't no other kids around when they done it. Just them. They took turns after they give us a shot."

Jack frowned. "Drugs?"

James nodded, his eyes clouding over. "They sent some doctor in to interview us, and they talked into a little tape recorder and then they come in and give us a shot. I kinda pass out, an' when I come to, they was doin' me in the butt. I was screamin'. It hurt!"

Interview, my ass! James began howling and rocking back and forth, bent double, clutching his chest in his crossed arms. Martin held him again gently until he quieted.

"How long were you in there, James?"

"A month maybe."

"Did they do that to others, too?"

Nod. "Not all of 'em. Only some. Them what they put in the back. Them they put in the front got out after a few days and never knowed nothin' about us in the back. They say they gonna kill me if I tell! An' they will!"

He began crying again, this time in stark terror.

"James, can you tell me who else was in the back with you?"

The boy numbly gave several names as Jack dictated them into his microcassette recorder. "Were there any girls there that got the same treatment?"

"Uh huh. They got all of 'em, if they looked like anything. Some of the boys an' the girls was took out of there some nights an' took somewheres else."

Frowning, Jack leaned closer and asked, "What do you mean?"

"Once I was took with a girl to the Town and Country motel out on Airline an' a white man had at me. She was took to another room with another white man."

"Did they give you drugs, James?"

"Every time. It made me crazy. I didn't know what I was doin'. I swear I didn't. I couldn't help myself!"

Jack knew there were some highly illegal psychotropic drugs that could render a person totally helpless. Maybe even drugs that would generate sexual arousal.

"What did the white man look like, James?"

"Which 'un?"

"Well," Jack paused, "any of 'em."

"The one that wasn't no deputy, he was funny lookin'. Squatty. Short legs, long arms. Bald on top an' a ring 'o black hair over his ears. Gold tooth in the front of his mouth. Wore a bunch of rings on his fingers."

Jack frowned, recollecting someone who matched that description. "Did you hear a name, James?"

"Warner. . .Bosco, or somethin' like that."

Jack thought for a long moment, a fleeting recollection of something in relation to this name that darted away. "Warner Bosco?"

"That's it!"

Humm, Jack thought. *Name sounds some familiar.*

"What was the fat deputy's name, the one you called jelly-belly?"

"Parker." The florid face of the pot-gutted deputy at the morgue flew into Jack's mind. Jack scowled and had to catch his breath. No wonder Parker was at the morgue.

"Did you see the doctor more than once?"

James snuffled, looking away, completely grieving over his own guilt. "He come in every few days an' talked to me an' I told him about what happened, an' he just talked into a little thing like you got an' didn't say nothin."

"Was it always the same one?"

James shook his head. "They was two of 'em, an' sometimes they'd come together and listen. Made me tell what happened and how I felt when them men was doin' it; they said it was in the interest of science, but I couldn't understand what that had to do with science."

"Do you know their names, James?"

"They didn't say."

"What did they look like?"

"One was a big man with a red beard. The other one, he was skinny, act real faggy, blond hair he comb straight back that hang down on the side, kinda young lookin'.

Jack sat back, frowning and gnawing the inside of his jaw as he thought of the descriptions given, then leaned forward and asked, "Who did they work for, James?"

"Didn't say, but I heard they come from the Orleans Parish Mental Health."

Jack became still for so long that Martin asked if anything was wrong.

Martin asked, "Somethin' wrong?"

"Ah, no," Jack said, clearing his throat, looking fleeingly at Vic, who sat unblinking, absorbing the information just revealed. Jack squinted as his mind raced over the few solutions presented.

After a moment, he asked, "James, do you know where these kids live—the ones in the back with you?"

"Yessir, some. Most live in the projects."

"Can you take me to see any of them?"

James' hunted look returned. His eyes glazed and he instantly retreated into his shell, pressing the side of his face into Martin's big chest, trying to hide.

"James?" Jack urged gently. "We need your help, Son. All you have to do is go with us."

James almost imperceptibly shook his head.

"Why not?"

"They kill me. They kill you. I don't wanna die."

Jack let out a pent up breath and asked Martin if he would come with him to the projects. A deep worry crease appeared between Martin's brow. He glanced at Estelle.

Jack pressed him. "Martin, this is for you, man, for you and Estelle," Estelle sat rigid, tormented by the cruel mental movie of what she had seen in the morgue, and now the threat of this new development.

Jack's features hardened. "I don't want to risk my life any more than you do, but everything depends on how many victims we can get to talk. If you don't go with me, I'll go alone."

Vic said, "I'll go with you, Jack."

Jack shook his head vigorously.

Estelle put her small hand on Martin's arm. "Go with him. It's for Dawn."

Martin' scowl turned to a hardened glare. "You ain't goin' alone." His expression changed from the grief he had been suppressing to what Jack thought may have been a flicker of a smile. "Nossir, we ain't goin' alone." There was an emphasis on the "we." He gently moved his arms from around the boy and walked to the phone.

Jack continued talking to James while Martin made two hurried phone calls. James gave up a name and address in the projects of one he knew about for sure. Martin poured a half mug each of the pungent brew of coffee for himself and Jack and left the room. He returned with a pint of Jim Beam and filled his coffee cup to the brim with the amber liquid.

"Courage," Martin said, taking a long quaff of the powerful mixture. He handed the bottle to Jack, who likewise filled his cup and took a long drink. The men looked at each other silently, as if they were about to storm an enemy beachhead.

"You got a gun, Lawyer Jack?"

Jack nodded. He always carried his revolver under the seat of his car when he drove around the city. Martin patted the bulge in his pocket.

"Well then," Martin said, topping his cup again with the whiskey, "we better get movin. Big storm comin' and we need to get done what we gotta get done."

Jack drained his coffee mug, then poured another inch of Jim Beam in his cup. He slugged it down as he stood and looked up at the six foot six Martin, who walked over to Estelle and gave her a light kiss and a hug.

Vic, who had been listening quietly to all of the dialogue, whispered to Jack. "I want to go."

"It's just too dangerous, babe. You need to stay here with Estelle. I'll be back here to pick you up after we see this dude."

Vic pondered this for a moment and then nodded. "You're right. Estelle needs company. I have a feeling there's lots more I can do after this."

Jack frowned, thinking about involving Vic in this.

Vic shook her finger in his face and said, "Jack, I am going to help you in this and don't you forget it. So don't be cutting me out."

Jack shook his head and looked at Martin, who pursed his lips and wrinkled his broad brow with a look that said "you better give in boy, cause you ain't got a chance in this argument."

"Okay, we'll see."

"We're going to be a team in solving this, Jack Chandler, and if you try to cut me out you'll be sorry."

Jack felt a thrill at having Vic as a partner, but the emotion was mixed because of the danger.

"I'll find my way home, and you better call me when you get back," she said, glaring up into Jack's face.

"Okay, I'll report back," Jack said, giving Vic a sharp salute.

Estelle said, her eyes tearing, "Martin, please be careful, I don't want to lose you too."

"Don't you fret none, Mama, you man gonna be back in a jiffy."

⁓

The streets were wet. Low clouds threatened more rain at any time. Gusts of damp wind tugged at Jack's open shirt collar.

Jack thought he had been in the house for hours, but looking at his watch, he saw he'd been there for only an hour. It was just past six.

Standing by his car were two of the biggest men he had ever seen. One was golden skinned, like Martin and Estelle, and the other's ebony complexion fairly gleamed. The light one was Harold LaMarque and the other was Julian Freret, both longshoremen who worked with Martin on the docks. Both were over six feet four. Harold was in the two hundred and fifty pound class, light skin with golden eyes and trimmed moustache like Martin's. He gave the impression of a huge tawny cat: wide of shoulder and narrow of waist. On the other hand, Julian was as wide at the waist as at the shoulder, a rhino at three hundred pounds of raw brute power.

Jack said, "I see what you meant when you said we weren't goin' alone."

Martin nodded grimly and then turned to the waiting, unsmiling men and told them what James had revealed and what they were going to do. They visibly bridled at every word Martin said. Jack could see the fury rising in them. He felt a helluva lot better about going into the war zone with these men. It would take an elephant gun to bring down either of them; they were a small army unto themselves. Nonetheless, he was going to carry his own .38. And he could see, in spite of the size and power of these men, they had a familiar imprint of iron in their pockets. They weren't taking any chances.

Harold and Julian both had huge calloused hands that engulfed Jack's when they went through the formalities of introduction. Neither smiled. They never said a word again to Martin or to Jack. The ride was silent and expectant as they drove through the wet streets.

Jack was glad his car had four doors so that these huge men could fit inside. *It's like the clown car in the circus,* he thought. He wondered how his little Ford could carry such a load, but it did, and after a short drive, they entered the projects.

There were blocks on blocks with nothing but winding, dirty streets among grim two story brick buildings, many vacant with windows broken. Idle men lounged on curbs or stoops holding bottles, smoking cigarettes and weed–their faces dark with hostility. Jack was nervous, even with the armed squad of linebackers he had with him.

34

The street lights that hadn't been broken were already on, although there was still plenty of light outside of the projects. The entire area seemed capsule of darkness, denying entrance to the light of day. From the litter, broken bottles, and trash everywhere, it was evident the street cleaners avoided the projects as well. Jack felt as if he was driving through an invisible menacing mass that pushed against the car, resisting their intrusion deeper into a no man's land of squalor and despair.

Jack parked at the address. The four piled out onto the littered sidewalk.

"Just a minute," Julian said as he walked over to three teenagers loitering around a stoop a few feet from the car.

He motioned for Martin and Harold to come over. The trio of boys sat back, eyes wide at the approach of the mammoth, ferocious men blocking out the light as they towered over them.

Julian grabbed one by the collar and lifted him off the step. He growled, "Where you stay at?"

The kid dropped the joint he was smoking and, with his arms dangling by his side as he was lifted bodily off the step, said, "This buildin'."

Julian dropped the cowering boy, who collapsed on the concrete step, then reached for another, who darted back. Martin grabbed him while Harold grasped the other by the arm.

"You all stay in this buildin'?" Julian demanded. There was no doubt in his voice.

Trembling, they all nodded.

"Well, then. You all gonna sit right here and watch this little white car. If anything happen to this car, we gonna turn you all's head around on you shoulders so you be starin' at you all's asses, and we can find you if we come lookin'. You understand, you little mutts?"

They nodded vigorously. They understood all right. Intimidation was the give and take in the projects. They had dished out enough of it themselves to their weaker brothers. This message was as clear as a bell on a still night.

Julian and Harold dropped their surly burdens onto the cement steps, dusted their palms together and walked up the trash littered stairs.

Chapter 5

The landing at the top of the stairs was illuminated by a dim, low wattage bulb. Jack was glad, because it masked the mess of refuse and litter laying about. Graffiti was scrawled on the walls and on the door. It reeked of cigarette butts, stale beer and urine. Roaches skittered from the dried body of a rat in the debris. Broken glass crunched beneath their feet.

T.V. sounds filtered through the thin walls. Martin knocked.

There was no answer at first, but Martin persisted until a tremulous female voice came through the door.

"Who is it?"

"It's Martin Delacroix and my lawyer. We ain't no gang and we ain't the heat. We need to talk to Tyrone and maybe help him. Would you please let us in?"

After a long delay, there was the clicking and snapping of several deadbolts. Finally the door opened a crack, showing three sets of safety chains strung across the opening. A small, frightened face peered through the crack at the white man and three dark giants standing behind him. Her eyes were wide and her thin lips trembled at the sight she beheld in the shadows of the stairway. She attempted to close the door, only to find Martin's booted toe through the opening. A low, terrified moan came through the crack, as if it was the end of the world.

Jack stepped up and talked through the crack. "Please, ma'am, we need your help. It's very important that you help us and there may be a chance you can. Please let us in."

There was a long uncertain pause. Jack could hear shallow, ragged breathing just inside the door. Perhaps the woman had never been asked for help of any kind.

She probably believed she could never give any help to anyone—helpless and hopeless, barely clinging to survival and the shreds of life itself.

After a sigh that carried all the suffering of mankind, the chains rattled down and the door tenuously opened. A tiny black woman cringed at the presence of the men standing before her. Martin and Jack tried a smile while Julian and Harold never changed expressions.

She reluctantly motioned for them to come into the sparely furnished but spotless living room. Jack could see a small kitchen through an open door and a short, narrow, hallway giving off onto what were probably two bedrooms and a bath. The men sat and the thin little woman stood before them, wringing her hands.

"Thank you, ma'am," Jack said gently. "I know anyone would be shocked to see such a group as us at the door, but we're calling on you for help, and we hope you can."

She looked puzzled.

Jack started explaining and she began to panic, appearing to be looking for a way to escape.

"Now, ma'am," Jack said, raising his hands to assure her, "we don't mean to cause you any upset or fear. We aren't here to get Tyrone in trouble, because we know he's had enough business with the law already. But he can help many others by givin' us just a little information. We want to bust their ass, if you know what I mean, and I mean bust it good!"

Her eyes darted to the hallway door. Jack asked, "Is he here? May I go in to see him? Or will he come on out? Now, if he won't talk to us, we'll leave right now, but keep in mind that they could do something to him again and to many others if they're not stopped. Somebody has to stand up and be counted; we're hoping that you and your son will."

The door to one of the bedrooms opened and "out stepped a strapping youth, late teens, with a gleaming, freshly shaved, bald head. He was wrapped in a towel, his hardened muscles glistening as if he had just stepped out of the shower.

The young man bristled with hostility, challenging his guests with his eyes. Here was a very street wise young man: tough, mean as hell, and full of ready violence. There were several homemade tattoos on his chest and arms, and an unidentifiable symbol had been scratched in blue on his cheek.

His baleful glare was met by the unblinking stares of the four men who sat saying nothing.

At length, Tyrone broke the silence. "What ya'll want?"

Martin explained the situation to him, Tyrone sneering as if it was no news to him and what Martin was saying was totally irrelevant. Martin finished and asked if he could help by providing information.

"You think I'm crazy? They put Tyrone right back in the slam and buttfuck me to death this time. I'm on the street and you ain't gonna get nothin' outta me."

"Tyrone," Jack entreated, "there's a beautiful girl, Martin's daughter, lying in the morgue right now because nobody ever came forward and helped. No telling who'll be next. Maybe you can stop this from happening to the next one. Why, you might even have a civil claim against the sheriff's department and get some money if you cooperate."

Tyrone's lips tightened as he watched Jack through narrowed eyelids. It was clear that this was a new spin on an old pitch for him.

"What kind of money you talkin' about?"

"I don't know. If you and enough others came forward, and we could win, there may be a good bit to spread around. It'll be handled in the Federal Court where the local bullshit makes no difference. We could file a big suit against the sheriff for all those who've been abused in Juvenile Detention, and that could mean bucks. I don't mean to sound vague, but I'm not gonna blow smoke and lie to you. There are no guarantees, but you might score. We may lose, but don't you think it's worth the try?"

Jack had Tyrone nodding, thinking about the money. Jack knew this was the only opportunity Tyrone had of making any major kind of money short of a life of crime. The money sounded good, but he hesitated.

Jack continued, seeing the uncertainty. "Tyrone, you may lose the case, and you may get nothing, or a little, or a lot. It's a crapshoot. Pass it up and you'll never know."

Tyrone looked plenty worried. He had lots to lose and he knew all about losing. Jack watched Tyrone wrestle with this new problem injected into his troubled life. A small tic developed in the cheek with the tattoo as he struggled with Jack's words.

The tough, posturing, surly Tyrone looked at his scared little mama who had turned gray while she listened to the exchanges. She knew the risk. She had lived in the ghetto all of her life and she knew the power of the law. If there wasn't direct reprisal by arrest on some specious charge, there could be simply a case of mistaken identity and Tyrone would be another morgue statistic.

"Your call, Tyrone. You man enough to handle it?" Jack said simply.

Tyrone's flared nostrils dilated as he grappled with the risks to himself and his little mama, who would be left alone if he were gone.

"Mothadear," Tyrone said to his mama, "I wants to do it. Them men give me the clap and used me every day, over and over, and called me they li'l girl. One time I bust that big 'un in the eye and knocked him out cold. They kept me another thirty days and really did me over that time. I ain't gonna never forget." He turned to Jack. "If ya'll tellin' me shit, you be lookin' at a dead Tyrone, 'cause you be killin' me as just like you be pullin' the trigger youself."

His mama buried her head in her hands and sobbed silently.

Tyrone dropped his arrogance and began to tell his story that began when he was nine. He never knew or had a father. He had been arrested for stealing hubcaps, bicycles, cigarettes, and everything that could be lifted by a kid. He had broken into houses and stores, and had sold drugs and pimped before he was fourteen. Now, he was nineteen, a powerful, vicious thug who had learned the ropes the hard way and survived. He wasn't like little James, who didn't have his pugnacious, combative spirit.

Tyrone gave names and addresses and the identities of those who had abused him.

"Them psychiatrists, Hotchkiss and Bormann, come in every week and I had to tell 'em everything that was done to me, and how I felt about it. They say they writin' a book and makin' a scientific study of some kind. If I didn't talk, they put more days on my prison stay."

"What did Bormann look like?"

"Big man. Red beard. He came every week. Talked into a little tape recorder about everything I said. The other 'un a l'il fag actin' dude."

"Did they take ya'll someplace out of the JD lockup?"

"Yeah. Town and Country motel. Some rooms had a big mirror on the side. I knowed it wasn't no mirror. Could see both ways. Somebody on the other side watchin'."

Jack frowned at that concept.

"You mean..."

'Yeah, I mean. Somebody on the other side watchin'." Tyrone's face showed a combination of fear and revulsion at that idea.

There was a moment of quiet as everyone absorbed the thought of a two way mirror in the bedrooms.

"Were others abused besides you?"

"Sho. The boys whored out after that, and most of the girls, if they wasn't whores before, went into the life after they got out. Some killed theyself when they got out."

"Were all the juveniles done this way?"

"Naw. Just some. Young pretty boys, good lookin' girls. Some would be picked out and picked up for nothin'. They usually come from poor families who couldn't do nothin' about it if they cared in the first place. Them doctors would say they was messed up in the head and then they could give 'em drugs and say they need what they called rehabilitation."

Jack was alarmed. Here was confirmation that certain of the "girl-boys," as Tyrone had been, and the attractive young girls had been carried to motel rooms for use by men who evidently paid someone well. He only hinted at their identities, but would not tell. He said that would be giving too much. He would be killed for sure.

"I heard talk about some high ups and the mob."

"Name somebody," Jack said.

"Some from the mob. Some come down from Baton Rouge. They all act the same. Them mafias, them laws, them politicians."

"I see," Jack said. "Just give me one name, that's all."

There was a pause, and Tyrone's eyes filmed over at the memory. "On me, Shep McConnell, an' on one of the girls, a dude name Aucoin. McConnell with the governor's office, cause he bragged about it, an Aucoin with the State Hospitals. They was a bunch of others. Once they put a dude name Bosco on me—say he was with the State Police, but I don't think so."

He told of the deputies, Jelly Belly Parker and Destrehan, a big black man with his high soundin' uptown talk.

Jack taped Tyrone's rambling listing of names and what they did to him and those he knew about. He met Tyrone's gaze. He knew that Tyrone felt he'd signed his own execution order, but both knew exactly what they were doing; both were moved by the same reason, and it wasn't money after all.

"Talk to some of your friends who've been through this, Tyrone, and get 'em to contact me. We need as many as possible, because I'm going to kick this city right in the ass and you'll help me do it!"

Tyrone didn't nod or smile. He was clearly frightened, already regretting his momentary experience with truth.

"We're doing what we have to do," Jack said to both Tyrone and his mama, "and it seems we don't have any choice if we intend to live with ourselves. Life's not worth livin' if we have to sneak around hopin' nobody is going to kick our asses. The asskickers are the ones who make it. You gotta choose what you're gonna be. I'd rather kick ass."

"Amen," Martin said.

Tyrone's face broke into a smile for one brief instant, showing large, bright, even teeth and a childlike innocence through the tough veneer of the projects. Jack shook his hand and the other three men shook hands all around. All of the men gave their phone numbers and addresses, and told them to call if there was any sign of trouble.

On the drive back, Jack dialed a number on his cell phone.

A deep, masculine voice with a Cajun accent answered. "Allo?"

"Nookie?"

"Yaas?"

"Jack Chandler, your lawyer."

"Hey, cher! What you doin' right here before this one big dam hurrican?"

"I didn't hear the latest. Been out of touch for the last few hours."

"Hoo boy, bad time, bad weather. This a bad 'un. Aurora, she clamb up the Florida Coast, now she in the middle of the Guff, tryin' to make her mind. Nobody knows what them hurrican gon' do. What you need?"

"I need your services. . .tonight."

Nookie Naquin, pronounced "knock-ann," was a Chitimachas Indian born and raised in the Gulf tidal marsh land thirty miles south of Houma, a city to the southwest of New Orleans. He was, among other things, a burglar. Jack had saved him twice from jail. Nookie's gratitude was boundless, particularly since Jack had represented him free of charge. It hadn't been Jack's idea, but Nookie believed in the barter system when it came to his costs. Nookie intimately knew the coast from Sabine Pass at the Texas border to the Pearl River on the Mississippi line. Many times he had taken Jack to catch big speckled trout and redfish, legally and illegally, as part of his fee. Plus he and Jack liked each other. Both could have been happy enough in an uncivilized society.

Nookie was a full blooded Indian, with the lighthearted ways of a thoroughbred Cajun. His ancestors were native Americans, having lived on the coasts of Louisiana for thousands of years. Cajuns were country French people, exiled from Acadia in Nova Scotia just over two hundred fifty years previous. The Cajun's powerful cultural influence had all but absorbed the Indian culture except for small pockets "down the bayou" where Nookie was born.

Nookie had a strong sense of family unity. He returned home several times a year to help his family during the trawling season when they pulled the big nets to catch shrimp. When times were good, they would bring home thousands of dollars worth of shrimp. Nookie's home on the bayou was positively serene, with no action but the wind rustling the marsh grass, the calls of the swamp birds, the kerplunk of a great fish turning over, or an alligator grunting after his dinner. But the marsh didn't hold Nookie for long at a time. During the off season, when he wasn't trawling for shrimp or working as a mate or skipper on crewboats for offshore oil rigs, Nookie hung out around the joints on Bourbon Street because he had an affinity for loose, wild women—and the city gratified his need for constant movement and action. Jack was convinced Nookie was a reincarnated pirate who haunted Barataria Bay and New Orleans waterways during the days of Jean Lafitte. He was also irresistibly charming.

Short and squarely built, Nookie walked with the grace of a natural dancer, or a panther. He had those soft, all seeing, liquid brown eyes that shared a secret smile. Sparkling white teeth showed through his dark beard and he let his wavy black hair grow to his collar. Like Jack he sometimes tied it up in a pony tail with a red ribbon. A small gold earring was in his left ear. Jack admired Nookie's ability to dazzle women.

He told Jack that he broke into a house in the Garden District where a refined lady owner caught him red-handed at her silver. When he turned on his Cajun charm and laughed at the situation with complete insouciance, she lowered her gun and asked if he cared for a drink. He accommodated her wishes completely and when he left at daybreak, she retrieved the items she really wanted, and let him take the rest. She collected the insurance. Jack envied Nookie's ability to *laissez-le-bon-temps rouler,*: let the good times roll. Nookie was totally carefree, perpetually happy, always with a pocket full of money.

Nookie also had the ability to make himself invisible. He could turn his back or look away, somehow blending into his surroundings like a chameleon. He explained this ability to Jack. He said he didn't put out any signals to anything around him, concentrating on the pavement or his shoes or something very close to him. He said people can feel you if you look at them. He just became part of the scenery.

Jack called Vic on her cell phone and told her what he and Nookie were going to do. She protested, saying she could get in and out of the morgue better than anyone because of her work in pathology. Jack didn't want to expose her to any more danger than necessary and besides, he wanted her completely out of the picture and not appear to be involved. She would likely be recognized, and for sure a cutie like Vic would surely be remembered.

It was dark when Jack returned home. The wind had picked up and the rain struck his face like pellets as he ran to his doorway. It was only when he heard Nookie chuckle a few feet away that he saw him leaning against a wall under the overhang of his own balcony. Jack jumped, feeling for his gun, then swore when he realized who it was.

"Nookie, you son-of-a bitch! You scared hell out of me!"

Still laughing, Nookie said, "Hoo boy, you jump like a shot rabbit."

"Damn! Don't do that, Nookie. You'll give me a heart attack. I got lots on my mind. Come on in and let's talk."

The phone was ringing when they entered Jack's office. It was Martin.

"Lawyer Jack," Martin said, "my phone been ringin' off the hook since we got back. Tyrone got things stirred up. A bunch of folks wants to see you. One of 'em told me I had better lay off if I knowed what was good for me!"

"A threat?" Jack asked.

"That was plain. Tyrone been talkin' out both sides of his mouth—coverin' his li'l punk ass just in case. He done called somebody."

"Well," Jack sighed, "we knew we'd be getting into it when we started this. Just take their names and phone numbers and I'll try to see as many as I can tomorrow. I may be out for a while this evenin'. I'll call you when I get back."

When he hung up, he hurriedly briefed Nookie on the situation and related his plan.

"I know you can find a way into the morgue and with the storm coming, nobody'll be watching it closely, Jack said. They think I'll back off. All we have to do is to move the body to another drawer–delay 'em a day or so till I can do somethin'. They won't suspect it'll be hidden in their own morgue."

Nookie thought for a moment and then grinned. "You goddam crazy, Jack. I stole a lot of thing in my life, but I never stole no dead person!"

"We ain't stealin' her," Jack protested. "We're just hidin' her."

"This gonna be a different kind of break in for sho!" Nookie said, slapping the palm of his hand on his forehead.

They raced up the winding stair to Jack's apartment. Jack changed into blue jeans and a dark shirt and took a six pack of Dixie from the refrigerator.

Nookie's old "pick-em-up," as he called it, looked like any other old run-out Chevy truck, with a few dents, bondo on a faded front fender, and a camper built in the bed. It had a four barrel carburetor, dual exhausts, and the motor ran like a sewing machine. It was muffled down so that it purred. The camper accommodated a bed, small stove and storage area. Nookie was self-sufficient and was never at a loss for sleeping quarters when there was a need, but he seldom had a need because any number of beds in the city were available any time he wanted.

"The cops can't catch Nookie," Nookie said airily. "Podnah, you gotta be ready and fast if you need to move, and this old green machine is like a damn roaming candle on the fourth of July. She'll make a hundred twenty an' I got her her center of gravity slung way low."

Jack felt vaguely relieved, but he didn't know why. Nookie had only been caught twice at his burglarizing and each time it was because of events beyond his control. Once, he had not counted on there being two different alarm systems in the house, and the other was when a random check of vehicles on Chef Menteur Highway caught him with a load of stolen merchandise. Jack had managed to walk him in each case and he had Nookie's enduring gratitude.

Nookie was one of the most skilled second story men in the city, but Jack really didn't want to know the details. He only knew that this man could get in and out of any building without detection, and he could outsmart any alarm system.

The windshield wipers smacked at the random sheets of rain as the men drove down the broad Tulane Avenue to Charity Hospital. Nookie turned into a narrow side street and parked alongside the Hospital building itself.

The rear window to the truck opened into the camper. Nookie reached into a little cabinet he had built at the head of the bed and removed two dark wool navy caps. He told Jack to put one on while he pulled his own down over his curly locks. Immediately their appearances were transformed.

Nookie said, "See, you might not be able to pick me out in a line-up if you don't see my hair. Pull it down over your ears and nobody could know you from the back; only if they see you head on could they know you."

Nookie crawled into the camper. There was a thump and the clank of tools and things being emptied out onto the floor. He clambered back through the window dragging a large olive drab canvas bag along with him.

Nookie had put on a pair of coveralls sporting a blue and white patch embroidered on the pocket that read "Louis," and on his left lapel was another that read "Bayou Maintenance." Around his waist he strapped a wide leather belt bearing pockets filled with mechanic's tools, and in his hand he had a clipboard holding sheets of invoice paper with carbons between. The heading on the invoice read "Bayou Maintenance."

Nookie handed a jacket with "Bayou Maintenance" on one pocket and "Myron" on the other, a clipboard and flashlight to Jack. "Wear this an' carry this, cause you look more like a boss, Myron. Hee hee. We come to fix the refrigeration unit inna morgue."

Jack could only nod his head in wonder.

"Here, wear these too," Nookie said, handing Jack a pair of heavy rimmed glasses with plain glass lenses. They won't recognize me, but you need something to draw attention beside youself. You see, people, they don't notice much; they stumble around kinda blind. We gonna give 'em something wrong to remember. Hee Hee!"

Jack put the glasses on. To the world, the pair were plumbers.

Nookie leaned back and looked at Jack. "Ma poo yi yi, you mama won't know you now! Where the morgue at?"

"We gotta go through the emergency room," Jack said, opening the door to the truck and bounding away through the driving rain.

They stopped running under the overhang sheltering the emergency parking and ambulance area. Several ambulances and hearses were parked beneath the shelter, with attendants, drivers and nurses swarming about loading and unloading their cheerless cargo.

Two orderlies, busily talking about the storm, pushed a low cart loaded with long, heavy-duty cardboard boxes to the far end of the overhang near a dumpster overflowing with vile smelling refuse. After the orderlies walked away, Nookie casually kicked half of the boxes from the cart into the street and pushed it toward the emergency room door.

"Nobody gonna notice us," Nookie said nonchalantly, "you just watch."

Jack led the way through the double swinging doors that opened into the emergency area. People scurried to and fro as the plumbers strolled casually through the bedlam.

The halls were lined with emergency cases. They pushed the cart through the milling crowds as if they were indeed plumbers who knew just what they were doing. When they passed a receiving area, where several nurses and attendants did what nurses and attendants do, nobody so much as looked up at them. They continued through emergency into the dim hallway beyond, with Jack holding his clipboard and flashlight, his symbols of authority and passport into the bowels of the big building.

Bumping the cart against the two large, grimy metal swinging doors, they entered a hall with doors along the way marked as laboratory, contaminated materials, supplies, and janitorial closet. At the end was an elevator large enough to accommodate the cart.

The elevator slowly dropped them to the first level of the basement where they found themselves in a dimly lighted hallway. Across the hall was a little plate on a door that read MORGUE.

Nookie grinned and turned the knob.

It was locked.

Jack caught his breath and Nookie held a finger to his lips and winked. "Keep a lookout," he said to Jack.

There was a light jingle as Nookie sorted through an assortment of odd looking wires and thin pieces of metal in a small leather wallet. Jack watched the hall behind them and in less than a minute the door swung open into a large dark room.

Nookie swept his hand down in a grand, eloquent gesture, indicating for Jack to push the cart through.

Noiselessly, they eased through the door and shut it behind them. It was pitch dark. Nookie played the little beam of a penlight around the room. The chamber was piled high with plain, wooden caskets on each side, and the point of his light found another door at the opposite side of the room. Nookie walked toward it and Jack followed, pushing the cart.

They listened for some time at the door for voices or activity on the other side. Finally, deciding it was safe, Nookie eased the door open. They had come in the morgue's rear entrance.

Jack whispered that the office was through the door in the far wall and somebody may be there. They tiptoed to that door and could hear voices on the other side. Jack's eyes were as wide as saucers.

Nookie chose a slender probe from his lock pick kit and worked with the lock until there was a soft snap as the door's bolt slid in place. "That'll give us time to get out if they try to come in." Nookie whispered.

Jack looked at the banks of drawers on all sides of the room. It was freezing cold in the room and he shuddered. The smell of formaldehyde was so powerful it nearly took his breath.

"Pooyie!" Nookie whistled, "dat's some bad stink, dat!"

"Yeah, but I would rather that."

"Hoo boy, you hit the head on the nail that time!" Nookie agreed.

Jack rolled out three drawers before he found the right one. Each of the others were occupied with sheet draped corpses in various states of decay. One had its head nearly blown away by what appeared to be a shotgun blast. Finally they found Dawn Marie.

"They haven't tampered with her," Jack said.

A grin came over Nookie's face. "Hey Jack. You know my coozan LaLa Matherne, the one they call Poochie? His friend girl, she say 'LaLa, you say you gon' take me to Florida.' He say, 'Shoop, I ain't tole you no such dam thing. I say I gonna tamper wit you." Hee Hee."

Jack punched Nookie on the shoulder and said, "Dammit, Nookie, get serious! Let's find a place we can move her to where they won't find her."

Each drawer Jack tried to open was either locked or filled. "Nookie, this damned place is loaded with dead guys. There ain't no place we can move her!"

Just as Nookie began applying his skills to open a locked drawer, the door to Sanchez' office area rattled. Jack caught his breath and grabbed Nookie on the shoulder. "Oh shit!"

Nookie made a motion with his hand for Jack to be cool. "I jammed the lock. They'll be a few minutes gettin' in, an' they won't find out it was jammed by nobody. Look like it froze up."

Jack was transfixed to the spot. "Fuck a duck!" He whispered.

Someone was trying keys to unlock the door. There was the sound of metal twisting in the lock.

Nookie's voice then became urgent. "We gotta split, Jack."

"We don't have a choice, Nookie, we gotta take her with us!"

"Take her with us? You gone foo foo?"

Jack pulled the drawer out as far as it would go and began to tug at the sheet draped corpse. He refused to remove the sheet, keeping it wrapped tightly around the rigid form that reeked of formaldehyde.

"Damn, Jack!" Nookie swore, "Let me hep' you."

They stood the little sheet draped figure alongside the table, and it remained upright. It was less than five feet tall.

Nookie paused, and whispered, "Hey, we got de tool bag!"

The office door shook and rattled. Loud, angry talking could be heard from the other side. Nookie took the long duffel bag, slid it down over the standing body and lifted it easily onto the cart.

Jack suddenly had an inspiration. He hurriedly whispered something to Nookie. They opened another drawer nearby and lifted a corpse and transferred it to Dawn Marie's drawer, and covered it with a sheet. Anyone simply looking in the drawer couldn't tell the difference without lifting the sheet.

"Jack, you coulda just traded places with her and dat udder one. It'd been all the same!"

Jack ignored him and pushed the cart toward the back door as fast as he could without ramming something in the dark.

Nookie jammed the lock between the storage room and the morgue. They quickly inspected the bag lying on the cart and noticed Dawn's cold chalky feet sticking out of the bottom. Nookie gave the feet a shove as Jack held the bag and the body slid all the way in until the head rounded the top. Nookie fastened the bottom so that it looked like any other filled duffel bag. But there was still something odd-looking about it.

They stacked the remaining empty boxes they had left on the cart all around the bag and when they were done, Nookie dusted his hands together with satisfaction, grinning. "Bayou Maintenance on de job," he said.

They pushed the cart into the hall and Nookie locked the door behind him.

With imperious indifference, the plumbers of Bayou Maintenance wheeled the cart down the hall past the busy attendants and nurses who attended the nightly harvest of the ill and injured. Jack pretended to check his clipboard as they strolled through the emergency area to the back entrance and the parking area.

A curtain of water poured from the lip of the overhang, splashing at their feet. Nookie ran through the wall of water and backed the pickup through the torrential downpour to the ramp. Jack opened the rear door to the camper and easily slid the bag onto the floor of the camper between a narrow bunk and built in cabinets.

Jack checked the time. It was only nine o'clock. He was amazed that it had been less than twenty-four hours since this craziness began. He had kidnapped a corpse, and he had no idea what to do with it.

They drove along Tulane Avenue and turned right on Loyola. The tops of the trees whipped and churned in the wind, and the streets were rushing rivers.

Nookie tuned to WNOE's weather report. "The U.S. Weather Bureau advised a hurricane watch from the Mississippi Sound to Matagorda Bay on the central Texas coast. Aurora has churned into the Gulf with winds of seventy-five miles per hour after it passed Key West and is now in the middle of the gulf picking up intensity. A hurricane watch is in effect across the entire central gulf coast."

"Mais yeah, this one damn big hurrican, Jack. If we already gettin' squalls with this much rain, she mus' be a real bad lady. When she sit around in the guff like that, she pick up steam and get mean as hell. Now what?" Nookie asked, hooking his thumb toward the camper in back in hitchhiker fashion.

"One thing for sure, she needs to stay cold. Got any ideas?"

Nookie frowned as he pondered the question. He thought as they drove, then raised his eyebrows wisely as if he had the answer.

"Nobody ain't goin' out tonight, or tomorrow. But Nookie, he got a idea. Cold storage locker, a freezer place down off Tchoupitoulas. Ain't nobody gonna be down there in the storm. Run by a generator. She'll keep."

Jack thought about this for a moment, then said: "Now I'm guilty of burglary, kidnapping a corpse, unauthorized use of a movable, and in a little while, freezing of a juvenile."

"Dat's a fact!" Nookie laughed, "Me too."

Jack said, "If the storm is as big as they say and if it hits the city, everything'll be shut down for forty eight hours at least. Things'll be so messed up and confused, I bet nobody'll even notice she's gone."

"You right about dat." Nookie said, nodding. "What you gonna do with her, you crazy redneck?"

"Damfino. I'll think of somethin'. Gotta get her someplace safe, so the right people can check her out."

Winos seeking a dry place stumbled along the gusty street in the rain.

"Where'll they go?" Jack asked absently, pointing at the bums hugging the dingy brick walls as they staggered through the rain.

"They'll find someplace," Nookie said sagely, "they know every hole—like roaches—come out when the rain stop."

Jack shook his head at the thought.

Nookie turned from Magazine onto a side street and drove slowly for a block or so until they hit the warehouse district. He then turned onto a one way street with warehouses on each side. Nookie jumped out and told Jack to get under the wheel.

Once again Nookie plied his art and an overhead door swung up, revealing a huge cavernous space with hulking black shapes in the darkness. Jack gunned the motor and the pickup jumped through the opening.

They entered a storage warehouse filled with huge, grotesque monstrosities. The headlights revealed a space, just wide enough to drive between high, rearing heads of jesters, crowned monarchs, serpents and alligators, and all manner of fantastic creatures, thirty feet or more in height, all leering and scowling down at him from the top of Mardi Gras floats stored in the big building.

The effect of the rain thundering on the metal roof, the glowering eyes of the creatures adorning the big floats, the body in the back, the acres of tinsel and glitter vibrating and jittering all about him from the incessant thunder, the danger Jack was plunging headlong into, took on a alien, other worldly effect. An immense clown, with a red ball nose as big a tire, animated during parades by rolling its eyes and moving its long arms, towered over the truck. A deafening thunderclap shook the building, and the clown began moving slowly. Jack's hair prickled on the back of his neck, knowing it was only an artificially animated thing to begin with, but clowns had never been funny to him, actually frightened him as a child, and a thrill of fear shot through him. Taken all together, as he drove slowly down the narrow fantasy corridor, with Nookie walking ahead of the truck, leading the way, it was a nightmare parade hovering in the dark, omens of what lay ahead.

Nookie pointed to a concrete block wall to his right. A large metal door was set in the wall with a chrome levered handle on the side. A two story float, with a crowned, bejeweled, twenty foot crawfish perched majestically on a great throne, was parked directly by the door.

"Dis is it," Nookie said.

Nookie inspected the lock to the freezer in the tiny beam of his penlight, his lock pick set jingling. In a moment, the door swung open and Jack felt a blast of icy air. Inside the freezer, corridors led off to the right and left from an enormous room with sides of beef and pork hanging in rows on ceiling mounted trolleys. Down one corridor, they found individual rooms filled with boxes of frozen foods.

"Wholesale storage," Nookie said, as if answering Jack's unasked question. "Some of dis stuff may get et at Arnauds or Antoines; silk stockin' restaurants. Some good eats in here."

Continuing to wander around, they found a small, isolated room in the very back, stacked with long empty wax-coated boxes.

They carried the duffel bag and its contents to the back room and slid it into one of the boxes and closed it. Jack read on the side of the box, "Swift's Premium Short Ribs."

On the way out, Nookie made a short detour and returned with a smaller wax-coated box, which he shoved into the camper. He snapped his fingers with considerable satisfaction then locked the door to the storage locker.

They drove out and Jack pulled the big door down."Thanks, Nookie. Will she be okay in there?" Jack asked.

"Mais yeah. In case the power go out, they got a generator what kick in and keep it all good in there. They ready for any kind of weather."

"Hey, Nookie, what's in the box?"

"You know me, dis a gold opportunity for Nookie to get some fine aged ribeye, sirloin an' T-bone. Man, me and my lady, you know—Pussy Beaucoup, we shore like them T-bone! Hey, hold on, I got more'n enough. Some of them T-bone an' ribeye been already cut in two inch portion, so I gonna' make a gift of some so you can have something good to cook tonight when you git in. If you need me, I gon' be down at The Sudden Exposure. You know my cell number."

"That's mighty kind of you, Nook. Now that makes me guilty of breakin' and entering a cold storage and theft of steak as well as accessory of theft of steak and receiving stolen steak."

"Mais yeah, cher," Nookie whooped, "Me too."

"Nook, you hang by your cell phone. Don't let the battery go dead. I got a feeling I'm gonna need you at any time for something or another. So don't leave town without calling me."

"Whoo boy, Jack. You think I gonna let something like this slip through my finger? This the best time I had in a while! My ear gonna be listenin' for you ring, hopin' you need me. I think we gonna be busy tonight or tomorrow."

They crossed into the Quarter and Nookie said, "This is where I always park my pick-um-up. Seems like I can always find this place empty for some reason, even in Mardi Gras." He pointed at a sign that said 'No Parking, Convent.' He chuckled to himself at Nookie's viewpoint on life in general. Life was to be lived, and everything not tied down was available.

Nookie dug some big steaks out of the waxed box and handed them to Jack. Nookie said, his eyes gleaming under uplifted eyebrows, "my lady love age T-bone. Poo-yi, it gonna be a great night for 'ol Nookie," he grinned lasciviously.

Jack slapped Nookie on the shoulder and closed the door behind him.

Hugging several large cuts of Kansas City ribeyes and T-bones, Jack ran through the rain and stood briefly under the overhang of his apartment balcony. The rain splashed on the sidewalk around his feet while gusts of wind tugged at his clothes.

The rain was getting cold. Puffs of wind blew spatters in his face, and though he was getting soaked, he continued to stand and gaze down the narrow street.

Jack was given to introspection at any time, and he stood in the rain and thought about himself and how he was always getting into predicaments to solve. *What the hell's wrong with me? Why can't I have a simple, uncomplicated life, make some money, get laid, go fishing, get drunk, read my books. Is this some kind of Karma?*

The falling curtain of rain created a nimbus around each street light. The shingles hanging in front of the stores down Royal Street rattled as they swung and jerked at their chains in the wind. A seagoing tug hooted and a police siren squealed down Rampart a few blocks away. A rush of affection for the Quarter ran through him. *This is a great place to live,* he thought as he walked the few feet in the rain to turn his key in the door.

Soaking wet, he dripped on the floor on the way up the stairs and into his apartment. He stripped and changed into jeans with no shirt.

Jack had no sooner opened a beer when there came a knock on the door. Vic stood outside, her hands on her hips with a scowl on her face. "You said you wouldn't leave me out of the action. What did you do?"

Jack held up his hands as she advanced through the door demanding an answer. "Mea Culpa, I'm guilty. I cut you out, but I don't think it would have been good for you to be recognized, and someone would have known you at Charity."

Vic sighed, giving in. "I guess you're right about that, but I knew that child, and I love her family and I am going to help even if I have to do it without you."

Jack's eyes crinkled, grinning his lopsided grin at this feisty woman and the fact that she had always gotten what she wanted and this was something she wanted. He had better give in. Vic noticed the huge steaks on the table. "Wow, these are wonderful. I don't think I've ever seen such fine T-bones. Where did you get them? There's enough for both of us."

While he recounted the venture in the morgue and cold storage locker, she listened, wide eyed and intent on everything he said.

"Wish I'd gone with you. That's kickass," she said, her eyes sparkling, caught up in the excitement of the telling. "You tricked me this time, but you're not gonna leave me out any more after this, Jack" she said, poking him with her small cafe-au-lait finger on his hairy chest.

"OK, I won't leave you out from now on. But things are heatin' up, and there are some badasses out there trying to cover up and they're gettin' serious."

Jack felt his heart thud as he looked at this vital woman poking him so seriously in the chest. The feeling was so intense it almost made his eyes water, and his breath caught in his throat. He wanted to take this fantastic being in his arms and hold her. This was a feeling he had never had before, but it was something beyond his expectations and hope. And because of it he was, for the first time in his life, vulnerable.

The steaks whispered in the broiler as they sipped merlot from long stemmed glasses. The apartment filled with the smells of roasting steak while the wind and rain battered the walls and windows in episodic gusts. Jack couldn't get his mind onto the evening. Neither could Vic. They would talk about the weather, and always return to the subject of Dawn, speculating on who and what and why. They were worried. This was something neither had experience in handling, the unknown, the dangerous.

Both completed preparing the dinner and brought two sizzling T-Bones, with baked potato, creole tomato and salad, to the table. They sat on the sofa and ate in silence on the coffee table, with Jack having more on his mind than he had ever remembered. He had to solve the problem about Dawn, run his law office with troubles of its own, and now how he could keep Vic from harm.

Vic seemed similarly pre-occupied, as their worried eyes met from time to time.

Then Jack realized how much he was enjoying the steak. "You know, there's something about this stolen steak. I don't think I've ever had one so good."

"Illegal, Jack."

"I think I could be an outlaw, Vic. Live on the cusp, like Nookie, where things are just more alive, more ah, delicious."

"Yeah, but you would sink your own boat, Jack. People are basically good, and sooner or later you'd cave. We carry our own justice system in us and you wouldn't last. If you wouldn't turn yourself in you'd find a way to get caught."

"Yeah, you right. But the idea's cool."

"The problem you have, Jack, is you should have been born when there were warrior poets, in days of romance, when people weren't so civilized."

"Yeah, I feel like I'm in a strait jacket—having to wear a seat belt, abide by rules, pay taxes, stand in line. There's something in me that just won't let me be part of this hypocritical world. They pat their feet to music I can't hear. And they don't hear mine."

"You're a wild men," Vic said, her eyes glowing like live coals.

Tension was building, nearing the end of their dinner. Neither looked at the other, except a surreptitious glance from time to time, and finally, Vic stood by the couch and looked directly in Jack's eyes. He went rigid and said nothing; he was tongue-tied.

They stared at each other for what seemed like a lifetime, and then she opened the door and turned to Jack, who hadn't moved. "Thanks for the dinner and company."

"Uh, no problem. It was cool."

"Yeah, cool. Call me before you get into any more trouble."

She closed the door behind her, and Jack clenched his teeth and groaned, "Goddammit!"

Something blew over on the balcony. The night and its troubles intruded. The temperature had dropped twenty degrees in the past hour. Jack felt a chill.

He brought the furniture in from the balcony, decided to do the dishes in the morning, and fell asleep on the couch. Just as Jack felt the velvet blanket of sleep close over him, he knew his life had changed. He didn't know if it was for the better or the worst. Either way, he was confused, when he had always been the totally confident stud in his love life.

Soon he was in the deep forests of dream, running away from the unconfrontable.

Chapter 6

DAY THREE

It was still dark, but the darkness was not from the hour, for it should have been daylight. He slid out of bed, walked to the balcony and watched the rain sweeping the streets below. He made a stout pot of coffee and took a steaming cup to the sliding glass doors. The curtain of water pouring off the balcony shifted and twisted in the random gusts, spattering the glass doors.

Everyone in south Louisiana would be holed up for the duration of the blow. The T.V. showed the location of the eye of the hurricane to be standing fifty miles off the mouth of the river, inching north. There was talk of evacuating the entire city, depending on the direction the storm would take. The roads would already be jammed.

He plugged and filled the tub. Water may be in short supply. Electricity was usually the first thing to go, so he took an old Coleman lantern and some candles from the closet and placed them around the room. Flooding wouldn't affect them on the second floor. There were some canned goods in the pantry, whiskey, beans and rice, and plenty coffee. He could make it.

The phone rang, causing Jack to start at the unexpected interruption of his speculations and plans. Who would be calling at this hour?

A deep, resonant male voice asked, "Is this attorney Jack Chandler?"

"Yes. Who's this?"

"I have some information that can help you."

"About what?"

"There are some things that go on at the Juvenile Detention Center that you ought to know about. I've been there."

"Who Are you?"

There was a long pause, and the voice said, "I would rather not talk on the phone."

"Can you come over here?"

"No." The voice was definite. "I must stay out of sight."

The man was intelligent, articulate and from the rich timbre of his voice, probably black, but with very little trace of New Orleans or southern accent.

"Where do you wanna meet?"

Jack was given an Esplanade address that was only fifteen or so blocks away, a section of the oak lined boulevard having a number of dilapidated and vacant buildings.

"It's a vacant house; come in the front door and meet me in the back. I'll be waiting. You'll get what you need."

"When?"

"Now."

The line clicked as Jack began to ask more questions. A dial tone droned in his ear, and slowly put the receiver down. *Stupid to go without back-up,* he thought. *Maybe I can get those linebackers who helped us out in the projects.*

Jack had learned Aikido and Karate from Vic, and a client had taught him some dirty street kick fighting tricks. If lucky, he could get away from trouble. Much of his skill depended on whether he had enough warning. Also, his .38 revolver gave him an edge—maybe.

Jack punched Martin's number. The phone rang many times, but there was no answer. Jack groaned, regretting he hadn't gotten the lion and the rhino's phone numbers.

He dialed again and let it ring for a long time. "Damn!" Jack swore. Then he remembered that Estelle and Martin were Catholic and were probably at early mass. They needed all of the spiritual help they could get during this most terrible of times.

Jack dialed Nookie's number: no answer. He called several others, including his drinking buddy, Sam Leviathon. Nobody was home, or just not answering.

Jack gnawed his knuckles and debated if he should call Vic. This could be the most dangerous yet. Should he expose her to whatever this call portended, or should he expose himself to her wrath for not calling her. He had promised, broken the first promise and promised again.

He thought of the way Vic looked as she left last night. She might be a tiger in the ring, but this was real life, and Dawn was dead—murdered, and he didn't even know who the enemy was. But the enemy knew about him! He squeezed his eyes shut and decided he had to protect her, and would rather her rage than expose her to danger.

But the choice was not his to make. A knock on the door startled him out of his introspection.

Standing in the doorway was Vic, excitement glowing on her face. "Okay, partner. What's on the agenda? It's Sunday, and I have the whole day free."

Jack finally found his voice, after he found his breath, for Vic was in a pair of white shorts, halter top, and her long black hair in a pony tail tied with a red ribbon. She was so animated the pony tail seemed to have a life of its own.

Jack filled her in, and told her he couldn't get anybody on the phone to go out in a hurricane and talk to a snitch with him. Jack thought, *This is another crossroad. Do I go or stay? Maybe this will provide material evidence. Maybe it's death calling.*

"I think we need to check it out," Vic said.

Again here was danger, and he was getting Vic into it. *How the hell did all this happen at once? I find someone like this and now I am exposing her to danger. How irresponsible can I be? How can I get out of taking her?"*

As if reading his mind, Vic said, "You're not getting out of taking me this time. You promised. We're a team, you said, then you tricked me into not going to the morgue with you. If you go, I go. Simple as that."

Jack hesitated. "Maybe we should wait until Martin can get his squad of brutes to run interference."

"And maybe the caller will chicken out and what he has will be lost?"

Dammit! Safe, sensible choices are never available in urgent situations, he thought. But then, he had never followed the safest or the most sensible path.

Jack cracked his knuckles and stared into space as he wrestled with the decision. *What's wrong with me! The road I take is usually the hard one."*

Jack's lips turned up in a half smile. At the very bottom of it, it was for the sensation: the ripping, gripping, edge that seemed to be the only paymaster that surrendered a full paycheck. There was no choice. The caller may be the grim reaper, but he had to know. "No guts, no glory," he said aloud, suddenly energized by his decision.

Vic's eyes sparkled, "Lock and load," she said, having heard Jack use the expression meaning to get ready for action. She spun around and raced downstairs, saying, as she ran, "I'll get my rain gear. Meet you by the front door."

Jack strapped on his shoulder holster and dumped the bullets from the .38 into his hand to inspect them. He then dropped the bullets back into the chambers, spun the cylinder and slid the revolver into the holster. Pulling on his old yellow slicker suit with a hood, left in his office by a sailor he had represented on a public drunkenness and fighting charge, he locked the door behind him and went down the stairs. Vic ran up the dark hall to meet him, wearing a pair of tight fitting jeans, a bright red slickersuit and a pair of rubber boots.

She walked up to Jack, her eyes glowing with excitement. He would smell the light fragrance she always wore. *God she fills the senses.*

Jack shook his head at the grit of his woman and they ran through the driving rain to his Ford. When he pressed on the accelerator, he knew there was no turning back.

Chapter 7

Night refused to let go of its hold and streetlights were still on at nine. Jack turned on the headlights. The wipers on full barely cleared the windshield enough to see. Rain came in sheets, hitting the windows like firehoses, and the car shuddered in the broadside gusts blasting through the streets. He tuned to WWL. The only news was about the storm.

"Aurora is moving in a direct line toward the mouth of the Mississippi. It should make landfall by late afternoon and then is expected to pick up momentum. The direction it takes when it passes Empire and Venice is anybody's guess."

Jack thought about Slidell and Mandeville, two small towns sitting hard by the north shore of Lake Pontchartrain. They could be wiped out if Aurora turned easterly and New Orleans could be inundated and blown away if it turned northwesterly. The huge, shallow, brackish lake must be whipped to a frenzy, beating at the concrete sea wall. It could become a nightmare if Aurora pushed it in either direction. Nobody in his right mind would try to cross the lake on the 24 mile long causeway over the lake. The bridge itself may get blown away in this wind.

They plowed through the flooded streets, finally finding the address in an area of large old houses built in the pre-depression 'teens and twenties by an affluent middle and upper class. Urban flight and the intrusion of lower income whites and blacks emptied them during the fifties. Rows of three and four storied empty-eyed homes stood side by side along the formerly elegant boulevard.

The address had once served as the Brazilian Embassy. Long abandoned by its diplomatic tenants and occupied by a lesser and lesser class of lodgers, finally bums and transients slept in the once sumptuous rooms.

They stopped in front and raced up the broad steps to a sagging front porch and stood under the overhang. A steady stream of water poured through a hole in the porch roof, beating on the hoods of their slickers. Jack's heart thudded against his rib cage from the brief exertion and the tense drive through the rain, but mainly because of who or what waited inside. A foreboding swept through him. He usually obeyed those signs. It was everything he could do to resist the urge to run back to his car.

Vic was tense, and didn't smile when their eyes met.

"Chill, Jack!" He muttered to himself.

He hefted his heavy five cell police flashlight made of tempered steel. The police used them as effective billyclubs. Carrying it in his left hand, he clutched the .38 in his right as he pushed on the solid mahogany door with his shoulder. Swollen from the moisture and rain, it resisted. He gave a solid kick and it scraped open wide enough for them to squeeze through.

Jack sniffed at the dank, musty air. They stood dripping on the marble floor of the small foyer. In the beam of their lights, the hall widened a few feet from the entrance. Beyond was a long hall that disappeared into the darkness with huge rooms on the right and left. Built long before air conditioning, the house had sixteen foot ceilings with tall windows that provided cross ventilation in the torrid days of New Orleans summer.

They inched forward quietly. Whoever waited inside surely heard him kick the door open. Even though he was expected, Jack wasn't going to blunder through the darkness with any unexplored dark doors or hallways to their back or flank. He would know what was behind them before moving through.

The floor was littered with beer cans, bottles, empty food wrappers, worn out clothes and shoes.

The room to the left had been a large sitting room with a large fireplace that had been recently used. The floor all around the hearth and the wall alongside was scorched and blackened with soot where fire had once escaped and for some reason hadn't burned the whole house down. To the right was a library study with sagging, empty shelves that reached from floor to the high, vaulted ceiling. Some of the shelves had been ripped down, perhaps to use as firewood. The room was as big as his whole apartment.

A wide stair curved gracefully from the hall around to the second floor. They passed alongside the staircase with backs to the wall, playing their *flashlights* into every dark corner.

"Stay by me," Jack whispered.

Vic nodded, shining her light on opposite walls from the areas inspected by Jack. At the far end of the hall was a large closed door, and on either side were two more tall open doors to rooms flanking the hall. One was a vacant dining room and the other appeared to be a parlor with its own fireplace, a room built for ladies to talk while the gentlemen sat in the library with their brandy and cigars. Rain poured through its broken windows. Rotten drapes of a forgotten color swung heavily in the wind, dripping from the deluge.

Jack looked into the rooms. Seeing nothing, he began to push the large rear door open when he heard a board creak from the dining room to his right. Reacting instinctively, he dropped to a squat and spun on his heel as a metal pipe swung over his head and crashed against the door. Jack's grip on the .38 was so tight he accidentally squeezed the trigger, creating a deafening blast as the gun roared like a cannon against the walls. The slug blew the brass doorknob away.

Jack fell backwards against the parlor floor. His pistol was kicked from his grip and sent skittering over the naked boards. The door behind them slammed shut, and Vic was left on the other side, beating on the door, screaming "Jack, Jack, open the door!"

As he fell, the flashlight slipped from his grip and spun into the rain drenched room. It revolved on the center of its own axis, spraying the beams of light strobe-like around the room. A huge black man stood over him, holding a length of pipe in one hand, and in the other, what appeared to be a long ice pick poised above Jack's neck.

Jack lunged to the man's side and kicked with all of his might at one of the tree trunk legs. He connected on the right side of the man's knee, and drove his foot forward. The man let out a soul rending screech as he collapsed, grabbing his knee. The pipe clattered to the floor.

As Jack rolled away on his stomach, a big hand grappled for his foot, gaining a grip on his pants leg. Jack struggled to get away, clawing at the board floor to escape the ice pick that was just inches away. The man stabbed down and the pick stuck through Jack's pants into the hardwood floor. Jack was sure that, at any moment, the slender instrument of death would punch through his leg and then through the rest of him, and Vic would be next.

"You a dead man, Chandler," came a frenzied bellow and a grunt as the pick was jerked out of the old hardwood floor. This was no stray drunk who was protecting his digs; it was the voice on the phone.

Oddly, it flashed in Jack's mind that the death weapon of choice was an ice pick—the weapon of an itinerant.

Jack twisted and blindly kicked out with his other foot. He struck something solid. The air was split by a scream that made Jack's hair stand on end. Then there was silence.

The hand still clutched Jack's pants leg, but it no longer pulled. Jack wrenched himself away and rolled against the far wall under the windows in the streaming rain. He lay in the cold pool panting. The floor had rotted out at the edge of the wall where the water drained through a large hole to the ground below.

He moved to a crouching position and hunkered there for an instant trying to decide what to do. He could hear Vic beating on the door and yelling for him. The large, dark shape of the man blocked the doorway. The flashlight lay still, its beam focused into the grate of the fireplace, away from Jack and the man crouching in the doorway, leaving them in deep shadow.

Jack felt about for his gun, but couldn't find it. He could hear ragged breathing and a slurred mouthing of sounds that weren't quite words. The only motion Jack could see in the shadows cast by the flashlight was a slight back and forth rocking movement of the man who waited in the darkness.

Was this the dread he had dreamed about? Was this the end? Who was this man? Jack had to know. He couldn't see his gun or the pipe that had been dropped.

After what seemed like an eternity, Jack eased across the room, grabbed the flashlight, and rather than look for his gun, he pointed the tightly focused beam directly on the face of the man in the doorway.

The face was as dark as obsidian, the eyes wide and staring. At first Jack thought the man was looking at him, but the vacant eyes were not focused. The dark lips moved, as if the man was trying to speak, but there were no words. Spittle drooled from the corner of the man's mouth. The big sausage-like fingers were stiff and trembling.

Jack leaned forward and put the light directly in the face, wondering at the man's strange moustache. He stepped back in horror at what he saw. It was no moustache.

Wedged into a flaring nostril of the man's nose was the wooden hilt of the ice pick. Pearls of bright red blood dripped from the handle and pooled on the floor.

The big man tried to move, but he had lost motor control. He trembled and babbled quietly as he smacked his lips and stared at Jack, but seemed unable to move.

Skirting along the wall to the side, Jack shined the light beam on the back of the man's head and saw the bright silver tip of the ice pick poking through the bristle of black hair. The thin steel shaft had entered the nose at an angle and exited through the skull at the crown. Blood and a silvery colored liquid oozed around the shiny point.

The man's huge body spasmed, lurched forward, and lay still. A sickening stench flooded the room as the man lost the contents of his bowels. Jack backed quickly to the other wall and covered his nose, trying to keep from throwing up.

Jack turned the knob of the door behind him. Vic stepped back, as the door opened, a small automatic pistol in both hands pointed right at his face.

"Vic, it's me!" Jack shouted.

Vic let out a pent up breath and said, "Thank God. You OK? Wow, what's that smell?"

"Yeah, I'm alright, but that sonofabitch isn't," Jack said, pointing at the dark form crumpled on the floor.

"Who is he?" Vic asked, standing with her gun pointed at the crumpled figure on the floor.

"I don't know, but I have an idea."

Vic inched forward, holding the gun directly on the man, and felt for a pulse at this throat, then examined the bright tip of the ice pick sticking through the scalp and the wiry hair. She looked at Jack with amazement. "Dead! What happened?"

"Lucky kick," Jack said, thinking of the icepack plunging into the floor just a fraction of an inch from his leg. He briefly told her what happened as he dug into the man's hip pocket, trying to avoid touching his stinking clothing.

The driver's license identified him as Leroy Destrehan, and other papers proved him to be a Sergeant in the Orleans Parish Sheriff's department.

"Vic, This man fits the description of the head guard at the prison, Leroy Destrehan, the one who had the first turn on little James and Tyrone, and maybe Dawn."

"If he did those things at JD, he got less than he deserved," Vic said, as Jack put the wallet back into the pocket.

Jack, the executioner, he thought. The lucky kick had driven the slender steel pick through Destrehan's brain. Now just a big, black piece of meat on the floor, his obscene career over.

"My gun. Kicked into the corner and there's a big hole. Just mud down there," he said, playing his light into the hole. "Not registered to me."

Vic frowned, looking around in the hole with Jack. "What're you gonna do?"

Jack said, "I'm not about to crawl under the house to find it. Lord knows what's under there. I only know we gotta get hell out of here. Destrehan's pals will probably be here at any minute.

They stepped over the stinking body and ran through the rain to the car.

The downpour had increased with gusts of wind growing stronger. The tall light standards shook as Jack drove down Rampart's broad boulevard. As he entered the narrow one way streets, the gusts lessened, but his light Ford met resistance as he headed into the face of the wind.

After parking directly in front of his door, they sat in the wind-rocked car for several minutes thinking over the situation. "OK," he said, "I've killed a sheriff deputy. Doesn't matter if I have been attacked and killing him was accidental. I'll be charged with murder if it's traced to me. Maybe Destrehan acted on his own, but it was likely he had told someone of his plans, or was following orders."

"This whole deal involves sheriffs' office personnel, including the shrinks of the Mental Health Unit either directly or indirectly, as well as some powerful politicians. I guarantee they'll get together to protect their anonymity. At least one of 'em is down, accidentally, and I'm a fool to think my luck would hold a second time.

Without that lucky kick I'd be a pincushion and I don't want to think about what would have happened to you."

"I'd have killed him, Jack. I had a gun, you know."

"Yeah, you probably would have. But we have a problem now. Destrehan's body will be found, but there would be no way the death could be traced to me. Plenty desperate men lived in those old abandoned houses, and the logical conclusion would be that the deputy had been murdered by an unknown drifter or some guy with a grudge. At least that's what I hope."

It was nearly noon, but the day was as dark as night. Not a soul was to be seen on the streets. The streetlights were still fooled. It was eerie.

Jack and Vic stamped the water from their shoes on the mat outside the door to the apartment before they entered. The rooms were cold and forbidding.

Jack thought, *I was always hoping to use some of my arsenal, and now I have the chance but everything changed since Vic. I can't put her in any more danger than I have already.*

The rain beat a rattling tattoo on the plate glass sliding door. The ivy and figvine had been torn away from the lace grillwork and was twisting like mad living things on the balcony. He knew it was a matter of time before it would all be ripped out by the roots. It was like being inside a drum being pounded by a spastic drummer.

"I can't let you get hurt because of me. There's only one thing to do now. I know they're gonna be after me now. They don't know you were with me today. I want to keep it that way."

Vic frowned. "You're not dumping me. I'm as much a part of this as you are now."

Jack didn't acknowledge her, but said, "Go to Estelle's and wait for Nookie. I'll find him and have him pick you up. Y'all get the body and haul ass to your friend's place in Mobile. I have an idea we aren't going to have long before they come after me. That damned gun had my fingerprints on it. If they find it, they'll know it's me, so you're gonna have to get outta here."

"What about you, Jack?"

Jack thought for a minute, and then grinned broadly. "It just hit me. I'm having a helluva time. I gotta get outta Dodge. They'll follow me, I'm sure. I go one direction, while you and Nookie carry the body to safety. That's the most important thing. You know I can take care of myself. I'll outrun 'em"

Vic frowned, "Why can't you just come with us?"

"I can't be sure they won't spot me somewhere on the road, probably have an APB out, and the game'd be over. They wouldn't stop you and Nookie."

A wicked smile lit her face. "I have a plan."

Jack leaned forward, knowing it had to be good for her to have that kind of look on her face.

"I'll steal an ambulance! I'll drive to Estelle's and wait till you call me after you locate Nookie. I'll pick him up, rip off one of the lab's ambulances and be on our way. Nookie can drive and I'll be a pathologist taking a body somewhere."

Jack snapped his fingers. "Why didn't I think of that? You better split. I have a bad feeling something is about to happen."

They stood for a moment looking at each other. A blaze of lightning lit the room like a welding arc, followed in a moment by a blast of thunder that made the lights flicker.

"That one was close," Jack said, "just a little more than a second between the flash and the thunder."

Vic's eyes softened and she laid a soft hand on Jack's.

Jack wanted more than anything to grab her and hold her. But the cold bars of the mental prison that locked him away from his desire slammed down. He stiffened, against the will of his own heart's desire. Like a stuttering man who can't get the words out he froze, his mind and heart in a battle he fought and loss.

At length, Vic jerked her attention away and grabbed her slicker as if irritated. "Take care, Jack."

She turned and ran out of the door, leaving Jack standing holding his breath as she disappeared down the dark stair.

Vic's leaving left Jack with a sudden vacuum of being totally alone. *At least she'll be safe,* he thought. *If they come after me I'll lead them away and Nookie'll take care of her.*

Jack gathered things he thought he would need, his derringer, his magnum revolver, some rope, a couple of knives, first aid kit, a couple of beers, and some trail mix. As he stuffed them into his backpack he noticed the ivy creepers growing on the gallery and covering the brick wall of the building had finally been ripped away with the wind.

For the first time he considered the idea of dying. He thought of his home in the pine hills of North Louisiana. He had been raised in the country, no different from any other white Anglo Saxon protestant community. He had worked at a sawmill until he had enough money to go to college, then worked at odd jobs until he got his law degree. It had not been easy. He knew no other way. His parents had died years before, and he had a sister in Texas who would probably miss him. That was all. *I hoped to make a bigger mark in life than I have so far. But I ain't dead yet.*

He turned on the TV and the anchor announced that the eye of the storm had passed the mouth of the river and was heading directly north up the Mississippi toward New Orleans. As he watched, he pressed Nookie's cell phone number and after a few rings Nookie answered: "Hey Jack, where you at?"

It was always disconcerting for someone to have caller ID and know he was calling. Nookie was state of the art.

"Can't talk right now, but I need to see you now!"

"I'm down by de Sudden Exposure. My l'il Pussy Beaucoup comin' on stage in a few minute. You gotta come down and see how lucky Nookie is, man."

Jack's attention was pulled away by the reflection of a blue flashing light reflecting on the balcony window. He raced to the sliding glass door to the porch and opened it just enough that he could squeeze through without the wind blowing the rain into the apartment. He peered over the balcony. Three men in yellow day-glo slickersuits piled out of a patrol car, its blue lights still blazing. They banged on the door to the apartment building until someone opened and asked what they wanted. Jack heard his name and froze in his tracks.

"Nook. The heat's just outside. I'm trapped unless I take the roof."

"Git outta dere, Jack, now. Come on now, I'll help you."

Jack stuffed his phone in the pack and glanced around as he heard yelling from the street.

He grabbed his back pack, slipped on the slickersuit and ran to the bathroom. He pushed the window up directly alongside the toilet and swung open the shutters.

The window opened onto a red tiled roof which provided a view, on clear days, of the Quarter rooftops and the steeple of the St. Louis Cathedral. He grabbed the sides of the window and launched himself feet first into the rain. He turned, shoved the window down and pushed the shutters together again.

The overhang of two large eaves were situated to the right and left of the recessed dormer window to the bathroom. Jack ducked under the one to the left, through a falling torrent of water, and backed against the wall, behind a liquid curtain, just inches from his nose. He couldn't be seen, but could press his ear against the wall to hear inside the bathroom.

It wasn't likely, if the police came into his apartment, that they would open the window, much less look out. Some tipoff water may have splashed in as he left, but that couldn't be helped. Maybe they would suspect he was on the roof, and if so, it would be a one-on-one if somebody came out. He could handle that.

The entire block was like one large building, with uneven roofs, with each house or apartment building joined by mutual walls, frequently sharing the same roof elevation. It was fairly easy getting around on the roofs, being careful on the slippery shingles and tiles, but it would be tricky going in this deluge and gusting wind, particularly since the pitch of some were quite steep.

A crash came from inside his apartment; he pressed his ear to the wall. They had broken open his door.

"If you in there, Chandler, come out wit' ya hands inna air!"

"Oh shit," Jack murmured.

There was movement in the apartment. He could hear the voices of the deputies as they searched the rooms.

"Hey," one shouted. "He got out the window. Look, there's water on the floor and on the windowsill."

Jack pressed against the wall, just inches from the open window, separated from the window by a sheet of water falling from the eave. The men inside gathered around the window.

They pushed the window up and swung the shutter wide.

"If the sonabitch went out in that," one said, "he probably drown by now." A head poked through the window and tried to look about, but immediately withdrew, dripping. Parker swore again. "Can't see nuthin'."

There was muffled talk and swearing coming through the open window. One said, "Hey Bubba, get out onna roof and look around."

"Bullshit, Parker," came Bubba's nasal twang, "You get your own fat ass out there. If Chandler put Leroy's lights out on Leroy's own ground, you think Chandler can't handle me on his? What kinda fool do you think I am?"

"Yeah, Parker," the third voice dissented, "You see all that iron hangin' on the wall? You think Chandler'd go out without a piece? He probably can shoot, too. If you got some goods on him, wait 'till the storm's over and arrest him proper-like. I don't think you got enough to pull him in from what I see."

"How you know he iced Leroy?" Another asked.

Parker said, "Leroy was gonna meet him. Said he could handle Chandler by hisself. Couldn't be nobody else!"

The first voice asked: "How could he have done that? Leroy was one badass."

"I dunno, got a ice pick inna face. Surprise."

"Yeah. Surprise to Leroy. But we ain't got no hard evidence, Parker," you sure don't have probable cause, came a protest from the third voice. "We done busted in Chandler's place without no warrant and there ain't no proof he done it! We can get in the shit for this!"

Jack remembered the name tag on the bushel-bellied deputy with the coroner at the morgue. *Parker! And he's got that accent. Must be the same guy. And he was in on the action with Leroy, according to James and Tyrone. He's gotta cover his tracks. If I was in the apartment, he'd find a reason to blow me away. They couldn't prosecute me. There's no evidence. His only choice is to eliminate me. That's why he busted in!*

Jack couldn't see the three faces standing back from the waterfall pouring through the window. He could only imagine Parker's flustered face. Parker had taken his shot and missed. His two deputies had seen him do it, and they knew something was wrong.

Just some police are bad, just some, and from the sound of this dialogue, the only real bad apple in this bunch was Parker. And he had missed his chance to hush the one voice that could give him a bad day. Jack was indeed going to give Parker a bad day at the first opportunity.

Jack continued pressing his ear against the wall beneath the overhang while the three deputies stood by the open bathroom window.

"You stay here, Bubba," Parker yelled over the storm. "Bastid's gotta come home sometime. He's quick, so blow him away on sight. You seen what he done to Leroy, and from the look of this arsenal, he's packing a piece. Don't take no chances—just do it. I'll cover you. After you blow 'em away, use one of his pieces for a throw down." Jack strained to hear what they said next, but he gathered that Parker had given Bubba one of his own arsenal to use as a "throw down" gun to use if Jack didn't have one when Bubba "blew him away." They would put one of Jack's own guns in his dead hand, proving the law officer had killed in self defense, justifying what otherwise would be cold-blooded murder, or an error in judgment.

Jack stared unseeing at the wall before him, knowing he would be shot on sight by either of these officers in spite of the deputy's previous protest. They were all in on the break-in now, and they were scared. Scared of Jack. Scared of having done wrong. Scared of being caught.

Jack's mind raced. *Can't go back in. Gotta get hell out of here, but where after I see Nookie? Who'd believe my story? Nobody. Ok, Jack, get a grip. Meet Nookie—go hide.*

Jack paused as he thought about Vic being brought into his problem. *They mean to wipe all evidence of their guilt clean. That now means Vic. Oh God! I finally found the woman of my dreams and have exposed her to being killed too. I can't let her get more involved than she is! She will be really pissed but I have to cut her out of the action.*

Chapter 8

The window was still partially open. Jack knew the rain was flooding his bathroom, but there was nothing he could do about it. He surely wasn't going to shut it with 'ol Bubba somewhere in there ready to do his best for law and order.

He pulled the yellow slicker's hood up around his head, made sure that all of the snaps were fastened and hitched the backpack over his shoulders. Then he peered through the waterfall to make sure Bubba wasn't in sight, and slowly edged out over the rooftop. In a moment, he was beyond the window's view, cautiously moving over the slippery red tiles on his hands and knees.

The rain hammered on his slicker. Jack feared a gust would lift him like a leaf to send him hurtling down to one of the gardens below. He clung to the peak of the roof while he inched along, head down to keep the pellets of rain from stinging his eyes and face.

He crawled the entire length of the block along a series of roofs, each with different slopes and surfaces. Several times he lost his grip, almost sliding to the bottom edge, but managed to claw himself to a stop and crawl back to the crest.

After a few tense minutes, he reached St. Phillips Street and edged to the street side of the eave. The two story roof dropped to a single story building. He easily climbed down a drain pipe to the roof of the lower story building and slid down the pipe to the sidewalk.

Jack began a slogging trot through flooding streets. The rain mixed with little pellets of hail stung him through his slicker, popping on it like being shot with bb guns.

Jack was a regular at the Sudden Exposure He knew the manager and some of the strippers who worked there. Nookie probably would be pretty loaded by now.

As a matter of fact, they all would probably be pretty high and raucous without the inhibiting interference of the heat or tourists. This was one day they would turn away even the hardiest crazy conventioneers or sailors drunk enough to drown in the storm to get there. Jack was sure that because of the storm, nobody would be there except some strippers, whores, their pimps and other regulars.

Jack looked like a hunchback with his backpack and slickersuit as he plunged through the ankle deep water toward his destination. His sleeves, feet and pants were soaked. Some of the cold downpour found its way down the back of his collar.

If I'm caught, I'll go to jail for some trumped up charge and wouldn't live through the first night. I got no choice. I gotta keep moving, and fast, hurricane or no, and this is gonna be one big damn storm. Boy is Vic gonna be pissed at what I am going to do.

Bourbon Street and the sidewalk was a flowing river. A gust of wind caught a badly dented aluminum garbage can lid and swept it clanging and clattering down the sidewalk directly toward Jack. He saw it coming and came to a dead stop, watching it spin toward him at a high speed.

The lid crashed noisily against the wall several yards from him then submerged in the street. *Man, that wind is picking up. Aurora is here.*

The neon lights along Bourbon created a lurid, multicolored haze through the pouring rain. Every night, year round, for twelve blocks starting at Canal, Bourbon was jammed with milling, strolling humanity, peering through the open doors into the darkness of the strip joints with barkers standing outside each door extolling the virtues of the merchandise writhing on stage within. But tonight he was the only one on the street.

The door to The Sudden Exposure was locked. Jack banged on the door and finally a very large man with a pock marked face slid the bolt open and angrily peered out. "We closed," he barked with a gravelly voice.

Jack recognized the face of the club's bull bouncer and said, "Bomber, it's me, Jack Chandler. Lemme in."

"Oh, it's you. Get ya' wet ass in heah! We havin' a hurrican party."

Jack was pulled into the darkness which engulfed him in the reek of old ashtrays, smoke and stale beer.

Dripping just inside the door, Jack let his eyes adjust to the dim atmosphere. Music, loud talking, and laughter filled the room. He recognized many faces. This was the late night hangout of the locals after everything else was closed, and now it was a Quarter party. Jack didn't see a tourist or a strange face in the house.

The star of the establishment, Pussy Beaucoup, whose real name was Norma Faye Lemoine, was strutting back and forth on the elevated stage in an old bathrobe under a series of lights that changed from blue to red to green in sequence. She loved her work and now she could perform without the ever present tourist, conventioneer, or the limitations placed on what she did by the law. The audience paid little attention to her, for she had just begun her dance, this time doing a new routine with the robe. Jack thought she would soon be stripped down to a g-string and pasties. She would take her time, but eventually would be completely stripped before the night was over, as would the rest of the strippers who simply liked getting naked in front of people in the first place.

She was no ballerina, but she was pretty, slender and well built, and could move her supple body in voluptuous ways that kept Jack spellbound. Her spine must have been made of rubber for her to have such a range of motion down there. That part of her anatomy seemed to have a life and personality of its own, and Nookie was all over it when they went home and turned out the lights.

Norma Faye was Nookie's woman, and the current beneficiary of what her dance promised. Jack had a flash of envy at what Nookie was experiencing regularly.

The room was large for a Quarter strip joint. It had two dozen tables, was fairly well-appointed and clean, in spite of the smoke and smell. The bartender and waitresses bustled about and there was a feeling of holiday. Some groups were playing bourree', a French card game similar to poker and bridge, in the light of candles at their tables, while others just talked and drank.

Here was a gathering of accomplices whose fortunes had brought them, through God knows what backgrounds, to settle in this little community of hucksters who lived by their wits. They were young and old, gamblers, procurers, hustlers, call girls, con men, thieves and road whores—all with the common day-to-day lifestyle of the urban gypsy who lived just within and frequently outside of the law. Jack knew many of them, having helped them out of scrapes with the law and each other.

Jack was the trusted legal advisor for many in the Quarter. He was called, among the natives, "Popeye," and his three hundred pound lawyer friend, Sam Leviathon, was called "Bluto." The two hung out together, acting and looking the part of the two characters when they got drunk together.

Jack hung his slicker over a coat hook just inside the door. He asked about Nookie, and Bomber pointed to a crowded table near the stage. He waded toward them through the crowd. Norma Faye opened her dreamy eyes, waved, in Jack's direction. He simply returned the wave. While Nookie was grateful for what Jack had done for him, he was a hot-blooded Cajun and he'd never tolerate anyone messing with his squeeze, and Jack wouldn't even consider such indiscretion now that he was slowly and reluctantly realizing that Vic was part of his life, so he kept his wave innocuous and innocent.

"Ah, ma fran'," Nookie burst out, standing and embracing Jack. "Ya'll all know Jack Chandler, best dam' lawyer in de city." A dozen patrons raised their hands and waved at Jack. There was Big Bennie, a brawny x-wrestler turned bouncer for another strip joint down the street; Bones, a gambler whose fame at manipulating dice was legendary; Harley Davidson, a TWA pilot who had been forcibly retired after being convicted of running guns and other contraband to several banana republics on his days off; and Sweet Tips, Harley's honey who worked as a B girl and stripper at the club. "Tips" worked the bar. When she wasn't stripping, she coaxed "Johns" into buying watered down drinks at exorbitant prices. Because of her blatant sexuality, and not a little because of her very high, pointed tits, she made more money than anybody, including Norma, in gratuities. Nobody ever complained.

"Hey, Jack," Nookie said frowning at Jack's intensity, "what happen?"

Jack pulled Nookie into a corner and, after looking around to see if anyone was watching, quickly related the latest string of events and his plan. When he finished, Nookie looked worried for a moment, then yelled at the bartender. "Brang Jack a triple bourbon and water!"

"You need a drank, Jack," Nookie said earnestly. After thinking for a moment, he dug in his pocket and handed Jack a set of keys. "My truck, she park where I always park her at. Get yore ass outta town. I'll call my li'l brudder, Noonie, in Pointe Au Chein, down da bayou, and tell him you comin'. You know him—wit' da big nose? He'll take you in if you don't get blowed in de river first."

When Jack told Nookie the plans, Nookie beamed, "Mais yeah, me I done tole you someting fun gon' happen."

Gritting his teeth, so that the muscle in his jaw bunched in a little hump, Jack told Nookie about Vic's involvement, and how terrified he was for her.

Nookie's brow furrowed in concern. "Hot Damn, Jack, dat sweet child shouldn't ought to be mess up in dis. She say she gon' steal an ambulance, and me and her gonna drive across de causeway in dis storm wit' de body? Dat's a foo foo plan! We get blowed in de lake and drown, beside, she can stay clear by doin' notting."

"Yeah, that's my idea. She is gonna hate me, but I am cuttin' her out of the loop. I'll get the body and drive it down the bayou, and she will just have to be pissed. Maybe never forgive me."

Nookie looked sidelong at Jack and grinned, as if he just realized something. "Jack, don't tell me! You hot for Vic? Mebbe you in love?"

Jack stammered and looked stunned that the emotion and thought he had hidden from himself could be so easily discerned by Nookie.

"I'm just concerned for her, that's all."

"Yeah right. She one fine thang, dat Vic. A prize ketch if ever I see one. Me I don't blame you. You got dat love drunk look. Hee Hee. Poo Yii, she as fine as my Pussy Beaucoup. Yeah, you right, she gonna be plenty piss, but you doin' de right ting. I'll pretend I don't know, go to de freezer and ack piss myself when de body ain't dere. Hokay? I cover yo ass best way I can wit' her, but you take care, cher, don't git youself drown or kill."

"I'll keep you posted on my cell. When the storm lets up, you two haul ass to Mobile and I'll somehow meet you there with the body. Vic has a pathologist friend there who will do an autopsy. If you don't hear from me, go ahead on anyway. With the storm, even cell phones go down."

"I done tole you cher, dis gon' be some fun, hah?"

Jack shook his head, realizing that he was grinning and having a great time. He guzzled his drink. "Thanks, Nook. I knew I could count on you."

"Yah. I ain't missin' out on this. You better you take that face of yours outside de city rat now if the heat lookin'."

"They ain't got nothing on me," Jack protested.

"You know dam' well that don' make no nevermind. I'm gonna call Noonie now an' tell him you on you way if he ain't lost his phones by now."

Nookie and Jack turned back to the stage. Harley and another man back in the crowd were staring intently at them. The two men quickly looked away, and Nookie grunted and said, "You see, at least one in here gonna pimp on you soon's you leave. So you gotta split, and quick."

Jack looked up at the stage. Norma Faye dropped the robe and was stark naked. It was all her. No plastic anywhere. *My God,* Jack thought, *that is one fine woman.* She began grinding her sacroiliac in ways that defied what he knew about anatomy and the limitations of motion of the human body. She could put a belly dancer to shame with the sensual yet near acrobatic things she could do with her body. Jack felt a catch in his gut, unable to avoid imagining what she would be like doing that in bed.

Jack looked at Nookie wryly with a foolish grin and Nookie grinned back, whispering in Jacks ear. "Can you believe dat? Dat's Nookie's woman," he said proudly.

Jack rumpled Nookie's curls playfully and then said, "Nookie, you're a real friend to help. I hope your truck and I make it through this."

"Jack, you worry too dam' much. She's old anyway. Time to trade her. So get outta here 'fore Aurora really hit. You probably gon' have to take the Loopey Long Bridge."

Jack thought of the high wind and the narrow Huey P. Long Bridge Nookie referred to, and said, "I sure as hell hope not. That sucker's narrow and high. The wind's kickin' ass out there."

"Lache pas la patate, Jack."

Jack grinned at the Cajun idiom, literally translated meaning "don't drop the potato," but really meaning "don't give up."

"Thanks, Nook. I keep a good grip on my potato. You keep a hold to yours. Take care of vic for me."

"You got it, ma fran. Nook gon' take care of you lady." He winked and slapped Jack on the back.

They shook hands and Jack slowly and reluctantly pulled on his slicker. Norma Faye was getting the attention she wanted, swiveling and slowly girating languidly, her firm breasts somehow moving in sequence, her eyes closed and the tip of her pink tongue barely showing between her red lips. Jack stood in the open door gaping back into the safety of the club. Bomber asked, while gaping at Norma Faye's gyrations himself, "You stayin' or leavin?"

"Leavin', dammit," Jack swore, and as he dived back into the rain, he saw one of the customers sitting near Nookie's table punch some numbers on his cell phone.

Jack found the truck a half block away. He gratefully heard the engine roar into life as he turned the key in the ignition switch. "Now what?" He asked himself.

Jack threaded his way through the empty, inundated streets to the warehouse and saw that Nookie had left the padlock on the big scrolling up door unlocked. His headlights pierced the darkness between the looming Mardi-Gras floats, but this time he didn't have time to afford the luxury of the eerie feeling he got before. He rushed into the freezer, lifted the waxed container containing Dawn's body and pushed it beneath a bed Nookie used as his emergency sleeping quarters in the back of the truck.

The relentless downpour on the metal roof drowned out all other sound, including the click of his Bic lighter as he lit a Picayune before cranking the truck for his flight from the city. Forcing his thudding heart to slow he had learned in a meditation class, he calmed and allowed the thundering clamor become soothing and magically interesting. His tension dropped to a quiet internal peace he had learned to invoke. The machine gunning thoughts running like rampant, chaotic traffic in his head slowed. He blew a smoke ring toward the towering dragon hanging over his head. *I think I will be a dragon. I am sorry to do this to you Vic, but it is for the best. I have such mixed feelings, but I cannot expose you to hurt because of me. I could not live with myself. If I live through this, I will just have to confront your anger.*

Leaving the big door by the ramp appearing to be locked, Jack accelerated toward whatever destiny lay before him with Dawn's frozen corpse as his passenger.

If I'm going down the bayou, I gotta cross the river. The ferries are probably closed so I gotta cross one of the high bridges in this wind.

The downtown Poydras Street ferry was closed, so Jack drove to the toll bridge that crossed into Gretna. The entrance ramp was swarming with patrol cars, blue lights on top of their units flashing. They may be looking for me! Maybe there's an APB out for me at this very minute and those squad cars bunched around the upramp could be stopping traffic just for me.

Jack drove by slowly. He saw to his relief that the police were diverting all traffic. A couple of eighteen wheelers had collided at the top of the bridge, now blocking all westbound traffic.

Jack let the clutch out slowly and headed upriver to the Huey P. Long bridge. He could only keep in mind one destination at a time. If it was blocked, he would have to drive north to the new Luling bridge or the Sunshine bridge at Donaldsonville. If worse came to worse, he would cross on the I-10 bridge at Baton Rouge. At least he was heading north, away from the storm and the sheriff deputy who wanted him dead.

If he could cross on the Huey P. Long bridge, he would have to head back south and west to Houma, then south from there to Pointe Au Chein, which would take him back into the western periphery of Aurora's sweeping path. If Aurora moved west, he would be driving directly into it. He was sure there would be plenty of blow southeast of Houma, but not as much as New Orleans was to get.

He switched on the radio. Aurora was moving again, heading directly toward New Orleans. The winds were approaching 200 miles per hour in its main path. The public was warned to evacuate the city if they could or stay indoors to avoid flying objects. Flooding was predicted in low lying areas and along Lake Pontchartrain, which seemed to be Aurora's target area. Jack accelerated up St. Charles Avenue and found himself in heavy traffic headed out of town to escape the storm's fury.

Branches of the huge live oaks writhed as if they were alive, snapping back and forth in the wild wind. There was an explosive crack as a body-sized limb fell into the street, blocking traffic. New Orleans Public Service, NOPSI, and the Police and Sheriff's department had their yellow slickered men out in force trying to clear the streets. They battled the wind directing traffic around fallen trees and limbs, trying to keep their own balance in the blasts that pasted their slickers to them like glue.

An ancient live oak, its huge trunk and branches designed for the mellow summer days of summer, leaned and slowly toppled over as Jack passed, crashing into high voltage lines strung over the street. The wires were crushed to the ground, and along with them came the utility pole and its transformer. An ear shattering blast was followed by sparks flying in every direction. Instantly the entire area blacked out.

Jack managed to avoid the arcing power lines submerged beneath the rivering streets. Cars were stopped and flooded out in the flood. Some were simply swallowed up by the fallen branches and trees; their frantic occupants clambering out trying to free the captive piece of dead steel from the clutches of the great oaks.

He zig-zagged through side streets. Moving as if in a dream, he careened through yards and by swing sets, over the broad lawns and down the sidewalk by Tulane and Loyola Universities. He began to think he was superman, that nothing could stop him on his quest for the Westbank even with pieces of slate from the roof of a house, careening off the hood of the truck like thrown Frisbees. Jack joined the wild melee of swinging limbs, rushing waters, and blasting winds–and in what seemed to be only minutes, he was at the long incline up the bridge. He felt as wild as the storm.

Flashing, rotating red and blue lights from a half dozen Orleans Sheriff and State police vehicles created dizzying, swirling patterns through the downpour. Cars streamed over the bridge to the west, but none returned from the other side to New Orleans.

Troopers and Sheriff's deputies were out, having laid flares along the foot of the bridge to mark the route to follow. Each carried ineffective flashlights, directing the foolhardy who wanted to cross the bridge.

The "Huey P.," as it was called, was high, narrow and scary on the best of days. It was called the Haunted Bridge because legend held that several workers were entombed alive in the colossal cement pilings holding the bridge in place.

Painted a dull rust-proof brown, the bridge was built by the late Huey P. Long, the governor who promised to make "every man a king," in a socialistic welfare state, in a backlash to the great depression. He put in free books and hot lunches at the schools; paved muddy roads; and built hospitals, colleges and bridges that spanned the many watery byways of the bayou state. Many of the larger bridges, like this one, sported a railroad track through the center with two lanes of traffic on each side. The grade to the zenith was steep, with low railings that would deflect the A-models of the thirties, but would be ineffective in the present. Two modern cars could pass, with just inches to spare, since the lanes were designed for much smaller cars, and only the heedless would dare to pass on that bridge even on a good day.

A string of tail lights of slow moving, bumper-to-bumper traffic headed up the steep slope of the bridge. Jack pulled the slicker hood down over his face as he approached the trooper directing traffic. Jack was asked to stop and roll down his window. He said, "Hey buddy, you know that camper is gonna make it hard for you to make it over the bridge in that wind?"

"Yassuh," Jack said in a Cajun accent, not offering more.

The trooper shook his head, as if he was seeing this dumb Cajun during his last few minutes on the earth. Jack rolled the window up and drove through the police cordon to the foot of the bridge and left the lawmen behind in the bilious shimmer of their lights below.

As soon as he reached treetop level, and all barriers and protection from the howling winds were behind and below, the blast hit him head on. The little car ahead of him shuddered nearly to a full stop. The camper jerked as if struck, and skidded to the right. Jack turned his wheel hard to the left, struggling to stay away from the railing.

Gunning the motor in low gear with all four wheels pulling, he kept the camper moving. The horizontal rain strafed the truck like machine gun fire. Blinding lightening flashed everywhere as bright as welding arcs, followed by deafening explosions. A fist of wind smashed the camper head on, and Jack was grateful. If it had come from his left, he would have been lifted over the rail and swept into the dark, muddy waters far below.

Jack reached the top where the bridge leveled out for a distance. A small car, two vehicles ahead, was swept to the edge, its left wheels suspended in the air and hung against the wrought iron banister momentarily. Jack gasped in relief when the little car was released from the grip of the huge gust and set back down.

There seemed a wild wind variable just at that place on the bridge, for the car ahead of him went through identical behavior when it reached the spot. Just as he reached the same point, the truck slid to the right, tilted against the railing with both left wheels lifted a foot or more from the surface of the roadway. Jack yelled, knowing that he was going over the low railing. The cars had not been flipped over because they were lower and didn't have as much wind surface as the truck. *Oh shit, why did I have to take this stupid bridge? Why didn't I go on upriver to cross where the wind was less and the bridge safer?*

The side of the truck squealed as the railing gouged into the door and fenders. The truck gently lifted and fell, as if being teased by a great, unseen hand. When the truck reached a forty five degree angle tilt, it was suddenly released and slammed back down onto the surface. Jack had been hanging on to the driver's door to keep from sliding down to the passenger's side when the truck was released, and as the wheels bounced back to the bridge surface, his head slammed against the driver's window. Lightening continued to blaze incessantly around the bridge, turning the world silver, followed by ear splitting explosions.

The bridge itself trembled, and the truck windows rattled in their frames. He thought he was seeing things when the entire superstructure of the old bridge was enveloped in a pulsating, spectral glow like a Halloween skeleton.

Jack's ears rang from the thunder and the blow on his head. He was as dumfounded at the ethereal shimmering, throbbing metal members of the giant bridge rising far overhead and the railings to his right as he was amazed at still being alive.

"St. Elmo's Fire," he mouthed, remembering stories of ships masts and sails being bathed in cold, green fire in storms at sea. He punched the accelerator and the tires spun on the wet roadway as he began his descent.

Far away, through the arcs of lightening and the streaming rain, long columns of taillights headed to the southwest, the same direction he intended to go. He knew the storm would get worse when the real peril of the maximum winds reached the area, and he hoped he would be skirting the worst of it as he traveled in a westerly direction. It could be much worse than what he had just experienced. Jack had seen news stories of vehicles being hurled about like bits of down by those relentless winds.

The storm batted the truck back and forth, and twice he was shoved to the rail again, scraping the side of the truck badly each time, but the tires weren't lifted off the road surface. Soon he was below tree level and on terra-firma. He thought of the old saying, "the more firma, the less terror," and now he knew for sure what that meant.

Power was out everywhere. Several police vehicles were at the foot of the bridge, with troopers and deputies staring up at the glowing bridge. Suddenly, the bridge returned to its old sullen darkness, as if someone had snapped the light switch.

Drowned-out cars sat dead all along the highway. Creeping along, he felt more than saw the road ahead, praying that all four tires stayed on the hard surface, because the shoulders were deep mush. Jack squinted through the brief clearing of each wiper stroke, his face almost pressed against the windshield.

Slowly, slowly he drove, pushing through the water as if in an amphibious landing craft, knowing that a surge or a wave would sunder his plugs and wiring, leaving him immobilized for the duration. He held his breath for long moments, unblinking, seemingly frozen in time.

It was almost impossible to tell where the roadside ended and the ditch began; the entire area ahead was a sea of dark water, barely illuminated by his headlights. He leaned to the left as if to resist the wind shoving the left side of the truck. When he realized what he was doing, he relaxed slightly, but his knuckles were white from gripping the wheel.

Chapter 9

Jack practically had the road to himself. The only others he saw were headed west and away from New Orleans. Normally, US 90 was thick with trucks and commercial traffic at all times of the day and night, this major east-west artery keeping the Big Easy supplied and fed.

The rain started in pouring like a cascading waterfall, and Jack had to drive even slower. He entered a swampy area. Dead branches from the tall trees on each side covered the road, and electrical wires had been blown down. Sometimes a very large limb had floated or been blown into the road, and he would have to get out and move it out of his path while leaning against the blasting wind. He had to keep his head down out of the stinging rain. He wished he had swimming goggles, as it was like swimming.

Several frightened deer nearly collided with the truck as they ran knee deep in terror, trying to find a high quiet spot. He saw many raccoons and opossums swimming across the road—their little red eyes appearing and disappearing as they struggled through the high water.

Traffic increased when he reached Raceland. More refugees headed southwest and away from the storm. That section of U.S. 90 hadn't been blocked by the police, allowing some traffic movement in the deeply flooded streets of the little town. Jack could see just ahead the silhouetted domed top of a little Volkswagen Beetle, one of the old air cooled models. It looked like it was swimming and partially floating in the roadway.

Jack wondered and worried about the souls living in little villages like Raceland, surrounded by bayous and cane fields, with floodwaters lapping at their doors. They were all Cajun, all hardy survivors. They would make it.

A large truck with a high wheel base and wide tires came roaring from the opposite direction and created a tidal wave that swept the Volkswagen off the road. Jack cursed the bastard driving the truck for being so thoughtless of those fleeing the storm. The small car washed like a cork into a ditch which had become a vicious little river.

Instinctively, Jack braked and pulled onto the shoulder. *Just keep driving, Jack, leave well enough alone.* The ditch was deep and the passengers surely in panic. Maybe it was a family with babies, or a little old lady. His brain seemed to go into a spasm. Personal survival versus intervention. His help may not result in help after all. He could die trying. He could die in the next few minutes.

He kept replaying the image of the tiny car lifting on the huge wave and being dropped into the ditch. *Another damn crossroads!* And he knew that once again, there really was no choice.

The VW began to float away. At any moment the boiling ditch could suck it into the darkness, maybe into the nearby bayou, where it would surely sink and trap the passengers. He knew Volkswagens floated, but not for long.

Jerking up the emergency brake, he charged into the roaring rain. He had seen a length of heavy nylon rope in the camper. Grabbing the rope, he tied an end to the trailer hitch and formed a loop on the other end of the rope as he waded into the neck-deep ditch. His feet were swept from under him and he pitched backward beneath the rushing tide. A bolt of fear shot through him. He could die right here! He clutched the rope to keep from being swept away.

The VW rocked as the current pushed it over an obstacle and surged rapidly away. Jack sucked in a breath and dived beneath the roiling current. He grabbed the bumper of the little bug car with one hand, looped the open noose over its curving end. It immediately tautened as a bowstring and the car stopped it surging into the maelstrom. He burst to the surface and pulled himself, hand over hand, out of the ditch and up onto the roadway. He could hear screaming from inside the VW.

The water on the roadway was knee deep, and Jack saw with relief it hadn't yet reached his exhaust pipe. At least the motor was still running. He released the emergency brake, making sure the four wheel drive was engaged, and slowly moved forward. The rope tightened. The truck shuddered.

Jack gunned the powerful motor. After a battle of wills with the elements and the weight of the car, the VW lunged out of the ditch and leaped onto the hard surface of the highway.

Jack splashed out and tugged at the VW door. A vacuum in the car held the door fast. He knocked on the window, and finally, the window rolled down slightly. In a blaze of lightning, he saw two girls sitting waist deep in water. They stared up at him, wide eyed and speechless, trembling from cold and panic, too frightened to speak. He jerked open the door and the water cascaded out.

"Get out of the car and come with me," he shouted over the storm.

They struggled out and stood by him in the pouring rain like drowned rats. He motioned for them to get into the back of the truck. They climbed in together, and after closing the rear door, huddled in the darkness on the bunk. Jack flicked on his trusty Zippo lighter to give a little light, threw back the hood to his slicker and said, "I'm Jack. That was a close call."

Both girls wore white very tight, abbreviated short-shorts and halter tops, and shivered from the trauma and cold. One began to sob while the other maintained control of herself. "We're freezing," she said.

Jack suddenly remembered that the icy box containing Dawn Marie was directly beneath their feet, and it didn't contribute to the warmth of the situation whatsoever. Knowing that Nookie was prepared for all contingencies, Jack searched around and found two army blankets. With trembling hands, the girls wrapped themselves in the warm wool and their shivering gradually slowed.

Jack found the switch to the little overhead light in the camper and snapped it on. His attention was riveted on the two waifs before him. It took him only a moment for his trained eye to see that they were about eighteen, and that under ordinary circumstances, they would be very pretty, and two vixens if he had ever seen any. One had long black hair and dark eyes, and the other was blond with a ponytail. Even though this man had been their savior, they were defensive and uncertain about this wild looking character who now confronted them in these close quarters with the rain and wind slamming the truck from all sides. Their eyes questioned many things. What were they going to do? What was he going to do?

"Well," Jack said, "here we are."

Both girls managed a wan, forced smile. The brunette said, "I'm Judy and she's Debbie."

"Where's home?"

"I live in Montegut," Judy said, shivering, "a wide place in the road below Houma. Debbie's from Shreveport. We're roommates at LSUNO. I thought we could make it home."

Jack thought of how he would be passing near Montegut, pronounced mon-tee-gew, on the way to his destination.

"I'm goin' to Pointe-Au-Chein. I'll drop you off."

Judy brightened, and then a worried look raced across her face. "What about my car?"

Jack shrugged. "Maybe we can start it, or I can pull you and we can find a place to park it until the storm is over. Do you want to try?"

Judy looked relieved and nodded assent, still dazed from the close call.

Jack got out again and went to the VW. He turned the key in the ignition and surprisingly, the motor fired to life. He thought of how Der Fuhrer had put together this little wonder car, and how, if Hitler had won the war, everyone, or at least all of the Germans, would be driving it. He threw the rope back into the truck and told Judy to follow him closely.

They drove for a short distance until they came to a closed gas station where Jack told Judy to park between two closely set outbuildings for protection.

He put their luggage in the camper and all three got into the cab. Judy sat next to Jack and the two girls trembled under their blankets.

"Hey, ladies, you're alive. You're no worse off for the experience, and you'll be home soon with your folks. And besides, this is fun." Jack said, grinning as he lit a Picayune without taking his eyes from the road.

"Well, this is sorta fun!" Judy laughed.

"Nothin' like this ever happens in dull old Shreveport!" Debbie said.

"See," Jack laughed, "this is an adventure."

Judy and Debbie lit cigarettes themselves and the miles slowly passed until they finally came to Houma, a city that was supported largely by offshore oil and gas. On the way, they told jokes, sang songs, and time passed swiftly with no major mishaps.

They turned south, buffeted by strong headwinds and dodging fallen power lines and limbs. Several times flying objects crashed into the side of the truck.

"Won't be long now." Jack said, pointing to a Montegut road sign. He looked down at Judy's upturned face. Her teeth were perfect, and there was something about her lips when she smiled. Her brown eyes glowed mischievously.

"Jack, are you married?"

"Nope."

Her smile became warmer and she slid closer to him. "We owe you, Jack. Don't we, Debbie?"

Debbie nodded quickly, suppressing a grin at Judy.

"Well," Jack said, "I ain't no hero, just was there at the right time. No big deal."

Judy traced the outline of Jack's ear with a slender fingertip. "You risked your life for us back there, Jack, and I for one would like to show my appreciation."

"Me too," echoed Debbie.

"Why don't you pull over? There's a bed back there," she said, pointing to the back of the camper with her thumb. Judy leaned over and whispered in his ear loud enough for Debbie to hear. "I've never made it in a hurricane."

"Me neither," Debbie said eagerly.

An erotic image sprang in his mind of action in the back of the camper with these hot little foxes, whose offer would fulfill the dreams of most men. He had no commitments, and he and Vic really didn't have anything going, and here was first class fun. He see-sawed, and hesitated, his breath caught in his throat.

Both girls dropped their blankets and pulled down their halter tops to reveal the hardening nipples of small pointed breasts literally calling out to Jack. They trembled, not from the cold, but from anticipation. Judy ran her tongue into his ear.

Judy reached down and grabbed his manhood which instantly rose to battle stations. Both Judy and Debbie said "wow," at what Judy was holding.

Jack's libido sat up and howled. He brought the truck to a stop beneath the darkened shelter of a gas station in Klondyke. The girls giggled and wriggled through the window of the cab that opened into the camper. Jack shucked his slicker and followed. The girls teased and tickled him as he worked his way through the small opening.

"Damn, this box is cold. What you got in there?"

Jack looked down and saw Judy's bare feet on Dawn Marie's frosty cardboard coffin and said, "Something frozen."

Jack knew that Nookie would have a larger bed than the small narrow bunk running along one side. Then he noticed the hinged cushioned bunk, and he lifted the top. It swung over to rest on a ledge on the opposite side of the camper, making a bed with a mattress already built into the top.

Judy and Debbie climbed onto the mattress and pushed Jack down, busily removing his soaking shirt and pants.

Jack guessed both were less than five feet tall, each weighing in at a trim ninety pounds. He gazed happily at their tiny waists and high firm breasts with nipples that stood out high and hard. Judy was an olive-skinned brunette, and Debbie was Anglo-Saxon and true blond, as Jack could readily determine in the sporadic arcs of lightning.

They swarmed over him, engulfing him with their bodies, nippling and stroking him in all of his favourite places. Finally, Judy mounted, crying out as she pressed his steel deep into her silk. Jack pulled Debbie astride his chest, and holding her tight buttocks in both hands, he drew her to his lips to access her down little garden that eagerly thrust itself forward for his kiss. He tantalized her hard button nipples with his fingertips. Soon Debbie's reactions told him the tip of his tongue was on target, igniting her ravenous nerve endings.

The rain thundered on the station overhang and battered the camper on the side while the blazing sheets of lightning create a strobe effect on the busy little group. The wind rocked the truck, which, along with the steadily booming thunder and light show, was a nice counterpoint to the rocking that was going on inside.

His attention strayed to the cold clay just inches beneath the carnal scene on the mattress. *Dawn Marie, your life was short, but mine is long—and it's good for me right now—forgive me, but I'm alive and I am going to enjoy.*

Jack could barely hold back. Judy squealed, went rigid and then collapsed alongside of Jack, kissing him gently on the lips. Debbie said, "my turn," eagerly taking Judy's place. She was very vocal and had an unexpected ability to contract certain muscles Jack had only heard about. After gyrating wildly for a few minutes, she spasmed around Jack and shrieked "I'm melting!" He became energetic in his thrusts and nearly slammed her against the top of the camper.

The girls cuddled closely around him, nuzzling and kissing him gently on the neck and ears, whispering how got it was. Cigarettes were smoked, and at length, they decided to get moving. Jack found a change of clothes in one of the little drawers build beneath the bed, discovering that he and Nookie were close enough in size for it not to matter.They climbed through the window into the cab and were soon back on the road again..

They broke out cigarettes and listened to the radio. Judy and Debbie couldn't take their eyes off of him in wonder.

They smoked and listened to the radio.

WWL radio gave regular storm progress reports. Aurora headed straight into Lake Pontchartrain and pushed a wall of water into New Orleans East. The southern part of New Orleans was flooding and many homes were now under water. A levee had broken and the flooding waters were threatening to inundate New Orleans East. Jack and his charges were in the western periphery of the great ring of galing wind, and since the storm was heading north, it could blow by in a day or so. The eye of the storm probably wouldn't hit Pointe Au Chein unless it veered to the west. That was unlikely, for in Jack's experience, hurricanes usually turned to the east once they made landfall, owing to the counter-clockwise rotation of the winds.

They drove alongside Petit Caillou, a bayou that paralleled the road to Montegut. The locals call it "li'l kiyou." Boats of every description were secured along its banks, having been brought inland from the Gulf for the most secure haven possible. There were offshore crewboats, used to carry personnel to the drilling rigs in the marsh and in the Gulf, yachts of the rich who had moved their huge pleasure crafts from New Orleans Yacht Club harbor, and shrimp boats with their tall butterfly nets standing erect on each side like huge resting water-borne crickets. Patrician and proletariat, all democratically bobbing side by side at this moment of truth, equal in the eyes of the storm, each available for consumption by the ravening winds.

All men are equal in a hurricane, Jack thought cynically, and me especially. Then, again, maybe not everybody had my experience tonight.

The girls chattered about what they were going to do during their days off until the storm cleared. Debbie had never been to the bayou, and Judy told her how her family lived. Judy's father, Ovide Cheramie, was an affluent shrimper. A self made man, he was one of seventeen children and had been born and raised on the bayou.

Jack glanced at her and saw the entire Cajun nation—how immaculate, industrious and frugal most of her people were. Of course, there were some who lived day-by-day, and after a big catch or payday, wouldn't work until they spent the money, but most were hardworking, responsible and fun loving.

The water of the bayou paralleling the road was level with the streets. Jack was afraid he soon wouldn't be able to discern the bayou from the highway. He was already relying on the location of the road signs to determine the edge of the roadway.

"Look," Judy shouted as she pointed out her street. I'm home! We made it!"

The girls whooped and cheered and hugged Jack, nearly causing him to run off the road.

Jack turned down the street and drove for a short way when Judy pointed to a large two story Acadian cottage built on a high, man-made knoll.

"Papa knew there would be storms and flooding. He brought in enough fill-dirt to make sure our house wouldn't ever get under water," Judy said proudly.

Jack drove up the driveway and saw that Judy's daddy was indeed a wise man. In addition to the "hill" the house was built on, it sat on sturdy brick piers high enough to park the family vehicles beneath.

"We got the only hill on the bayou," Judy laughed.

Jack pulled up the emergency brake.

"Ladies, it's been a hoot. Time to bid you all adieu."

"Thanks for everything," Judy said quietly, gently rubbing the inside of Jack's thigh. He felt the old stirring down there again, and Debbie reached across Judy and placed her hand directly on his rising manhood and squeezed.

"We're gonna give you a call when we get back in town," Debbie said.

"Yes, we are. I know I am." Judy said, sliding her tongue in his ear."

"You better knock it off, ladies, I don't think Mr. Cheramie'd understand if he looked out here and saw this truck bouncing in his driveway."

Judy raised her eyebrows quizzically, and Debbie caught her breath at the aspect of an immediate return engagement.

Pushing Judy away, Jack said, "You all gotta get inside and stop those folks from worrying. And I gotta get my ass down the bayou before I can't."

"Come in and meet Mama and Papa. Please?" Judy pleaded. "They'll want to thank you for saving my life." She moved close to Jack. "You did, you know. But they won't pay you like I'd like to, she said with a wicked chuckle."

"Me neither," Debbie said, huskily.

Jack thought of the days ahead and whether he could survive a real onslaught by these two. *Well, what the hell, heroes are made they say. And this one may be made more than once.*

At that, Judy grabbed Jack's ponytail in both hands and gave him a hot, passionate French kiss, pressing her body against his. He finally managed to push her away, and she grinned at the effect she had achieved, as it was very manifest.

He opened the door and stood in the cold rain for a few moments, allowing his body to return to normal. The girls ran to the house and beckoned him to follow.

They entered an immaculate kitchen lit with candles and storm lanterns. The kitchen opened onto a large dining room with a long table, around which sat at least a dozen people noisily talking, laughing, playing cards and drinking beer. A small portly lady sprang from her chair and ran to Judy, embracing her as tears welled in her eyes.

"Judy. I was so worry. We done called de stet pleece 'an all! Dey got a all pointed bullet out fa you."

"That's an all-points-bulletin, Mama," Judy said, laughing and hugging the little round lady.

A thin, gnarled little man walked slowly toward them and glared at Judy. "Mais jamais! You shoulda call. You worry yo' mama."

"I thought I could make it, Papa."

The little man rubbed at an itch in his nose, and a suppressed tear glistened in his eye as he chided Judy. "W'aal, you safe—dat's all dat matter. Hey," he said, his features breaking into a smile that made his eyes dance, "who dis you done brang wit' you?"

Judy introduced both Debbie and Jack, then quickly babbled all of the details of their mishap, Jack rescuing them, and the drive through the storm.

"Sacre! "Hot Dam, boy!" he said, slapping Jack on the back and handing him a Schlitz. "You save mah li'l Judy life! Shoop! Dat call for a celebration!"

Jack remembered the thawing going on in the back of the truck and began hurriedly, "Mr. Cheramie. . ."

Judy's father interrupted him saying, "Hell boy, call me E-Boo. Dat's what dey call me aroun' here. Li'l owl. Ain't no Mister aroun' dis house unless you a stranger, 'an you ain' no stranger here, never mo."

"Thanks," Jack said, taking a lengthy swallow of the icy brew. "I gotta get to Pointe-Au-Chein quick. Some friends down there expecting me."

E-Boo stared at Jack for a moment. "What you goin' down to see *dem* for, boy?"

Jack remembered that Nookie was an Indian, in his opinion as noble and fine a group of people as he had ever met. But many Cajuns had a bias against them for reasons only they knew, if they had any reasons or thought about it at all. They both lived about the same way, and Jack couldn't tell the way a Cajun acted from a Sabine Indian. Nookie called himself a Cajun and had the same carefree spirit of all Cajuns.

A short, heavyset man with a beard stood up and said, "Man, you ain' gon' make it. De road gon' be flood an' dey gon' fin' you floatin' in de marsh."

Jack had to get Dawn Marie into refrigeration soon. Things could get pretty rough in the truck if he didn't. He had to try it regardless of how much he was tempted to stay with these people. Maybe Noonie would have enough ice to keep things settled until he could get her to the pathologist.

It was clear, from Jack's determined look that he was going to try for reasons of his own. E-Boo and the rest became very quiet and studied him with obvious regret that they couldn't change his mind.

"You et yet?" Judy's mama asked. Seeing that Jack hesitated, she bustled into the kitchen and fetched out a plate on which she had piled some fried fish and shrimp, a length of spicy rice and pork sausage called boudin, and some hot, buttered French bread. She covered it with aluminum foil and put a cold six pack of Schlitz in a bag.

"At leas' when you drown you ain' gon' drown hungry!" she said, and as she laughed, her belly bounced and they all roared.

"Thank you all. I gotta chance it," he said, turning to walk out.

Just as he reached the kitchen door, E-Boo said, "Hey, Jack. If you got no place to sleep, I dock my big boat–Miss Judy–on lower 665 in the bayou by Naquin place. All dem people on lower 665 make good hands. When it come a blow, it's a safe place to put my boat. Keys to the cabin is hung on a nail over the door. You plenty welcome to stay on her till the storm blow over if you want."

"Thanks, E-Boo, I may do just that!"

Judy, Debbie, E-Boo, and the man with the beard walked out to the truck and stood in the driving rain and waved goodbye as Jack backed down the driveway and back into the storm.

Chapter 10

The Cajun's love of life was contagious, and it had wrapped Jack like a soft old coat. Simply sitting around a table talking and drinking coffee or beer was a pleasure. They laughed easily, loved company, and made a person feel more than at home. They were clannish and protective of each other as a family, but once you were accepted, you *were* family to them. Jack had been adopted as a member of the Cheramie family.

The smell of the spicy fried fish and boudin filled the cab, and with his free hand, he dug through the crinkly foil. Then he cracked open a beer and nested it between his legs while munching on the delicately fried speckled trout and shrimp.

The radio said that the wind exceeded one hundred seventy five miles per hour in Venice and Port Sulphur, which lay just below New Orleans. Aurora was barging straight up the river toward New Orleans. Someone had dynamited the levees that normally would have kept the rising flood away from the lower end of the city, but now that the protective barrier was down and the water was diverted from the silk stocking lakeshore homes toward the poorer section of town. Jack knew that whoever blew the levee would never be brought to justice. Carlos Mendez, mafia don of New Orleans, lived in one of the mansions on the lake that was spared by the hand of the man with the dynamite. New Orleans levees were not built anticipating category five hurricanes, and another had broken, flooding the entirety of New Orleans East.

Jack grimaced, remembering an old Irish folk song: "She was poor but she as honest." He began to sing as he drove on in the pouring rain.

> It's the same the whole world over.
> It's a shame, a wretched shame.

It's the rich who gets the pleasures
and the poor who gets the blame.

Jack thought, *in this case, it's the poor whose ass gets wet, but if the levee break lets water into New Orleans East, the middle class will be flooded.* New Orleans expanding East into below sea level areas, dependant on levees, was an invitation for a tragedy like this.

Taking La 665, Jack headed south again, this time angling into the headwind. The wind and rain and rolling tide on the roadway nearly held him at a standstill. He was grateful to Nookie that his engine was so hardy, and that somehow, at least until that point, it had not drowned out, for there were many times Jack knew for sure that the entire engine had been submerged in small tidal wave.

Finally, he reached the tiny village of Pointe-Au-Chein, which translated means "fork of the oak tree," but his actual destination lay several miles to the south, at the end of the road where the bayou met the marsh and fingers of the upper Gulf of Mexico. For a time, the road followed a small winding bayou through low, sparse hardwoods of water oak and cypress. The woods abruptly ended at the edge of the salt marsh, which, if it had not been raining, Jack would have been able to see for miles in every direction over a sea of light brown marsh grass. An occasional oak or cypress stood along the ridge on which the roadway was built. There was nothing to block the wind's fierce winds, and Jack felt a malignant intention behind that steady fusillade coming straight at him.

Oh God, if it gets any deeper she'll drown out!

The truck whipsawed and yawed, seemingly held to the road by the bumper-high water. His brakes were all but gone, saturated long ago. He would be stopped dead in his tracks by the force of the wind and water were it not for the powerful motor shoving the truck against them. He constantly expected the wind to make a sail of the flat side of the camper and simply flip it into the marsh.

Logs and limbs floated toward him, some steering straight like torpedoes, striking his bumper or tires. It was a good thing the water was as deep as it was, for any less and the floating flotsam and jetsam would hang beneath the truck and block his wheels. If that happened, he could go no farther. Inside the truck or out, he was at the mercy of the storm. If he had to go outside for any reason he simply would be blown away and found only by Alligators who seldom had left overs.

On several occasions, the log-like submarines were animate: alligators blown from their marshy homes onto the highway. Jack counted two dozen before his attention was riveted on a huge treetop that bounded toward him and lit on the truck like a tarantula. Its flailing limbs, nearly stripped of leaves, grappled for a hold on the cab before it tore free and blew over the camper to the rear. Jack knew he could never forget the sight of that treetop, twice the size of the truck, flying like a nightmare thing right at him. Nookie's truck looked like it had been in a war.

The wind blew harder. The windshield took several blows leaving a half dozen running cracks. He felt his way more than seeing. There was almost no light coming from the headlights. He thought the headlights must be full of water, or one of them had blown.

Finally, he arrived at the settlement at Lower 665. It was at the bottom of the state and at the end of the road. He made a left turn, crossed a small bridge, and continued south on a narrow shell road that paralleled the bayou. Gravel was expensive and had to be hauled in a long distance. Shells were dredged from the waterways and lakes and laid down on the roads to give a serviceable surface in the bayou country.

The waterway was packed with berthed shrimp boats. In a quiet bayou like this, deep enough to accommodate large shrimp vessels, it was the safest place that could be found anywhere short of leaving the area entirely.

To a stranger, the community would be a curiosity. Situated on a narrow, three-mile-long oak-lined ridge, it was barely wide enough at any point to afford a one lane road. The grip of several oaks and a single house on either side of the road was all there was before the land gave way to the salt marsh at their back door.

Jack entered the ancient world of the Chitimaca. Here were native Americans who stayed unto themselves, and except for their houses, powerboats and modern cars, their lifestyle wasn't so different from the way their ancestors lived. The marsh and the sea provided everything they needed for food or money from trapping, fishing, crabbing, and shrimping.

They weren't part of the Cajun or Anglo communities. They seldom married outside of the group, and remained isolated in several areas of the lower bayou country. Keeping apart, they were excluded–in a way, exiled by their own choosing.

The alienation probably came from three hundred years before when Iberville tried to decimate the Indian population and his scourge didn't reach them. The Chitamacha had originally dominated all of southeast Louisiana and the French, in an effort to control the Mississippi, had rallied other tribes against them and literally chased them into near extinction into the swamps and marsh. They spoke French with a patois of their own, probably with a little of their ancient tongue thrown in, and they didn't consort with many in the nearby city of Houma. The women were usually extraordinarily beautiful and bright, with long black hair, huge dark eyes and mellow dispositions. The men were mild and easy going, as well as proud and intelligent. The men's deeply tanned, smiling faces were furrowed by the sun and wind of the sea, and they were impervious to heat or cold.

The marsh, bays, bayous and gulf were their life and livelihood. Their fare was shrimp, crabs, oysters, fish, alligator, possums, raccoons, nutria, ducks, geese, and every other wild thing that thrived in the marsh, bayou and gulf. Of course they knew every inch of the very complex network of bayous and waterways in the marsh. One could become lost or could hide forever in there. Jean Lafitte the pirate managed to evade the law for years in the Baratarian marsh near New Orleans.

Many lived in mobile homes or shanties, and some had houses built on stilts away from the high water of floods on their little spit of land. Their children's playground was a small front yard on the bayou with the back of the house literally hanging over into the marsh. Just a few years before, the entire area was meadows and wooded high ground. The sea and coastal erosion had eaten all but this tiny thread of land, and a few more hurricanes would probably wash the last vestige of homeland from beneath these people.

Jack knew Nookie's great uncle–toothless, wizened and over ninety–living in a shanty on a tiny island of high ground to the south. His house was separated from Lower 665 by over a mile of marsh and open water. During the old man's youth, his home was high and dry, connected to the rest of the mainland, but erosion and hurricanes had washed away the connection, and now there were bits of land here and there, still occupied by the hardcore oldsters who insisted on not giving up their landed legacies, staying until the bitter end. The entire area had been forests, farms and grazing lands until the last generation, when it suddenly was changed by the elements.

Once Jack was sitting on the dock having a beer after returning from a fishing trip when the old man paddled his tiny pirogue up the bayou across a great expanse of open water from his island home that during his life was connected to the mainland. Jack had looked into the merry eyes set deeply in his craggy face and knew that he was looking at eternity, for this old man didn't know or care about time or age. He was timeless as life itself, and Jack felt a pang of envy at not ever having tasted as much life as the old man knew at that very instant. The old man lived moment to moment, just as his ancestors had lived. Jack wanted to touch this old spirit, and he did, though they didn't speak the same language. Jack gave him a beer and they squatted on the dock, grinning at each other, smoking Jack's Picayunes and drinking beer as the sun set.

The limbs overhead whipped and snagged and fought each other. The current in the road flooded in from the marsh, pushed by terrific tides. The power was out, but candles and lamps lighted the windows of most of the trailers and little stilt houses, telling Jack that many of these rugged people had decided to ride out the storm in their own homes, like they had done for generations.

Jack was at the end of his trek and stopped at a house with a screened porch built just a few feet from the edge of the roadway. Just several hundred yards further, the last thread of land ended, and the road dropped into the marsh. He always thought of it as the end of the world. Several unusually large steel shrimp boats were moored in the bayou that he had not seen before. "Miss Judy" was painted on the bow of one.

With his head down, Jack raced against the blast, pulled open the screen door and entered the porch. He knocked on the inner door, which was immediately opened by a serious-faced woman of around sixty who motioned for him to come in.

The house was lit by storm lanterns and candles, giving it a warm and welcoming aspect, something like Christmastime. Sitting around in the large room were a dozen adults and probably more children than that. A table was loaded with seafood, including shrimp cooked in several ways, and the room was redolent with freshly brewed coffee.

The woman who came to the door looked sternly at Jack and said something in French, as if expecting him to understand. And he knew what she said, though he didn't understand the words. She asked if he wanted a cup of coffee. Jack nodded. She turned and went into the kitchen. Coffee in every South Louisiana home is not just a drink, it is a ceremonial ritual of compelling social import and turning it down when offered is a faux pas and may operate as a discreet impediment to trust and real understanding.

Noonie, Nookie's brother, came from the back of the house and shook Jack's hand. "We ridin' it out," he said. "De whole family come when dere's a storm. More'll be comin." He pointed to a chair and said, "Make youself to home. Nookie called before de lines went down, tol' me a l'l about you problem. Don' you worry. You okay here."

Jack flopped down on the old couch, sighing in relief. He felt like he was still driving, the motion continued in his head as he gradually settled down and relaxed.

They all welcomed Jack. The children obediently sat on the floor, playing games or talking quietly. The adults spoke alternatively French and English, depending on whether they were talking to Jack. Their conversation contained occasional English words or phrases scattered throughout.

Jack thought of the surface differences between the French Cajun and the Indian Cajun, as he called them, and found none, except the Indian took life more seriously. They clung to their old ways, and even spoke in a patois among themselves that was neither French nor English. He knew from what he had observed and what Nookie implied, they held to mores and customs they kept to themselves, ways that had their roots deep in time they never showed to any outsider, even to him. The idea that anybody could find anything wrong with these people eluded him. He thought they were beautiful.

"Aurora, she turn a li'l bit west," Noonie said, "look like she goin' up de Mississippi. We gonna get lots of wind."

These people know enough about high water and storms to tell the weatherman a thing or two, Jack thought.

The old uncle was there. He said something and Noonie repeated it to Jack in English. "Big wind cause high water in city. We okay."

"He knows weather," Noonie said, "He like, howyacall, a barrowmeter. He know from the stars and the feel–says the air talks to him. He say its all alive and tells him things."

The old man grinned at Jack, his barren pink gums gleaming behind his thin, weatherbeaten lips.

Jack relaxed, knowing if there was anyone he could rely on for many truths, it was this old man.

The woman returned from the kitchen with a cup of sweet, black coffee and watched intently as Jack took his first sip. Her name was Lizette–Nookie and Noonie's mama, the mother of sixteen children and still attractive with a nice figure. She refused to learn English and spoke French to Jack, even though she knew he only understood a few words. Somehow he always understood what she meant. Jack gingerly allowed a few drops of the scalding liquid past his lips, enough to taste, and he smiled and nodded that it was perfect. She smacked him on the back and returned to her kitchen.

They discussed the storm, asked about Nookie, how Jack's law practice was doing, why he wasn't married, and did he have a girl friend. Jack was brought in like a long lost son and given refuge.

Chapter 11

Jack ruminated over the plight of his friends. Though they fought it in their own way, their unique culture, like the Cajuns, was being diluted, blended and swallowed by Americans. He was observing the effects of sociological change from only one point on the great graph of time, but he didn't like it worth a damn. At least he could enjoy the vestiges of a great culture first hand.

Noonie, a muscular, bronze man who carried himself with the pride of a chieftain, returned from the kitchen with a strange looking duck he had mounted himself. "Me, I shot him in de marsh," he said proudly. The duck was black with a white head and a white lightning blaze on the breast like nothing he had ever seen. They speculated on the bird for a long time, and concluded finally that it had obviously been lost or caught in a storm, and found itself in Noonie's sights in the Louisiana marsh.

Nookie's family made a decent living trawling for shrimp in boats that ranged from sixteen to a hundred feet in length, using long nets that would fan out near the bottom when pulled behind the boat, scooping up schools of shrimp and whatever else was unfortunate enough to get in the way. Sometimes they used huge butterfly nets affixed to the side of the boat like giant wings that they would submerge and drag alongside.

They built their own style of boats from a design handed down through the ages. The Lafitte Skiff's bottom was nearly flat, with a small keel running the length and an upswept bow. Each time Jack had visited them during the off-season, at least one was under construction in somebody's yard. The whole family helped, and that meant all of the brothers, uncles and cousins.

Jack often saw the outrage in their faces at pollution or destructive fishing and hunting. It was more than anger; it was a deeper, older, primal feeling. Jack could tell by the smoldering embers behind their eyes as they described those dumping trash and game-taking methods they considered as iniquitous. Such things violated a law higher than man's. Jack thought of the buffalo and the hunting grounds in the west, and how those tribes fought back. The taking of their resources in the waters of the marsh and gulf was more subtle and usually legal, but they were just as destructive to their way of life.

Jack's pulse slowed and his tense nerve endings relaxed in the warmth of the room and the safety of friends. There was something musical in their language, rhythmic and hypnotic. It was like a dream, and the room and the people in it began to change. At first, it was as if he was viewing the scene from above, and then he became part of the group. The present collapsed and merged into a dreamy state. The same people were in the room, but they were different. The time was different.

He was in a large tribal shelter with the men and women talking about the same things, but they were dressed in skins, sitting and squatting around a fire, with an animal spitted over the flame. Naked children played a game with little sticks on the dirt floor. The smoke spiraled upwards, through a hole in the ceiling. The room was hot and crowded, and he could smell the closeness. A high wind howled outside, blowing the smoke back through the open chimney hole.

An eerie feeling of deja-vu swept over him. He was naked except for a soft, animal-hide loincloth. A spear lay across his lap and a razor-sharp bone knife was at his waist. His hair was long and black, and the taste of partially cooked meat was strong on his tongue. He could understand every word spoken. And he was alive! At that moment, he became more certain of who he was than any time in his life. He remembered! Something fell away from him and disappeared, a husk he didn't know had been there, and he seemed to rise, free of his body.

Jack sucked in his breath and looked down at his rain-soaked clothes. He looked all about to assure himself that what he had just seen, or been, was an illusion. It had been so real! For that single instant, he had become someone else—or was it someone else? He had been in the head of that other man, blending with a primitive mind that was yet his own mind, set in another time and place. Jack knew it was not his imagination or a dream. But somehow, it was linked to the images of the interminable dream that had made the nights of his life a living hell. It was something he remembered down through time.

He knew things. He not only knew the wind was beating the outside, he was the wind, and the smoke in the house, and the smells of the bodies and the cooked meat. He was the world outside and not just part of it. He was everything, and he had no doubt about it. He questioned nothing. He belonged. These were the people. It was so simple. He knew who he was.

The tension in him dissolved and he felt a calm that was at once volatile yet serene, completely alert yet at rest, poised and ready yet at repose. He delighted at the subtle strength he felt in his body, nerve endings sending him messages about his surroundings he never knew were there and a sense of grace that pervaded his entire being. The only word that came to describe the way he felt was the word delicious. He felt like he was purring.

Jack sat as still as a stone, reliving that moment of some other time and place and body, still feeling the thoughts of that other time with total certainty, feeling the limitless energy and confidence that had been his just the moment before. He'd brought all this, and something else back through time, but wasn't exactly sure what it was.

He was different. Sheer power had coursed through his entire being. He could still feel it in him; a vitality borne of the wind and rain and earth–a wildness, yet as still and as quiet the deepest pool.

In that brief twinkling, Jack had united with himself across the gulf of time, and he again knew the freedom he had lost and longed for all of his life: a soaring quiet, a peaceful rapture that transcended everything he had ever known or thought about. Yet he was part and master of them, and he was still Jack, "Night Cat," or whoever, they were the same–but he was himself. That seemed entirely too simple to have meaning to anyone else, but it meant everything, because he knew–knowing was certainty–and certainty was truth. *He* was truth.

The wind creaked the walls of the uninsulated shiplap board house while the boats in the bayou, straining at their hawsers, bumped on the dock. He could hear more things, clearer and deeper, and they told him more. A sweet sense of joy filled him with something he had been in that other time. A hot tear tracked its way down Jack's cheek as emotion coursed through him. He knew he had just moved through an experience that changed him, for he still carried with him the enormous certainty of that long haired barbarian with the spear, and he knew he was once that man. He was a spirit yet a man, a resting lion, a savage, and the power of that knowledge gave him a peace he never dreamed possible; he had come home to himself. He felt his lips pull apart in a wide smile of wholeness fulfilled. He didn't give a damn! Defiant! Free! Insouciant–even carelessly arrogant.

The old man had been watching him closely throughout the interval of his vision and nodded gravely and made a sign, holding his two forefingers downward along each side of his mouth like fangs, and hissed "haaaah!" Jack returned the sign, and both laughed. For sure, he had perceived Jack's totem, the Lynx.

Nookie's mother, Lizette, watched the interaction between the old uncle and Jack and said something in French. The old man nodded, and as she spoke to the group, they became quiet and looked back and forth between Jack and the old man. For some reason, Jack wasn't embarrassed by the attention focused on him, and listened uncomprehendingly as the old man and woman talked.

After a series of exchanges, Noonie leaned forward and said, "Mama, she say you a old one. Mon oncle," he indicated to the old man, "he can see tings, you know. He say he trust you, so ah tell you. He say he don' know whar you come from, but you var' var' old spirit 'an he like you."

The old man nodded as Noonie spoke to Jack. Obviously the old man understood some English, but spoke none. Noonie continued, "He say you welcome here any time, cause you brang good luck."

The old man spoke again. His old voice was shrill and breaky. Noonie translated. "You hunter, he say, 'an you strong. You got no tribe. He seen a big cat in you, bigger dan any cat he ever seen, so you ain' from nowhere aroun' here. But you always welcome as a fran'."

Jack nodded in understanding and turned to the old man and gave him a cigarette. They quietly smoked Jack's Picayunes as the group continued their light, merry kidding and bragging among themselves.

Jack had been accepted fully into the fold. He felt like he had come home after being away for a long time.

Jack drank another cup of the sweet, hot coffee, and accepted some roasted duck he knew had been taken out of season. He wiped the grease from his mouth with the back of his hand, at once realizing that such a method of cleaning up was new to him—he usually used a napkin—but it felt natural to do it that way. And for once, he didn't give a damn what anybody thought. He noticed the old man smile, his eyes twinkling as he watched Jack's gusto as he polished off the duck and slugged down the boiling coffee.

Damn, I feel good, Jack thought, glancing around the room as he stood to leave.

"I'll stay on the 'Miss Judy if that's OK with you. I know where the key is. E-Boo said there's plenty room. Been a rough day—need to hit the sack. I want to thank you for your hospitality and great food."

Lizette nodded, and slapped him on the back. Everyone told him they were glad he was there.

Jack pulled on his slicker and Noonie followed suit, saying, "Nookie say you got someting need ice down. I help you. I work as skipper on Miss Judy beaucoup time for E-Boo."

The wind and rain was stronger than when Jack had come in. They could barely stand. Grappling their way to the truck, they ended up falling to their hands and knees, crawling the rest of the way.

The rain stung Jack's hands and face. He retrieved his pack and the rest of the beer and wrapped the rope around the cardboard coffin, which had developed a frost over its surface, to secure it from breaking open and its contents flying into the churning bayou. He tied an end around his waist and the other end around Noonie's waist. They lined the box up so it wouldn't be broadside to the wind and crawled to the edge of the dock.

The Miss Judy was a hundred fifty feet long, made of steel, and was the state of the art in blue water trawlers. She was made fast to the pilings of the dock, fore and aft, with rubber tires secured to the side of the pier as bumpers. The gale hit her broadside, stretching her heavy hawsers to their limit, pushing her away from the dock and bumping her back again, rocking her in a rough rhumba that Jack realized he would have to endure once aboard.

They wrestled the cold box, now soaking and softening in the rain, over the side onto the deck. Jack opened the hatch under the deck where the shrimp were stored. A rich, fishy aroma rose from the hold, and Jack descended the ladder, shining his flashlight inside.

She was as clean as a pin. Jack knew that E-Boo would maintain his boats like this, with pride. Jack would have to start the generator to keep the lights on, but that would be no problem. It usually ran twenty four hours a day when they were under way.

Noonie slid the box through the hatch and pointed to a metal door. Jack could barely keep his footing with the big boat's unpredictable ramming and butting against the tires on the dock while it dipped and rose in the boiling bayou. He thought that the freezer locker would be hot, and it would take a long time to get the mechanism to start its thing, but when he opened it, a blast of frigid air rushed out. Evidently, Miss Judy had known work up until the very eve of the storm. Jack would have to start the generator to keep the refrigeration going, but that would be no problem. It usually ran twenty four hours a day when they were under way. He shoved the box into the large compartment and clicked the door shut.

The key was on a nail above the door, as promised, and the door opened to the wheelhouse. Noonie pressed a button, and somewhere below an engine fired into life.

"De generator," he said, as he flipped a light switch. A bulb, dim at first, glowed brighter as the voltage grew stronger.

"De freezer back on, too," Noonie added.

There was a comfortable four bunk sleeping area behind the wheelhouse, a small galley with a stove, and a refrigerator full of food, still cold. "Ah been out on dis boat many time wit' E-Boo. Dis his best rig." Noonie said proudly. "Nice boat."

Noonie said E-Boo would trawl the blue water for the big shrimp catches. They would stay out for a week, or until the hold was filled, and then return to offload.

Noonie grinned showing a big gap between his two front teeth and said, "E-Boo, he ain't like most shrimpers, him. He'll go right back out again. He don't wait till he get broke befo' goin' out. Dat's why he got all dem boat and live in dat big brick house."

Storms meant little to Noonie, having lived with the sea and the elements all of his life. He said that there had been some big storms when they had to evacuate, but his mama's house always escaped damage, and his family made it the place to huddle together at times like this.

"All mah brudder an' sister pass mama house evah day," Noonie said, meaning that they all stopped by to see her daily. They were a close-knit family, most of whom lived nearby, depending on each other in many ways.

When Noonie turned to look out at the driving rain, Jack studied his rugged profile against the dim light of the wheelhouse. Silhouetted were the high cheekbones and noble humped nose of the American Indian. A war bonnet would make it complete. Noonie would look like the Chief on those old Indianhead nickels.

"I gotta get back in befo' it get more worser," Noonie said. He waved and ducked out into the storm.

Jack had to hold to the walls to keep from being thrown down. He thought of a cement mixer with the incessant splashing, tossing and thumping on the tires. After a cigarette and another beer, while sitting in the captain's chair behind the wheel, Jack searched the boat for something to read, and found nothing but a few playboys hidden beneath the mattress. Must belong to one of E-Boo's sons, Jack thought.

A ten inch board had been built along the side of the bunk to keep the sleeper from rolling onto the floor. Jack was thankful for it. He stretched out on the hard mattress with his hands beneath his head and adjusted to the rolling, bumping motion.

He felt peculiar, but not unpleasant, for he wasn't tired, in spite of his hellacious day. He had invoked a vision that changed him, without having to sink to despair and marginal death to create the necessity. He was calmer. The old feeling of dread and fear of something behind the curtain or around the corner was gone. The remarkable thing was that he wasn't afraid of failure any more. Maybe that's how the Indians of old found their totems, in a vision, a recollection of their own past.

Jack was incredibly aware of every instant, and he knew he was safe, for he was dangerous and liberated from the smothering fear of failure and death. He could not fail. It was impossible. The life force he had felt while sitting with the tribe in his vision returned, coursing through him. He grinned, lying in the dark, remembering the long hair, the taste in his mouth, and the wild freedom that lived in his heart.

Still smiling, he drifted off.

The deep woods were dark. He was attuned to every shadow, movement and sound. He knew the follower was behind him in the darkness, as always, just beyond his vision, and he didn't look back. He trotted along easily. He was pursued, but wasn't afraid. He continued to run, easily this time, over the icy streams and through the deep carpets of evergreen needles beneath the towering timbers.

The forest ended abruptly at the edge of the glacier. He leaped onto the broad flat surface of a huge boulder, listening to the soft, steady tread on the forest floor behind him. Someone, or something, leaped to the boulder and walked up behind him.

Jack slowly turned around.

Standing there was a half naked savage with long black hair tied back in a thong. Jack looked into his own face staring back.

"Jack, all you had to do was to stop and look back; you never had to run. Your fears weren't yours in the first place. Your people carried them through time. I do not need weapons, for I am not afraid. You are complete, as I am, as we have been since the beginning.

He stood, unmoving, as the figure stepped forward, melted into him, and disappeared.

Alone on the boulder, Jack felt an uncontrollable sense of wild, exultant well-being sweep through him. He thrust his fists into the air and shouted at the heavens, "I'm free!"

Jack sat bolt upright on the bunk, panting and laughing, knowing he would never dream that dream again.

Chapter 12

DAY FOUR

The full fury of the storm struck New Orleans in the early morning hours and continued for the entire day and up into the following night. The huge whirling vortex of the storm was over fifty miles in diameter, battering and grinding everything in its path like the threshing machine of an angry god. The Pointe-Au-Chein area was in its western periphery and received enough wind to do millions of dollars in damage to property and crops, but it didn't compare to the losses in New Orleans. Lower New Orleans, below sea level to begin with, became a lake many miles wide with nothing but roofs showing. In New Orleans East, because of the levee breach, the waters from the lake and river made a lake out of modern subdivisions with not even the roofs showing. Some residents in the Belle Chasse area and lower sections of the city refused to leave and drowned when the wall of water crashed through. Many couldn't open their doors against the tidal wave and were forced to stay in their homes as the water rose past their windows in minutes. Others took what refuge there was on their rooftop in the gale force winds, only to find that other creatures were looking for refuge as well. Big cotton mouth moccasins, vicious and aggressive by nature, sought the same high places already occupied by the hapless humans trying to hold on in the windy dark. Many died from snakebite.

Jack listened to the news of the storm on the radio. Slidell, a small low-lying city on the north shore of Lake Pontchartrain, was the expected recipient of the lake's waters until the perfidious winds switched direction and headed straight up the Mississippi. If it had made landfall a few miles to the east and continued its northerly march, it is possible that the shallow lake would have been pushed in its entirety—crabs, catfish and all—to devastate the little St. Tammany Parish city. Instead, it unleashed its payload and windborne fury into the poorest part of New Orleans.

The winds tore away everything that wasn't nailed down. Within a hundred yards of Jack's retreat, two cars and three mobile homes were blown into the bayou, and a huge oak was torn from the earth and thrown through a trailer. Luckily the families had evacuated.

During the night, Jack woke when he heard a car door slam. He got up and saw a Jeep wagon in front of Lizette's house. One of Lizette's sons—Cookie, a six-foot-six linebacker for the Minnesota Vikings—had battered his way through the melee to be with his family. Several other family members found their way home, leaving safe havens to be at Mama's to help if need arose.

Time drifted slowly, dreamily, and it all seemed surrealistic. Jack fought through the wind to Lizette's house during the day. Each time, the house was always packed with family members, all seeming to have a joyous family reunion.

Jack ran out of cigarettes and took to rolling his own from some rough cut Prince Albert pipe tobacco in a can he mooched from Noonie. The formaldehyde and freezer was doing its job, so far, and probably would continue to do so as long as Dawn Marie remained in a suspended frozen state, but Jack couldn't count on his luck holding. He would have to move as soon as possible. He just didn't know where to go.

If Nookie's truck would run, he would meet Vic somewhere and they would go to Mobile together. He would have to circle the city, for more than likely, there would be an APB out on him.

There was more to this than just the pressure from that jelly belly deputy Parker. From the information given by Tyrone and little James, Parker and Destrehan both were the worst of them, but Jack suspected that men were involved who were tight with the highest officials in the city and state government. They could cause some big trouble to keep their names out of the limelight.

I got no choice, Jack thought, *I gotta get the body somewhere for a thorough autopsy and analysis for drugs, then get more of the names of those involved. I gotta hit 'em so hard and fast that removing me from the scene wouldn't matter, then some other enterprising attorney—or DA for that matter, would have enough to work with. The fact that the kids gave the names won't be enough—that'll make lots of smoke, but no fire, with no corroboration other than the testimony of the kids themselves. I gotta get her to Mobile to that pathologist Vic was talking about. She mentioned his name—Jester McConothy. I could find him if I could get to Mobile.*

Wait a minute! Tyrone and James gave some names, and said they had been taken to a Motel—the Town and Country on Airline highway! Holy shit! It was rumored to be owned by Calos Mendez, mafia godfather. Mendez possessed untold power in lots of little dark corners the light of law and justice never penetrated. He controlled major politicians.

Jack had had been told that the Governor had to get Mendez's support to get elected. If those guys were tied in any way to Carlos, or his thugs, they could call on him for a favor and Jack would be silenced in ways Jack preferred not to consider.

"Well, one thing at a time," Jack said out loud, amazed that his blood pressure hadn't risen as he considered all these dire thoughts. He found himself smiling and completely at ease. He was having a ball!

Day Five

The storm blew past early on the second night, and Jack woke before daybreak to a serene calm, the big boat lying on still waters. A thick fog grew out of the bayou and spilled over onto the road and Miss Judy's deck like a living blanket. He could barely see Lizette's house across the narrow roadway.

Jack stirred from the bunk, knowing he would have to make his move in a few hours. His little vacation was over. The faithful generator still chugged away below, and that was the only sound except a couple of car doors slamming in the road just a few feet beyond the dock. It was long before dawn and Jack looked at his watch; it wasn't quite five a.m. *Who the hell could be driving in at this time of the morning so soon after the storm?*

Jack pulled on his jeans and looked out of the window of the wheelhouse. A sheriff's car with its blue light flashing squatted in front of Lizette's house. Jack squinted against the glare of the light and saw the large form of a sheriff deputy swagger to the front door.

Parker!

Jack slipped through the door and crouched on the deck less than fifty feet from the front door of the Naquin home.

The fat deputy banged on the screen door while a gaunt, anxious deputy stood behind him, nervously playing his flashlight into the cars and trailers all around.

Lizette and several men came to the door and pretended they didn't understand what Parker was talking about. Parker was infuriated at the fact nobody seemed to speak English. The Naquins knew what to do in cases like this when one of theirs was sought by the authorities—pretend not to understand.

Several men gathered around Lizette, making a frail attempt at understanding what it was all about. They all shook their heads and looked at one another quizzically as if they never had heard of Jack. Parker shouted Jack's name, saying that someone had overheard Nookie and Jack talking in a bar about borrowing Nookie's truck and coming down to Nookie's home, and sure enough Nookie's wrecked up truck sat right there in the headlights of the deputy's vehicle, so Jack had to be around somewhere.

Parker stamped his feet and cursed while the skinny deputy with him quailed at his rage, equally afraid of the swarthy faces that surrounded them in the dark. Parker shouted, "Ah'm gonna search de house!"

Parker was getting nowhere. He pushed Lizette aside, and as he did, Cookie Naquin bent his six-foot-six frame weighing in at two-hundred-seventy-five pounds as he exited the low door.

"You pushed my mama," Cookie said in English, placing himself directly in Parker's path. Parker stepped back, recognizing the young giant for the football hero he was.

"Sheriff, you come down here from New Orleans acking like you got some right, trowin' you weight around. I gonna forgive you for layin' hands on my mama, but if you keep on messin' wit' ma' people, I gonna git involved personal. If you got a legal warrant, you get on after it, but if you ain't, git one 'an come back."

The deputy edged his way back to the sheriff's unit, opened the door, and reached for something on the seat. Jack saw that his friends were getting into trouble because of him. Cookie would easily beat Parker half to death before he would let him in the house, but he could get himself and some of the family killed in the process. It would be Jack's fault.

Jack quickly lifted the bow and stern lines from the pilings on the dock and hurried back into the wheelhouse. He turned the key in the ignition, and the great diesels in the belly of the Miss Judy roared into life, fracturing the stillness of the night air and belching smoke just as the deputy leveled his riot shotgun at Cookie's chest.

The entire group froze in place. They watched the huge trawler slowly pull away from the dock.

"Stop, stop or I'll shoot," Parker shouted. He drew his revolver and pointed it at Jack, who was standing behind the window of Miss Judy's wheelhouse.

Cookie reached out with a huge hand and crushed the tendon in Parker's wrist. The gun dropped to the ground from the deputy's limp hand. The skinny deputy then leveled down on Jack with his buckshot-loaded pump shotgun. At such pointblank range, he could hardly miss. Noonie had quietly approached the deputy from the rear. He pushed the barrel upward just as the deputy pulled the trigger. Fire erupted from the barrel and its deadly missiles went wild into the early morning sky. Noonie snatched the gun away, glaring into the deputy's terrified eyes, and shucked the shells in the magazine onto the ground. Then he threw the gun back onto the seat.

Jack watched the action through the window of the wheelhouse as he steered the big boat away. He prayed that his friends wouldn't be endangered because of him.

It was impossible to hear what Parker was saying over the rumble of the big diesels, but it was obvious he was yelling. The skinny deputy retrieved his shotgun and shells and both men ran to a twenty foot Lafitte Skiff moored nearby.

Jack's friends stood by helplessly as Parker and his deputy piled into the boat and pushed off from the dock with a paddle. Parker busied himself at the wheel, and in a moment, the boat lurched and smoke rose from the stern.

Jack stepped back into the wheelhouse and headed south down the bayou toward the gulf, not knowing where he was going, knowing little of the waterways or bays, or even how to get to the big open water of the gulf in the foggy dark. He had some vague recollection of direction from his fishing trips, but that had been in the clear daylight with maps or with his friends who needed no maps.

The marsh was a labyrinth of canals, bayous, dead end lagoons and lakes, all looking alike, even on a bright sunny day. Jack only knew he should go south.

A new quiet settled around him as the giant diesels below rumbled smoothly, and he shined the huge spotlight ahead into the thickening fog. He patted the little automatic in his boot and removed his big revolver along with the box of ammo from his pack. He dropped a handful of loose bullets in his pocket and slid the pistol under his belt.

"Let 'em come on."

The fog, light at first, thickened into a solid wall of gray as Jack passed into the marsh. The powerful beam of the big spotlight on top of the wheelhouse barely penetrated fifty feet into the dense morning fog.

Jack remembered that the bayou meandered for several miles and then spilled into a large bay which joined other bays by intersecting bayous and canals, separated by long stretches of marsh. Many times before, after riding in a small boat at high speed for more than an hour, he had reached the Gulf of Mexico. But which of these canals should he take? They all looked identical. He could easily run aground or wind up in a dead end canal.

The fog closed in and at times he couldn't see beyond the bow. Jack's only consolation was that his pursuers would have the same problem, and they had no big light. But, being in the smaller craft with greater speed in the bayou, if Parker knew his business, he could catch up with Jack, and at any moment he could be boarding Miss Judy. Jack had his little automatic in one hand and the revolver on the dash, waiting for the inevitable confrontation.

Jack had never piloted such a huge boat before, but he had been shrimping in one like the Miss Judy, and knew a little. They were fairly simple. She drove like a car with all of the controls at his hands. *Great, but how do you stop this big sucker?* The chrome controls gleamed in the reflection of the big light above. Jack knew that he could throw her in reverse and give her full throttle to avoid running aground if he caught himself in time. That would slow her, but maybe not stop her at the speed she was going.

Actually, it was impossible to tell *how* fast he was going. He could have been sitting still; the only way he knew he was moving was from the laboring of the diesels.

The tach and the speedometer told him he was doing fifteen miles an hour—blind. The fog seemed to move along with him, like a pocket of white fluff surrounding the boat. Finally, he gave up and let off on the throttle. There were several tricky little turns up ahead. Even in the broad daylight, it was hard to tell which fork to take, and there were several decisions that had to be made immediately. What the hell was he going to do? He would be going by guesswork only. And as far as he knew, only one of the choices led to the deep water of the Gulf; the others would run into smaller and smaller canals until he ran out of water. He pulled back on the throttle and slowed the big boat so it was barely moving.

Jack's skin prickled. He felt a presence at his back. This is it!

He whipped around, his finger tightening on the trigger, ready to empty the revolver into the fat bastard.

But it wasn't Parker standing behind him; it was a kid! Jack's mind was a tumult of wild readiness to kill. His target was a scrawny twelve year old boy, yawning and knuckling his eyes.

Jack's guts rolled when he realized that in another instant he would have pulled the trigger. He thanked his hunting experience for never shooting blind. He let out an audible sob of relief as he lowered the pistol and pushed the safety button back on. The delay could have cost him his life if it had been Parker, but it wasn't, and there was no reason to dwell on what could have happened.

Jack's nerves turned to jelly as the realization struck him. He nearly blew that kid's head off with those .38 hollow points. Limply turning back to the window, he saw the edge of the marsh looming ahead. He spun the wheel to the right and rammed the throttle in full. The motors roared and the big craft veered away from the bank, as he straightened the heading of the boat to what he thought was in line with the bayou.

When he got the boat under control, he asked, "Who are you? What are you doing on the boat?"

"Bubbie. Veron's mah daddy," the boy said timorously. "The house was so crowded. . ."

There must have been over two dozen people in Lizette's house, including the children and the big linebacker. Jack could easily understand how someone may have slipped out during the night to find another place less hot and crowded—especially after the danger had passed.

Jack explained what had happened and where he thought they were. Bubbie sprang forward and ran out to the bow, peering into the fog. In a few moments, he returned, grinning.

"We still in de main Bayou. Go slow. Ah get out dare 'an point which way you go," he said, leaving before he got an acknowledgement. Jack was thankful this little mariner was aboard; it could save his life.

Jack was still tensed as Bubbie ran to the bow, turned and gave him the "OK" sign.

The fog cleared suddenly and Jack could see for several hundred yards ahead. Bubbie ran back to the wheelhouse and Jack asked him to hold the wheel while he looked around. He walked to the stern and watched the wall of fog recede into the darkness behind.

Jack started to turn back to the cabin when a Lafitte Skiff broke through the fog at high speed a hundred yards to the rear. Parker was at the wheel and the deputy hung over the bow, evidently doing for Parker what Bubbie had been doing for Jack.

The skiff would be upon him in seconds at that rate of speed, and he needed his revolver and reloads to hold them at bay. There were two of them and they had a shotgun.

The skiff bounced over Miss Judy's high, rolling wake, making at least thirty miles an hour, closing the gap between them rapidly. The deputy came to his knees and pointed toward Miss Judy, while yelling to Parker over the noise of the motor.

Parker lifted the shotgun and pointed it just over the deputy's head at Jack, an easy target for a scatterload of buckshot.

The skiff slid over a submerged object, and the bow shot skyward. There was a resounding thud. The boat came to an abrupt stop as the foot of the outboard struck the log, or whatever it was. The flat bottom of the skiff slammed down and slapped the surface of the bayou with a crack that sounded like a high powered rifle. The deputy, still squatting and pointing his shotgun at Jack, catapulted over the water, airborne for thirty feet before splashing down ahead of the skiff.

Parker and the deputy screamed at each other as Parker tugged at the outboard to release its foot from the object.

Jack raced back to the wheelhouse, and seeing his way clear for some distance ahead, rammed the throttle forward as far as it would go. The Miss Judy roared and leaped like a huge cricket, churning the bayou to froth, its tall outriggers chattering high above.

"Whoa!" Bubbie's eyes protruded at the demonstration of power.

Jack was glad when the fog closed back in around them, but the flip side of being concealed was that he had to slow down again. After a few minutes, he reluctantly pulled the throttle back and the big trawler wallowed down to a slow, forward drift.

"What happened?" Bubbie asked.

"It was a bad man in a skiff who wants to kill me. He was nearly on us, but he hit a floatin' log or something'. Stopped 'em dead, like they hit a wall. The deputy was on the bow like you were. Launched him into the bayou like he was shot from a slingshot." Bubbie grinned as Jack described the bad guy flying over the bayou.

"Swimmin' wit' de swimps," Bubbie said, his bright, white teeth gleaming against his tanned face.

"And the gators," Jack said. "Hope it blew his motor, but we can't take that chance. Get up front, Bubbie, let's get to open water."

Bubbie ran to the bow, where he held to a rope and peered into the gray wall ahead. Pitch darkness slowly gave way to the gray brightening of a dead white world with no more visibility than when it was night. It was well past daylight and Jack knew the fog had to clear soon. He imagined the marsh being completely blanketed in a soft pillow of silver so thick it felt like a cool, damp towel on his face.

On these bayous, just twenty four hours before, waves ten feet high thrashed through the marsh, driving all wildlife somewhere to the north.

The character of the water began to change; the smell of salt was in the air. The placid smack on the hull changed to a slight chop, which became swells and whitecaps. They weren't in a bayou any longer. It felt open on all sides, and waves began to surge against the bow, causing the big boat to roll and wallow slightly at first with seas growing heavier as they moved southward. *We must be in one of the big bays,* Jack thought, just as Bubbie excitedly ran to the wheelhouse.

"We outta da marsh. We in Lake Barre. Stay sout'. In a li'l while, we gon' pass Timbalier Island an' be in de guff."

Jack sighed in relief. He no longer had to fear running up on the bank and being stuck in the marsh with Parker somewhere behind. He turned his attention to the next problem. Where could he go? He had to go out of state, that was clear. He had to contact Vic and get her friend in Mobile to help.

He tried his cell phone several times, but nobody answered. The battery was almost gone. *Damn!*

If it was working, the closest phone would be at Grand Isle, Louisiana's only occupied island, located somewhere between where he was and the mouth of the Mississippi river to the east. Maybe he could call Judy's daddy and tell him about his fix. He couldn't use the radio because Parker, who could still be behind, may be listening on the skiff's radio.

Jack gave a little more throttle. Miss Judy rose on the swells and planed out smoothly, smacking the wave-tops with gentle thumps as she drove south. Bubbie told Jack they should be around Cat Island Pass and would be in the gulf in a few minutes.

"I need to get to Grand Isle," Jack said.

Bubbie raced to the bow, walking the pitching deck like a trained acrobat, and after five minutes, returned grinning. He pointed to the left of the wheelhouse and said, "Grand Isle is dat way. We in de guff now. Dat way," Bubbie said, still pointing.

"How far?"

"Hour, maybe. Da fog gonna clear in a li'l. You jus' head eas' by souteas', you can tell by dem big oil platform out dare."

Jack remembered, from his many fishing trips at Grand Isle, the huge drilling platforms several miles south of grand isle in the gulf. The particular rigs that Bubbie spoke of were three platforms, a hundred feet high and a thousand feet across, linked by catwalks. Owned by Freeport-McMoran, it was like a small city on huge spider-like steel legs sunk deep into the seabed squatting over a huge deposit of sulphur, oil and gas. There were smaller, single installations dotting the face of the Gulf as far as the eye could see in all directions.

"Are we clear of land, Bubbie?"

Bubbie nodded eagerly, pointing at the compass, indicating that Jack should turn to the southeast. To the south was nothing but open water to the Yucatan Peninsula, and Cuba to the east by southeast.

Jack relaxed and stoked up a Picayune.

Suddenly, the morning sun smacked him in the eyes as they broke through the fog into a bright, clear morning. Jack looked over the stern and saw a fifty foot high wall of gray wool he felt he'd been travelling in for years.

Jack shoved the throttle to its maximum and the big boat crouched as the diesels grumbled before the vessel surged ahead. Bubbie stood by the open door with a big grin on his face. He probably had never gone that fast in such a big boat before. His family usually had the smaller, wooden Lafitte skiffs that were no bigger than fifty feet, and to him, the Miss Judy was the Queen Mary. The tall rigging bearing the long trawl nets swung and chattered in the wind.

Jack laughed out loud at being released from the prison of fog and at the sensation of speed with all of the vibrations, sounds and the clattering rigging above. The swelling sea became azure blue. The big boat yawed and rolled more than he expected in the long, deep troughs of the open sea. His pistol slid from the dash and clattered to the floor of the wheelhouse. As Jack stooped to pick it up, the window exploded, shattering shards of glass throughout the wheelhouse, followed by the loud report of a gun.

Jack squatted on the floor beside the wide eyed Bubbie, who pointed at the window. "Somebody shot," he stammered.

Having been lulled into complacency, Jack had to reorient himself, knowing it had to be Parker. He told Bubbie to hold the wheel steady, without raising his head to see where they were headed—anywhere but to the rear would be clear.

Jack crawled over the broken glass through the door and peeked around the corner. The skinny deputy was not in the boat. He must have been left in the bayou. Parker strained to see in the cabin from his pounding skiff. He tried to keep the shotgun trained at the wheelhouse window while he steered the pitching craft alongside.

Parker was a big, easy target, and he didn't see Jack crawling through the wheelhouse door and crouching beside a large box built into the deck. Jack could easily take Parker out with his .38, but he couldn't just murder the man.

Jack watched as Parker dropped back to the trawler's stern. Banging and bouncing against Miss Judy, Parker tried to lash the skiff alongside. After several unsuccessful tries, he dropped a line over a ratchet and pulled the two boats together. Jack counted on Parker being clumsy and unable to maintain his balance on the rolling deck, but he was dismayed at the surefootedness of a man with such a ponderous gut. Parker vaulted on board with ease. A maniacal gleam came in his eye and he pushed the safety off the riot gun, dropped to a crouch, and advanced to the wheelhouse of the pitching and rolling Miss Judy.

Miss Judy nosed into a swell and a wave rolled over the bow, engulfing Parker, knocking him to his knees. He fell on his side as the boat rolled in the big swells that had become large breakers.

Jack motioned for Bubbie to get down and hold the wheel straight so the boat would take the most beating in the swells. On his hands and knees, Jack closed the door to the wheel house behind him to protect Bubbie and crawled around the starboard side. Parker slid and skidded his way around the port side of the wheelhouse toward the bow as Jack inched along the opposite side of the cabin toward the stern.

Buckets of spray from the deepening swells and large waves surged over the port bow, drenching Parker and causing him to loose his footing. The boat lunged bow down into a large swell, and Parker fell on his belly and slid forward. The bow pitched upward, and he slid back on the slippery deck, holding the riot gun high, cursing and screaming.

Parker slammed into the draw works built into the rear of the wheelhouse. The mechanism consisted of three 12" iron spools, around which were wound finger-sized steel cables to raise and lower the tall outrigger booms standing vertically on each side. Huge nets were attached to the outriggers.

Miss Judy rode a swell for a long instant, and Parker regained his footing. He gripped the shotgun in one hand and leaned against the cable-wound spools of the draw works. He lifted his gaze and spotted Jack kneeling on the starboard side of the wheelhouse trying to regain his own balance. The glee of insanity distorted Parker's features. He leaned forward, pressing his gut over the metal spools to give support, and pointed the shotgun at Jack, who was only a few feet away. Parker began squeezing the trigger.

Jack quickly grabbed a metal lever on the draw works and jerked it down at the same moment that Bubbie swerved and slammed the throttle to full, shoving the fat man's gut over the gears. The large open cogwheels and draw works moved, interacting against each other, but this time, Parker's pants were caught in them.

The nets above, hanging from the outriggers booms, already rattling and swaying with the rolling of the vessel, rapidly descended.

Diverted and thrown off balance by the surge of power, Parker pulled the trigger. The gun erupted in Jack's direction, but the sudden change in direction, coupled with the distraction of having his pants drawn tightly into the gears, had its intended effect. The shot went wild and over Jack's head into oblivion. Parker shucked out the empty shell and pumped in a live round as the gears went about its mindless business of gnawing at Parkers pants with their hungry rotating teeth.

Parker's florid, bulbous face showed surprise. He tried to push back from the rolling spools and let out a yelp of pain. The gears had tightened his pants so that they were knotted across his crotch, pulling the inseam of the deputy's tropical trousers tightly around his genitals. He dropped the gun and began to tug at his pants, undoing his belt trying to remove them, screaming in agony.

The big gutted man's jugular protruded and his eyes bulged while the gears pulled him inexorably into its matrix, eating into his groin. Parker bellowed as the boat pitched and rolled, and the gears pulled the pants ever tighter. Parker was helpless—eaten alive by a machine that mindlessly carried out a kind of retribution. Jack crawled over the slippery deck toward Parker and looked up. The outriggers had dropped to the sides and were about to release their nets into the sea.

Parker shrieked for help. Jack pushed the lever. The gears stopped their chomping on Parker and the outriggers began to rise. The gears reversed, but Parker's pants were still caught, and the mechanism pulled him in from the other direction.

Jack worked the lever until the machinery shut down completely. Parker leaned onto the gears and babbled. He stared at the blood coursing down his legs and mingling with the salt water that continued to crash over the bow as Miss Judy pounded in and out of the swells.

Jack approached Parker as one would a wild animal, then cut the man's pants and underwear off entirely with his razor sharp hunting knife. Naked from his gut down, Parker fell face first into the foaming water on the deck, screaming, jabbering and cursing. Gazing down at his groin, Parker saw only a stub squirting red amongst a mass of curly pubic hair where his penis had once hung. His pants had washed to the stern and floated in the foam there.

Parker stopped screaming, slowly comprehending the situation with his no longer long genitalia. His eyes bulged and he let out a little yelp as he launched to the stern, rolling over and over, leaving a bloody trail in the water. He grabbed his floating pants, scrabbled around in them, and came out with a small, flaccid piece of pale flesh.

A wild look came over Parker's face as he worked himself up to a standing position. His eyes slowly turned to Jack, who still sat on the deck holding to the one of the levers to keep from sliding into the blood. Parker fumbled at the snap on his holster, slid the .45 out in a slippery, bloody fist and raised it toward Jack.

The bow of the boat lifted itself from a trough and Jack kicked off and slid through the foam toward Parker. He slammed into Parker's gargantuan gut with his shoulder, and sent the big man skating backward to the stern. Parker sat hard on the fantail for an instant with his arms flailing to keep his balance, and then toppled off into the boiling propwash.

Jack signaled for Bubbie to cut the engines. Parker surfaced like a blowing whale with glazed eyes, holding his dick high in his right hand.

A wedge-shaped fin appeared within six feet of him. Parker's eyes bulged. His mouth opened in a silent scream and he disappeared in a crimson stain that gushed to the surface. The bright red water frothed with activity as several other fins appeared. Jack stared over the back of the boat for some sign of Parker. There was none. A pale, tubular-shaped object bobbed to the surface.

I didn't know they floated, Jack thought vacantly, as a gray shape emerged from the churning waters and plucked Parker's precious from sight. As the Miss Judy drifted away from the widening red spot, Jack leaned over the pitching boat and vomited.

Chapter 13

Bubbie let up on the throttle and brought the Miss Judy around to a southeast, heading at an angle that would not give such a pounding. Jack slid down and sat on the deck with his back to the starboard rail, staring numbly at the rolling blue sea. He couldn't shake the look on Parker's face when the fin sliced the top of the big swell. Parker must have lived a lifetime in the instant he knew he was going to be chopped and diced alive by the worst of nightmares. Chopped and diced alive. One predator dining on another. *There was plenty to go around,* Jack mused. *Parker was a smorgasbord.*

When Jack reached the wheelhouse, he asked Bubbie to look under the bunk and bring him the pint of J.W. Dant someone had hidden there. He shook out a Picayune and poured half the bottle straight down his throat. He felt instantly relieved as the fiery amber liquid scorched a path on its way south, and once again he turned his attention to the business at hand.

Jack grinned at Bubbie, extending his hand in thanks for help in saving his life. "Pal, you saved my cookies back there!"

Bubbie beamed at the acknowledgment, accepting Jack's vigorous handshake. He knew that his quick thinking in pushing the throttle on full while making a sharp turn of the wheel made Parker's gun miss Jack at point blank range and caused him to fall into the moving gears.

"You know, if he had nailed me, you would have been next."

Bubbie stopped smiling, obviously absorbing the fact that Parker would have left no witnesses.

"But he didn't get us, and now you got a story to talk about to your grandkids."

Bubbie's eyes rekindled and he quickly smiled broadly.

Jack rumpled the boys' hair and said, "hold her steady as she goes while I clean up this mess.

He swept the splinters and shards of glass left from Parker's shotgun blast, and Bubbie secured the Naquin family skiff astern by a long tow line.

Jack fiddled with the radio and discovered that his friends in Point-Au-Chein were standing by, waiting for a call. E-Boo was there, worrying about the Miss Judy. Jack told them of his destination at Grand Isle.

"Mais no," E-Boo said, "Gran' Isle been blowed away, mah fran'. Dare ain't nothin' lef' hardly on dat whole dam island. You gon' have to brought Miss Judy back here."

Jack thought for a long while, and then he said, "E-Boo, you owe me a big one for savin' Judy's life. I'm callin' in the debt. I'm headed for the gulf coast–Gulfport. I'm goin' to the public marina and you can pick up the Miss Judy there. I gotta job to finish and I need to get to the coast."

E-Boo didn't like his best boat being piloted by a novice, regardless of whether the novice had saved his daughter or not.

"Now, Jack, you bettah wait a minute."

"Sorry, E-Boo, that's the way it is. Both tanks are full, and I'm sure she'll get there. Call Nookie and tell him to contact Victoria and meet me at the public dock in Biloxi.

"Why don' you jus' come up de rivah an' I'll meet you in New Orleans?"

"That'd take just as long. If I get there before you do, Bubbie will keep Miss Judy safe. He was a stowaway and saved my life."

There was silence at the other end. E-boo resignedly agreed to relay the message to Nookie.

Soon they were in sight of a series of smaller uninhabited islands called Isle Dernieres, or Last Islands, and Timbalier Island. These high points of land were once part of a much larger inhabited island before the storms and erosion literally took them apart, leaving several small, scattered fragments of high ground.

Jack thought as he passed them that he would like to camp out on the islands and fish, laze around in the sun and sleep and dream, listening to the cry of the seabirds and the surf on the long, remote, white sandy beaches.

They passed several of the high drilling platforms that were like small villages built high over the water, with a steady, but rotating population of fifty to a hundred men at any given time, doing shifts that worked the rigs all day and night. Helicopters often hovered like great mosquitoes, moving crew and supplies back and forth to the beach, as they called it, and an occasional crew boat boiled through the sea doing the same job, just taking longer to do it.

Jack loved the mournful moans of the fog horns on the rigs. He had tied up a boat many times on the rigs and dropped a line two hundred feet down through the clear blue waters, watching his bait drop into gigantic schools of huge bluefish and red snapper, and suddenly one would turn and take the bait and there was a tug that fairly wrenched the rod from his hands. Jack found himself smiling at the thought.

Finally, Grand Isle came into view in the morning sun. Even from a distance of several miles Jack could see the devastation. Bubbie handed him a pair of binoculars and Jack scanned the island. Just a few days ago, there had been a hundred camps and homes lining the beaches. Now there was only flotsam and jetsam, flattened vegetation, dead fish and debris strewn the entire length of the island, with only a few timbers left standing here and there.

Route La 1 is the only way to get to Grand Isle by land. Like the road to Pont-Au-Chein, which it roughly parallels, it runs south to the bottom of the state through the marsh, ending at the big island. Grand Isle is seven miles long and a mile wide. About fifteen hundred permanent residents live there, working with oil and mineral interests, as it is a terminal for offshore helicopters, crew boats and offshore drilling companies. The population swells to fifteen thousand during the summer for the beaches and fishing. It is far from any other settlement and has the feel of an island, remote and removed from the hurried ways of the world. Elaborate, expensive camps sit alongside mobile homes and run down beach houses, lining the beach overlooking the gulf. The bars, seafood restaurants and fishing supply businesses boom in the summer, but the hurricanes over the years have, like the barrier islands, taken away, bite by bite, pieces of the island. Jack sighed, as he scanned the island for signs of life and saw only destruction, where the elements were trying to reclaim its own from man's works. Grand Isle looked as if it had been bombed.

Jack had spent many pleasurable weekends on the island, in the little motels, camping out, on boats, surf fishing on the beaches, going far offshore into the blue water deep sea fishing. The waters in the gulf out from Grand Isle are teeming with fish.

Many times he and and a ladyfriend of the moment would camp on one of the smaller islands surrounding Grand Isle and go crabbing out from the island beach. They set poles in about three feet of water and tied long horizontal lines from pole to pole. They dropped strings from the lines and tied chicken necks or other animal organs to the drop lines, and let them down to the bottom. They drank beer and lazed along the beach, and periodically ran the lines by walking along them with a basket, lifting the bait and huge blue crabs would be attached, still eating the meat. They shook the crabs off into the basket. Later they cooked them live in a cauldron of boiling spices, potatoes, ears of sweet corn, garlic pods and celery. They would then crack the shells and consume the sweet spicy meat with ice cold beer. It was a feast, made perfect by often being the only human beings on the small island for days at a time.

Jack smiled at the memories, hoping there would be many more like them in the future, preferably with Vic–if they could make it through what the future had to offer. There were more like Parker out there, and while two bad guys were down, he knew he had only scratched the surface. And while Jack's hunches were always right, this was much more than a hunch. This was serious and deadly, and Jack was having the time of his life.

The great Freeport-McMoran platform colossus drew near, and Jack looked up at its house-sized cement legs reaching a hundred feet in the air to the first level of catwalks and floors. Its mammoth trunks extended into the sea floor below and held high above the sea an area that served as an operational surface where humans could ambulate and work, busily sucking the essence from the primeval deposits slumbering far beneath the seabed.

With Bubbie's help, Jack got the knack of steering with a minimum of discomfort. When he had first hit the open water, he had been pounded and jolted as the bow struck the waves and swells at the wrong angle. Soon Miss Judy was rolling gently between the big swells. Occasionally, the wave form would change and he would nose into one, causing a huge splash of spray to cascade over the bow. The gentle swaying motion lulled Jack into a trance as he watched the turquoise horizon tilt back and forth lazily beyond the bow.

After an hour or so, Bubbie punched Jack and pointed off the port bow. "Da Mississippi."

The water had turned from bright blue to muddy brown in every direction. To his left and north was a faint haze that suggested land, otherwise, they were in a copper sea. *The great bowel of North America,* Jack thought, *donating the continent's fertilizer to the Gulf.* The Father of Waters branched and split into web-like canals and bayous through the marsh as it neared the Gulf, and the dark sienna in its throat fanned an ugly brown stain for many miles into the sparkling blue waters. Jack knew exactly where he was, and all he had to do to get to New Orleans was to turn left at this point and he could follow the sinuous stream north; within a half day he'd be home.

Jack noticed some charge on his cell phone. He punched Vic's number into his cell phone. It rang! Then there was the voice he had been fretting over answering the phone. He knew she would know it was him calling because she had caller id.

"Jack? Is that you?"

"Yeah, baby, it's me. I'm OK."

"You sonofabitch!"

"Vic, I can explain. I just didn't want you involved any more. When you hear what happened you would be glad."

Jack could hear her seething, but then after a pause, she said, "Jack, are you OK?" She then let out a sob. "Thank God you are safe. Where are you?"

All was good between he and Vic. "At the mouth of the Mississippi, in a big shrimp boat, headed for you, wherever you are. I hate to get you into this."

"Jack," Vic said in exasperation, I wish you'd stop saying that. I'm doing this because I want to do it. So knock it off. What're you doing in a shrimp boat?"

"On my way to you."

"How big is it?"

"Hundred fifty feet. Shrimp trawler."

"Who's the pilot?"

"Me."

There was a pause, as Vic took this in. "Jack, what do you know about a boat that big?

"Enough."

"Tell you all about it later. I'll need for you to meet me somewhere along the coast. Can you get to Mobile and do what we planned?"

"Yes."

""There's a marina in Biloxi. Find out where I can dock and the boat will be safe until the owner can come from Houma to get it. We gotta get off, my cell doesn't have much charge left. Find out and call back in thirty minutes. We're about three hours from Gulfport."

"Gotcha. Call me in thirty."

The charge on his cell phone was almost gone. He switched it off and turned to Bubbie. "Have you ever been to Biloxi?"

Bubbie's shrug indicated he had never been anywhere but in Louisiana waters.

"Well, we're just gonna have to find it," Jack said.

Thirty minutes later Vic called and said there was a berth he could use short term at the Biloxi marina. He then called E-Boo and told him where to retrieve the Miss Judy.

Just after South Pass, Jack made a gradual swing to the north through the Chandelier Sound. To the left were the Chandelier Islands, a thin string of sandy beaches just above sea level. To his right was Ship Island, with its old Spanish fort. The Mississippi coast was straight ahead. Jack gazed ahead at the mainland until he could see the harbor at Biloxi, with its many large pleasure boats riding at anchor and moored in the little port.

Jack brought the Miss Judy easily alongside the pier, and came to a stop with a gentle bump on the tires hung on the side. Bubbie sprang to the dock and looped Miss Judy's big nylon lines over the pilings like a professional deckhand.

Jack walked to the end of the dock and then to the parking area beyond, but he didn't see Vic or Nookie. He returned to the boat and found that Bubbie had a pot of coffee on.

They drank the coffee and cleaned the head, wheelhouse, and kitchen, then swabbed the deck. Jack checked his cargo and found her still acceptable for polite company.

It was afternoon when they saw a familiar figure running up the pier, followed by a swarthy dark man with a beard, who only was walking fast. Nookie didn't believe in running.

Jack heaved a sigh of relief and, turning, gave Bubbie an "OK" sign.

"You made it!" Jack shouted.

Vic's eyes glistened. She wiped away the tell-tale moisture that had coursed down a brown cheek.

Vic wore a pair of white shorts and a red halter top. Her long black hair was up in a ponytail, tied back with a white ribbon. She looked like a sexy college co-ed.

Jack felt the familiar tightening of his gut as he fought the urge to grab her and kiss her hard. Vic trembled as they faced each other. He grasped her slender fingers in his, and their eyes locked in the long knowing of something as old and basic as time. Vic regained her voice and Jack was mesmerized by the way her lips and tongue moved as she spoke. They had a sensuous but humorous animation. They had to be soft and warm. Bubbie looked from one to the other, obviously trying to understand the relationship. Nookie rolled his eyes.

Vic turned to Bubbie. "Who is this?"

"This is Bubbie, Vic. Bubbie, this is Vic, and you know Nookie. He saved my life this morning. Jack gave a very short version of his experience, holding a grinning Bubbie around the shoulder as he praised him for his part in the struggle.

Nookie mussed Bubbie's hair. "Bubbie daddy, Veron, is my brother. Dis my nephew. Jack, you left some thing out, I know you. Hey Bubbie, now you tell me what happen."

Bubbie's eyes got big, and he commenced to rattle off a long breathless tale in French, getting more and more excited as he talked, interspersed with a few English words. From time to time Nookie interrupted with a question or an exclamation.

Finally, Bubbie ran down, and Nookie turned to Jack and said, "Poo Yii, you all done had some excitements. Damn, I wish I had been there! Like I tole Vic, you land on yore feet."

Jack shrugged, beaming at Bubbie. "I owe you, Dude! Now we gotta get moving."

Nookie then told the whole tale to Vic whose eyes got wider as the story was told. She extended her hand and Bubbie timorously held it, blushing. "We gotta get the cargo outta the cooler. I need a hand, guys."

Bubbie stood wide-eyed as Jack tugged the wet box from its temporary crypt and without hesitation, Nookie grabbed the other end and they lifted it up the narrow stair and laid it on the dock.

The box and its heft looked altogether too familiar to Bubbie, even though he was only twelve. He physically backed away and looked at Jack with a strange expression.

"Tell E-Boo I have to take what's in this box to a doctor in Mobile. This lady here is the head doctor at a clinic at Tulane Medical School, and she's helping me with a very serious legal case involving murder. Thank E-Boo for me, and tell him that if it hadn't been for him, and you, I would be a dead man."

When Jack referred to the glossy skinned babe in the shorts as "Doctor," Bubbie raised his eyebrows.

Jack noticed his look, and said, "I know what you're thinkin', Bubbie. At twelve you know a lot more than people think you might. She's a doctor. Gimme a card, Vic."

Vic fished a little white card from the tight back pocket of her white shorts and handed it to Bubbie. It read:

Victoria Keens-Dennison, M.D.
Department of Pathology
Tulane Medical Center
New Orleans, Louisiana

Give that card to E-Boo when he gets here. And Bubbie, I really do owe you my life."

Vic bent and kissed Bubbie lightly on the lips and said, "I owe you for saving Jack too."

Bubbie flushed crimson and simply grinned, not knowing what to say.

"Time's wasting and we gotta get hell out of here right now, Bubbie," Jack said as he and Vic lifted the cold box and began walking away. "It's been a real rip, Bubbie. Thank all of your folks. I'll be down to see you soon."

Bubbie stood on the dock and watched Jack and Nookie wrestle the sagging box down the long pier to white king-cab pickup parked at the end. Jack looked back and saw Bubbie touching the tips of his fingers to his lips. *Bubbie knows more than I do about how her lips feel.*

They placed the box in the bed. They looked back and waved at Bubbie, who stood on the dock watching them. He slowly lifted his hand and waved back as the Silverado spun out onto the Gulf Highway.

They didn't speak for many minutes. Vic's pony-tail whipped in the wind as she accelerated along the highway paralleling the seawall and long sandy beaches as they drove through Biloxi. Jack grinned at Nookie through the rear view mirror. Nookie's eyes glittered and his white teeth shone through his black beard. This was grand adventure!

Vic studied Jack as she drove, stealing a glance at him every few minutes. She finally said, "Jack, there's something different about you. I can't put my finger on it."

Jack turned his cool gray eyes on her and smiled, remembering the soaring feeling of the barbarian with the long black hair. There was no doubt now. No doubt at all. They were one.

Vic shook her head as she drove, but she could hardly take her eyes from Jack's big grin.

The truck sped along the beaches and lowland scrub pine lands for over an hour, and soon they were in the old city of Mobile with its live oak lined streets. Vic drove into an alley alongside a one-story cement-block building and parked in a large four car garage alongside an ambulance.

"This is it," Vic announced, pointing to the large double doors at the rear of the building. "He's expecting us; let's get her inside."

Jack gaped at Vic's white shorts and slender coffee and chicory legs as she slid both from the driver's seat. Their eyes met at Nookie and Jack lifted Dawn Marie's sodden box. Jack felt the old electricity run through him, and stars fell on Alabama right there in the parking lot on Mobile Bay.

"Goddammit," Jack said.

"Goddammit," Vic said.

Nookie watched the two, shook his great head and sighed.

The back door opened directly into an operating room, with a polished terrazzo floor, bright overhead light and chrome on everything. The odor of chemicals and formaldehyde was nearly overpowering, and Jack's eyes began to burn. As they placed the now tattered box on the floor alongside the table, Jack squinted and coughed.

Nookie frowned and said, "pooyii, dat make my eyes water, dat."

"Smells great to me, Jack," Vic laughed. "That's perfume to a pathologist. We bathe in the stuff!"

At that moment, a short, rotund, rosy-cheeked little man in a white coat bustled in.

"Vic, yew fine thang yew!" He gave her a lengthy hug and grabbed her tight derriere in both of his chunky hands with more than a fatherly caress.

Vic's eyes glowed with conspicuous thoughts Jack found totally objectionable. He looked from one to the other quizzically, and finally Jester burst out in laughter. Nookie's took it all in and frowned.

"Ahem," Vic faltered for a moment, and Jack could have sworn she was blushing beneath that lustrous brown skin. "Ah, Jack, Jester and I once—ah—were close friends—long ago."

"Yeah, long ago," Jester said, "I asked her to marry me, but she turned me down. Don't know why. Ah'm ever thang a woman'd want, that's plain to see, am I not?" Jester stood with his arms outstretched, inviting Jack's appraisal as to his desirability, looking every bit a jolly humpty dumpty with a beard.

Jack and Nookie were introduced to Jester McConothy, MD, forensic pathologist and coroner for Mobile and Baldwin Counties.

"In case you're concerned about this old son-of-a-bitch's qualifications," Vic said, "he's from Selma, Alabama–graduated from Harvard Medical School with honors, earned two advanced degrees in surgery and pathology, then did three years in Nam' on a med-evac team."

Jack's initial shock at this little man's uninhibited grabbing of Vic's ass dissipated slightly as Vic related his credentials. She continued with Jester's lengthy introduction. "He has written tomes and lectured all over the place, including Europe, and now is a guru to the cops. He solved several murders for them with his analysis of victim's bodies. And, he's a good 'ol boy to boot. And to top it all, he thinks it would be a disgrace to give up his Alabama accent."

"Part of that's wrong," Jester said. "Ah'm from Sunny South, about twenty miles southeast of Selma. Ah don't want nobody to thank ah'm from somewhere I ain't from. Ah'm a country boy and proud of it. And whut do yew mean, accent? Yew're the one with a accent."

Jack felt an immediate kinship with this Southern rebel, even if the man knew Vic much better than was confrontable.

"Glad ya'll could come over," Jester said. His eyes danced at Vic's exposed navel and swelling breasts barely concealed beneath the brief little top. He rubbed his hands together in anticipation of the project she had brought.

"What's new?" Vic asked.

"Heh heh," Jester said, laying a stubby finger alongside his upturned nose, "Just solved another one for the local gendarmes. Found a body in the bay. Early twenties. Analysis of stomach contents did it. Sprouts." A mischievous grin spread over his round face. "Ain't nobody eats sprouts 'less they from Lost Angeles–and shore 'nuff, boy been missin' from Santa Monica fer six months. Don't know why they like them damned thangs. Bean sprouts!"

"What we got here's not that exotic, Jester," Jack said. "It's not a pretty thing to look at."

"Well, what the hell yew got in 'at box, boy?"

"What's left of Dawn Marie, the victim."

"Tell me about it."

Jack drew in a long breath and launched into his story, beginning with the visit to the morgue. Finally, he wound down and watched Jester's reaction.

"Son, yew took on a damned big job if what yew say's true. Stole the body from the' morgue an' in th' process two men got theirselves killed. Hum. Waal, let's proceed with the' proceedin's."

The autopsy was the part Jack had dreaded since the beginning of the saga. He asked Jester if it was absolutely necessary that he should stay and watch, as he and Vic removed the canvas bag from the box and laid it on the autopsy table. He hoped that they would say that he should leave, or at least give him the option to go, because while he didn't think he was squeamish, he wasn't sure he wanted to see what they would do to Dawn, and odors completely revulsed him.

Vic and Jester looked at each other and grinned widely, sharing some mutual bit of humor. Jack looked back and forth at each of them across the canvas bag where they stood side-by-side. Pathologists love to shock the queasy stomached lawyer who talks so knowingly about this very thing, but who seldom sees it.

"If yew're gonna tell about it, Jack, yew better see it first hand, hadn't he Vic?"

"Jester's absolutely right, Jack. If you try this case about the young lady reposing in this bag before you, you should be able to tell how she was abused and tell of it from what you see–so keep your chin up and let's get her out of there."

Nookie excused himself, saying he had to call his woman and smoke a cigarette.

Vic undid the knot on the end. Jack could see Dawn Marie's coal-black hair through the opening and stepped back.

"Hey, Jack, we need a little help here," Vic grinned. "Hold her by the shoulders while we pull the bag away."

Jack froze and shook his head. The two doctors stood at the end holding the bag, waiting with feigned impatience, Jack closed his eyes and held his breath. He reached into the bag and grasped two hard, icy shoulders, holding on as the doctors tugged on the other end. The bag slid off smoothly, and Jack gasped as the naked form, as hard and stiff as a board, banged down on the top of the operating table.

Jester's twinkling eyes hardened. He slowly approached the side of the table and stared at the trim young body before him. The body had changed to a deep rosy hue, but the gashes and abrasions on the inside of her thighs were highly visible. So were marks on her wrists and ankles. A puckered, inch long incision just under her left breast was smeared with dried blood and her groin and pubis was caked in a mass of gore.

Jester's face darkened in anger.

"This young lady was brutally murdered while she was bein' raped. She was raped and mutilated. Whoever–whatever–stabbed her in her heart while he raped her and kept on rapin' her after she was dead!"

Jester made a choking noise as he fought down the rage that gathered within him. "Ah don't need to do an autopsy to see that. Ah can feel this child's pain!" He let out a long anguished moan, as if he was reliving Dawn Marie's last moments. "Ah kin feel it! Her terror. She knows she's gonna die. She's drugged! Argh!"

Jester stumbled away from the table holding his head with his hands, as if trying to keep the thoughts and images away that seemed to be tormenting him.

"Hey, Jester," Vic said, gently steadying him by holding his shoulders with both hands. "Hang in there."

After a moment, Jester said, still breathing heavily, "Goddammit, ah wish that wouldn't happen. There's energy pictures or somethin' that hangs around. Hits me like a train wreck. Ah can feel and even see thangs that happened. This little child died a horrible death. Through the smoldering anger, Jester asked Jack, "Yew know who done it?"

"Not positively," Jack answered. "But two men died in the last three days tryin' to stop me from lookin' into it. I know from two other victims that there were quite a few involved in doin' this to kids, includin' the two that died."

"Did they give drugs?"

"The two other male victims said that they gave them something that made 'em crazy. I figured it was something like LSD or somethin' else that acted as an aphrodisiac."

"Goddammit!" Jester snarled, "this poor darlin' died cravin' sexual release from a drug they give to her. She didn't have a chance."

Vic and Jester pulled on rubber gloves and smocks and Jester handed a smock to Jack. "Here, put this on—we may need your help."

Jester hooked a small microphone around his neck that was connected to a microcassette recorder in the pocket of his smock. He began what he termed "a complete autopsy," dictating for the record every step he took and every observation he made as he went along.

First, he took a series of pictures with a Polaroid and then with a twin lens Hasselblad as he described what he saw as he took the pictures. She was rolled over, and pictures were taken from the back, and from every angle.

"Preserve this evidence!" Jester grunted.

So far, so good, Jack thought, standing a few feet away from the proceedings, his eyes filled with dread for what he knew was coming.

"Now," Jester said into the microphone, lifting a scalpel from a tray, "I am making an incision at the scalp line." He held Dawn's long hair up and away, and Vic lifted the upper body. Jester made an incision that encircled the scalp, traced the incision with a small Black and Decker saw, freeing the skull cap. This was lifted away, hair and all, to reveal a much convoluted organ: the brain. A fetid stench reached Jack's nose as he watched Jester carve this beautiful little girl to pieces.

Jester continued to record what he was observing and doing as he proceeded to surgically remove the brain for weighing. He placed it in a formalin solution container for a more detailed exam later.

Jack resisted gagging, but just as the freed brain was laid in the weighing pan, he raced for the back door and puked his guts out for the second time that day.

Chapter 14

Jack and Nookie chain smoked on the stoop outside for over an hour. Finally, he heard his name called, and with considerable trepidation, they peered into the lab. A totally objectionable odor hung in the air and Jack wrinkled his nose. He was grateful to see a sheet over the lump on the table, and he tried not to think about what lay under there after Jester had completed his imponderable work, however efficient. The two doctors removed their rubber gloves, gleaming and slippery from their ghoulish fiddling.

Jester had returned to a somewhat normal state of humor, but storm clouds still gathered around him, even though he managed the little grin reserved for the squeamish when Jack cautiously re-entered the room.

"Ah hope yew git the sons-of-a-bitches did that to her," Jester said, his eyes as hard as stone.

"All I know is that two of 'em went to their reward," Jack said. "Don't know if we'll ever know who did it, but from Destrehan's and Parker's reaction, it probably was one or both of 'em, and maybe more. If it was Parker, he got what he deserved," Jack said, pulling his lips into a thin smile. Vic frowned at his next question. "You say the gear tore his dick off?"

"Uh huh. Ripped or tore it off through his britches. The damned thing floated, bobbed up to the surface. That shark must have thought it was breakfast the way he went after it."

Both Vic and Jester frowned while Jack described Parker's radical emasculation and subsequent fish food. The shock had worn off and Jack's attitude was very cold about the demise of both Destrehan and Parker. He even found it faintly amusing. It was certainly appropriate if they had raped and murdered Dawn.

"Goddam fish don't care what they eat," Jester said, shaking his head. After thinking for a moment, he said, "Well, whoever it was that did it was hung like a mule, cause he tore the top of her cervix out and destroyed her vagina," Vic said. "She must have been in agony."

"That little thing that fell out of Parkers britches couldn't have done all of that damage," Jack said.

Jester shook his head. "Don't thank yew can tell anythang by that. Tumescent, that thang could'a been a horror to this little lady. Ennyway, we got plenty samples—all we could ever use, an' plenty pitchers fer evidence—ah'll git 'em developed 'an send yew copies. We'll send the specimens to th' crime lab in Fort Worth an' have every chemical and drug scan run known to man. Yew gonna git plenty evidence, boy. Yew gonna kick their ass! An' ah been glad to h'ep ye—it's free—a public service."

"Thanks," Jack said, "I can hang the Sheriff's office with this evidence. I can't prove who did it, only that it did happen. That's enough for this one case. I know there were others that were raped, and maybe some were killed for all I know. They were taken to motels around the city for the use of some politicians and maybe even some boys in the mob. That's what scares me."

Vic and Jester stared at Jack for a long moment. Finally, Jester asked, "What yew gonna do?"

"Get back to the city," Jack said, "and get this child a decent burial. See if I can get some more evidence on who else was involved and take my shot, if somebody else doesn't have me in his crosshairs."

"We'll see to it that she's sent back properly and given a free burial, on the city," Vic said. "I'll also make sure that the full report is sent to the U.S. Attorney and to the D.A."

"An' Ah'll even git in touch with somebody ah know in the Attorney General's office in D.C.," Jester volunteered. "They ain't gittin' away with this!"

"I'm sure they'll say that the only ones involved were Destrehan and Parker, if they admit that, but some real investigation can turn up the rest—I hope," Jack said, lighting a Picayune. "I could use a drink after all of this."

Jack pulled his cell phone out of his pocket and saw the battery was dead. "But first, can I use your phone?"

Jack called Estelle.

"I have Dawn here in Mobile, Estelle."

"Oh thank God, Lawyer Jack. We been prayin' steady. We thought they had done killed you too, an' we was the cause."

"I'm going to turn the autopsy report and the body over to the authorities, Estelle. I don't know when she'll be released for burial, but I wanted to let you know that everything's gonna be okay. She's being readied for transport back to New Orleans."

Estelle moaned and let out a racking sob. He allowed for the grief seizure to dissipate and then said, "This'll all be over soon. It's going to create quite a thing in the city, and there are lots of others involved, as you probably know by now. I'm leavin' in a few minutes, but she'll be here till the arrangements can be made."

"Thank you, Lawyer Jack, for all you done done. Ah know you done everything you could—but I jus' don' know what to do! I miss my baby so much!"

Estelle broke into another spell of uncontrolled wailing, and in a moment she said, "I'm sorry. I jus' can't help it. It's all too much, Lawyer Jack!"

"I know, dear. By-and-by things'll be better. I don't have any idea what you're goin' through, but I do know that time is the great healer of all things."

"I know, Lawyer Jack, but it's the worse thing that could happen."

Jack tried more reassurance before they hung up, but he felt totally helpless. There was nothing he could do or say.

Jester adjourned to the inner office. He passed around glasses and filled each with what he called "real sippin' whiskey" from a quart mason jar. The liquid was a clear as crystal and had a smoky bouquet. Jester said it was made from corn at a local, illegal still from an ancient formula passed down the Appalachian Chain. It was affectionately called "splode," from the immediate explosive effect on the imbiber.

The liquor was smooth taken straight, flavored with forests and lakes and hidden places, memories of earth and timelessness. It warmed the cold spot in Jack's soul that had iced over during the past traumatic days. As he and Nookie listened to Jester and Vic's reminiscences about old friends and old times together, the familiar, desolate deja-vu of being an outsider swept over him. He was reminded that he was a lone wanderer in time, searching for something that may be just on the other side of the next rise, and may not even exist at all; he only knew that he had to keep moving.

It was dusk when they left Mobile, and nearly nine when they reached their apartment building. Jack observed that someone had thoughtfully flattened all of the tires on his car.

"Parker's doin's, I bet," Jack muttered as they entered the building.

Nookie said, "Mais, dis been one good time for 'ol Nookie. I got a feelin' it ain't over and we gonna have some more fun soon." He waved a cheery goodbye and walked away down Royal as if he owned the whole town.

Jack pulled open the door to his apartment, expecting it to be trashed, and his entire evening would be spent getting things straight. But Estelle had been there, and not only was the apartment neat and clean, there was a cold six pack of Dixie in the fridge. There was also a pot of savory red beans and rice with sausage and some still warm cornbread in the iron skillet on the stove. The room was full of welcome home smells.

Jack's armory had been confiscated, or stolen by Parker and his crew, and so were his favorite cuff links, his LSU class ring and a set of crystal wineglasses. Several clothing items, including a tuxedo and an expensive leather jacket were missing. Pushing aside the clothes hanging in the closet, Jack pressed a raised button of wood near the inside corner. There was a faint click and a door swung inward, revealing a small room large enough for a small bed.

The old homes often had secret closets and hideaway rooms for runaway slaves or places to hide their valuables from tax collectors. They were taxed according to the number of rooms in homes, and used large Armoires to hang clothes and other belongings in rather than closets, as they were not classed as rooms. But in the more well to do homes, constructed to secret orders of the owners, frequently one or more rooms like this were used as hideaways or safes for personal papers, jewelry and baubles hidden in the walls or floor, or to hide runaway slaves.

Jack was glad he had put some of his special guns, swords, knives in there as well as some gold coins he had squirreled away. They were safe from the "confiscation" by Parker's partners. Jack said nothing about the theft of his guns, but Vic knew he was fuming.

They stuffed themselves and tried to relax. They didn't turn the lights on, eating by candle light, hoping to stay quiet enough not to give anyone the idea they were back. Vic was certain there would be a warrant for her arrest, and Jack was sure the killers were scouting for him and he was dead meat as soon as they spotted him. They listened to the evening sounds of the Quarter.

With an effort, Jack kept his eyes from straying to Vic's shapely legs, the color of midnight honey, and her flat belly with its little smiling cleft, inviting an animated, tactile discussion with his own. Vic's soft brown eyes seldom moved from Jack's blue ones. Lost in the soft meadows of her gaze, he felt a melting within, chunks of an inner mental glacier began crashing into the warm seas of his longing. He knew where he was going and what was about to happen and finally it didn't matter.

He reached to touch her hand, and paused long enough to realize he was going through with what he had craved to do since meeting her, and surrendered to the moment. She placed her soft hands on each side of his face and drew him close. He leaned over every so slowly toward her upturned lips.

The phone rang.

The magic of the moment exploded in a puff as it rang again. Jack shook the cobwebs from his head while Vic drew a long, exasperated breath and looked sadly at Jack.

It rang again.

They looked at each other, afraid to answer. He moved toward her again, but stopped and backed away.

After six rings, he apprehensively picked up the receiver. He tried to change his voice to a gutteral "hello."

"Hey Jack, you ol' son of a bitch, you got a cold? It's Fred Campbell, what the hell you doin'?"

Jack was annoyed for more reasons than one. He loathed the patronizing tone Campbell used when he wanted something. He looked at his watch. It was almost nine.

"Havin' some private time." His voice was brittle.

"Well, tell her to put her clothes on," Fred laughed, "I got somebody you need to meet."

Jack frowned, thinking back on their previous conversation just days before. Fred had coolly refused to help when he had every ability to do so by a simple well placed phone call. The bastard's got some gall after hangin' up on me like that, Jack thought. He could've saved me all this shit if he had wanted to.

"What's up, Fred?"

"Meet me at the Plimsoll club. Somethin's come up that could be a hot opportunity for you. Somebody big's got his eye on you and I don't want to tell you anything more right now, but you look like a hot commodity."

"I've had a rough few days and need to grab some winks," Jack said in a tired voice, referring to some badly needed sleep.

"Winks can wait, good things like this can't. Meet you there in thirty minutes."

The phone clicked and Jack heard Campbell's familiar dial tone.

"Dammit," Jack swore out loud.

"Who was that?

"That was Fred Campbell: confidant of governors, congressmen and U.S. Senators, lobbyist in congress and the legislature, and slick as owl shit. Deals are his stock in trade."

"What does he want?"

"Wants to meet me at the Plimsoll club right now to discuss some hot deal for me!"

Vic raised her eyebrows. "Odd timing, wouldn't you say?"

"Yeah. Fred never does anything for nothin'. There's a hook somewhere, you can bet."

"Plimsoll, huh? Wants to impress you. Are you impressed?"

"Yeah, Fred don't make calls for old times sake. He's from my home town. We got to be friends when I worked in the legislature when I was in law school. He's about seventy, I guess. He used to quote his mentor, Earl Long: "If you can't drank it, eat it, or fuck it, piss on it". Fred's gonna to get 'mileage,' as he calls it, from everything and everybody he knows, and he's one slick son of a bitch. His favorite expression is 'Admit nothin', deny everything, and when in doubt, allege fraud.'

131

"Sounds like a real charmer," she said, rolling her eyes. "You better get over there and see what he has up his slippery sleeve."

"Yeah, I guess I better," Jack grunted, resenting being manipulated by this master manipulator, and concerned about Vic's safety if some of these unknown people would find he was in town. He had no fear for himself.

"Vic, please don't be as stupid as I was just then in answering this phone. Hang here till I get back. If I have to call, I'll let it ring once and hang up, then call again. Don't answer otherwise. Keep the lights out, and I'll check this out."

Before she turned to leave, she placed her long warm fingers alongside Jack's face and said, "I'll be careful. You be careful," then brushed her lips lightly over his. Her breath was sweet. Jack froze as she walked to the door. Her eyes danced at his reaction. She left without turning around. Jack thought he was going to have a heart attack.

Jack showered and shaved, put on a suit and tie, and waited for a cab. He patted his nearly empty pockets and looked at his sad old Ford with its four flats.

෯

The International Trade Mart, an unremarkable but sturdy, twenty story office building, stands on the bank of the Mississippi River in downtown New Orleans. Atop this redoubtable edifice, resides the private Plimsoll Dining Club, named after the mark painted on the hull of a ship that shows how deep it may ride in the water after loading. Samuel Plimsoll pushed a bill through the British Parliament in the early 1800's to prevent overloading, and since then, all merchant ships bear the mark.

Jack pressed a button on which was imprinted the simple word, Plimsoll. The doors shooshed together and the elevator rose rapidly to the top floor. Standing at the door as it opened was a balding butler type, whose officious, pompous manner told Jack this was the maitre'd. As Jack stepped onto the plush maroon carpet, he gave Jack a professional once over.

The maitre'd said, in a very formal tone, "Good evening, Mr. Chandler, this way please." He turned to walk through a richly appointed foyer toward a large dining room.

Jack followed obediently, sniffing at being so readily recognized and expected. The subdued strains of a Haydn divertimento were accompanied by the clink of silverware and crystal and quiet conversation as waiters in tuxedos glided like ethereal phantoms to serve elegantly dressed couples and businessmen at their tables by candle light.

The club occupied the entire top floor, which was encircled by large windows, giving a clear, hawk's eye view of the entire city and the river in both directions. Jack followed the maitre'd through the softly lit room to a table in a remote corner, at which sat two well dressed men.

132

Fred Campbell stood quickly and pumped Jack's hand, grinning his boyish, mischievous grin. "Jack, yew old hound dog, it's good yew could make it. I want yew to meet Claude Cabal."

Sitting alongside Fred was an urbane man wearing a three piece suit that seemed to have melted around him in perfection. Savile Row? Armani? Brioni? Jack didn't know but figured six grand easy. The watch lying loosely on his wrist was a Vacherun Tour de l'Tle! Jack had seen pictures of them, but never thought he would see a $1,250,000 watch in the real world. And that haircut, thought Jack, looking at the sculptured gray head, cost more than my last suit.

Jack's hand was gripped warmly in a very smooth, manicured hand that he recognized belonged to the legendary entrepreneur, king-maker, mover and shaker, Ansel Claude Cabal. Here was the senior partner of the largest law firm in Texas, Cabal and Alsop, reputed to have a thousand lawyers on the payroll. Jack's heart stopped momentarily before he felt warning bells go off in his head. Why would this man want to meet him?

"Pleased to meet you," Jack said, looking directly into Cabal's blue eyes that made Jack think of Arctic skies.

"And it's my pleasure, Jack. Fred told me about you; it's all been good, very good. And please call me Claude." The west Texas syllables emerged from lips that smiled while the eyes didn't.

Cabal's manner was casual, relaxed, neither oily nor smooth, and completely at ease. The man was totally in control, charming, intensely interested in Jack, and Jack was worried. Nobody of such magnitude, or for that matter, of any magnitude, had ever granted Jack such a compliment by simply shaking his hand. He felt an embarrassment of sudden personal riches by just being himself. He knew this man had the ability to endow anyone with that feeling—a man of infinite finesse, the mark of quiet power. A man to whom you could not say no.

"I put you two together," Fred said, pushing his chair back and standing, "and I got some other fish to fry so I'm gonna skedaddle and let ya'll talk"

Cabal rose and shook Fred's hand, thanking him for the opportunity to meet Jack. Then Fred gripped Jack's hand tightly, winking hard at him as he said goodbye.

Cabal had a quiet dialogue with the wine steward and finally said, in perfect French, "Chez Chapoutier. Le Pavillon, s'il vous plait."

"Oui, c'est bon, m'sieu," the steward said, beaming with admiration at this American who had the manners and finesse of a Frenchman.

"Pas de quoit," Cabal replied.

Jack watched the exchange. Hearing the learned discussion of wines, he knew that the French wine ordered by Cabal may not be the most expensive in the house, but it was right up there. He was always surprised at how much he remembered from his year of French at L.S.U. An intense desire to go to France made the language stick. He definitely respected this smooth talking Texan, whose manners were Gallic enough to charm the fawning wine steward.

Jack was fascinated at the ritual. The steward's eyes glistened and his nostrils dilated while Cabal performed the ceremony of corking, sniffing and tasting the wine. Here was clearly the master, one to whom the steward could grant deserved reverence. Jack feared the little man would kneel and kiss Cabal's manicured hand.

As the wine was being poured, Cabal turned his Texas magic on Jack. "You had the moxy to set your own practice up in New Orleans, with no help or mentor. That takes confidence and determination, Jack." He raised his glass in a little salute.

Jack nodded, and felt mesmerized in the grip of those blue eyes.

A trace of a smile worked on Cabal's lips. "Fred tells me you're a quick study and a persistent and tough son-of-a-bitch. That's what I need in a man for the position that's open. I am looking for that man. That's why I had to meet you before I filled the position."

Jack couldn't have been pried loose from the table by a crowbar. His attention was fixed on Cabal. *Where is this conversation headed?* Cabal continued. "You see, the European community will soon become a country of states like the United States. With the Euro, unification and Germany at the helm, it is likely to form the most powerful economic force on the planet, bigger than the Pacific Rim consortium. I have varied interests in oil and gas in the near east, plus certain joint enterprises with Microsoft, MCI and Motorola, supplying software, hardware and communication services to the common market countries, the untapped markets of Russia and China, and numerous other investments that need overseeing."

"My associates and I have certain, ah, interests we want protected, and we need good, stable, reliable men in selected locations to make things happen. Men who have qualities my researchers see in you. My firm has branch offices where it counts in Europe. I understand you have an unusual facility for languages and for computers, in addition to your other talents. I am looking for someone to operate out of my Paris office."

Jack feared he might wet his pants when he heard the word Paris. His dreams could come true. He could "do" Europe at last. But the question was, why?

"I see your apprehension, Jack. If you are selected, there's a training program. You'll have the best minds in the field to help on the job. I wouldn't expect to dump a man, regardless of how qualified, into a position he couldn't handle. He would be required, from time to time, to travel to the near east to our interests in Kuwait, Iraq, Egypt, Stuttgart, Brussels, Stockholm, Singapore, and so on, but the main station will be in Europe. He would have the chance to manage the entire European operation if things work out well."

Attempting to still his swimming emotions, Jack stammered, "But..."

Cabal smiled paternally, as he reached out and firmly grasped Jack's shoulder. "Now, let's talk money, if that's what you are thinking about. The starting salary is $250,000 a year, with annual increases of $50,000 until $500,000 is reached and then there is available a partnership share if there is interest at that point—that is, if everything goes according to plan. A five year contract guaranteed. And there are perks: a car, furnished apartment, credit cards, etc. I know this is sudden, but the reason for my success is I do diligent research and then act quickly, and I want to make this decision by tomorrow afternoon.

Jack's jaw hung slack, almost dizzy with the mental image pictures of what this whole thing offered: Jack's dream of a lifetime.

"Why me?"

Cabal's manner became soft and paternal. "Because of those I have winnowed down to from the selectees, you not only have the qualities I need, you are honest and tell it like it is. I can trust you. You are a rare breed, Jack Chandler. I should have an answer for you by tomorrow at four. This will give you time to think it over. I will personally call you to set up another meeting to finalize the documents. We will meet at Jacob Forbes office, my affiliate here in town.

"If I'm chosen, and if I choose to accept, when will this start?"

"Immediately. You would have to wrap your business up in forty eight hours and be ready to fly to Paris by day after tomorrow.

"First I have to take care of a little business myself that would only take a few days."

Cabal pursed his lips thoughtfully and shook his head so slightly the movement was almost imperceptible. He seemed to be withdrawing, backing away ever so slightly. Jack felt himself being drawn into the vacuum. It was almost a whisper when Cabal said, "I'm sorry Jack, this position must be filled immediately. It is a very important post. I won't hold it open that long."

Jack thought rapidly about Dawn Marie, and relying on his own ability to move things fast, felt he could do both. But this fabulous offer was just too coincidental with the Dawn Marie thing. He ignored the gripping in his guts sending up red flares.

"Jack, I've known about this assignment for a year, and during that year, I've reviewed dozens of men with more experience, more brains, and more sophistication than you. But you have them all in the right proportions, Jack. I think you're the man for the job."

Jack's realized he had been holding his breath. His head swam in this sea of promise. "Okay, okay, I have someone I need to talk it over with. Then we can meet and firm it up as you wish."

Cabal's teeth sparkled in the knowing smile. Jack thought every part of this man is perfect, from the top of his coiffured head to the tips of his of his gleaming slippers.

"I knew you would see it that way," Cabal smiled his great smile, "it is a fabulous opportunity for you Jack, and for both of us."

Jack heard the words, but Cabal's voice and eyes were what held him. He's Caligula too, a small voice in his head told him.

Jack felt he could turn Dawn Marie's case over to another attorney that evening and the result could still be the same, even if he wasn't involved. There were plenty lawyers willing to pick it up and run with it. He thought of the best man he knew, Scott Love, and other asskickers he had worked with--Lewis Unglesby or Rick Caballero in Baton Rouge.

They shook hands and Cabal said, as he signaled to the waiter for the check, "I will call you at four."

Jack walked back to the elevator. As the elevator door closed, Jack looked back and saw Cabal signing the check and then raise his eyes to Jack. Jack felt a chill. What's wrong with this picture?

The bronze elevator plunged to ground level and Jack's spirit soared in exhilaration at the abrupt change in the direction of his destiny. He refused to accept that anything could be amiss as he floated on dreams of shooshing down alpine slopes, the antiquities, the museums, trying his hand with baccarat at Monaco, He was near meltdown. To think, he could be in Paris in forty-eight hours actually living out his lifetime fantasies. And a five year guarantee!

A cloying reservation gnawed at the rim of these images of the eternal dessert offered by an impresario politician and a man he had only met tonight; a man whose reputation was known around the globe as one who could make or break presidents with the lift of his eyebrow.

Reason returned as Jack's heels echoed on the polished terrazzo of the first floor. He hailed a cab and forced his euphoria to abate, trying to understand what happened. *You know damn well cherries don't fall from trees for no reason. Life doesn't operate that way. Things are hard won, not dropped in your lap. Of course they want me to drop Dawn. But why? If somebody like Cabal is involved in this, wanting me out of the picture,* how deep does this thing go?

Jack's emotional rollercoaster came to another stop. *I have to drop Dawn Marie's case, and rely on Cabal's contract with me. No contract is worth more than a court says it's worth, and this man has judges and lawmakers sticking out of every pocket. Hell, I might not even live long enough to make any noise. Jack thought of the Arabic Fellaheen who were given every earthly pleasure—women, food, and hashish—and told them they were in heaven, and to return to heaven, they had to perform some task, like 'assassinate' someone. That's where the word assassin came from: hashishan. Am I offered the reverse: don't do something and be rewarded with heaven?*

Jack shoved the increasing paranoia aside and became reasonable. *Naah! I'm lettin' my imagination run away with me. His offer's legit.* He tried to ignore the cloud of doubt hanging before his eyes, but it wouldn't go away. He prayed it would.

Vic had on a thick terry-cloth robe. Jack excitedly told her the whole story. By the time he was through talking about the wonderful opportunities, interlaced with bits of doubt, Vic was shaking her head.

Jack stopped mid-sentence. "It's bullshit, isn't it?"

Vic nodded. "It *is* bullshit."

They were a quiet for several seconds, with Jack allowing the exhilaration of the past hour to drift away like the dissipating shreds of fog from the levee on a sunny morning.

"If it is bullshit, how deep does this bullshit go to have a cat like cabal try to draw me away from the inquest?"

Vic shrugged. You don't know, I don't know. All I know is it's nearly one, and I've been waiting for nearly three hours and I want to take a swim. Nobody should be down at the pool at this hour."

Jack swallowed hard at the thought of what Vic had on beneath the robe. Probably that damn yellow bikini.

He started to protest about the danger and she said, "Jack, nobody shot you, arrested you, or did anything while you were out. Do you think they don't know you are back in town? If they were after you they would have you already. Campbell knew. Who else?"

Jack wrinkled his brow, trying to think of a rebuttal as Vic slid the tall door open and started down the stairs. "Wait, I'll get on my swimsuit."

"Meet you at the pool," Vic said, continuing down the dark stair.

Jack debated over his trunks. He was usually conservative and thought out his next move, but in a moment of uncommon impulsiveness chose a very brief Italian speedo one of his old girlfriends had given him a year or so before. It left no doubt he was a man.

A powerful mix of fragrances struck him as he approached the pool area. Sweet Olive, ginger lily, and cannibas. Weed! Jack had tried marijuana once and he didn't like the feeling of euphoric careless non-control. He thought people acted stupid when they smoked it. He had to block the primitive images of a large council hogan with men in animal skins sitting around a fire smoking spirit weed from a long pipe passed from one to another. *Damn, I'm getting these pictures too often. My imagination is running away with me.*

Vic lay on one of the chaise longues. He stopped in his tracks. She was wearing that yellow bikini. Her dark ginger skin looked soft and smooth, and her breasts swelled in the small bra. But most of all was that high rising bottom, and that proud mons pubis below a flat muscled belly.

"Uh Oh," Jack mumbled, "we got company. Didn't count on that!"

Vic's eyes traveled the length of his muscled body, stopping at the bikini. She smiled wickedly and tilted her head. She mouthed the words, "Wow."

Seeing the others around, Jack tried to cover himself. "Gimme that towel," he whispered to Vic. "I gotta go change!"

She shook her head and laughed, then pointed across the pool. "There's Ernie!"

"Oh, shit," Jack said, attempting to hide himself with both hands. Vic grinned at Jack's discomfort, and grabbed Jack's hand and wouldn't let him leave. The regulars were around the pool. Several others Jack didn't know were sitting around a table near Ernie's slave quarter apartment, a water bong on the table, and Jack could see they were passing it around to each other. Ernie stood alongside, his hands on his hips. His face was florid, and Jack could see he was talking rapidly at someone sitting at the table.

Jack looked over the crowd disgustedly, realizing they were all stoned and there was no way he and Vic could have a private swim. Archie the artist and Ann the CPA were arguing, as usual, over the fact that Ann wasn't giving him enough, and Archie was telling her that there was plenty pussy in the Quarter. She informed him so all could hear that he was free to get it if he wanted, but she was outta there if he did. They slurred, read and reread the text of their time-worn argument everyone in the patio had heard over and over.

Ellen, the old maid stewardess, surfaced from a long underwater dive, a beatific expression on her plain face as she purred, "I'm a submarine."

Lloyd Murchison, the law professor, had unsuccessfully made advances toward Vic for over a year. Murchison's efforts had become comical and Jack wondered how far he would go before he had to offer to mop up the floor with him. It was clear to everyone that Vic was not interested, but he continued using every ploy to get her attention. This time he had a new little blonde sitting on his lap. She had removed her bikini top and Lloyd was languidly tantalizing a taut nipple with the tips of his fingers as she traced the outline of his ear with her tongue. Lloyd was again demonstrating his amorous skills to Vic, who regarded the display with boredom and more than a hint of disapproval.

Though Vic wore the bikini around the pool, being from a fastidious, straight-laced background, she disdained such public demonstrations. Jack's eyes fell back on the velvet skin of this little tawny lioness. Jack felt the thing in him growl. *What's wrong with me. Why can't I move in and at least try? She probably would throw me out, but I can't even start. What's wrong with me?*

Ernie spotted Jack. "Jack, honey," Ernie Hotchkiss lisped, "do stop drooling over Vic's pussy and come talk to me. I've got something you want." Ernie leaned on the wall of his apartment for support.

Jack snatched the towel from the longue, and covered himself. Vic laughed out loud.

Ernie was doing something other than weed. He narrowed his eyelids, drew his lips into a thin line, and looked across the pool at a large man with a red beard who was talking intently to a fragile, pale young man smoking a lavender Sherman in a long jade cigarette holder.

Jack considered Ernie for a moment, then turned to look at Ellen floating on her back and spouting water from her mouth like a whale. Lloyd announced that he and his blonde were adjourning to his waterbed, while Archie and Ann continued their frustrated argument. Nobody noticed his exchange with Ernie. They were all so stoned nobody cared or noticed. Vic shrugged and dived into the pool, leaving him standing there, looking at Ernie, holding the towel over his bikini.

Ernie's eyes dropped to Jack's towel and his nostrils dilated. "Oh God, what are you hiding?"

"Nevermind. What do you want?"

Jack's emotions ran between contempt for Ernie as a human and real compassion for any man who was in Ernie's situation. It must be miserable, being a man wanting another man, dramatizing all that femininity, evidently always on the edge between hysteria and suicide. Jack could sense Ernie's tattered emotions and inward scream for any kind of peace.

"Have you ever done window pane?"

"LSD? No. Don't intend to," Jack said stiffly.

"Well, I just did a hit and I feel like I'm coming and going at the same time, and I dooo mean coming," Ernie giggled.

"Is that what you have to tell me?" Jack said impatiently.

"Oh no," Ernie smirked, tossing the blonde shock of hair from his eyes. "I have something to give you," he hissed, glaring at the red bearded man across the pool.

"What is it?"

"Its not what you think, although I wish it was." Ernie minced with a hand on his hip, as if insulted. "Besides, you're a breeder–tsk tsk, such a waste." Ernie turned toward the door and said, "You'll be surprised." He crooked a beckoning finger and opened the multi-paned French door to the first floor of the slave quarter apartment overlooking the courtyard.

Jack hesitated, glancing around surreptitiously to see if anyone was looking before he followed the swishing, weaving Ernie into the apartment. Ernie looked feverish. His eyes glistened oddly and there was a strange expression on his narrow features. They walked the short distance through a sumptuously appointed living room with an ornate Empire Period fireplace and mantel, with carved nude busts of hard breasted stern faced women, above which hung a nude painting of a pensive well appointed Adonis. The room was done in white: with white carpet and a snow white fur rug lying on the floor in front of the fireplace, which was surrounded by a circle of deeply cushioned white sofas. Jack thought it looked like a blizzard had hit the place.

Ernie grasped the curving rail to the spiral staircase, and pushed himself dramatically up the stair, tossing his head peckishly, muttering to himself, "I'll show that slut!"

The top of the stair was a gauzy bedroom with a canopied oval shaped bed that literally filled the room, around which was draped a filmy mosquito netting, not unlike a huge spiders web. Jack shuddered, getting a picture of Ernie being a spider and someone willingly walking into the threads of the soft snare.

A trace of incense filled the room and a life-size bronze replica of Hercules and Diomedes. The two curly haired, naked men were wrestling, one holding the other upside down while the upside down man gripped the other by the dick in a not too friendly manner.

Ernie stood unsteadily, noticing where Jack's attention had gone. "Like it?" he lisped suggestively.

Jack jerked his attention back to Ernie and said nothing that would betray his case of nerves at being alone with Ernie in his apartment. He still held the towel protectively over his front.

"Don't be nervous, sweetie. Here," Ernie said petulantly, thrusting a large folder stuffed with papers at Jack. "You want this."

Jack stared at the folder. The first page read "Records, Observations, Notes, Manuscript/First Draft: Libido and Prisons. By Rudi Bormann, M.D." Lifting his eyebrows inquiringly, Jack gazed back at Ernie.

"Yes. They belong to that bitch down by the pool. He has been fucking around on me for years and I just found out. This should show that slimy slut a thing or two. Take it. You can nail his hairy ass to the cross with what's in there!"

Jack flipped open the folder and his eyes fell on a statement written in longhand and initialed by Bormann, "I observed Deputy Parker make the young black male disrobe. He bent the young male over the bed and, after anointing his member with Vaseline, plunged it to the hilt and proceeded to ejaculation. Time: 1 minute 36 seconds. Effect of stimulant on subject inmate by act: undiminished. Stimulant: Y2."

"Shit," Jack gasped, realizing he held a legal nuclear device in his hands.

"See, didn't I tell you?"

"I can have this?"

"Yes," Ernie smiled viciously, "but only if you use it to destroy him." Ernie pointed down toward the pool.

"Who is Bormann?"

Ernie spit the words out: "The whore down there with the red beard. We're through. He had the gall to bring that hussy Randy to my place. He brought her here!"

Jack backed to the stairwell, covetously holding his prize, and hurriedly walked out of the apartment, past the pool. Just as he reached Vic, who was drying herself by the pool, he heard a noise from Ernie's upstairs balcony. Everyone looked up. Ernie was bent over with his back to the pool. He pulled his swimsuit down, revealing the cheeks of his ass and dangling genitals.

Ernie screeched at Bormann. "See that, you slut, take a good look. You'll never see it again," he shouted. He then shook his ass all about, pulled up his swimsuit and looked haughtily over the balcony at Bormann, who stared slack-jawed at the posturing, sneering Ernie.

"I got your ass now, butthole, "Ernie shrieked. "We're through. I gave your precious manuscript to Chandler. He is going to have your ass in ways you never want to know. Here's your shit!" A tornado of clothes, books and objects flew over the balcony onto the courtyard, some splashing into the pool.

Wanting no part of this, and having a treasure in his two fists, Jack pulled Vic along with him into the darkness of the corridor and raced to his office.

"What are you doing?"

"You'll see. Lets go to the office, quickly. We have what we need to hang the bastards!"

They ran to their apartments and changed into jeans and T shirts. They met in Jack's office.

It took over an hour to copy the entire file while reading the gross and nauseating entries by this monster who called himself a man of medicine.

"O My God," said Vic, "If these documents were true, Bormann actually observed and documented the rape and murder of Dawn Marie by Parker, Destrehan, and someone named Malborn Mourier."

"Yeah, that name twigs something. I can't remember exactly what. This name had been affixed to an invisible man—the closet billionaire, the Howard Hughes of the south—awesome power and wealth, but never seen—maybe as powerful as Cabal."

They completed copying and ran upstairs. Jack dropped the copy in the original envelope on the coffee table. Jack pushed back the clothes in the closet and opened the hidden door to the little secret room. He placed the original on a small shelf, and looked around at the things Parker had not found. His better guns and knives, and Vic's jewelry. He took out a sawed off twelve gauge shotgun pump and checked it for shells. It was illegal, as its barrel was too short and held six high powered shells of large buckshot, with capacity to wipe out four men in one shot standing side by side at a hundred feet. He laid the shotgun alongside the sofa, then turned to Vic.

"We have enough to nail the sheriff's office and all those named in the document, if we can get Ernie to say Bormann did it. But we have a ways to go yet. That's not enough to nail 'em. I have to work all that out. I'll send it out to a lawyer willing to kick ass, and we'll see if Cabal is gonna put his money where his mouth is."

It was nearly three and the two stared at each other, realizing it was another intersection. Feeling the old mental paralysis invading him, Jack tried to think of something to say. "Murchison's trying to show you his style."

"Yeah, some style..."

"He's got the hots for you."

"Not my type. Besides, that's reserved."

"What do you mean, reserved?"

"Just what I said," tightening her lips and glaring at Jack, "reserved."

Vic walked out and rumbled the big doors closed behind her. Jack stared at the closed doors, listening to her footsteps as she whispered down the stair. He groaned between clinched teeth. "Goddammit! Goddammit! Goddammit!

Chapter 15

Jack reeled from exhaustion. He fell on the bed, fully dressed, ready to pass out. Something nagged at him, an uneasiness, a feeling that couldn't be ignored. *Bormann knows I have it. He's gonna want it back. I'm too damned beat to go out. Hell, he might just try to break in.*

Jack bunched up the covers, placing pillows under the sheets so it looked like he was in the bed, and laid a pallet on the far side. He laid the shotgun alongside the bed, turned out the lights, plopped on the pallet and fell asleep.

Day Six

An hour before dawn, Jack woke to the sound of a light jingle of keys at his apartment door just before it was opened. Bormann entered with a short, squatty man in a green leisure suit and a felt hat pulled down over his brow.

The beam of a flashlight played over the living room.

"Bosco, there it is," an urgent whisper was heard and Bormann snatched the folder from the sofa. "Whew! That was close," he breathed.

Without checking his step, Bosco walked into the dark bedroom and pulled a revolver fitted with a silencer from a shoulder holster. Casually pointing the gun at the form under the cover, he snapped off six shots at close range with reports that sounded like a cough. He then turned and said in a gravelly New Orleans accent, "Now you ain't got nuttin' ta worry about. Da muddafucka's dead!"

"Thank God," Bormann gasped, clutching the file to his chest, "I can't imagine what would have happened if these papers had gotten into the wrong hands."

"Yah, you woulda gone to da same place dat asshole just went in dere, an' da man woulda had Bosco to make da hit."

Bormann sucked in his breath in terror. "I was writing a treatise on my studies in the prison. I could have made a name for myself in the psychiatric community."

"Well, you ain't gonna write nothin,' dockta. You gonna gimme dat. Da man wants it. You some stupid to write shit like dat wit his name in it. Hand it ovah!"

Bosco flipped the cylinder out on the revolver and six empty, warm, hulls fell into his hand. He dropped them into his coat pocket and then slid six more live rounds into the waiting empty chambers. He clicked the cylinder back in place and pointed the gun at the open mouthed Bormann.

"Give it!" he ordered. "When they find your body, they'll say that bastid killed ya"

"But he's dead, in the bed!"

"Dockta, you so stupid."

Bormann trembled as he laid the fat folder in the short man's outstretched hand. Bosco's finger tightened on the trigger just as the folder was passed over.

The unmistakable ratcheting of a shell being pumped into the barrel of a shotgun broke the silence. Bormann and the hit man froze.

Jack said, "hold it right there assholes," it came out more of a growl than in words. A thrill ran through Jack as he spit out "I got this baby loaded with Number two buckshot and at this range I can take both of you out with one shot." Jack eased into the light with the sawed-off shotgun pointing at the pair standing by his sofa.

"Drop the gun on the sofa, fat man," Jack said. "Easy does it. Make sure you leave plenty prints."

Bosco, his back still to Jack, dropped the gun on the cushions.

"Put the folder down. Easy now. Don't be stupid."

Bormann laid the folder alongside the revolver.

"I'm gonna give you two a chance. You can leave, and I won't have to clean your bloody shit off my carpet. I suggest you walk slowly out of the door with your hands on your heads."

The pair put their hands on top of their heads, and started to the door. Jack picked up the folder, stuffed it into his backpack, and followed them through the door into the hall.

"Now, down the stairs slowly boys. The safety's off and I'm nervous as a cat." Jack was as calm as a smooth lake. This was one of the delicious moments he lived for.

They walked down the stairs to the front door of the building. "While you're at it, fat man, leave me those keys you used to get in my apartment. I don't want to see you again."

The gray dawn spread its light through the early morning fog. Street lights were still on, but Jack could see down the damp street without them.

Warner Bosco slowly shoved a pudgy, ring covered hand into his coat pocket and held out a set of keys between two fingers.

"Drop it! Jack ordered.

The keys clinked on the wooden floor.

"Now, walk away, and don't stop till you are out of buckshot range."

The pair trudged down Royal toward Esplanade Boulevard, their steps echoing against the closely set buildings. They waddled as fast as their big bodies would carry them past a baffled street sweeping machine operator, who watched them bumbling away down the street with their hands clasped over their heads.

Jack retrieved the keys from the floor and rushed upstairs and changed to his usual jeans and T-shirt. He raced down to Vic's apartment and banged on the door.

Finally, the door opened a crack. Vic squinted through two safety chains stretched across the opening. "Is that you, Jack?"

"Yeah. Let me in, hurry!"

The door closed momentarily, and the chains fell away.

Still half asleep, Vic stood before Jack stark naked. Jack's eyes feasted on her for a moment before she pulled on a robe lying on a chair.

Grabbing Vic by the arm, Jack led her to the kitchen. "Sit down and listen."

"What's going on?"

"Trouble, mama. Big ass trouble." He told her what had happened and then said, "We gotta get this manuscript to the U.S. Attorney or to the D.A. immediately, before they nail us. They'll be waitin' for us, and probably in force now. So we gotta hit 'em before they hit us by gettin' this in the hands of the prosecutor as soon as he opens his doors this morning."

Jack paused to catch his breath.

Bosco referred to "da man," and I don't know who that is. May be this guy Mourier, who knows?"

Vic stared wide-eyed at Jack. "Now I remember his name. Some kind of financial wizard—major interest in oil, banks, even the media. And they say he's a weirdo. Goes in disguise, avoids any publicity. Nobody even knows what he looks like. If he's in it, we may have some real problems, Jack."

"That's what I'm sayin'. I've been in the shit since this started."

"We're in it, Jack. My name's on Dawn's autopsy."

"We gotta get outta here and take a ride, then get to the U.S. Attorney's office as soon as it opens at eight."

Vic dressed hurriedly and they raced through a maze of hallways. Having once been several century old mansions now combined to make apartments, there were several entrances, sealed for security purposes, but there were some that only the tenants knew about that still satisfied the fire code.

They passed the courtyard and Ernie's apartment and entered another long corridor that ran behind the slave quarters. At the end of the hall was a security door that could be opened by pushing a horizontal bar. Jack hit the bar on the run and the door swung open onto a small alley with a locked door leading into another apartment complex directly ahead, a wall to the left and a wooden gate was to their right.

Jack's key opened the lock on the gate and when he pushed it open they were on Orleans Street. Vic's parking garage was only a block away. When they closed the door behind them, it fit so well into the gray cypress wall, the only way he could tell a door was there at all was by the nearly invisible keyhole hidden in the grain.

Jack began "I'm sorry I got you into...." but was stopped mid sentence by Vic. "If you say that one more time, I swear I am going to bust you one. This is our problem, we're a team, and you're not going to carry this deal alone. So knock it off!"

Jack shook his head and gazed at her. He flushed as he felt a huge flood of emotion wash through him. He knew what the emotion was, but it just couldn't be. He had never felt this way about anyone, but she was somehow beyond his reach. While he was a renegade and outside the loop of society's considerations of correctness, he was in mental quicksand. It was agony. In his North Louisiana bible belt upbringing there was never any overt display of emotion, no hugging in public, and couples seldom showed their affection for one another. As a matter of fact, Jack had never thought much about husband and wives actually loving each other. They were only married, living together, somehow tolerating it, as was the case with his parents. Maybe that was the problem. Maybe he was doomed for a life of despair.

The fuel gauge registered empty. "Damn," Jack muttered. His mind raced. What gas station would be open at this time of morning? It was just after six and traffic was beginning to move in the Quarter. Delivery trucks rumbled down the narrow streets and yawning early workers carried steaming cups of coffee to their cars. Jack wished he had a cup of coffee.

Vic slid behind the wheel and started the engine. "There's a Texaco down St. Charles at Lee Circle," she said. "Let's hope it's open and we can make it."

All of the streets in the Quarter are narrow and one way. Vic's truck was on a street going the opposite direction from their destination. She needed to circle the block and head back up Royal to cross Canal, then the eight or ten long blocks to Lee circle.

"Don't take Royal," Jack said. "They're probably watchin' the front door and'll see you when you turn the corner. Go down Dauphine!" They turned onto Dauphine and sped through a stop sign, nearly colliding with a long black Cadillac with dark shaded windows.

The driver raised his fist and cursed, immediately slamming on his brakes as he passed through the intersection, nearly causing the truck following close behind him to crash into his rear. Jack recognized Bosco as the driver and his passenger as Bormann, probably driving around the block to catch Jack as he left. The Cadillac couldn't back through the intersection and follow Jack since the driver of the truck blocking him was cursing and threatening to whip Bosco's ass for stopping in front of him so abruptly.

Vic pressed the accelerator to the floor and ran every stop sign before getting to Canal at the end of the Quarter. Bormann and his hit man chauffeur would be searching for them. Jack hoped Bosco would surmise they would take a zigzag exit to lose him, so Jack told Vic to continue straight ahead. Bosco would be coming from their left and would be a block away unless they were stopped by traffic. Jack figured he would do best to continue on to his destination via the shortest route–straight up St. Charles as he had originally intended.

They raced through the red light at canal, and sped up St. Charles Avenue. Vic skidded into the Texaco. Jack slid his VISA card into the slit on the pump and punched "credit."

The mouth of Vic's gas tank was on the far side, away from the pump. She pulled the long black hose over the bed of the truck, placed the steel nozzle in the tank and began filling.

The Cadillac skidded up at an angle, an arm's length from where Vic was standing. Bosco clinched a short black cigar between his teeth. The tip was a live coal. His voice was gravel rasping on gravel.

"Thought you could get away in that big pickup? I can see you a mile, you stupid assholes."

Vic looked down at a scarred-faced man whose flat eyes told her much more than the words that spilled from his snarling lips. Vic and Jack knew they were both dead, regardless of what they did.

Holding the nozzle in the tank, still fueling, Vic stood transfixed, scarcely two feet from Bosco's open window, staring into the muzzle of a big forty-five automatic pointed straight at her nose. There was no way to run and no place to hide.

"You think ya smart, punk?" He said to Jack. "I'm a pro. Ya think ya could get away from me? I'm gonna send ya niggah girlfrien' back to Africa in a box if ya don't gimme that file like a good boy; I know ya got it with you."

Jack hesitated, regretting that Vic was along. There was nothing he could do but get the file. He knew he was as good as dead even if he gave it to Bosco, but moving toward the truck like he was going for the file would buy a little time. Bosco was probably a crack shot with that forty-five, and the best Jack could do would be to give him a moving target.

Bormann was pale behind his bushy red beard. He nervously pulled a brown Sherman from a pack and snapped on a little flame with a slender gold Ronson lighter.

The expression on Vic's face turned to fury. She slowly pulled the nozzle from the gas tank and pointed it straight into Bosco's leering face.

Bosco sneered in disbelief. He laughed, showing broken yellow teeth with green stains at the gum line. "Ya gonna shoot me with that, bitch?"

"Yeah," Vic smiled as she squeezed the lever to the maximum. A wide stream of premium gasoline gushed straight into the fat man's open mouth and eyes. She held the lever down, filling the car with high octane fumes. The .45 roared. The slug struck the steel nozzle, knocking it from her hand, and ricocheted past Vic's ear and smashed the glass face of the gas pump.

The interior of the Cadillac glowed red for an instant as the fumes ignited from the open flame of Bormann's lighter. Vic quickly stepped back and ran.

Bosco's face blossomed like a rose, puffing with blisters as the skin on his cheeks and eyelids swelled and popped. He blindly squeezed the trigger, shattering the windshield. The inside of the car erupted, with Bosco as the kindling.

Bormann flung open the door and fell to the street howling, beating the flames licking at his clothing.

Bosco pressed the accelerator and the flaming Cadillac shot across the street up onto the grassy knoll of Lee Circle and slammed into a park bench. The entire car disintegrated in a shattering explosion as the car detonated. The roof blew off and a small mushroom cloud lifted before the stony, unseeing eyes of Robert E. Lee, standing high on his Corinthian column in the center of the mound.

Bormann ran in circles, squealing and fanning his blazing, gasoline soaked pants. Jack tackled the crazed man and rolled him on the pavement. In a moment, he had Bormann's clothes extinguished and then removed the smoldering garments. Jack burned his hands slightly in the process and Bormann had some third degree burns on his legs and buttocks.

Wailing sirens came from all directions. Jack pushed Borman, stumbling and whimpering, toward the truck, shoved him in, and got in the back seat behind him. Vic gunned away from the scene before the police arrived.

"Head toward the river," Jack shouted.

Vic spun out, burning rubber.

"You're in deep shit, Bormann," Jack said as they accelerated through the streets. "They know what you've done, and you're a state's witness to murder and God knows what else. You're gonna need protective custody or those bastards are gonna ice you down."

Between sobs of terror and pain, Bormann asked, "What are you going to do? What can I do?"

"Well, if you live through this to testify, you can expose the worst crimes this city has ever seen. You gotta cooperate."

"I need a lawyer."

"You need to find a hidin' place first," Jack said, "and a guarantee of safety for quite a while. You wouldn't last five minutes on the street, or in jail. There are plenty guys like crispy critter Bosco back there on somebody's payroll who wants you quiet, very quiet. You better cooperate or I'll take care of you myself. I've seen three men die in the past week, and I'd gladly add your notch."

Bormann quailed at the intensity of Jack's words. It was clear that Jack was outraged enough to follow through on the threats. Bormann began bawling like a baby.

"Shut up, you worthless son-of-a-bitch," Jack said quietly in Bormann's ear.

Bormann stopped crying abruptly, and looked at Jack through calm, superior eyes of an English Lord whose dignity had been outraged beyond belief.

Bormann drew himself up straight, and said, with his lips turned down in a sneer, "You have no right to treat me in such fashion, sir. I am a doctor of medicine."

Jack had heard of such personality shifts before and realized that he may be talking to another person entirely—the first having submerged, and this new one bubbling up from somewhere to handle this situation.

"Doctor," Jack bit off the word, "you are an accessory to murder one, and a murderer yourself, in my opinion. Your damned papers prove that and other things even worse. You're goin' to jail if you don't get the chair. So shut up if you want me to save your worthless life."

Bormann became very quiet. His eyes darted. He jerked on the door handle and started to jump from the moving car. Jack doubled his right fist and slammed it into Bormann's neck just below the ear and Bormann collapsed unconscious.

Jack was amazed he had been able to react so instinctively and so fast. Vic frowned at the fleeting smile on Jack's face she could see in the rear view mirror.

It was still early, but they had to find somewhere to hide. Vic's truck was very conspicuous. Jack hoped the sleepy attendant hadn't gotten the license number in all of the confusion, but he couldn't expect such luck. He knew there would be an A.P.B out for a white Silverado pickup. He only needed until eight when the office of the U.S. Attorney opened. Then he'd march Bormann up the steps of the Federal Court building, hoping for asylum.

Then he remembered. The warehouse on Tchopitoulas was only three or four blocks away. Maybe it was unlocked.

In a few minutes, they drove up the ramp and Jack opened the door to the old warehouse. The hasp had not been securely screwed into the wall, and with a few deft motions, Jack was able to jerk it from the wall and he quickly rolled the door up. He pulled the door down as Vic drove the car through the grotesque corridor to the cold storage locker and got out.

Jack dialed a number on his cell phone. Nookie answered the phone after ten rings.

149

"Allo?"

"Nookie, I need your help!"

Nookie listened for a moment and quickly got the picture. "Jack, you koo-yon, you done stir up some shit, you. Yeah, I can get you."

"Bring a robe or a pair of pants."

"What size?"

"Hmmm, waist about a forty."

"You got it, cap. Lache pas."

Jack touched Bormann on the nose with the tire iron. Jack's rage at the injustice of everything that had happened had reached meltdown. He became coldly certain. This animal didn't deserve life, and the bastard might even walk away free in the so-called justice system. He lifted the iron rod, feeling perfectly justified in smashing Bormann's head in then and there. Bormann fell back, making a mewling sound.

Jack snarled right in Bormann's face, "You don't deserve the gift of life. You're irresponsible."

Bormann screeched, holding his arms over his head, trying to melt into the seat.

Jack suddenly felt ecstatic. He had decided what he was going to do. Holding the tire iron in the air he screamed in Bormann's ear, "You set it up. Destroyed Dawn and others for your crazy damned book and then let her be killed before your very eyes. She didn't mean a damned thing to you—nobody does. I'm gonna execute you myself, right here and now."

"Jack, stop," Vic screeched, slapping him hard on the face. Jack shook his head, blinking away the madness. He stamped his feet at his aborted short-cut to vigilante justice.

"The son-of-a-bitch might get off, Vic."

"Yeah, you crazy bastard," she said, "and you'd hang and I'd have to testify that I saw you murder this excrement."

Jack calmed instantly, still relishing the wildness of his potential head bashing. He drew a few deep breaths, then laughed.

"Thanks, you're right—but damned if that didn't feel right for a moment."

Bormann was bent over in the seat, hugging his knees and trembling.

"Bormann—you pissed on my seat," Vic shrieked, shoving him out of the truck onto the floor of the warehouse. "Jack, look what you made him do—he pissed on my seat."

"It'll dry," Jack laughed, "and by the way, we got a ride. Nookie's comin.'"

Bormann huddled on the floor of the warehouse and leaned against a rear wheel.

Jack said, "Bormann, your life ain't worth a plug nickel. No lawyer's gonna get you out of this one, and if they don't get you, I will. I promise you that. If the law cuts you loose, I'll find you. I just might cut you some slack, though, if you tell the whole story to a jury."

Bormann didn't reply. He hugged his knees and stared blindly at the floor.

Jack chain-smoked and paced the floor until the warehouse door rolled up and Nookie drove in sitting like a Maharajah in a Gleaming pink, 1959 Eldorado Barritz Cadillac convertible with huge tail fins. The top was down.

"Where'd you get this thing? Jack asked, amazed at the size of the car.

"Bouree' game. A pimp's car. Who dat what said 'don't give a sucker a even break?'"

"W.C. Fields," Jack answered. "Thanks for comin'."

Nookie slapped Jack on the back, and said, "My li'l truck got busted up a li'l, so I need a car! Like her?"

"She's a beauty, Nookie—that's a fine ride for sure."

They fitted Bormann with a pair of black and white checked pants Nookie said belonged to Pussy Beaucoup's mama's boyfriend, who was a cook at the Bon Ton cafe. Borman was seated in the front by Nookie.

Jack called Judge Mahoney at home. Jack knew Mahoney didn't get to his office before nine, and it was just past eight.

The judge answered. "Judge? It's Jack Chandler, remember me? I came to your house before the storm and you signed some papers for me."

"Oh yeah, Chandler. How'd it go?"

Jack explained what happened, interspersed with questions from the judge. It took several minutes for Jack to unravel the whole story as briefly as he could, judiciously omitting any reference to the name of Mourier, named as the murderer in Bormann's papers, a name linked with money and power but a man nobody had ever seen.

"Whew," the judge whistled, "Boy, you took some chances. What can I do for you?"

"I need to get into the U.S. Attorney's office when they open at eight-thirty. I got Bormann here. He's a wreck, with some bad burns, and he's scared shitless, Judge. He's gonna need a doctor and protection."

"Yeah," Mahoney said, "If what you say is true, the bastid gonna need protection from me."

"Right, Judge. I don't see how he can avoid being a prosecution witness. So I need to get directly in to see the U.S. Attorney himself, and not some assistant. Can you set it up so we can walk straight in without all the red tape?"

There was a pause at the other end of the line, and then Mahoney said, "Yeah. Yeah. I'll call Charlie Leone himself. I can get to him if he's there. Where ya at? I'll call ya right back."

Jack gave the number and in ten minutes the phone rang.

"It's set up," Mahoney said. "A security guard'll be at the front of the buildin' waitin'. They'll take ya'll straight to Charlie. Lotsa luck, pal."

"Thanks, Judge. Keep your fingers crossed."

As they started to leave, Nookie said, "Hang on. Gotta get a li'l someting."

"Nookie disappeared through the locker door and came out a few minutes later carrying a box, steaming with icy mist. He placed it in the trunk. "Mah l'il Pussy Beaucoup she does love dem age T-bone." He winked at Jack and Vic who just shook their heads.

Chapter 16

Nookie drove the trio up Magazine over to Camp Street, occasionally waving at the street people loitering along the way. At a stoplight, a wino walked up to the gleaming Cadillac and said, "I heard you got Jackknife Jackson's car and now I believe it."

Nookie stopped at the Camp street entrance. Jack sprang out and opened the passenger door.

Bormann's eyes were filled with terror as he looked in every direction before stepping out. With Jack pulling on his arm, he staggered to his feet.

Jack nearly laughed at the checked pants adorning Bormann's bottom half, thinking he looked like someone he once knew at a used car lot.

Immediately two dead-faced men in dark in suits rushed out. One asked, "Jack Chandler?"

Jack nodded. They looked at Vic and Nookie.

"I'm coming, too," Vic said.

"Vic," Jack said, "I'll be fine now. The danger's over with what I have here." He patted the manila envelope stuffed with Bormann's notes.

"Take Vic home. Hold this." He slipped Nookie his .38 revolver. "Stay with her till I get the A.P.B lifted and then take her back to the warehouse to get her truck."

"You bet, boss," Nookie said.

Vic and Jack's eyes held each other for a moment. "Be careful," said Vic, as she touched the back of Jack's hand.

Jack grinned. "I land on my feet, mama."

As Nookie drove Vic away in the huge pink automobile, Jack and Bormann were hustled up the steps through the metal detector machines to the elevators.

Bormann was limping from the burns on his leg, and Jack became aware of his own appearance. He had slept in his clothes, and looked like it. His hair was uncombed and he needed a shave. Bormann looked much worse.

An intense, thin, pock-faced man behind a mahogany desk watched them suspiciously as they paraded into his office.

"Chandler?" he asked, without any formal introductions.

This was the big cop, Charlie Leone, Jack thought. *Here to make a name for himself and do what he's told for the good of peace, order, and the administration that appointed him. Maybe run for congress or senate—even governor if he makes a name for himself and doesn't screw up. He's an employee, just like the rest of 'em, but with power of the anointed and the temporary bark of the big dog. The other party gets in, he's back on the street as a common lawyer just like me. What the hell, he puts his britches on one leg at a time just like anybody else.*

"Yeah," Jack answered, laying the folder on the desk, "and this is Rudi Bormann. You can read about him in his own papers he wrote himself."

Leone waved for them to sit in the deep leather chairs in front of his desk. The seating arrangement was situated so that visitors would have to look up at Leone, the classic strategic positioning used to intimidate.

Pain was beginning to set in, and Bormann rocked, grimacing, holding his leg. "I want my lawyer," he groaned.

Leone looked at Jack inquiringly.

Jack said, "Yeah, he needs a lawyer, but hear what I have to say and then let him call one. Won't make any difference one way or the other. While I'm tellin' you about it, better get a medic. He's got some burns on his leg."

"Mahoney filled me in on some of the details. How's about you givin' it to me straight," Leone growled, motioning to the guard to bring a nurse in.

Jack told the story from the beginning, leaving out reference to Mourier, showing Leone the notes and excerpts from the documents in the folder with Bormann's signature on most of them. While Jack and Leone talked, a nurse came in and split Bormann's pants with scissors, then applied salves and bandages to a large bright red place on Bormann's left thigh and calf.

When Jack finished the story, Leone whistled. "Sheeit! This is a blockbuster! Yeah, you better call a lawyer, Bormann. I'd rather not hear anything else right now. But you aren't goin' anywhere. Call from this phone on my desk, and meanwhile, I'm holding you for the DA. It's probably his jurisdiction anyway. Sounds like accessory to murder at least, if this'll hold up."

Bormann dialed a number. "Robert, I'm being held for accessory to murder at the office of the U.S. attorney. You better get over here. No. I don't have time to explain. Just get over here, now, at the Federal building on Poydras—in Charlie Leone's office. Yes, I mean Leone himself—do hurry!"

"I heard about Destrehan being killed by an itinerant. Nothing was said about you being involved, Jack," Leone said, being less menacing and addressing him by his first name. They were on the same side now, and maybe this was the star that Leone could hitch his wagon to that would carry him to the sweet ambrosia of political Valhalla.

Jack could drive that wagon. Leone approached it with extreme care, knowing that honey would get more flies than any amount of vinegar; and being nice to Jack wouldn't hurt—at least for a little while—hell, it may even last if it was worth it in political dynamite.

Jack knew what Leone was doing. Bormann's criminal case probably was under the jurisdiction of the Parish DA, Delahoussie, and he would relinquish that to him willingly. What Leone smelled was a motherlode of PR in getting Sheriff Sessums, who he personally detested. Jack knew Leone would try to hold on to the action against the sheriff if he could keep it from the State Attorney General or DA's office. It was known that Sessums was tight with Delahoussie, and any excuse would be enough to avoid bringing charges against the sheriff's office.

A brisk young man named Robert, wearing a dark three piece suit, strode in. Spying Bormann, he said, "Rudi, you look like hell. Mr. Leone, I need to talk to Bormann in private."

While Robert and Rudi conferred, Leone and Jack drank coffee and smoked while looking over the papers.

Leone found the section where Bormann had documented Dawn Marie's murder and began reading out loud, occasionally stumbling over an illegible word in Bormann's handwriting.

Data: "8Sept96. Subj:Delacroix/B/A/F.

Experiment purpose: Coitus reduce effects of induced arousal?

Initial/IV2ccDemoral. 45min/delay. IV1cc"X"/&1/2cc Y1

Restraints/removed garments/no resistance

Obs:Respir. intensified/pupils dilated/arousal/pelvis pumping.

Participants in experiment: Parker/Destrehan/MM

(MM wants ultimate experience = wildcard)

Action: Parker climaxed immediately. Destrehan extraordinary large. Subject screamed. Internal damage suspected. Obs abrasions and lacerations on thigh and groin area. Bleed profusely. No diminution of drug reaction.

Obs: MM inserts stilleto into subj heart/moment of climax. Subj. expires. MM: "Get rid of it."

Leone was sweating when he finished the long handwritten summary. "Those bastards! Those slimy, rotten, sons-of-bitches," he swore, slamming his fist down on the desk. "Who is this MM?"

This was the moment of truth, Jack knew, the moment to see what Leone was made of. He said slowly, watching Leone as a cat watches a dog, "Turn the page."

Leone angrily slammed the page over and scanned the top sentence. His eyes stopped moving, as if disbelieving what he was reading. Malbourn Mourier was MM! He made a small sound in his throat as he caught his breath and looked up at Jack, his mouth open and eyes wide. He appeared to have difficulty in keeping his equilibrium as if those few words pronounced his own death sentence. What dimension of power, or evil, could cause a man like Leone, accustomed to every kind of criminal, to nearly strangle?

Jack watched Leone's reaction. "Makes your job interesting, don't it, Charlie?"

Leone's face was ashen. Fear flooded his features and his hand shook as he tried to light another cigarette. He pushed his chair back from the desk and walked to the tall, multipaned window behind his desk and gazed out on the rooftops. It was very quiet in the room. It was obvious he had to turn away to regain control. Leone narrowed his eyelids to slits and turned back to Jack, his lips turned down in an inverted U, about to say something when Bormann and lawyer entered the room.

Bormann wasn't cheered by the presence of his lawyer or by the advice he had been given, as evidenced by his downcast eyes and slow limping tread back to the chair he had vacated in front of the desk.

"Got a proposition to make to you." Robert the lawyer said.

Charlie was already dealing with the mixmaster in his own head and wasn't ready for any new revelations or propositions. He said nothing. Robert understood the silence to mean that he was to continue.

"My client asks for asylum and immunity in exchange for his testimony. He wishes to be given a safe house, under twenty-four hour guard, and a change of identity, and he will cooperate fully under these terms. Before we agree to anything, we must put this in writing and properly authenticated as a full immunity with the guarantee of safety."

Beads of sweat popped on Leone's brow. Suddenly, Leone energized from what appeared to be an inspiration. "This is a copy of the documents. Where are the originals?"

"I have 'em," Jack said.

"I'm ordering you to turn 'em over to me immediately."

"No dice, Charlie. I need 'em for the civil trial, and they are very safe. If anything happens to me, they'll be in the hands of someone who'll use 'em properly."

Leone's eyes bugged and he looked as if he was going to have a stroke. "You son-of-a-bitch," he panted, obviously directing his fear at the wrong target, "You're obstructing justice. I could put you in jail."

"Okay. Put away. I could use the rest, but you got your indictment right here," Jack pointed at Bormann, "and his testimony is all you need anyway. Cut him loose, and he's a dead man—and he knows it. Put me on the street and I may be a dead man, but somebody else with more stroke than I have'll stand in my shoes, and others in his. This game's over. Give Bormann what he wants, and during the process of my litigation, I'll work with you to get you the indictments you need."

"But I, I can't, I mean, I. . ." Leone stammered.

"You're scared shitless, and for the same reason Bormann's scared. Mourier snuffed that little girl, and you know who you are dealing with. If you don't handle this, I'm walking out of here to the Times Picayune, U.S.A. today, Time Magazine, U.S. News, all of 'em, and I guarantee your name will be in headlines on the front pages. You gotta fish or cut bait."

"This is the domain of the Parish DA," Leone said quietly, too quietly, averting his eyes from Jack, a tic developing under his left eye. "I'll call Delahoussie and see what he says."

Leone made a call and then said, "The first Assistant will be over in a moment. He said if the facts are like I say, you got a deal."

Jack looked at Leone without blinking. *Leone rolled over entirely too fast, I wonder...*

"Okay," Jack said, "recall the A.P.B on the white Silverado, and while you're at it, check and see if they got any warrants out on me."

Leone groused and placed a couple of calls. "There ain't nothin' out on you, and they're recallin' the A.P.B out on the truck. Leone asked sarcastically, "Anything else, counsel?"

Jack said, "I need access to a computer and printer. I have some things to do myself."

"What for?" Leone asked, frowning.

"I'm gonna file a damage complaint before I leave this building."

Jack called Vic, so Nookie could take her to get her car.

He was given a small room with an old Royal manual typewriter, some worn out carbon, and wrinkled onion skin that looked as if it had been left out in the rain. He laughed out loud at the "royal" treatment, and said, "screw 'em."

Some of the keys jammed, and the ribbon made an almost unreadable copy, but Jack tediously typed a complaint entitled, "Martin and Estelle Delacroix, individually and for the use and benefit of the estate of their deceased minor daughter, Dawn Marie Delacroix, versus The office of the Criminal Sheriff, Orleans Parish."

Federal Court requires only a brief statement of the facts rather than an elaborate particularization of each and every detail, so Jack synopsized his factual complaint by stating that the sheriff's department, through Leroy Destrehan, Alonzo Parker, and others, raped and murdered Dawn Marie on or about the 8th day of September,

1995, which was known or should have been known by the Sheriff himself. The complaint was only a page and a half long, but he finally had a product that would pass muster as a legal document. He grinned, knowing this little page, as miserable as it looked, typed with that nearly deceased typewriter, if proven, could topple the existing political power in New Orleans, for the Sheriff was the power, and this would catapult him right out of office by an enterprising opponent.

Jack hustled down to the office of the clerk and filed the petition. He left a copy to be served on the sheriff by a special deputy and kept two copies for himself. He considered giving one to the Times Picayune immediately after leaving the courthouse, but something told him to hold back. Jack knew to obey those little hunches.

When Jack returned to Leone's office, assistants from the DA's office were present, having just completed the signing of the documents granting immunity and a safe house. Leone's drawn features were totally void of expression, but his eyes betrayed something—and Jack hoped that it didn't mean more surprises.

Bormann was surrounded by deputies, assistant DA's, several witnesses, two secretaries, a recording machine and a VCR on a tripod trained on Bormann. Jack sat in the corner watching Leone begin the questioning with the preamble about Bormann giving this statement in exchange for immunity and guarantee of safety. Bormann spilled forth a full, sickening explanation of Dawn Marie's death, along with admissions of setting up and witnessing over a hundred documented rapes, sodomies, and perversions over a five year period at the Juvenile Detention Center, at other adult detention facilities, and at private motels in the New Orleans area—implicating by name other doctors, politicians and men whose identities had never surfaced before. Jack took notes. A growl rose in his throat at the horrors so blithely related by this creature sitting before him who held himself out to be a healer and human being.

After the interrogation, Bormann, in cuffs, and his lawyer were taken to another room. It was agreed a medical doctor would be called to treat him and if necessary have him hospitalized for his burns. Jack assumed Bormann was being provided with a safe house and guard, in keeping with the agreement.

Jack and Leone stared at each other. Leone's demeanor and attitude had swung in the last hour from euphoric optimism to bristling, menacing hostility.

"Are you gonna charge Mourier?"

"That's my business, Chandler. If you don't get me that original, I'm gonna arrest you. I got the power to do any damn thing I want, and you know it. Don't fuck with me."

"C'mon Leone, get real, you got a confession," Jack said. "You got the man himself, and he identified those writings as his own. You don't need the original. But I assure you, it'll be available when you go to trial if it is absolutely needed. I want it for my trial. You'll have to get a court order and I'll get a protective order to stop you, so we'll be wasting each other's time with this issue; it's safe, don't worry. Nobody can find it, but if anything happens to me, I've left instructions with several people I trust who'll find it and use it properly." Leone turned beet red as Jack delivered his little speech. The tic on his cheek intensified; he looked as if he would explode.

Jack walked toward the door, folded his papers and slipped them into the pocket of his jeans. He turned around and said, "Keep Bormann safe."

Leone visibly winced.

"Get out!" Leone whispered huskily, pointing to the door with his finger trembling slightly.

Jack's eyes met Leone's, and there seemed to be an audible crackle of conflicting energies in the air. Jack closed the door behind him, still feeling those malevolent eyes boring into the back of his head.

Jack's life had been filled with men who wanted him dead or paralyzed. He couldn't understand why people reacted that way to him. Ever the nettle in the drawers of those in authority, Jack sometimes wondered, and even worried about it. What was it about him that caused some men in authority to do backflips?

All I do is look 'em in the eye and expect 'em to level with me, Jack thought. They always get nervous and attack, and it's usually big shot hot dogs like Leone.

Jack laughed, realizing he had always worried about this phenomenon. Now it was just slightly amusing. It was their damned problem, and not his that they reacted that way. Must be something in them—guilt or fear he ignited by just looking at them. *That makes me dangerous,* Jack realized, smiling at the image of his alter ego walking through enemy territory.

⁊

It was just past noon. Vic met Jack in his apartment. They sat on the balcony and talked. Jack noticed she wouldn't look at him directly, and her lips were drawn into a tight line. Finally she said, "Jack, if this deal with Cabal come through, what are you going to do?"

There was a long pause. Jack's eyes darted as he tried to deal with the answer. "It's bullshit. We agreed it's bullshit. It ain't gonna happen."

"If it's not bullshit. Then?"

"It'd be a helluva deal, you gotta admit that."

"Yeah, a helluva deal," she said, glaring at Jack. "So you would leave this evening if they came through?"

"Hadn't thought of it since we talked, but it would be stupid to turn it down."

Vic stood suddenly and walked to the wrought iron railing and looked away. She pinched off a glistening tear forming in her eye, and took a deep breath. She turned, and looked steadily at Jack. "OK, lets see what happens."

Jack had been holding his breath, watching Vic as she seemingly was wrestling with some decision, and exhaled noisily when she evidently allowed a reprieve.

"I'm starving. Lets go to Tujaques," Jack said, breaking the tension.

Vic nodded, still less than her usual peppy self, and Jack was all confusion, but had a place to go and a reason to go there and that temporarily delayed the necessity of dealing with an issue that demanded resolution.

Everything in the Quarter is within walking distance. It was clear and balmy, drenched in the blend of the midday smells of the fruit and vegetable vendors on Decatur and the confectioners' sugar and strong coffee of the Morning Call. The hoots and toots of the riverboat traffic just behind the levee blended with the clip clopping of the horses pulling the little fringed surreys touring the Quarter. Everyone was trying to put the Quarter back together again after nature's recent vicious attack.

Tujaques didn't use a menu. It is small hole in the wall kind of restaurant with an ancient bar on one side of a partition and the restaurant with its dozen or so tables on the other. A formally dressed waiter brought course after course, beginning with salad, then appetizer of shrimp remoulade, baked chicken and boiled brisket with horse radish with a vegetable, and finally bread pudding with rum sauce and coffee. The powerful coffee looked like ink in the little glass tumbler used as a cup.

They ate quietly, discussing the events of the day and what Jack expected of the civil suit. Vic was subdued and introverted. Jack avoided any discussion of Cabal and the possible trip to Europe.

A pale, moon faced man watched them from a corner table. The man didn't blink or change expressions. Jack remembered seeing this face around, but it was always so nondescript and forgettable that it was almost like no face at all. It was flat, maggoty-white, and expressionless; Jack had always dismissed him as being one of the Quarter freaks who either had too much or too little of something that qualified them as residents.

Jack felt the impulse to move and face the other direction. Every time he raised his eyes the man was staring at him. The Quarter was filled with kooks, creeps, and the socially disenfranchised. Weird happenings and bizarre people were part of Jack's world. That was one of the reasons he liked it. He looked, and kept his distance, knowing the people were an indispensable part of the color. But this man's gaze had no feeling in it—it was just a stare, unblinking, bland and dispassionate. Jack wondered if the man was even perceiving him; he was like a blind man, a staring corpse, but he knew that the look was meant for him. The man's brows were nearly invisible and his eyes colorless, the big pupils like holes in a flaccid bloodless mask.

Vic noticed Jack's discomfiture and turned to look at the man. She frowned and curled her lips in a distasteful expression, communicating to Jack she saw and felt the strangeness.

Jack realized he was rushing through a meal he normally would have leisurely savored. *Damn, I am letting this little creep get under my skin.* He gulped his coffee and they left. When he rounded the corner, he felt compelled to look back. The man stood on the corner watching them.

Jack's skin crawled at the feeling engendered by this maggot-man as he named him, and they picked up their step back to Royal.

Vic had to check with the lab and stopped at her apartment. They stood at the foot of the stairs. Jack pretended not to notice the tears welling in her eyes. Just before she slammed the door behind her, she said, with a poorly suppressed sneer, "Your man Cabal is not going to call."

Jack smiled slightly at her unintentional rhyme. "Not with what just went down," he said, moving up the stair.

Jack closed the door behind him and felt a pain in his chest. It was something like grief. He wanted to go to Europe more than anything, but now the equation had other factors. What about Vic? How can she fit in to the old plans to "do" Europe. He had never thought of bringing anyone along, and this was all entirely too much to deal with.

I need a drink, bad, Jack thought. But first he went to his office.

It was nearly three. Jack quickly showered, shaved, changed clothes and packed everything he could in his ragged suitcases. He called Sam Leviathon, whom the Quarterites called Bluto, and told Sam's voicemail about the case and that he was sending him a letter all about it. He also asked him to sell his office stuff if he was gone. Jack hastily typed out a letter that succinctly explained what had happened, giving instructions on the case, including the location of the original manuscript in the secret compartment.

He ran to the corner and dropped two letters into the mail slot, one to Sam and the other to Baton Rouge maverick lawyer, Don O'Donovan, who, with Sam, would take the case and run with it regardless of the names involved. He also typed a set of instructions on what to do with his guns and other memorabilia to Estelle, who would box them up and send them to his parents in northern Louisiana. Finally, he was set.

Jack had finished all he had to do and for the first time in two hours he thought of Vic. It hit him like a hammer. If Cabal was going to follow through, he would be leaving any moment for the life of his dreams. But would it be? Vic would be back in New Orleans with Mr. America, and Jack couldn't abide the thought.

He took a fifth of Glenfiddich he had been keeping for a special occasion. This was a combination celebration and calamity. So the occasion was special. Maybe the smooth as silk scotch would help him through.

He took a final look at his office, leaving everything just as it was, in a big mess. He sipped the mellow scotch straight as he sat at the window looking out on Royal Street. His heart jumped in his throat each time a taxi slowed in front.

At six the phone hadn't rung, and he drank in observance to it not ringing. At six thirty he paced in front of the window, drinking to the world kissing his ass. At seven he was singing Waltzing Matilda with an Irish brogue and toasting the tourists and traffic passing in front of the window. At eight Vic found him drunk as a lord.

❦

Vic held up the nearly empty bottle. "Good stuff you're drinking, Jack." She poured herself a glass and pulled as chair up alongside him; he was bleary eyed and having difficulty talking.

"You's right, it's bullshit," he slurred.

He fumbled in his shirt pocket. His pack of Picayunes was empty. He wadded the rumpled pack into a ball and threw it at the window. He dug in the ash tray for butt, and finding one that showed promise, singed the ends of his eyelashes trying to light the short stub. "Fuck'emsumbitches," he muttered.

The phone rang. Jack tried to stand, but stumbled over a low table. Vic gently pushed him back into the chair. "You sit right there," she ordered.

"He's not available right now. Can I take a message?" Vic listened intently for a few moments, wrote something on a pad by the phone, then said, "Leave a message and I'll get it to him. Who, me? I am, ah, just straightening things up around here." She hung up.

"Straighten up? Whash you mean, straighten up?" Jack squinted to get Vic in focus.

"Just what I said. You're a mess." She handed the written message to Jack.

Though Vic's handwriting was small block lettering, the print swam before Jack's eyes, and after trying to read it, he finally handed it back. "You read."

"Before doing anything on your federal complaint, call me. We need to talk: 852-9966. Clancy Sessums."

"Shesshums? Sheriff?"

"The same."

"Hells bells. I just shued the shumbitch."

"I think you better sober up before you do anything. C'mon, let me help."

Vic pulled Jack from the chair and pushed him up the winding stair to his apartment. Smiling all the while, she removed his tie and coat and made him lie

162

down. Jack mumbled about the room moving around, how he knew all along the deal was bullshit, and he really didn't expect to go in the first place.

Jack opened his eyes to see Vic smiling down at him. She pressed her hand over her mouth, and her eyes brimmed with tears.

"Whassamatter?" Jack asked.

"Nothing. Nothing at all is the matter, now."

He closed his eyes, and just as he was dropping into a dead sleep, he heard his door close and Vic's unrestrained whoop as she danced down the stairs.

Day Seven

The sun had been up for three hours when Jack opened his eyes to be greeted by a blinding hangover. He was never able to drink large quantities of alcohol without being a basket case the next day. After several cups of strong coffee and a cold shower, he found the note in Vic's handwriting on his coffee table.

Jack thought of the note for a long time, wondering what the sheriff personally would want from him. He expected to hear from a lawyer first, and then a response would usually be filed denying the allegations of the complaint and the slow waltz toward the courtroom would begin.

But here, the defendant himself had called, and this man was no stranger to the way things worked. The sheriff of any parish, and particularly Orleans Parish, had power not unlike an absolute monarch over his subjects and vassals.

Rhonda, Jack's part-time secretary raised her eyebrows as he came in looking pale and in pain. Managing a sheepish grin, he said, "Had a little scotch last night." She nodded knowingly, and went back to work on her nails.

The Times-Picayune was on his desk. Jack scanned every section to see if there was any reference to the suit he had filed, and found none. He worried about that. The media would normally leap from its kennels like hounds, baying to the whole world that they were on the scent of some sensational excrement, which, real shit or imagined, would arouse the public's sense of smell to red alert. There wasn't the slightest reference to the lawsuit or the murder.

Hell, if he called me, I can call him.

Jack was put through to the sheriff immediately. "Mr. Chandler, I would appreciate your taking no action on your suit until we have had a chance to talk."

"What do we have to talk about, Sheriff?"

"Well, we shouldn't use the phone. Can you meet me somewhere so we can talk, just us two?"

"I don't know, Sheriff. Usually there's an attorney somewhere in the woodpile who calls me rather than the defendant himself. I feel strange with this. Extraordinary."

163

"You and your suit are both extraordinary, Mr. Chandler."

"Yeah. That's what I mean. The whole damned thing is out of the ordinary," Jack said, holding his hands over his eyes and squinting against the shaft of morning light streaming through the window.

"It would be beneficial."

"Beneficial?"

"Let's leave it at that," the sheriff said quietly. "I have something of benefit to you and your client that may make this whole thing painless."

"I'm all for avoidin' pain," Jack said, knuckling his temporal to stop the lightning bolts from jabbing the back of his eyeballs.

"Meet you at noon at the carousel at City Park."

"Alone?"

"Alone." Jack agreed.

After hanging up, he leaned back in his squeaky old wooden swivel chair and considered the situation. "Damn, I wish I had somebody to talk to about this," he said out loud.

"Did you say something, Jack?" The secretary asked, pausing between desultory strokes of her nail file.

"Never mind. I gotta meet somebody at the carousel at City Park in a little over an hour. Do I have any calls?" "As a matter of fact, you have three. One from Sheriff Sessums, one from Estelle, and another from a girl who said it was from Judy of Montegut."

Jack smiled as the image of a hot young Cajun girl whose blatant sexuality and open promise during that windswept night in Nookie's camper filled his mind. It may be a message from her dad about the boat. "Rhonda, call this Judy person and find out what she wants."

"Oh, this Judy person said it wasn't anything important. She said, 'The subject was still was open to discussion,' whatever that means," Rhonda said, lifting her eyebrows twice, and then giving Jack a wan, knowing smile.

Jack shook his head and thought, *I don't think I'll call her back. Just trouble.*

He called Vic's number.

"I got your note."

"Good, I thought you'd find it. How you feeling?"

"Like shit. Sheriff wants to meet."

"What about?"

"Damfino, but I'm gonna find out. Meetin' him at the carousel at city park. My cell'll be on. Shouldn't take long."

"Jack, be careful. This is a bad man to let all this happen. Don't trust anything he says."

"Not to worry. I won't be alone."

"Who's going with you?"

"My echo, my shadow, and me. We three. We bad!"

"Jack! Stop it. You're making no sense."

"Maybe not, but I'll call you back in a bit and let you know what happened.

He called Estelle and told her he had filed suit and she could come by and pick up a copy of the petition. He didn't say anything about meeting the sheriff.

Jack thought the serene quiet in the big live-oak filled park was ethereal, almost eerie, as if under some spell that somehow dampened the sounds of the busy boulevard just outside. Jack mused that there was a sprite who ruled the park and brooked no outside nonsense, who blanketed the wandering bayous, the swans and geese, the wide green areas and live oak groves with the peace known before the rude advent of man.

The park attendants had stacked huge piles of limbs blown from the grand old oaks in the open areas. Several immense century year old, moss clad oaks lay crumpled on the ground, their big muddy roots clawing the air. Acorns, leaves and small twigs covered every inch of the ground, and the reeds along the edges of the ponds were flattened.

The New Orleans City Park had kiddie rides and a huge old- fashioned carousel with elaborately carved horses and loud tinny music. Jack could hear its thumping drum and distinct chiming rhythm as he walked under the old live oaks toward kiddieland. They had wasted no time in getting it up and running.

It was the middle of the week, a school day, and the park was nearly empty. Only a few pre-school age children were on the rides as their parents or governesses crooned or languished nearby. There was only one single adult male in the area, and from the casual confidence exuding from this man, Jack knew it was Sessums.

Before they came together, Jack felt something inside move in protest, a low growl only he could hear caused the muscles of his throat to vibrate quietly. They shook hands and introduced themselves. Sessums was a balding, short man. He wore a white linen suit and white oxfords, and had the manners and bearing of a courtly gentleman of the old South.

"I apologize for putting you to this trouble, Mr. Chandler," he said with an easy smile and what Jack thought of as borne of sincere honesty. We need to talk in private. I hope I am not inconveniencing you."

Jack wasn't prepared for this. He could read most men in power, for they were usually forceful or incredibly smooth in a studied, deliberate way, but this man was completely effortless and could pass for a gentle, affable, country doctor.

Jack said nothing, it was Sessums' party.

Sessums' gave an easy smile. "Would you like to sit?" The sheriff inclined his head toward a park bench down the sidewalk.

Sessums sat, crossed his legs, and turned to Jack in a confidential manner. "I initiated this little meeting, so I will get directly to the point. I know a little about you. Of course, we have means of knowing that kind of thing. You have no record except some parking tickets and once you ran a red at Carondelet and Louisiana. You are clean—and a decent kind of man. I think I can talk to you honestly without the interference of anything you have to hide. You are straight and to the point, and I like that in a man. You have done a remarkable thing in this case, and I think you intend to follow through with no motivation except that of righting a wrong. And a wrong was done. A horrible wrong. The buck stops here—at me. I know you will have difficulty in believing this, but I knew nothing of this. I am shocked, to say the least."

Jack lit a Picayune and tried to figure where this was going, having a hard time not believing this apparently guileless man who dealt regularly with the worst of humanity in one of the largest cities in the United States, a man who dined on Louisiana politics daily, a-la-carte. It didn't add up. But there was a grumbling in his throat and an incipient wildness growing in his chest he couldn't check.

Sessums continued. "I've talked to the DA, and to Charlie Leone, and as you know as an experienced attorney, we should be able to resolve this matter quickly."

"How?"

"You make a suggestion. Some resolution that would bring this entire matter to a close, muzzled, with no public mention as to how it was done."

Jack actually growled, and tried to suppress the rising within at this velvet trap being spread by this velvet salesman. "Sheriff, if you're talking about a settlement, there are lots of other kids whose lives have been ruined by those sons-of-bitches, and I don't think any money settlement for one little raped and murdered girl is going to handle the rest without getting into the whole picture."

Sessums looked at Jack with what seemed to be honest understanding and he said softly, "Are you going to right all of the wrongs of the world?"

"I sure as hell would like to right this one, and it's a big one with lots of similar wrongs that all need airing."

"Yes, I know," Sessums said in his quiet way. "And you can make a lot of noise, and with the evidence you have, you could win one and maybe two or three—but only if Bormann was available to testify. If not, then you only have a case against me for one death—one horrible death for sure, but only one case. Destrehan, Parker and Bosco are now retired, as it were, through your good services, and there is no one else."

"What do you mean, there is no one else? There's Bormann."

Sessums almost smiled as he said, "Bormann, your prime and only witness, took his own life last night at Elmwood Plantation Sanitarium. You are going to have a very difficult time with your case, Mr. Chandler."

Jack's heart stopped. The vital witness. The case for little James, Tyrone, Dawn and all the rest depended on Bormann's testimony. Gone! Probably murdered. Without Bormann, the manuscript would be inadmissible as hearsay, and the only case would indeed be against the sheriff's department. Ernie Hotchkiss, the little homo shrink, would take the fifth and slide. Sessums would duck and avoid the bullet by professing innocence.

Sessums got the reaction he expected–Jack was stunned. "You can hammer on me, Mr. Chandler, for I am ultimately responsible for the operation of the detention facilities. You and the press can make a huge deal of this, and you will be smothered in calls from ex-cons who claim they have been abused. Is that what you want? I don't think you want to start out your practice like that.

Sessums went on. Jack felt his social veneer crumble. As he listened, growing quieter and more certain. "You have potential, Mr. Chandler, of being a fine, respected attorney with as much political influence as anyone in this state. You may even run for office one day–a high office, if you wanted. But with this legacy, you may not be able to. Of course, if you orchestrated it right, you could dig a few dollars from the mountain of offal you would have to sift through–with your own hands–but is it worth it?"

Jack's head throbbed and his senses reeled at what he was hearing. He hadn't fully thought out what he would be doing if he went ahead–and for sure he would be inundated by calls from the sleazy element of convicts and ex-convicts. He didn't want that. But he still had a big stick that he could use to beat this gentleman over the head with, and possibly unseat him from power in so doing. Sessums knew it. And Sessums knew Jack knew it. But it was as if two people were listening, one was trying to analyze and the other ready to pounce and Jack held on with effort. It took every ounce of restraint to hold the riot within him in check.

Sessums observed Jack's reaction with undisguised pleasure. Thinking he was seeing Jack dissolving in defeat, as he was accustomed, he continued, a wry smile working his thin lips. "Now that Bormann is gone," Sessums continued, "you have only a case against my office, and it's against me. I can and will make it difficult for you, to say the least. I have inhibited the dissemination of this in the press, but there is a limit on how long I can restrain the issuance of it. I will make your life a living hell. I have the power to eliminate you and no questions will be asked, but I also know that someone else will just take your place. So the matter must be remedied swiftly and thoroughly."

Where was this man leading? Sessums was no fool. Was Jack?

Jack didn't respond. The two men sat only two feet apart, looking, without blinking, into the other's eyes.

Sessums always got what he wanted. He was accustomed to unquestioning acquiescence, and he had no doubt that a tete-a-tete with this insignificant little lawyer would resolve the bothersome interlude.

"I suggest you entertain a reasonable settlement."

"What did you say?" Jack asked incredulously, as if he hadn't heard Sessums the first time. Somehow Sessum's face and words melded with Jack's image of Cabal's face and honied words and he felt a sense of deja vu over and above his rising disdain.

"I said, a reasonable settlement."

"What're you talkin' about?" Jack asked.

"Money. Money, Chandler. The thing that makes the world go round and what you don't have much of. You have $3,532.98 in savings and $334.57 in your office checking account at Hibernia National Bank. You've settled cases before. This is just another case. It doesn't involve you personally. These people are insignificant—and black. Settle it and move on. You're going places. I could use a sharp cookie like you on my staff if you want a job with lots of perks."

Jack's stomach churned and the headache returned like the winds of Aurora, now blowing harder from the opposite direction.

Jack thought of Sessums as a Chess Grandmaster quietly saying "Check," knowing that there was no escape for the king.

"I guess Mourier walks. You walk, too?"

Sessums nodded, his lips turning up in a restrained smile of victory.

Jack hadn't expected this. As a matter of fact, he hadn't known what to expect. And until this moment, he hadn't known where he was going. He was at another crossroad. He could easily end this and have some money for the first time in his life. He felt what seemed like a rising tide within him he knew he couldn't hold back much longer.

Destrehan, Parker and Bosco got their reward, and properly. But perhaps the worst of the lot stood right before Jack, unpunished and probably unpunishable. Sessums had created and continued the climate for these unspeakable crimes. Through Sessums' machinations and Mourier's money, they would all walk. What was this all about? Had it really all just been about money?

Jack could hold on no longer. A wild, exultant feeling of power surged through him and a sound came from his lips he thought was derisive laughter.

Resting Lynx opened his slitted eyes and looked at Sessums.

"No, damn you," he hissed.

Sessums leaned back, defensively holding up his hands at the looming image and spitting cry of a big cat.

Sessums regained his composure. "You little son-of-a-bitch, I'll crush you before you can get started. You don't know what you are dealing with."

Jack smiled and actually growled, "And you don't know what you are dealing with."

Sessums backed away from this wild man who moments before had seemed to be uncertain and faltering. This was something outside of his experience.

"You're insane," Sessums said, spinning around and rushing to his sheriff's unit.

Jack's spirit soared. Several nursery school children passed, herded by their teachers. The children smiled at Jack and the teachers frowned, quickly ushering their little charges away from this strange man standing in the park grinning at nothing.

Jack gradually returned to mother earth and began to think of his next step. He figured Sessums was already moving, probably on his cell phone, to do something to head him off. He can put me in jail for something and try to put me out of commission. Better get some help. Maybe a junk yard dog. Time to call Sam Leviathon, he's as mean as they come.

Jack punched in Sam's office number on his cell phone.

"Tell him it's Jack Chandler with a crisis."

A moment later, an older man answered. "Yeah, Jack, what's the crisis?"

"Sam, I'm into some deep shit and I'll probably need some help, personally. It's right down your alley. May not mean any money, but there will be lots of ass kicking, maybe yours, surely mine."

Leviathon laughed, and said, "Jack, you sure got a way of stirrin' my interest. Go on, you know what I like."

Jack started at the beginning, interrupted only by a few "damns," and "oh, shits," from Sam.

"When you said deep shit, you weren't shittin'," Sam laughed a big belly laugh. "Realistically, you've filed a civil case asking for money damages–that's the only thing you could do. You can't make the DA or Leone bring criminal charges if they don't want to. If you can prove what you say, there's a chance of some money damages, but Sessums' gonna make it hell to get it."

"Sam, I swear I never thought much about money. It was just something out there. I don't have any idea what a court would award–never thought much about it."

"Waal," Sam drawled, "a Federal jury's drawn from the silk stockin' crowd in Covington and uptown, the Klan types in Jefferson Parish, as well as from the broke dicks in the Irish Channel and the projects. And most of 'em are gonna be white, and your clients ain't. I doubt if a jury's gonna award a helluva lot unless you really get em' fired up at Sessums. From what you say, you got enough matches to start a fire, but what's the life of your little black girl worth to a bunch of white blueblood Catholics and Redneck Protestants? You know as much as I do. Maybe a lot, probably nothin'."

"Sam, I thought I knew all I needed to know about Sessums. What do you know?"

"Mainly scuttlebutt. Bad to the bone, to hear tell of it. He was a deputy for Leander Perez's Gestapo heirs down in Plaquemines Parish before he came to New Orleans. You know Perez?"

"Yeah, Perez ran Plaquemines Parish like Hitler ran the Third Reich."

"You bet," Sam grunted. "When Sessums moved to New Orleans, he wormed his way up the ranks by settin' one guy against another by lies, blackmail, buyin' whores, or whatever was needed to move up another notch. The slick, bad cop who never walked a beat or made an arrest. All crooked, political shit."

"He's smooth, that's for sure."

"All his opponents dropped out for some reason. Probably extortion or payoffs, and finally he spent a fortune on a very dirty campaign for Sheriff against his ex-boss. Nobody really knows where all that T.V. and walkin' money came from."

"I knew most of that, except the part about where he got his money. Somebody with money is in this deal. What the hell have I got myself into?" Jack said.

"Jack, this could go pretty deep. You gotta figure a way out."

"I don't see any way out at this point," Jack said. "I started rollin' downhill on this damn thing and now I can't stop. Will you stand by if things get hot?"

"Hell yeah, Jack. You know I like a good fight. Call me at home if things get rough; I'm around the corner. You got my number."

"Okay, Sam, bombs away."

"Yeah, you crazy bastard, bombs away yourself."

Jack hung up and counted the change left in his pocket. Just enough to catch a taxi back home. As Jack waited for his ride, he thought about Sam Leviathon.

Nearly seventy, six-feet-four, in top shape, weighing in at over three hundred, Sam was well named. Born and raised in Punkin Center, a tiny, Anglo Saxon settlement north of New Orleans, he'd joined the Marines in the fifties, serving as a first sergeant in Vietnam.

A war correspondent took a photograph of Sam that appeared in Time Magazine. A huge, dirt streaked grinning marine was pictured with arms outspread, holding two live enemy soldiers high in the air by the seats of their baggy pants. The picture was captioned, "Marine at work."

After Vietnam, Sam played bass in a Quarter jazz band at night. During the day he taught history and coached football for Warren Easton, the toughest high school in the city. He returned from work late one night, and not having any identification with him, was arrested for vagrancy by a couple of too-ambitious hot-dog cops. The Marine sergeant in Sam awakened during the confrontation and two of New Orleans finest went to the hospital. Sam spent several days in the city jail without bail or able to call for help. He resolved, during his tenure in the vermin infested cell with miscreants and perverts, that he would become a lawyer and right the wrongs of the world. He worked his way through Loyola Law School in night school, becoming the defender of the defenseless and the most ruthless and capable criminal lawyer in the city.

After a near physical altercation involving a divorce case, when Sam and Jack represented opposite parties, they became good friends. They played chess, discussed philosophy, chased women and got drunk–always got drunk. Their Quarter friends called them Popeye and Bluto because they acted like sailors on shore leave when they made a good fee.

Jack called Vic and started the two remaining stolen steaks sizzling on the little hibachi stove on the balcony. Jack told her about the meeting with Sessums and his talk with Sam.

"Sam's ready to move if Sessums tries anything," Jack said. The way I figure it, Sessums'll try to block the litigation. He's gotta smear me and the case, and all I have is you, Nookie, Ernie, and Jester with the evidence he's sending in, and a dead Bormann. Dawn's body should be safe somewhere; I'm sure Jester has it in safekeeping."

Vic smiled and said, "Sam's probably drooling for the chance to jump into this. He says he is the biggest redneck in the Quarter."

"Yeah, he's right about that."

Vic's brow furrowed. She asked, "Jack, just what is a redneck?"

Jack chuckled, took a pull from his Dixie and said, "Sam defines a redneck as an Anglo-Saxon with a pioneer spirit, and Sam definitely has a pioneer spirit."

They both laughed at how Sam fit the definition perfectly. They were quiet for a long time, absorbing the afternoon, listening to the tourists walking on the street beneath them. Jack smiled at the hoots of riverboats and ferries, and the lonely wail of a clarinet threading its way through the narrow streets.

"What's going to happen, Jack?"

Jack closed his eyes, the remnants of his hangover still gently throbbing behind his eyes.

"I dunno," he said, "All I know is I'm goin' with the case. That's all I can do. Bormann's manuscript can't be used as evidence without someone to identify it. It's hearsay. I may be able to get Ernie to identify it, but a smart defense lawyer can make it tough to get in evidence. Ernie'll probably clam up anyway. There's Bormann's video confession, but it'll be hearsay too and I guarantee politics'll prevail and a judge won't let it in."

"What about Jester's testimony? And mine?"

"That'll cinch the rape and murder. It's worth a judgment against the sheriff's office, but it won't prove who did it."

The phone rang. Jack thought it sounded like someone screaming.

"Jack. They busted into my place and stole her and all of the studies!"

"Who is this? Jester?"

"Yeah. It's me. The bastards broke in and knocked me colder'n a door-nail. When I came to, my lab was trashed, she was gone, all the stuff was taken—includin' the pictures, negatives, notes and videos, and they busted my Hasselblad."

"When did it happen?"

"Bout midnight. I was finishin' up the summary so I could send everything off at once when they broke in. Gave me a knockout injection that lasted for hours. Wrecked my place. Had that Hasselblad for 30 years. Sons-of-bitches! Place crawlin' with cops. Lab looks like a boiler room with all the black dust they smeared everywhere checking for prints. Found nothin'. They were wearin' gloves."

"Any clues?"

"Nothin'. Pros. Somebody's got some high-powered connections to pull this off."

"What you gonna do?"

"I want their ass for sure now! When I realized there was nothin' I could do in Mobile sittin' around with my thumb up my ass, I headed to see you and Vic. I'm on my cell on the outskirts of the Quarter—just checkin' to see if you're in. See you in a minute."

Jack told Vic what Jester had said and her expression was mixed horror and fear. "What're we dealing with, Jack?"

"Sessums. And we ain't through yet. I'm callin' Sam."

Jack dialed a number and explained the situation.

He hung up and said, "He lives a block down the street. He's comin' right over."

Sam huffed up the stairs and looked like a combination of Paul Bunyan and the Pillsbury Doughboy standing in the doorway.

Sam, still puffing, said, "I made it!"

Jack handed him a beer and Sam said, "I did some checkin' after you called the first time. One of my contacts tells me that Sessums has a big piece in the Winner's Keepers casino in Biloxi and in Harrahs here, and in Grin and Bare It, the gentlemen's club with the naked waitresses."

"Never been there," Jack said. "See no reason for a hungry man to go to a steak house if he doesn't have any money."

"There's fancy little rent-by-the-hour apartments on the second and third floor, they tell me." Sam said, lifting his eyebrows in the fashion of Groucho Marx.

"Why, Sam," Vic chided, "you don't mean you had to go to a place like that?"

"Didn't have to. Just curious. Not a bad bang for the buck," he said, shrugging his big shoulders, looking at Vic with a foolish look on his face.

Vic shook her head and raised her big brown eyes to the ceiling. "I'll never understand men if I live to be a hundred."

Sam's leer dissolved and he turned to Jack. "You opened up a can of worms, little buddy. There's no tellin' what that mean bastard has up his sleeve. I bet he thinks he can get rid of the case by gettin' rid of you. Shows how paranoid he really is."

A cherry red Corvette blew its horn beneath the balcony, and Vic said, "That's Jester, I'll let him in."

She ran downstairs and in a minute she led Jester in, his round face florid from the rapid walk up the stair.

Jester waved his short arms as he animatedly described the masked men who broke in and knocked him out.

Vic asked, "You didn't save anything?"

"Not a damned thing! You know how I am, Victoria. It's gotta be done right, and it was a pretty big package–I needed to get the autopsy report transcribed and pictures developed and all," he said, with a trace of guilt.

"Don't feel bad," Vic said, touching his arm. "You did a great job, and it was less than eighteen hours from the time we left when they hit you."

The wailing of police sirens several blocks away shattered the peace of the Quarter. Everyone became very still as the oscillating howling came closer, drowning out all other sounds or thoughts. Three sheriff units with red and blue lights blazing on top, followed by a white van, screamed around the corner and screeched to a stop just below the balcony.

There was fear in Vic's eyes.

Jack smiled wanly. "It's beginning. Advice, Sam?"

Sam's eyes twinkled. "Is this the fun you were talkin' about?"

Chapter 17

Jack watched the busy scene below as Sam, Vic and Jester backed through the apartment door. Twelve deputies in black SWAT protective gear sprang out of the police units, bristling with weapons. Several carried riot shotguns and two had tear gas rifles. Jack noticed that "Elmwood Plantation Rest Home" was printed in small letters on the side of a van. Three muscular men in white coats stood outside of the van while the officers positioned themselves defensively behind the police units.

Jack stood in full view on the balcony with his hands in the air, and said, "Up here."

The muzzle of every gun swung upward and trained on Jack as he grinned down at the small army below.

"That's him," one cried. "He's armed!"

Jack saw one of the officers stiffen. Jack dropped to the floor of the balcony. A blast thundered down in the little canyon of buildings on Royal Street and the rain gutter on the building behind Jack disintegrated, swinging down with a dull clang.

"I'm not armed, you idiots," Jack screamed.

"Don't believe him, he's a cop killer," one screamed. "This un's a homicidal maniac."

Jack scrambled back into the apartment as a wild melee of shotgun fire blasted through the balcony floor where he had lain moments before. Still on his hands and knees, he shoved the door to the apartment closed just as a tear gas canister thumped against its glass pane. Saffron smoke gushed from the canister, creating a yellow screen against the plate glass window. Several other canisters lobbed over the balcony and crashed against the glass door. Fracture-lines and crazing appeared in the glass, but it didn't shatter and no gas entered the room.

The gunfire stopped as the front entrance door of the apartment building crashed in. Deputies swarmed up the steps and approached Jack's sliding door.

A big grin spread over Sam's wide features. "This *is* the fun you were talkin' about, Jack."

"We can only hope," Jack said, as he pulled open a drawer to a table by the sofa and removed a pair of handcuffs. He snapped one on his wrist and the other on Sam's. Momentarily baffled, Sam frowned, and then his face widened in a big grin when he realized what Jack was doing. Sam opened the door to keep it from being smashed in by the charging SWAT team.

A squad of grim faced men stopped in their tracks as they came to Jack's door and found the huge Sam Leviathon blocking the door with his hands in the air, Jack's arm dragged up held in place by the cuffs. A dozen men bearing shotguns, assault rifles and tear gas launchers crowded around the door, pointing their weapons at Sam over each other's shoulders.

"Ya'll goin' to a party, boys?" Sam asked, grinning down at the tallest of the officers.

A pinched-faced little Sergeant pushed his way through the crowd of deputies and screamed in the stilted staccato voice of command he had learned at the academy, "Move out of the way or we will have to remove you. We have orders to shoot to kill Jack Chandler if he resists arrest for murder of two sheriff's deputies and one citizen, Warner Bosco."

"I'm Mr. Chandler's attorney, and I have advised him to turn himself in peacefully, allow himself to be processed, booked and given bail."

"We are ordered either carry the subject's body to the morgue or his living person to Elmwood for psychiatric evaluation and observation."

"Sorry, boys," Sam said, shaking their shackled arms. "This is a package deal. You take both of us to the station together and properly book him in, or you drag my carcass with him, and that's nearly a quarter ton of dead meat."

The scowling sergeant whipped out his cell phone, pressed a few numbers, and explained the situation to his senior. The rest of the team continued scowling and pointing the dozen gun barrels directly at the Jack and Sam, who stood grinning in the doorway.

"Gonna book both of you," the sergeant sneered after snappily placing the phone back into its holster.

Sam asked, "What are you arresting me for?"

"Resisting. Obstructin'."

"Here's my hand—put the cuffs on. Am I resisting? And am I obstructing you in arresting my client? I offered to bring him in peacefully. There are many witnesses here."

There were some sniggers from the SWAT team at that. "What witnesses?"

"If your witnesses won't come forward, then we have two more," Sam said.

The sergeant jerked his head around and asked, "Who?"

"Doctor Victoria Keens-Dennison and Doctor Jester McConothy," Jack said, moving aside to allow the group to view Vic and Jester standing just beyond the door.

Both Vic and Jester waved cheerily at the SWAT captain and his troops. "We heard it all, sergeant," Vic said. "Arrest us, too. We have been harboring these two vicious criminals you're arresting."

The sergeant looked stunned. There were witnesses! Doctors at that! The men with guns began to glance at their sergeant for guidance, who was obviously surprised at the unfolding of unexpected events. His face reflected there was no doubt at the beginning of this excursion that cop-killer Chandler was morgue material. Jack knew this little martinet's orders left much to his discretion, and it was clear he wanted to take no prisoners.

"If you are gonna arrest us," Sam said, "please get on with the program. Of course, I will charge you personally for false arrest, malicious prosecution and kidnapping and then sue you personally for civil damages. So take me and my client to the station either as lawyer and client or as your prisoners both under charge."

The sergeant's face flushed beet red at Sam's threat.

A decision had to be made. The sergeant said, trembling in exasperation, "All right, both of you come with me. I'll decide which one on the way Mr. Butt-in Lawyer."

With two fingers, Sam extracted a business card from his shirt pocket and handed it to the captain. "My card."

The sergeant dropped it like it was a hot coal. He shouted at the SWAT team still standing with guns poised like a puffed up porcupine. "Carry this prisoner to bookin'. Take his lawyer, too!"

Jack grinned at Vic and Jester as the shackled pair was led away. "Come down to the station and drive Sam back," Jack said. "I may not come back with you. I expect they won't set bond very quickly, and when they do, it's gonna be sky high."

"Oh yes, they'll set bond," Sam said. "They got to. We can't let 'em keep you in there overnight. You won't last."

The parade of police cars, sanitarium van and Vic in Jester's corvette, convoyed to the courthouse. Jack and Sam, still shackled together, were led to the booking desk where Jack was ordered to unlock the cuffs.

"I don't have a key," Jack said, grinning.

"You son-of-a-bitch," the sergeant whispered, inclining his head toward a door leading to the prison holding cells "you're gonna learn some respect when I get you in there."

Jack asked, "What am I charged with?"

The sergeant at the desk said, "Murder of Leroy Destrehan, Major Parker, Warner Bosco—and Negrofeelya."

"Ah, that's necrophelia." Jack corrected, "Do you know what that means?"

"Grabassin' a black person, you idiot."

Sam and Jack laughed and Sam said, "Close enough."

"Where is the bail bond officer?" Sam asked.

"Ain't here," the sergeant said.

"Then who is duty judge?"

"Judge Maus," the sergeant grinned, showing large blunt teeth.

"The worst one of all," Sam moaned, "Mickey Maus. Case of chronic constipation, dyspepsia and ulcers. Joy to the world."

Vic and Jester, having finally found a parking place, rushed in. "How much is the bond?" They both asked together.

"Not fixed yet," Sam said. "I'm gonna call the judge and get him to set it now."

At that moment, Sheriff Sessums walked into the room, the placid, satisfied look of the Southern aristocratic gentleman never leaving his face. The other sheriff's officers stood back in shock as the high sheriff himself put in an unannounced appearance.

"Ah, sir," the arresting sergeant said, "we apprehended the subject as ordered, sir."

Sessums nodded. "Yes, I see. I wanted to see Mr. Chandler after his arrest, but I hear that he has come together with his attorney, Mr. Leviathon."

Sam reached for the phone, ignoring Sessums. He said, "I'm callin' the duty judge to set the bond."

Sessums smiled his bland smile. "Why don't you do that, counsel?"

In a moment, Sam had the Judge on the phone. "Judge? Sam Leviathon here. Jack Chandler has been arrested and I am here to make sure that bond is set for him."

"You already know about it? You already set the bond? Well, ah, that's great!"

Sam paused, and scowled, and then held the receiver out from him and looked at it as he hung up.

"Well?" Vic asked.

"Two million dollars. A bail bondsman would charge ten percent to post that kind of bond, and Jack and I don't have anything like that. We sure as hell don't know where to get the whole amount."

Sessums lips worked into a half smile and he winked at Jack. "Tsk tsk," he said, shaking his head slowly. "Chandler, that's a lot of bond. Looks like you are my tenant. Welcome to Parish Prison."

"Hold on there, boy," Jester said, bellying up to Sessums and talking right in his face.

"Who are you?"

"I'm Doctor Jester McConothy and this here's Dr. Victoria-Keens Dennison, pathologist at Tulane Medical Center. We did an autopsy on that little girl. She was raped and murdered."

Sessums blinked, but his expression didn't change and he didn't move back as Jester pushed his humpty-dumpty belly against him.

"I have no knowledge or proof of that. Where is your report?"

"I think you know all about it, Sheriff. So me and Dr. Victoria here are gonna do you a big favor. You keep that cell for a real criminal. I'm gonna post the bond!"

Sessums' mouth fell open.

"It's gonna thin out my account pretty much, but I'm gonna write a check on my money market account so you can't get your hands on this boy and give him time to do what he has to do."

Jester wrote a check for two million and handed it to the sheriff.

"I want a receipt, sheriff. And I want to tell you one thing before we leave here. I probably wouldn't have been here to do this for Jack except for the fact that I want the son-of-a-bitch who stole Dawn's body and trashed my lab to pay. They busted my big Hasselblad, the bastards!"

Sessums said, with his condescending look, "I can't accept a check."

"Wa'al alright then,' Jester barked in Sessums' face. "I'll call my broker and he'll be right over with the cash you little pipsqueak."

Sessums flushed, gripping Jester's check so tightly that his knuckles were white.

"You're gonna cause us all to stay here till he comes, and you bet he'll have a cashier's check that is good as cash. You talk to the head man at Howard Weil."

Jester quickly punched some numbers on his little hand-held cellular phone and said, "Bernie? Jester McConothy. Tell this man if I have any money on account, and if you can bring it all over to Parish Prison for bail."

There was a pause, and Jester snorted, "Hell no. It ain't for me. For a friend."

Jester handed the phone to the Sessums. After a moment, Sessums handed the phone back to Jester, scrawled out a receipt, and handed it to Jester, saying nothing."Mr. Chandler," Sessums practically hissed, "I didn't count on you having such affluent friends. Maybe we should have set the bond higher." He paused, and said thoughtfully, "But then, maybe that would have posted it too. Nonetheless, this is just round one of as many rounds as I choose, or you choose, I should say. You still have these charges against you, and I'll hang you in the papers and convict you in the court. Nobody'll touch you in this city—you'll be a leper—an untouchable."

A faint smile pulled at Jack's lips. He stood perfectly still and listened to Sessum's speech. When Sessums ran down, he whispered right into the sheriff's face, his pupils seeming to change to vertical slits, "I land on my feet. You won't survive this case.

You better run and hide because you're toast." Jack continued to stare at Sessums for a long moment.

Sessums seemed to hold his breath, his eyes becoming wider. Jack then smiled, and with his free hand, made a motion like a magician and the key to the cuffs appeared between his fingers. He unlocked them, placed them his pocket, and slowly turned to Vic, both grinning big. Sam pulled Jack's pony tail and Jester punched him on the arm as they walked out of the building.

"The least I can do is treat everybody to dinner." Jack said, "Where do you guys want to go?"

Jester said, "I'm cravin' some oysters. How's about Felix's Oyster Bar on Bourbon?" Everyone agreed.

"Sessums can't make the charges stick," Sam said.

"Yeah, he took a quick shot hopin' he could snuff me before I lucked out again. He's probably not even interested in pursuin' the charges now that I'm out. He lost the first move, and the chance, thanks to you," Jack said, looking at his three good friends.

An eviction notice was stuck on his door with a thumbtack.

The balcony was shot full of holes. Now it would leak for sure, and the sliding glass door to the balcony was shattered.

"I guess I better call my landlord."

"Who's your landlord?" Jester asked.

"A shrink," Vic answered.

Jack dialed a number and said, "Pete? It's Jack. Yeah, I'm out. Got your notice. Sure, I understand. I wouldn't want a maniac livin' in my place either. But are you kickin' me outta my office too? From the way it looks, I seems as though I may not have much business now, but it would give me a place to operate from while I get. . ."

Apparently interrupted mid-sentence, Jack listened to the voice for a long moment and then he said, "Hey, man, don't kick me outta my office. It's gonna be hell findin' a place to store my junk and to restart my practice."

Jack pinched his lips as he listened to the man's voice, which proceeded to tell him that he was a paranoid schizophrenic with dementia praecox and a twist of delusional grandeur, a manic depressive, and several other psychiatric diagnosi thrown in for good measure.

"By any chance, Herr Docteur," Jack said snidely, "do you have any connection with the New Orleans Mental Health Clinic?"

There was a lengthy pause and the answer was yes, as if it was a question rather than an answer.

"And did Sheriff Sessums give you a little call telling you that it would be lots of fun just to kick old Jack out in the street?"

The voice turned cold and said, "Get out. You have forty-eight hours. If you're not out by then, your belongings will be placed on the street. I'm holding you personally accountable for every bit of the damage to the building. When you leave it, you leave it broom clean and in the exact condition you found it when you moved in. If you don't, I have lawyers who would love to sue you."

"Sue me, sue me, what can you do to me, you fuckin' frootloop, you know I will file a protective order and stop your bullshit. I can stay here as long as I like and we can just take it on to the court of appeals. You better get your lawyer busy because you can't do this as long as my rent is paid and I'm paid up for another month. If you evict me illegally I'll have your next year's salary." Jack said as he slammed the phone down.

"Luck strikes again," he said.

Jester said, moving toward the door. "Let's eat!"

The quartet rolled out into the Quarter streets like four Yankee conventioneers from Milwaukee ready for a party. Jack sucked the warm evening air in, with its cargo of stale beer and cigarettes breathing from the open doors of barrooms, mingled with the rush of jasmine from narrow brick-lined passageways. The jazz bands thumped and wailed down the street.

Smiling, Vic watched Jack, her eyes glistening. She snaked an arm around his and held tight. Their eyes met and Jack's pulse sprinted at the touch. Jack led the troop down Dumaine, turned the corner at Chartres and looked up at the looming spire of the St. Louis Cathedral.

Dozens of artists had set up their easels on the sidewalk alongside of the tall cast iron fence surrounding Jackson Square and in the area directly in front of the great Cathedral. Tourists sat happily on folding chairs as artists did their portraits and caricatures. Other artists painted Quarter and plantation home scenes. Jack smiled up at the balconies on the several floors of the Pontalba House, dripping with fern and overflowing flower boxes hanging over the narrow brick street alongside the park.

The crowds of the summer were still around, undiminished, as if they didn't know vacation was over. The younger tourists were missing, being back in school, but there were increasing groups of Japanese and Europeans wandering about, their cameras snapping everything, including Jack and his entourage.

On the corner of St. Peter and Chartres, a white faced mime tried to escape from an invisible room and a clown juggled flaming brands while riding a tall unicycle on the opposite corner.

Jack marched his troop through the crowds down St. Peters Street. They crossed Royal, sophisticated and sedate with its antique shops and art galleries, the refined and elegant aunt of Bourbon, the raucous blacksheep of the Quarter family of streets.

They turned left on Bourbon, where packs of little black boys tap danced on the sidewalks around hats that collected oddments of change. A one man band sat on a wooden Coca-Cola crate and tooted "Do you know what it means to Miss New Orleans," on his kazoo. Honkytonk pianos thumped and banjos plunked in several bars, and the keening clarinets and trumpets of jazz bands came from every direction.

Bourbon has ten blocks of strip joints, bars, cheap gift shops, ambulating whores and transvestites, packed each night with drunks and cavorting conventioneers. Bourbon is a land of make believe where you can experience riskless degradation—a one time shot at the shoddy and sordid without getting any on you. An ersatz depravity, it's a tiny cosmos of innocuous shadows of sin, where you can smell, taste, feel and walk through the seemingly seamy and wild side and return to Wichita to wink knowingly at friends who can only guess what wickedness you had known in the Big Easy. But real wickedness is available if wanted, for a price.

The barkers held open the doorways so the prancing mares on the little stages could be seen twirling pasties and grinding groins to the thumping rhythm of CD players behind the bar. Occasionally a barker would yell, "Its Popeye and Bluto!" Twice, strippers yelled from the stage at them. At the "Sudden Exposure," Pussy Beaucoup was on stage and sent an extra bump and grind their way.

Vic said, "You two are well known in high places."

Sam and Jack grinned. Jester said, "You all make my life in Mobile look like Sunday School."

They entered Felix's and were greeted by little men in white aprons behind the oyster bar. "Hey Popeye," one said, leaning over the bar, "what's happenin' man? Hear they shot up ya place. You da talk of da town."

"Nothin' to it," Jack said, "I'm fine. Look at me."

The oyster shuckers grinned, and said, "Popeye, you da man!"

They ordered two dozen each, for starters, and frozen mugs of Michelob draft. The oysters were clear, firm and salty.

Vic was hesitant, punching at an oyster with her little fork. "Jack, you know I don't do these. It looks bad, like, like—"

"A lougie?" Sam asked.

"Eek," she said, "yes."

"Can't believe she's squeamish, considerin' the stuff she works with every day," Jack said.

"But that's different," she said, turning her lips down and frowning at the plate of gray lougies.

"Let me show you."

Jack mixed some sauce in the little glass bowl in the center of her plate.

"Simplement. Mixa ze ketchupa and ze little horseradisha, una dasha de le Tabasco et ze Lea and Perrins Worchester saucea avec ze squeeze de ze lemone, stir, and la voila! Dipa ze lougie in ze saucea, puta heema on ze crackier saltina, place heema in ze mousea, and ummm, marvellment!"

As Jack demonstrated the sequence, Sam and Jester followed suit, step-by-step, as in a drill team of oyster eaters, down to the groan of pleasure as the little mollusk dropped to its destiny.

"And, Sam said, "make sure you cross your legs when you swallow him. Like so." He crossed legs and pressed them together tightly.

This brought a laugh from the table next over.

"OK then, I've lived here for years and never did these, but here goes." Vic prepared her oyster, and bravely put the whole assembly in her mouth with her eyes closed. She chewed a moment, and then her eyes popped open and she busily prepared and devoured another, and then another. "Wow. I had no idea! I can't believe I have been missing this all these years!"

The oyster shuckers and several others, including some tourists, witnessed the initiation ceremony. The crowd applauded, held their mugs of beer high and someone said, "To the new convert!"

The shuckers continued shoving trays of oysters on their table until three dozen oysters apiece later, gluttony demonstrated and abated, Jester wiped the crumbs from his whiskers, saying, "Jack, are you scared?"

Jack shrugged, as if the thought hadn't occurred to him. "Not really," he said. "It's funny. A week or so ago, I'd have been scared shitless. But now, it don't matter. I know things'll turn out right, and I don't know what to do next. Goin' with the flow."

"Well, I've seen enough to know you ain't goin' with no flow, Mr. Popeye Chandler," Jester said, half seriously. "I bet you never went with the flow in your life."

Thinking about it for a moment, Jack said, "Guess not. You're right, but lately I don't fight it like I did. Like fightin' the wind. None of the stuff I ever worried about ever happened."

"You are different than you were, Jack," Vic said, looking intently at him. "I can't put my finger on it, but you seem more relaxed than before all this started, and that doesn't make sense."

Jack nodded, thinking of his new awareness and how it began and what it felt like then, and how he still felt the same.

"You've changed, Jack," Vic said, "Do you know that?"

Jack said, "Yeah. You're right. Somethin' happened to me one night when I was at Pointe-au-Chein. I realized I've lived before—in another body."

Vic smiled suddenly. It was like the sun had broken through the clouds. Jester cleared his throat and chuckled.

Sam frowned and said, "Huh?"

"I guess you call it remembering, but it was more, like I had returned to a time and place wearin' skins and havin' long hair. It was like I was there. I had a spear and a sharp bone knife, and I lived alone on the land. I never felt so. . .well, like. . .me; *really me*. I know who I am, and was, and always have been—whether I wear skins or these clothes—it's me. I don't worry any more. I am where I am, and wherever, that's okay. The idea of death doesn't bother me anymore. I'm gonna live forever. I think I've lived forever. Always been me."

"I'll buy that when I see it," Sam said. "Nobody's proved to me there's a damned thing after you die. I don't buy all that heaven or hell stuff—don't make a bit of sense to me."

"Sam," Jester said, "You're mixin' what currently passes for religion with what Jack's talkin' about."

"Yeah, Jack," Sam snorted. "You're different. You always were a cocky bastard, ready to take on the world—now you don't seem to care. There's a right smart of danger about you nowadays."

"You're lucky," Jester said, nibbling on a cracker. "Not everybody gets to experience that, Jack. I remembered somethin' too. That's why I became a doctor—it's what I am."

Jack smiled, his eyes quiet and knowing. "I don't worry any more. I'm ready for anything, even dyin'."

"I'm glad to know you, Jack," Jester said. "I'd be proud to have you along if I ever had to go in the jungle."

"Me too," Vic beamed so brightly at Jack one would think he should melt like butter.

Sam said, "There ain't no doubt, you're different, Jack. But you always had screwy ideas."

Sam, Jester and Vic launched into an intense discussion of life and death and spiritual speculations.

Jack drifted, getting a far-away look, as the other three chattered about their new-found mutual interest of past lives and philosophy. The conversation became a hypnotic drone and the walls of the building fuzzed and disappeared.

He sat cross-legged alongside a log and a small fire. The hide of a bear was stretched on a frame of bent branches in the sun. Chunks of meat hung from leather lines extended above the flames.

Beyond the mountains was a walled city where men went about on the backs of large animals. Their weapons gleamed in the sunlight with edges sharp enough to kill with one swift thrust. He dreamed of these blades and knew he would have to kill for one or break into the city and steal.

Jack blinked the illusion away and blurted out, interrupting the spirited discussion, "That's it!"

The others stopped talking and looked at Jack as if he had gone crazy.

"I know what to do," Jack whispered, his eyes gleaming with excitement. Jack punched a number in his cell phone.

As he waited for it to ring, Jack's attention was drawn to the table near the door. It was the maggot-man with the dead face looking with malevolence directly at Jack. Vic noticed Jack's hesitation and followed his gaze. She caught her breath and tugged at Jack's sleeve.

"Jack, thats the same man. . ."

"Yeah," Jack said, interrupting her, "at Tujaques. Maggot Man."

Sam turned to look at the man and shrugged. "Quarter freak."

Jack handed Vic a hundred and told her to pay the bill. "Order a Dixie to go for everybody."

When Jack looked up, the man was gone. "He's a damned phantom," Jack said to Vic, pointing at the table. She gasped and said, "he was just there a moment ago!"

A familiar voice answered the phone after a few rings.

"Nookie? You busy tonight?"

Chapter 18

As they approached the Marquis de Mandeville, there were a number of people on Jack's balcony.

Jack said, "What the. . ."

Vic put her hand on his arm. "Don't panic. I called Estelle. She brought some friends to help clean up the mess the cops made."

Estelle and Martin beamed as Jack walked in. Julien Freret and Harold LaMarque, the lion and the rhino, stood beside them. The balcony and the roof had been patched, and the sliding doors replaced with new ones. The place looked as good as new.

Martin asked, "Did we do right?"

"Do right! I guess so," Jack said, letting out a long sigh in relief. "I can't thank you all enough."

Martin laid his big hand on Jack's shoulder. You don't have to thank us, Lawyer Jack. We ready to help you do anything. There ain't enough we can do for you."

Jack gave them a quick summary of what had happened, omitting the fact that Dawn's body was missing.

Jack went into the bedroom and returned wearing a pair of black pants and black shirt and sneakers. He had his big skinning knife on his belt and a headlamp he used for hunting.

The phone rang. It was for Estelle.

Her face contorted in horror as she listened. Finally, Jack heard the click as the other party disconnected, and Estelle let the phone drop to her side, staring into space and then at Jack.

Vic touched Estelle on the shoulder and said, "What is it?"

Estelle began to tremble and let out an anguished moan that brought Martin bounding up the stairs. He held her trembling shoulders and shook her gently, "Estelle–Estelle, baby. Whassa matter?"

"Yo' mama called. Said she heard on the T.V. they found Dawn Marie's body in the river–drown. It in the morgue. They been callin' to get me down there to identify– ahh, what's happenin' Lord. Why this? What's happenin?"

Martin's eyes blazed in anger as he held her close.

"What?" Jester nearly shouted. "That's impossible!"

"Oh, my God, my God," Estelle keened.

"Battle stations!" Sam said, reaching for the phone.

Jack looked at his watch. It was nearly midnight. "Martin, this is not true. It's gotta be part of the Sessums' game."

"Yes," Vic said. "Dr. McConothy and I did the autopsy. We verified everything that Jack suspected. He filed the suit against the sheriff."

"I didn't tell you two that Sessums called me out to the park this morning for a discussion. He offered money to settle the case, and I told him to go to hell. This is just part of his scheme to stop me. Jack told the rest about the body being stolen.

Martin erupted, "You mean somebody done stole Dawn Marie?"

Jester nodded slowly. "Broke in my lab, knocked me out, ripped my place apart, stole the documents, pictures, and everything."

Six men and women in addition to Jack, Jester, Sam and Vic gathered around. The room throbbed with frustration and rage. The hate was so palpable that it pulsed like a living thing.

"Now, they're tryin' to knock out the last shred of evidence by sayin' she drowned," Jack said. "There's lots of money and power behind this, Martin. More'n I told you about. They've tried to ice me for days, and so far I've been lucky. The attack on this apartment was supposed to make me fight back so they could kill me, but it didn't work."

"What can we do?" Julian Freret growled.

"Nothin'," Jack said. "I've got another trick up my sleeve, and I'm askin' all of you not to do anything rash, regardless of how angry you are. I don't blame you."

His big nostrils dilating, Martin asked, "We gonna go to the morgue?"

"You're right, but only these doctors and your lawyers should go," Sam said, interrupting. He stood the same height as the three big black men, and standing, he looked them dead in the eye. "We gonna get a court order to allow Drs. McConothy and Vic here to see the body and represent you at the exam. I can legally stop any crap they might come up with."

"We comin'," Julian said. His face held the unequivocal look of intention without reservation.

Martin said, "Yeah! We comin'."

Harold said, "We ain't' sittin' by no mo'."

Sam snapped a nod and looked at Jack. "I'm gonna call Maus and tell him to call the morgue to permit us in immediately—if his mama will put us through."

Sam dialed Maus's home phone, and after many rings, an aged woman answered, apparently annoyed from being wakened at midnight. Maus picked up on the extension line. He was furious. "I'm not duty judge tonight, Mr. Leviathon."

"Judge, all I'm askin' is. . ."

There was a click, followed by a dial tone.

Sam held the phone in his hand and looked at it dumbly. "The little shit hung up on me! They got to him too!"

Jack reached for the phone and dialed Mahoney.

"Judge. Jack Chandler. As usual I got trouble. Need another court order."

"You in jail?"

"No, judge. My two doctor friends who did the autopsy went my bail—two million. You already know the story, nobody murdered Destrehan, Parker or Bosco. It's what you think it is: Sessums is still tryin' to cover his ass. He took his shot and missed again. They wanted to put me in Elmwood, the same place that Bormann supposedly committed suicide. I was next in line till the cavalry came to my rescue."

"What you want from me?"

"Dr. Jester McConothy, the forensic pathologist who did the autopsy, had a break-in. They ripped off his entire file, the report he was submittin', all of his pictures, trashed his lab, and stole the body."

"Busted my Hasselblad," Jester muttered.

"He was one that went my bail," Jack told the Judge. "Now, it's reported they found her body in the river—drowned. They got something at the morgue, Judge, but it's not her. Guess they're hopin' that this'll end the case by sayin' this was Dawn. I need for you to order the coroner or the morgue people at Charity to allow Dr. McConothy and Dr. Victoria Keens-Dennison, Tulane pathologist who assisted in the autopsy, to look at that body tonight."

"Why tonight, Chandler? Can't we do it in the mornin'?"

"Can't wait, Judge. We gotta put a stop to it tonight. I dunno who the duty judge is."

"Well, I been anointed as duty judge this evenin'. That's why I wasn't surprised when the phone rang. The only reason it's me is 'cause there wasn't nobody around. Okay. I'll call. If ya want, I'll sign a order. A call'll do. It better. I'll go down there myself an' kick some ass if they don't let ya in and do it."

"Tell 'em me an' Sam'll be there too," Jack said. "We'll have a power of attorney to authorize us to act for the parents. Can we go right now?"

"Have at it."

"Thanks, judge."

"You're okay, Chandler. But watch ya back."

"Thanks, judge."

When Jack hung up, Sam asked him, "Go?"

"Go."

∾

At half past twelve, two doctors, two lawyers, and three longshoremen walked with grim resolution down a dark side street toward the rear entrance to Charity Hospital. With Vic and Jester on either side, Jack led the way, several yards ahead of Sam and the longshoremen. Jack turned the corner and standing in their path were five sturdy men wearing ski masks and holding baseball bats. They were all in the two fifty weight class, and Jack knew professionals when he saw them. Jack, Vic and Jester stopped in their tracks. Jack waved his hand behind his back to warn Sam and his wrecking crew, who halted just around the corner out of sight.

The masked men slowly approached, smacking their bats in their open palms.

"Gentlemen," Jack shouted to gain momentum, and at the same time to warn those behind, of the menacing quintet, "are you the assholes we're to take apart tonight?"

The men stopped, seeming befuddled for a moment. "No," one said, "you're da asshole gonna take a swim inna rivah."

The others laughed at the clever repartee' of their companion.

"Well, Jack said, "I wanted to make sure, because we have a can of whupass we are just itchin' to open up. I'd like for you to meet some friends who've got the can opener."

Jack stepped to one side and, sweeping his hand in an eloquent gesture, Sam and the gigantic three stepped around the corner. The black men, already boiling with fury, wore terrible grins; Jack saw Sam's eyes dance in anticipation. *Wonderful!* The five holding the bats stepped back at the sight of the three black behemoths, rhino, the tiger, Martin, and a white whale—each with the rage of battle exuding from their pores.

Sam gleefully asked, "Shall we, gentlemen?"

The bellow emitted from that corner could have been heard on any African veldt where predatory beasts were feeding. The masked men stumbled into each other in confusion.

Jack darted forward, delivered his practiced street fighter kick, shattering the knee of the bat man on the right. A shriek of agony tore from the man's throat and went down like a tree felled by a lumberjack.

190

Martin ripped the mask from the one he had chosen to demolish, grasped the man by both ears, and kept slamming his head against the brick wall over and over until long after the man was unconscious and flopping like a rag doll.

Rhino and the tiger took their prey by such surprise that they snatched the bats from their hands and commenced to kick and beat the previous batbearers into the sidewalk. Jack had to stop them all before they stomped the life from the twitching human lumps barely breathing alongside the man holding his knee and screaming in pain.

Sam's quarry broke and ran, but after a brief chase, Sam and Jack caught him. The man swung the bat in a roundhouse fashion. Sam ducked, and just as the bat whizzed over his head, Sam jerked the mask from the man's face. It was one of the deputies who had shot up Jack's apartment. Sam brought his knee up between the deputy's spread-eagle legs with all the power he could muster, lifting the big deputy a foot off the ground. The scream could be heard for blocks. Jack smiled at the idea that this cretin was the tail end of his own gene pool and wouldn't be able to spawn any more of his kind.

The man collapsed on Sam's knee, howling. Sam dragged him by the hair back to the corner and dumped his writhing form on the pile of moaning men.

"Damn," Sam said, looking about at the human rubble lying about like rumpled laundry, "I feel cheated. There wasn't but one apiece!"

They dusted off their hands and walked to the rear entrance ramp.

Jack stopped at the desk and spoke to the reception nurse. "It would behoove you all to send an ambulance down to the corner. Some men appear to be in need of medical attention. Looks like they've had hell stomped out of 'em."

The nurse lackadaisically turned to an orderly and said, "Wouldja send somebody out back? Hoodlums fightin' again." To Jack she said, "Somethin's always happenin' back there. They oughta keep a deputy posted out there at night."

"I think there's a deputy out there now," Jack murmured.

"Whadja say?" The nurse asked, seeming to notice for the first time the grinning faces of the squad of fullbacks.

"Nothin, just mumblin' about law enforcement."

The morgue was filled with angry-looking Sheriff's deputies and several men in white coats. Surprise registered on the officer's faces, evidently anticipating Jack being brought in feet first. Instead, he came in on his own two feet with his mouth working, and in the company of five very healthy specimens, including a gorgeous black woman in skin-tight jeans. His group still had the light of fight flaring in their eyes, and it looked as if they would just love to bang some more heads together.

The deputies gathered around the door to the morgue. Sam confronted a man in a lab coat with a name tag verifying his doctoral status and said, "I'm

Sam Leviathon. This is Jack Chandler, Dr. Jester McConothy, Dr. Victoria Keens-Dennison, Martin Delacroix, Julian Freret and Harold LaMarque. We're here to view the remains of one alleged Dawn Marie Delacroix. Judge Mahoney has called ordering this, and we expect to be allowed in immediately without interference or delay."

The doctor said nothing and opened the door to the morgue. He led them to the tray and slid it open. Three armed deputies followed. A vile smell of corrupt flesh flooded up from the tray. The doctor expected for the group to rush from the room gagging, but he was disappointed as Jester stepped forward and pulled the sheet from the lump lying beneath.

The form of the body was barely identifiable as human. Tattered remains of hair stuck to the skull, rotted flesh hung from the bones, and sunken eyeballs stared from a wasted face.

Jester and Vic took wooden tongue depressors from their pockets and probed at the reeking mess that once had been a vessel of human life. After a few moments, both straightened up and grinned at each other.

Jester pulled the cover back over the putrefying mass and said, "Shut it."

The doctor looked puzzled.

"Who is that supposed to be, Doctor?"

"The tag says Dawn Marie Delacroix, sixteen years old."

"Bullshit," Jester said.

Martin, who had stoically stood by like a Roman sentinel the whole time, let out a breath of relief.

"That woman is at least fifty. She died of a crushing blow to the skull, and not drowning. I would warrant there is no water in her lungs. She has been dead now for at least a month. The state of decomposition is advanced, but her teeth alone plainly show all you need to know, Doctor. Her bone formation is that of a woman with advanced arthritis, and her hair was red, not black."

"That's right," Vic said firmly, "and I suggest, Doctor, that if you and the coroner attempt to pawn this pitiful thing off as the body of the murdered and raped child, Dawn Marie Delacroix, all of you will be charged with malfeasance in office, and I'll see to it that you never practice medicine again."

The doctor raised his hands as if to protect himself from the rain of words.

Sam held a sausage-sized finger inches from the doctor's nose. "Retract and correct that news release, immediately. This coroner's office is involved in a conspiracy with the sheriff to cover up a series of despicable crimes."

Martin and his longshoremen friends, still holding their unabated anger in check, let out a low, menacing growl that caused the doctor to back away and the deputies in the room to reach for their sidearms.

"I'm personally taking this to the U.S. Attorney General for prosecution," Sam continued. "The correction must be prominent in the morning's Picayune and in all the media."

Jack led the party from the morgue through the emergency exit. Lying on stretchers along the halls were the foiled assailants, three of whom were still unconscious and being vigorously administered to by a team of interns and residents. The two who were conscious saw Jack's group approaching and instantly ceased whimpering and moaning and laid on their stretchers wide-eyed and quiet.

"Good evening gentlemen," Jack said in passing, giving the wounded a crocodile smile. "I do hope you have a nice day."

Lamarque and Freret smiled for the first time. It wasn't much, but beating hell out of those five moved all of them momentarily from total effect to a little cause. They returned to the apartment and Martin's group left.

Jack looked at his watch. It was almost two.

"Nookie'll get me into Bormann's office," Jack said. "There's gotta be other records, or somethin', somewhere."

"Jack, I want to go with you," Sam said.

"Sam, you'd be a bull in a china shop. This may take bein' quiet and catlike, and that just ain't your thing. Me'n Nookie'll do it."

"I'm going with you," Vic said adamantly.

"Now look here, Vic. I'm not gonna let you get arrested for breakin' and enterin' and maybe gettin' hurt."

"I don't care. I'm going, whether you like it or not. If you leave without me, I'll never speak to you again," she said, dashing into the bedroom.

Jester said, "Better let her go. Her mind's made up, and you'll rue the day you didn't let her take some risk with you."

Jack sighed and said, "I don't want to expose her any more than I've already put her through."

Nookie blew his horn in the street below and Jack looked over the balcony. Nookie grinned up at the group looking over.

"Hey, you koo-yon. You ready to do somethin' else crazy? I am. Hee Hee."

"Park that long bottle of Pepto Bismol, Nookie. Everybody knows your car. We gotta find some other way to get there."

"Here's my keys," Jester said, handing over a small set of keys to his Corvette.

"Too obvious, too. Alabama plates. Sam?"

Sam scratched in his pockets and came out with a single key and placed it into Jack's palm. He sniffed.

"Sam's got a car that looks like he's been in the stock car races. It'll do fine. Where'd you park?"

"On Dauphine, around the block. Be careful—don't dent the right rear quarter panel—that's the only good one left."

Jack put his big knife and a small derringer into his pocket, tested the headlamp, and dropped a six-pack of cold Dixie into the pack.

"Gotta have rations," Jack said.

"We'll hang here, you got plenty scotch," Jester said.

Vic came out wearing what appeared to be a black body stocking that fit so well it looked as if it was painted on. Her dusky skin, jet black hair tied back, and black sneakers would make her invisible in the shadow.

He said, "Okay, you'll do. Let's haul."

Nookie's appraising eyes consumed Vic as she walked slightly ahead of them. Jack noticed Nookie's gawking at Vic's muscular derriere. Nookie gazed at Jack, his eyes comically wide.

Jack's reaction was of resentment at Nookie looking that way at his woman. *Hold on, Jack. What am I thinking? She's not my woman.*

Nookie said, "I be damn, Jack. We got some good help this night." As they reached Sam's old Chrysler, Nookie said, "Hoo, boy. This car been in Vietnam or someting?"

"Just superficial, Nook. Looks bad, runs good."

"Like someting else I know—looks bad, feels good."

The two men laughed at the old joke and got in the ravaged car.

Vic sat in the middle and Jack drove. Nookie asked, "Where we goin'?"

"New Orleans Mental Health, and wherever that leads."

"What we lookin' for?"

Jack brought Nookie up to date.

"Shoop!" Nookie swore, "I see why you need to find someting. Else, you case est mort, it is dead."

"Just keep a lookout, both of you. We probably'll be followed from now on."

Nookie spotted a car driving without lights a block back. "Hey, Jack, we got a tail sho' nuff."

As soon as they came to the next corner, Jack made a quick turn to the right and then another to the left and doused his lights. He backed into an alley and they sat quietly behind a large dumpster while an unmarked Ford raced past.

Jack shifted into low and eased out of the alley.

There was little traffic. Fifteen minutes later, they parked in the shadows behind an aging, three story brick building.

"Your skills now, Nook. Show Vic what you can do."

Jack and Vic huddled around Nookie as he bent to the lock on the back door. He removed his little leather kit with the wires and pins, inserted a couple in the keyhole, and after jiggling it for a moment, the bolt snapped open. Nookie said, "Voila!"

Vic slid a small penlight under the watchband on her left wrist allowing her to use her hands and still have light. "Now, that's a damn good idea! Me a thief. Why didn' I think of that, me!"

Jack strapped the elastic band to the headlight around his head and hooked the battery pack on his belt.

Bormann's office was next to Ernie's on the second floor along a narrow hallway.

Nookie worried the locks for a few minutes, then pushed the door to Bormann's office open. Once inside, they saw that the door to Ernie's adjoining office stood ajar.

Bormann's office was furnished in the style of the flamboyant Empire period of the Napoleanic epoch. Everywhere they saw carved faces and bosoms of hard-eyed men and women, some with wings and hooves, staring from the drawer pulls and corners of the desk, credenza and large armoire. Framed pictures of Freud, Wundt, Jung and other unsmiling, goateed men were interspersed with various certificates and degrees hanging on one wall.

One of the pictures showed a younger Bormann among a crowd of other men standing before an austere looking building, evidently set somewhere in Europe. On it was written, "May your career be as shocking as your internship at Leipzig." Signed, Jodl."

Nookie pulled open the drawers in the high chest behind the desk. "What's dis?" he asked.

Jack focused his headlamp on a small machine with dials, switches and a set of leads with alligator clips at the end. "That's an invention from hell," Jack said, spitting out the words. "An electro-convulsive shockin' machine. Plug that baby in, stick those leads on some poor bastards temporals, put a towel between his teeth, throw the switch, and fry his brain. Gives him a convulsion. State of the art for these so called doctors. Keeps him quiet for a while—gives him a bigger problem than he had in the first place. Pretty barbaric. They don't have any idea what it really does or why—or even care—they just keep on doin' it and get paid big bucks for it, usually with our tax money."

Nookie curled his lips in disgust and threw the device back into the drawer.

Jack and Vic pulled out more drawers and found boxes of papers, neatly stacked in stapled bundles, each with lead sheets describing the contents.

Jack read a few of the titles to himself, each of which had been authored by Bormann, some jointly with Hotchkiss. "Employment of Pain, Drug, Hypnosis to Adult Males", "Reaction of Adolescent Males to formula Y2", "Resolution of LSD Response", "Anal Sex Therapy", "Sex Therapy for Pre-pubescent Males", "Human-animal Coital Forms", "Enigma of the Mind: A Puzzle Without an Answer, Sexual Response in Infants."

Jack and Vic fanned through the remaining titles to the studies, all authored by Bormann.

"Prolific pervert," Jack said.

"I feel degraded just touching these neat little stacks of paper," Vic said, wiping her hands on her pants.

"You want to take these with you, Jack?"

"Maybe. Let's see what else we can find."

The door behind the desk led to a small storage area with several filing cabinets filled with case histories. One small cabinet was actually a fireproof safe with a combination lock.

Nookie's eyes gleamed in the glow of the flashlights beams. Spitting on the tips of his fingers he said, "This gon' be that piece o' cake," as he began turning the dial slowly while listening to the tumblers.

As Nookie worked at the safe, Vic shined her light around the walls. A long mural-like oil painting hung just above the window in the storage room. It appeared to be a pale python coiled around a nude man. After studying it for a moment, she said, "Jack, what do you make of that?"

Jack studied it for a moment and said, "It's supposed to be symbolic of phallic domination. The snake is actually his dick; look, it's got one eye. I know exactly how that poor bastard feels."

Nookie looked up from his work at the painting and said, "That fool got plenty trouble, him."

"That's all men think about," Vic sniffed.

"With trouble like that, babe, that's all he can think about," Jack said.

"Ah ha! This l'il rascal safe he be plenty tough, but he ain' fool me," Nookie whooped, pulling the heavy drawer out.

"Will you look at that," Jack said, focusing his light into the drawer.

Several neat rows of videocassettes in plastic boxes filled the drawer. A typewritten note was taped to each. One read, "A. "6.3.10, 000-128, JD, BMA,YS2A/LSD adm. FolderC/92. B. "6.6.10, 129=263, T&C, BF, YS2A/PB adm. folder c/92," and then had a series of other symbols and abbreviations from A through C on it.

Nookie looked puzzled.

Vic said, "Either June 3rd or March 6th, 2010, digital numbers, Juvenile Detention, Black Male Adolescent, the drug administered, cross indexed to his notes on the experiment. Elementary, Watson."

"Brilliant, Holmes," Jack said in a British accent, "I was about to say the same thing."

Nookie searched the building for something to pack the videos in while Vic and Jack stacked the canisters on a table nearby. Beneath the videos were several layers of folders, each marked with a letter of the alphabet.

"The referenced files, Watson," Vic said, pointing.

Nookie returned with a large cardboard box and a heavy case with a handle on top. "Ah found this on a shelf in that l'il room," he said. "You want to take him too?"

Nookie lifted out a portable T.V. with built in V.C.R.

"Hey, that'll work," Jack said. "We need one to see what's on these videocassettes."

Vic and Jack placed the cassettes and files in the box and carried it into Bormann's office, finding nothing else of interest.

They weren't ready for Ernie's office.

"Ma poo yi-yi," Nookie said as they played the beams of their lights about the room.

It was byzantine fantasy splendor, complete with a delicate fragrance of jasmine. Heavy brocade drapes covered the entire window wall from ceiling to deep piled Persian carpet. The only item of furniture was a low table, no more than eighteen inches from the floor, with an ebony, inlaid mosaic surface of a pentagram; each S-curved leg was adorned with a naked, winged figure and one cloven foot. A large deck of tarot cards was stacked on the table, and huge crimson cushions were strewn about the floor. A large painting of Hieronymus Bosch's "Garden of Earthly Delights," with its macabre portrayal of miscreants and the grotesque, filled the wall opposite the window. There were no books, certificates, or other identification except the plain plate on the hallway door giving Ernie's name.

"Looks like a whorehouse for the freaks," Jack said.

"I wouldn't know," Vic sniffed.

"Me neither, hee hee," Nookie said.

"Nook," Jack said, "you live in one!"

A thorough search of Ernie's office was unproductive. The only thing found was an address book. "Well, we've plenty of stuff to study. Gonna take hours," Jack said.

"It's only a little after three," Vic said. "Why don't we check Bormann's apartment?"

"I don't know where he lives," Jack said.

"6060 St. Charles."

Jack turned to Vic and asked, "How'd you know that?"

Vic held up the address book and said, "There's plenty names in here. Maybe we should take it along."

"A thief'll steal anything," Jack said throwing up his hands.

Chapter 19

Bormann's address was three stories of Victorian gingerbread with at least ten thousand square feet of living space. They stopped at a gate in a high masonry wall at the rear of the house. Nookie quickly had the gate open and parked in a three-car garage.

The door from the garage that opened into Bormann's kitchen was slightly ajar.

"Somebody done beat us here," Nookie whispered.

They stood by the door until Nookie said, "I been around places enough to know. Ain't nobody in there. I can feel somebody if they in there, and they ain't."

A huge Chambers range was on one side of the kitchen. On the other were two Sub-Zero refrigerators and a twenty cubic foot freezer filled with packaged meat. An array of every conceivable type of cutlery, pot and pan hung from an island over the center of the kitchen. A wine closet with labeled pigeon holes and filled with bottles fit under a stair-well. Two huge sideboards were stuffed with the finest crystal and silverware.

"Hoo boy," Nookie said, his brown eyes gleaming in the reflection of Jack's headlamp, "Bormann shore know how to live, dat boy. You know, some thief might come in here an' steal everything that prevert had accumulate. I think I might have to come back and take some of this stuff into, howyacall, 'protective custody?'"

"I wouldn't touch any of it," Jack said. "Tainted. I couldn't look at any of it without thinkin' about Dawn Marie and all the others."

"Shoop. This coonass don't worry 'bout no taint. Only thing worry me is how many load it gon' take to git it all outta here."

The living room area was plush with a walk-in fireplace, grand piano with candelabra, and a gigantic painting of nude satyrs and boys dancing in a circle, all heroically endowed. On the wall opposite the fireplace was a study, its fireplace sharing the same chimney, with fourteen foot bookshelves that reached the ceiling. Jack hungrily read the titles to the hundreds of leather bound volumes.

"I'd lift these myself, except for the rest of my life I'd feel dirty just havin' 'em in my place."

They searched every drawer and tapped on every wall for secret panels and found nothing. Jack noticed one large book extended out slightly from the rest. He pulled it out and laid it on the table. It fell open, revealing a large, hollowed-out area in the middle, but nothing was in the hole.

Studying it, Vic said, "Jack, does the size of that hole look familiar? It's about the size of a videocassette."

"I tole you all, somebody done been here," Nookie interjected.

"Ernie!" Jack and Vic said simultaneously.

"Who else?" Vic said.

"Could be Sessums," Jack offered.

"Yeah, could be, Vic said, "but they didn't get to Bormann's big cache in his office did they? Whoever got what was in that book, assuming there was something in it to start with, felt that the stuff in the office wasn't as important."

In the small private courtyard, statues of nude mythical gods peered through the ferns. Prometheus gazed yearningly across the pool at a slender, winged footed Mercury. Melted candles puddled in sconces on the vine-covered brick walls around the patio, and small burners hidden around the pool contained the dusty residue of incense.

"Quite a pad, huh Vic?" Jack said.

"Cozy digs."

"But me, Nookie, I feel funny. Like somebody watchin'," Nookie said. "Like somebody don' want us to be here. And I git a kind of funny feelin' about what been goin' on here."

"Me too," Jack said. "Bormann's probably pissed at us bein' here and is right here with us tryin' to get us out. Let's look at the rest and get hell out of here."

"Hoo, Jack," Nookie said, looking around nervously, "you don' suppose his ghost is in here wit' us, do you?"

"Sure, Nook. Where the hell do you think he went? To Heaven? To Hell?"

"I guess so, ain't that where we go?"

"Like the song says," Vic said, turning back to the double French doors leading into the house, "it ain't necessarily so."

"Let's get hell out of here," Jack said, "Sun's up."

"Yeah. This place feel like it got the gris-gris laid on it. I'm comin' back, but it make my skin crawl."

Nookie found a large brown paper bag and opened the freezer. He filled the bag with items labeled T-Bones and Rib-eyes. As he locked the door behind them, he said, "You know, Norma, dat Pussy Beaucoup, she love dem T-Bone."

Day Eight

A thin layer of fog hung in the street. The mellow morning light slowly turned the city from umber to gray. The great cathedral tolled six o'clock, as the drowsing Quarter opened a sleepy eye and blinked away the night.

Sam and Jester snored, one on the sofa and the other in a lounge chair. Nookie placed the box filled with the cassettes and documents on the kitchen table.

Jack said, "I'm going to make some coffee."

"Mais, yeah, that hit the head on the nail," Nookie responded. "I could use a cup, me."

Sam and Jester stirred and came to life.

"Any luck?" Sam asked.

Jack said, indicating the box. "This stuff. We grabbed it all and split. Maybe it'll tell us somethin'."

Stacking two dozen videocassettes, several manila envelopes of photos, and the manuscripts on the table, Jack flopped onto the sofa. He lit a cigarette and sighed. Unhinging a long, sharp blade on his pocket knife, he slit one of the envelopes across the top. He then dumped the contents onto the table just as Vic returned from putting a kettle of water on to boil. Everyone watched an assortment of Polaroid and thirty-five millimeter photos tumble into a pile. Vic idly picked one up and drew in her breath audibly.

She whispered hoarsely, "Oh, my God!"

Everyone leaned over her shoulder and uttered oaths at what they saw in the photograph. Destrehan was locked in anal copulation with a small black boy whose face showed mortal torment.

The group stared at the Polaroids and thirty-five millimeter photos piled on the table as if they were coiled rattlers. Then they queasily picked through them, each of which revealed men engaged in some sort of sexual act, all with juvenile boys and girls, both black and white. Each envelope contained dated photographs that documented the drug used and a page number which evidently further described the activity in detail.

Jack said, "I'm gonna be sick, boys and girl. I assume these movies are gonna show the whole damned thing. Sessums' goons may have taken your evidence, Jester, but this stuff'll blow him to hell and back if it's all what I think it is. Let's see how this is documented."

Vic flipped through the files and located a page corresponding with the data on the back of a particular photograph involving a little black waif looking like James. The written account chronicled the entire event. It described in detail the administering of a designated drug, its effects, the sex act, how the "subject" reacted, and if sex abated the effects of the drug.

Vic studied the cassettes, the dates on the envelopes, and the journals detailing it all. "The dates on the videos and journals go back three years, ending on the day before Dawn was murdered," she said, lifting her eyebrows.

"The bastard kept records like his buddies did in Auschwitz and Bergen-Belsen," Jester said. "He had to record Dawn's deal too!"

"Ya know damn well he did," Sam said. "It's in his big journal. These are his little notes as he went. The big journal's the summary Jack gave to Leone. So he must have a detail—maybe even a videocassette. That'd nail their ass!"

Vic picked up the earliest of the accounts and read the first few pages. "Says here there were hidden camera rooms at Juvenile Detention and at the motel, and that they were operated by himself and, guess who. . ."

"Bingo!" Jack said, narrowing his eyelids, pumping the muscles in his jaws. "I'm gonna pay Ernie a visit!"

"Wait," Sam said, "don't you think we oughta look at one of those videos before you get too excited."

Jack took a videocassette at random from the box and slid it into Vic's V.C.R. Bormann was seen entering the room while a little black child of about twelve years old sat wide eyed on the bed. He administered an injection into a vein in the bend of the boy's elbow. Bormann left the room, and the little boy began to tremble. Soon he was rolling and tossing on the bed, writhing and masturbating. A fat man entered the room and forced the little boy to perform oral sex. Then the man flipped the boy over and entered him from the rear. The act was quickly over. The man dropped the boy on the bed and left the room.

"I've seen enough," Jack said, turning the V.C.R. off.

"Hoo boy, me too," Nookie said. "If I ever see that fat fuetbetan, ah gonna fix him. Ah got a 'lectric cattle prod what'll make a bull jump a barb-wire fence. He gonna know what that feel like to that l'il boy."

"Don't worry, Nookie," Jack said, grinning at Vic. "Vic already handled him. That was Warner Bosco, the crispy critter of Lee Circle."

"Hot Dam. That was about right for him."

"And look you all," Jack said, "that was just a tiny bit of this video. How many other things are on this one, let alone others."

Vic looked at Nookie and asked, "What does fee-bee-tan mean?"

"Hoo, a lady don't wanna know. It mean every bad thing a Cajun can say about somebody. If you want a fight, just you call a Cajun that. You got a fight."

Jack said, "enumerating every curse, put-down, rotten unforgiving expression of disgusting low life you can think of, and some you cannot put into words but just get the idea of, and you have it."

"I see," Vic said, "I learn something new every day. You're right, the epithet is mild as regards Bormann and Ernie."

They sat silently, smoldering in rages of various intensity.

"How could he get away with it?" Jester asked.

"Easy," streetwise Sam said. "He was a kind of pimp. He got paid. Bosco was a John, and he didn't know he was bein' filmed or participatin' in an experiment. I bet Bormann had lots of cash stashed somewhere."

"Uhm," Nookie said.

"Nookie," Jack said, "promise me if you find lots of cash in Bormann's place you'll throw it into some kind of a fund so we can help some of those victims. You can keep lots of it, but let's get somethin' to these kids. They probably feel there's no justice at all after what's happened to 'em."

"You right," Nookie said, "this one time I gonna burgle for somebody beside Nookie."

Jack said, "It's nearly eight. I'm gonna choke the truth outta Ernie, right now."

"This Ernie live here?" Nookie asked.

"Yeah. I might need help gettin' in, Nook. As far as I'm concerned, Ernie's already past the point of mercy. The fucker's mine!"

The whole group fell in step behind Jack. He stopped and said, "Hey, I don't want you guys to get into the shit just because I'm about to."

"Shut up, Jack," Jester said, pushing him gently ahead.

"Yeah, Jack," Vic said, this involves everybody now. You're not going to hog the glory." She grabbed his arm and pulled him down the hall.

The sun gilded the second story of Ernie's slave quarter apartment, leaving the rest of the courtyard in shadow. The cool, moist air in the little greenhouse environment around the pool caressed Jack's face as he strode with grim purpose to the many paned French doors of the apartment. The deep throated moan of a riverboat could be heard over the rooftops.

Nookie's lockpick set jingled as he examined it for the right thin metal probe. He poked around in the keyhole for a few moments, then a faint snap could be heard from within the door. He pushed down on the ornate little lever and the door quietly opened.

Jack leaped up the spiral stairs, followed by Vic, then Jester, Sam and Nookie. They made no attempt at being quiet.

Ernie was naked and sprawled on the bed clutching a pillow. Slack jawed and gray, drool spilled from the corners of his lips.

Jester pushed Jack aside and pressed two fingers into the side of Ernie's throat.

"Overdose," Jester whispered, pointing to the bedside table.

Two empty prescription bottles laid among a dozen yellow pills that were scattered on the table top.

Vic examined one, and said, "Valium, ten milligrams. It's empty. He must have taken the whole bottle. Looks like he pulled the plug."

"Suicide, unless we can save him. He's still with us, but barely." Jester said. "Need to pump him out and maybe a massive transfusion. No tellin' what or how much of it he took, or how long ago. Can't give him ipecac to make him throw up, but we gotta empty his stomach."

Vic dialed for an ambulance.

Jester moved Ernie to the edge of the bed. Although unconscious, Ernie clutched a pillow locked in the crook of his arm.

As they pulled the pillow free, Jester said, "What's this?" feeling something solid inside the pillow slip.

Jester shook the pillow and a videocassette bounced onto the carpeted floor. Jack snatched it up before it stopped rolling and held it high.

"This is it! Gotta be!" Jack exulted. "Hold the call, Vic."

Vic pressed the button, disconnecting the line just as the hospital answered, and asked, "Why?"

"Look," Jack said, "I know it's takin' a chance, but Ernie's life ain't worth a plug nickel if he's in the hospital, even if he can be saved. They'll see to that. If you can save him, let's keep him till we need him. He's the key to the whole case and the videos. If we can get him to testify, hell, we can nail Mourier–Sessums too, and all of those other bastards we don't know about who'll show up in the stuff we got from Bormann's office."

"Vic, go git your bag," Jester ordered.

Vic sped down the stairs and Jester said, "I think I can save him, but it's gonna be close. It could mean my license, but I don't give a damn at this point."

"We gonna kidnap this'un too, Jack?" Nookie said, grinning.

Jack turned to Nookie and couldn't help laughing at the quizzical but sincere look on the swarthy Cajun's face. "Nookie, you said 'we,' so I guess you want in on this kidnappin' too?"

"Mais, hell yeah. You don' think you gon' leave old Nookie out of the rest of the fun?"

Sam slapped Nookie on the back. "Nookie, you're a real trooper. Me'n you woulda had a helluva good time in Seoul."

"Sam," Jack asked, "if we can keep Ernie alive, do you think we can make him testify?"

Sam's eyelids narrowed knowingly. "There's more'n one way to skin a cat," Sam said. "Get him out of here alive with his mind fairly intact, and we'll handle that little step. I practiced 'street law' for long enough to learn a few things."

In a few minutes, Vic returned with her little black bag, lugging another large case up the stairs.

"What's that?" Jack asked.

"Portable respirator and a stomach pump. I got lots of stuff stashed away. We have everything we'll need in there."

Nookie gazed around the apartment at the statue of the two nude wrestling men and the webby appearance of the room. "You know," he said abstractly, "this is all very queer."

Even Jester stopped what he was doing, and they all looked at Nookie incredulously. Jester said, "No shit, Sherlock."

Everybody laughed, and Nookie laughed at himself.

Jester and Vic quickly connected the parts to the machine and pushed the nasogastric tube down Ernie's throat.

"This thing'll flush and suck at the same time," Vic announced as they readied to pump Ernie's stomach.

Jester peered over his little half glasses at the three men standing by the bed watching the flurry of activity over Ernie.

He said, "Boys, if ya'll wanna stand around with ya'll's thumbs up ya'll's asses, that's okay by me, but me'n Vic's about to get to work here and ya'll might not think it's too purty to see what he's got in his stomach. Its gonna be real evident in just a minute."

"I'm leavin'," Jack said quickly, heading for the stair.

"Don't bother me none," Sam said.

"I bet," Vic said.

"We're in the way, so we'll watch T.V. downstairs while you two do your thing up here," Sam said.

Nookie curled his upper lip and said, following Jack down the stair, "Ah gutted me a many a deer, an' cleaned many a possum an' coon, but people's different."

"Just so you'll know, Naquin," Jester said, pressing a tube through Ernie's pale lips, "we ain't gonna skin or gut Ernie."

"Wouldn't bother me none if you did," Nookie said.

"Me neither," Jack said from the bottom of the stairs.

Jack made coffee while the two doctors worked upstairs. After a few minutes, Jack heard Vic say, "Look, there they are." Jack bounded back up the stairs as Vic pointed at some small round pills in the container. "They weren't all digested."

"Alright!" Jester said, "That means we might not have to use any anti-seizure drugs, but we gotta get him on an I.V."

Jester applied some activated charcoal to absorb the residual and flushed it out.

"I think we got about all of it," he said after a few more minutes. He withdrew the tube and Vic assembled all of the equipment, flushed the stomach material down the toilet, and cleaned the apparatus in the tub.

Ernie's eyelids fluttered open slightly.

"I'm Dr. McConothy, Ernie," Jester said. "We've just pumped out your stomach; I think we got it all in time. You just about did yourself in, but you're gonna be okay."

Sam and Nookie came back up the stairs.

Ernie was propped on some pillows breathing easily with his eyes closed.

"He's going to make it," Vic said. "We need to keep him quiet for a few days."

At that moment, the bedside phone rang. Ernie moved sluggishly to answer and Vic gently restrained his hand as she lifted the receiver.

"Hello."

There was a pause at the other end of the line. "Oh, do excuse the ring," a lisping male voice said, "I must have the wrong number."

"What number are you calling?"

"892-4403."

"Who are you calling?"

There was another pause, and the voice said, "Dr. Hotchkiss."

"Dr. Hotchkiss is not free at the moment; who may I say is calling?"

"Ah, er. Well, who is this?" the voice asked, suddenly becoming demanding.

"I'm Vic. Is there a problem?"

"I might ask you the same question," the petulant voice protested. "I am an old friend of Ernie's. I received a note from him saying that he was going to kill himself. Is he alright?"

"Yes. If you want, I'll call him. He isn't feeling too well and just dozed back off."

"Oh no, don't do that. Just tell him that Bruce called. Ernie has threatened suicide so many times, I just never know about him. You know, cry wolf and all that," Bruce said.

"I understand. Does he have your number?"

"Oh yes. By the way," Bruce probed, "are you a friend?"

"Yes, I live in the same apartment complex and I am just visiting because he wasn't feeling well. Brought him something and he went back to sleep. Answered your call before I left."

"Are you sure he's okay?" Bruce asked suspiciously. "He never sleeps past eight. Stays up all night. Don't know how he does it."

"I've thought the same myself. Anything else?"

"No. Maybe I should come over and check. Good-bye." Click.

Vic replaced the receiver and looked questioningly at the rest of the group. "His name is Bruce. Ernie left a suicide note. He's suspicious. Sounds as if he is coming over. Could be trouble."

"Can the boy travel?" Sam asked both doctors.

Jester shrugged. "Dicey. Gotta be careful if he's moved. Why?"

"I got a camp in the swamp around Lake Maurepas. Gonna need a place to stash this evidence anyway. Sessums has power, and his goons can do anything, including break in, so nothin's safe in the city. Jack, you and Ernie and the evidence gotta be tucked outta sight for a while."

"I'll pack Ernie's things," Vic said. She pulled a suitcase from a closet and began placing clothing items in it. "I better leave these," she said, swinging some gossamer-thin women's lingerie' in her hand, including a red garter belt and black sequined hose.

"Yeah, Jack might be tempted," Sam said, grinning.

"You might, you big faggot," Jack said, thumping Sam on the shoulder with his fist.

"I don't think you need to worry about Jack," Vic said, looking Jack straight in the eye.

Jack's heart thumped an extra beat as Vic stood erect, straightening up from packing, her breasts and pubis pressing against her skin tight black leotards. Without thinking, Jack wet his lips with the tip of his tongue. Vic smiled at his reaction.

Jester asked, "Just where and how far is this camp?"

Sam said, "Take I-10 to LaPlace exit, then across to a landing on Blind River where I keep my boat. From there by boat up Blind River to Lake Maurepas, and from there to a bayou called Little Mississippi. A couple miles up that to a walk through the swamp for about a quarter mile. It'll be a trek. We'll have to carry our boy on a litter."

Jester, still sitting on the corner of the bed, rocked thoughtfully for a long while and finally said, "Okay. But we gotta be easy, and quick. How big's your boat?"

"Big enough. Twenty four foot. Got a little cuddy cabin we can put him in for the ride. Gonna need a stretcher to get him from the landing to the camp."

"Fair enough," Jester said. "Jack, get your stuff. We'll go in two cars. Nookie, can you get us a stretcher?" Nookie's eyes gleamed at the opportunity to use his skills for a good purpose and said, "Mais yeah. You know Nookie's the number one, howyacall, 'procurateur?' I think that's what they call that."

"You right, Nook," Jack said, a procurer cum laude."

"Lawdy Lawdy Miss Claudie," Nookie said, "I think Nookie better get movin' to get this stretcher. I'll pick up some other thing we gonna need while I'm at it."

"Whatever we do, gettin' the hell out of Dodge quickly would be advisable," Sam said.

"We'll need a little help getting Ernie out of here and up to your apartment," Vic said. She thought for a minute and then said, "Maybe you should wait till dark. It will look very strange having to carry Ernie to your boat."

"Not to worry, babe," Sam said, "we'll make it go right."

"Wait for me," Nookie said, "ah gotta idee. Be back in a hour."

The crew emptied Ernie's pantry and refrigerator. Sam and Jack carried Ernie to the sofa in Vic's downstairs apartment.

After two hours, Jack began to worry. Nookie had always delivered what he promised, but there were times when he would get distracted by a lady's smile or an irresistible procurement opportunity. Jack paced the floor and chain smoked. Finally, the door buzzer sounded to Vic's apartment. "Who is it?" Vic whispered.

"C'est moi, Nookie. Ya'll bring all yore stuff out now. We gonna travel together. Come see."

The still limp Ernie and all the supplies were carried to a panel-van with benches along each side and a litter down the center.

"Nookie, he earn his keep," Nookie said, beaming at his acquisition as Ernie was put on the stretcher.

"Where did you find the van?" Jack asked, amazed.

"It was there. Nobody was in it. So I took it. We only borry it nohow. I done switch plates and put a Bayou Maintenance sign on the side. Nobody gon' pay no never mind. We'll drop the payload an' bring it back."

"Where'd you get the stretcher?"

"That's easy. Me, I paid me a visit to that fancy marina at the Lakefront and borrow two 'luminum masts from some l'il sailboat and took the sail. All I had to do was cut the sail wit' my pocket knife and wrap him around dem 'luminum pole. I prop him on some concrete block I found by a house on the West End by the Lakefront. Will that do?"

"Perfect, Nook, just perfect. You're an acquisitions agent impresario," Jack said.

"Yeah, and I'm a dam good thief an' procurateur too," Nookie said sagely.

Nookie drove and Jack rode shotgun. The others rode in the back with Ernie, who moaned and sat up. Vic gave him an injection and he laid back down and relaxed.

"He's gonna need glucose," Jester said. "Vic, me an' you'll go up to your office and "borrow" some things.

The doctors opened the rear doors and hopped out at Tulane Medical Center on Tulane Avenue, and Nookie slid the van into a no parking zone and waited. In a short time, Vic and Jester returned carrying two large bags each.

They inserted a hypodermic needle into a vein in Ernie's arm and taped it down. Then they hung a plastic bag of glucose to the ceiling of the van, then fixed a long plastic tube to it and to the needle.

"Like the med evacs in Nam," Jester said, looking at the glucose bag swinging and swaying as Nookie barreled along Airline Highway.

"They evacuated me just like this during the Tet Offensive, bottle of glucose and all. See my scar?" Sam said, rolling up his sleeve to reveal a nasty scar encircling his upper arm. "They wanted to take my arm off at the shoulder, but you see it's still there."

Ernie opened his eyes and tried to comprehend the strange party he found himself with.

Jack felt him looking, and said, "Ernie, you're gonna be fine. We're taking you someplace safe."

Ernie, still drugged and barely able to hold his head up, frowned. He dropped back on the pillow and stared wearily at the ceiling and the swinging glucose bag.

"Hey boss," Nookie said to Jack while looking in his rear view mirror. "I think we got another tail. A l'il pickumup been with us since we left the Quarter."

"I guess that can't be avoided. At least where we're goin' they're gonna have a hard time slippin' up on us."

In twenty minutes, Nookie turned north off the Interstate.

Sam said, "To the right is Lake Pontchartrain and to the left is Lake Maurepas. We're on a narrow strip of land separatin' the two big lakes."

Great blue herons, white egrets, and cranes stood motionless in the shallows on each side of the road. One plunged its pointed beak into the water and, after flipping its finny find into its beak, moved its head up and down to work the little fish down its throat.

The air became dank and humid, smelling of mud, the remains of squashed turtles and other roadkill lying on the roadway, along with the perfume of an offended skunk somewhere in the vicinity.

"If I didn't know different, I'd think I was in a boat," Jester said.

The swamp gave way to higher ground. In less than an hour, they were at Blind River Campsites and Marina. A gravel road meandered for a mile among small frame shacks and trailers.

Blind River was three hundred feet across at the landing. On the opposite side was swamp and wilderness. To the left of a concrete launching ramp was the Blind River Landing Bar and dance hall, part of which was built out over the river to allow boaters to tie alongside and disembark. It was large enough to accommodate a country band and several dozen, mostly drunk, patrons who had a "shit kickin' time" every Saturday night. This was in the Southeastern part of Louisiana, with residents mainly being rednecks from Mississippi and a scattering of Cajuns imported from Cajun Southwest Louisiana. Louisiana is divided into four parts: The northern half is white Anglo Saxon protestant, the Southwest quarter is Cajun French, the Southeast rednecks, and New Orleans a mixture of cultures and races.

To the right of the ramp was a series of large, metal buildings built alongside the river. Sam told Nookie to turn onto the road that ran alongside the sheds.

Nookie drove slowly, noting the size of the huge cruisers floating in their berths.

"Kiiyow," Nookie said, "that's some big fine boat in them shed. You got one like dat, Sam?"

Sam pointed forward impatiently, indicating for Nookie to keep driving.

Soon the large metal buildings, all filled with huge cabin cruisers and sailboats, gave way to smaller sheds with corrugated tin roofs.

Sam told Nookie to stop at one of the doors built into the tin wall. He opened the doors to the van, wallowed his way to the ground, and swung the door to the shed open, revealing an antique Chris-Craft cabin cruiser floating in its little moorage. A small fishing boat buzzed by, creating a wake that caused the old cruiser to bounce against the rubber tire bumpers nailed to the rickety walk alongside the boat.

Sweeping his arm into the shed, Sam said, "My canoe."

With her hands on her hips, Vic surveyed the boat. "Frankly, Sam, it looks a lot like your car."

"Yeah," Jack said, "runs good, looks bad."

"Just like something else I know," Nookie said. "Look bad, feel good."

"Mr. Naquin, if you think I don't know what you're talking about, you are the dumbest Cajun," Vic snapped. "Besides, you said that about Sam's automobile."

Nookie drew his head down into his collar and put his hand over his mouth.

"That's alright, Nookie," Vic chided. "I'm accustomed to being around men—and men with much less savoir-faire than you."

Jack heard a sound from the back of Sam's boat and walked along the little boardwalk to the stern. A man wearing a red cap in a little aluminum fishing boat alongside was frantically pulling the crank rope to his outboard.

"Hey you," Sam shouted, "what are you doing. . ."

Sam was unable to get the words out of his mouth before the little outboard fired into life. The skiff spun in a circle and rammed into the side of the shed before the man gained control. He twisted the control handle and the little boat planed out on the river surface and disappeared from view as he passed around the front of the boatshed.

Jack turned and looked at Sam, who was frowning with an odd look on his face.

"What, Sam?" Jack asked.

"I know that little snitch. Little two-bit hustler. Represented him when he was charged with shopliftin'. Got a rap sheet a mile long of petty stuff. Probably a stake-out."

"Wa'al, they know where we are. Let's get the patient on board," Jester said.

There were few boats on the river, since it was the middle of the week, and all that could be heard was a dog yapping at something in the campground, the water smacking at the piers, and the other boats in the sheds.

The rotten four foot long carcass of an alligator gar bobbed and bumped against the hull of the Chris-Craft, minnows pecking at the long body of this primeval fish, its long snout filled with needle sharp teeth. The odor of the decayed fish filled the enclosed boat shed.

"Lots of big gar in the river," Sam said. "Speed boats and skiers always hittin' 'em. They float to the top."

Jester disconnected the I.V. glucose drip and the supplies were quickly put on board. Ernie was ported out last and laid on the bed in the cuddy cabin below.

The cruiser was in need of paint; there were some dings and scratches all along the sides and bow. The inside, however, was in excellent condition. The teakwood finishing was unmarred, though in need of cleaning, and Jack thought of how fine this boat could be if cleaned up.

"Built in 1940, the year I was born." Sam said.

"It's a classic," Jack said. "Why don't you fix it up?"

"What for? I just go back and forth to the camp in it."

Jack shook his head.

The motor growled and the exhaust burbled quietly as Sam backed into the river. Sam shoved the silver throttle forward and the big boat's powerful engines came to life. The sleek craft leaped and planed out instantly on the glassy river.

"Ma Poo Yi Yi! Look bad, run good!" Nookie shouted at the man wearing red cap, now sitting idly in a small aluminum fishing boat near the ramp.

As they drew rapidly away from the landing, Jack watched the man run to the landing and scamper up the ramp to the public phone booth alongside the bar. *Gotta be one of Sessums' weasels,* he thought, *there's nothing I can do about it.*

The Chris-Craft hummed on the surface like a great mosquito, making the big sweeping turns of the river without so much as a drop of spray. On each side of the river were deep swamps. Huge ancient cypress trees, dripping with Spanish moss, hovered like bearded old men over the river's edge.

They passed a floating houseboat built on pontoons made of barrels. A rusted Schlitz sign hung at an angle, and a woman sat on an old chair on the deck fishing among the cypress knees alongside the bank.

Sam waved, and she waved back enthusiastically.

"That's the Blind River Annex," Sam said. "Clarice Fontenot's lived there and run that bar for fifteen years I know of. When I come down, I always stop and have a beer and shoot the shit with her. She's a good 'ol gal; lonesome, and tough as a boot. They say she killed two of her husbands, but on the river, you hear lots of tales, most just lies. She's a real river rat.

"How far now?" Jester asked.

"Ten minutes to Maurepas, up Little Mississippi for another five, then we walk about a quarter mile through the swamp. You'll be okay back there."

CHAPTER 20

Lake Maurepas opened before them, so broad it looked as if they had reached the sea. The opposite shores to the north, east and south were below the horizon. The cruiser sliced through the slight chop with rhythmic little smacks against the hull.

Sam gently turned the wheel to the starboard and the boat smoothly eased right to parallel the northwestern shore of the big lake. White egrets roosting in tall dead cypresses watched their passing. Some took wing and flew lazily back into the swamp.

They entered a bayou with shacks along the right bank and old houseboats floating on barrels or pontoons.

"Little Mississippi," Sam said, pointing to the bayou. "River Rats," he said, indicating the run down little camps.

"Who lives there?" Vic asked Sam, pointing at the shacks.

"Usually fisherman who run lines, nets and crabtraps in the lake. Some on welfare, some just bums, alkies and druggies, and occasionally somebody like us might just have a cheap place to come to get away from it all. Only way to get here is by boat, and it's quiet and peaceful."

He throttled down as he reached the camps to avoid making a wake, then slowly proceeded up the bayou. The bayou twisted and turned, becoming narrower and shallower. Finally, he steered to a small dock on creosote piers beneath the low hanging limbs of a cluster of large cypress trees. Nookie jumped onto the pier and made the cruiser fast to the pier.

"So far, so good," Sam said. "Now for the trek. That's why we put everything in ice chests. We're gonna have to make a coupla trips. Get Ernie and the videos and stuff in first."

Feather-light Ernie was lifted over the edge of the boat to a stretcher on the dock. Vic and Nookie took as much as they could carry.

There were more items than Sam was willing to leave on the boat while they were gone. He said, "Nookie, bring some of those boxes and lay 'em on top of Ernie."

Ernie groaned in protest.

Jack said, "Shut up Ernie. Hold this box."

Jack rested a large box on Ernie's chest and placed Ernie's arms around it. Then he laid another box on Ernie's legs and said, "Don't move or let these drop, or we'll leave you out here for the alligators and snakes."

Ernie's blurred eyes sharpened suddenly. He looked about as if seeing his environment for the first time. He lifted his head and stared out into the darkening swamp and his mouth fell open.

He whimpered, "Are there snakes?"

"You bet." Sam said, "I'm gonna show you the granddaddy of cotton mouths and maybe a hundred young'uns right by the trail. They're mean as hell and'll attack if you get too close. They chomp down and won't let go. You never seen anything like it—they grab hold, wrap around you and squirt you full of poison. You have to pull 'em off, if you're able. And nothin' hurts bad as that, I hear. I think you better consider stayin' close to the camp when we get you there."

Ernie locked his arms and legs around his boxes. "Please don't put me down," he begged. "Snakes terrify me. I'll be good."

Jack looked at Sam knowingly. "Well, then, Ernie. Maybe you'll consider tellin' us everything you know about what you and Bormann did."

"Ye-ye-yes," Ernie stuttered, "I'll tell everything. I'm going to die anyway. I don't want to die of snakes."

"You got a deal, Ern," Jack said.

Sam led the trekkers through the swamp. At first, they walked on a ridge beneath oaks and cypresses dripping with Spanish moss that bordered the bayou. Then the ridge turned away from the bayou, dropping to a swampy bottom.

At that point, they walked over a long, rickety boarded walk built inches over the boggy areas. It was laid over log pilings pounded into the mud and water below.

Sam said, "Me and some of my clients who owed me fees built all of this. Ain't real sturdy, but if you're careful, you can get there without gettin' wet."

Jack and Nookie sniffed the swamp air and grinned at each other. "Feels good, huh, Nook?"

"This Coonass at home inna woods," Nookie said.

The pathway led deeper into the swamp. Sam's felons had driven posts and logs deep into the marshy bottom with sledgehammers. Treated four-by-fours had been laid parallel on each side of the path on the tops of the posts and nailed in place. Rough cypress boards had been nailed to the parallel four-by-fours, creating a boardwalk through the mire. Some boards had loosened and the logs below had rotted, resulting in a wavy and sometimes unstable footing when a board would sink or even snap when stepped on.

Jester stepped through one and pulled a sodden, muddy shoe free. Sam laughed, "Oh yeah. I forgot. Watch your step."

"You watch your step", Jack said. "I'd hate to dump Ernie."

Ernie squealed, "Please be careful!"

The swamp closed in and the trees became taller, forming a thick canopy overhead. The sun was setting, creating deep shadows and darkness in the swamp. An occasional flop and burble could be heard from the darkened rushes nearby. A rat faced nutria scurried into the palmettos. Several curious crows circled above, cawing their raucous taunts.

After ten minutes of walking, Sam said, "Right up here is gator slough. It's got some big 'uns in it, but the cotton mouth's have a spawnin' area there. Damnedest thing you ever saw."

They approached a dead stream thirty feet across, with the walkway built just inches above it. The dank foliage dripping with Spanish moss above seemed to press down, and a light mist hung over the dark, still waters. The muddy banks were almost at water level. As Sam stepped on the bridge, his weight smacked the limber boards down into the water, creating waves around the crossover.

The water around the bridge quickened and came alive.

"Look, there," Sam said, inclining his head toward the water on each side.

The slough became agitated, as if it were a living thing.

Jack said, "Sam, move your big ass. Let's get hell outta here."

Ernie, clutching the boxes tightly, prone on the stretcher and only inches away from the surface, stared at the churning muddy water. The heads of a dozen large snakes lifted no more than two feet from Ernie's stark face.

Ernie let out a screech that could be heard for a mile.

Sam and Jack picked up speed, the boards bending into the water under their feet with each step. They finally stepped onto more solid swamp ground away from the slough.

Ernie continued to squeal.

"If you don't shut up, Hotchkiss," Sam said, "I'm gonna personally throw your worthless ass in there with them snakes. And that ain't all they got in there. There's a dozen gators bigger'n you that call that their bedroom. Where you're concerned, it could be their dinin' room."

Ernie stifled his screeching and tried to control his gasping breath.

When everyone reached the opposite side of the slough, Nookie exclaimed, "Godomighty!" pointing into the water.

A python sized cottonmouth at least eight feet long and twelve inches in diameter slithered over the walk where they had just passed and disappeared into the slough.

"That's him: granddaddy," Sam said. "They're my watchdogs. Not many people come in here after dark when they learn about my snakes. Look there," Sam pointed further down the slough. There were what appeared to be bumpy floating logs. "Gators," he said.

The ground rose slightly and the walkway became a sandy loam path through a copse of water oaks.

"Home sweet home straight ahead," Sam said.

The tin roof and chimney of a large cabin showed through the trees. As they drew near, a house built eight feet off the ground on creosote piers came into view. The cabin sat on the edge of a quiet little lake, dotted with graceful moss hung cypress trees. A wide veranda hung over the water, and a long net was hung on the side of the high porch to dry.

Beneath the house were two twelve foot aluminum boats locally called bateaus, a large barbecue pit, metal chairs and tables, two extra large hammocks suspended between the piers, and generally everything needed for doing nothing for extended periods of time.

Sam said, "Three bedrooms, kitchen, livin' area, porches, and you wouldn't believe it, but I drilled and got artesian water—hit an aquifer—pure and sweet. Drink from the tap. Indoor plumbin', but got no electricity, except a bunch of batteries for the radio and phone. I have a little generator that'll convert the juice so we can use V.C.R. and T.V. I don't run it unless I have to; too damned noisy. Usually use lanterns or candles. Makes you get everything done before dark."

He reached up, unlocked a trapdoor and pulled a set of stairs down. "Nobody can get in unless I ask 'em in," Sam said, pointing at the steps in the high trapdoor. Just as everyone started to ascend the steps, Nookie said, "I got a l'il present. He held up a three foot long snake by the tail as thick as his arm. Everyone jumped back and Nookie laughed.

"He's dead, don't you worry.

"Where the hell did you get that?" Jack asked.

"Wa'al, them snake havin' a l'il family meetin' back there, so I just reduce the population. You just grob him by him tail, like this," he said, sliding his hand down to the snake's tail. "You whip-snap him like this," Nookie explained as he popped the snake like as bullwhip, "and then you break that bad boys neck. Cotton mouth ain't bad eatin', no."

"You eat it, Naquin." Vic said, curling her lip at the thought.

Nookie squeezed the jaws of the big snake, causing the mouth to spring open, revealing a sallow white interior with two curving fangs, both dripping with a pearly substance.

"That's the way to milk snake," Nookie said, allowing a tiny pearl of the venom to drop on his forefinger. "Poo yii, when that bad boy grob ahold to you, he just chomp down and don't let go. That hurt real bad and kill you dead, yeah. Don't take long, neither."

They again started up the steps when Vic said, "Now look what you did, Naquin. Ernie fainted."

Ernie lay passed out on the stretcher, his eyes rolled back and his tongue protruding slightly.

"That's hard on a city boy, Naquin," Jester chided, "specially a little girl one."

Realizing the full impact his "demonstration of natural competence" had on Ernie, Nookie was chastened considerably, and he said, "Ma poo yi yi. I plumb forgot. I'm sorry. I'm gonna do my best not to skeer that boy no more."

Standing on the porch overlooking the lake, Jester asked, "Sam, how the hell did you get all this stuff in here?"

"Took a long time," Sam said. "Swamp's not always this wet. Lots of people owe me money, and favors. Walked every bit of it in. All the material in the cabin came from old houses, mills that were torn down, even some churches. I don't think I bought anything but the nails and the plumbin' stuff. Me'n my felons built all this. They use the camp too—keep it up for me. I come up here every couple weeks just to get away.

"Boy," Jester said, "when you come here, you're away from everything, that's for damn sure."

Ernie was given a bunk in a small corner room. The whole upper cabin was like a high screened porch with windows all around to provide cross ventilation. Vic snapped an ampule of ammonia under Ernie's nose and he jerked his head, coming wide awake.

"I think you better get another I.V.," she said, connecting a plastic bag to a hook on the wall above Ernie's bed.

Jack and Jester watched Vic insert the I.V. Jack rubbed his chin thoughtfully and asked, "Ernie, are you willin' to talk to us?"

Ernie nodded weakly.

"You get some rest, and we're gonna get settled in, then we'll talk in a little while."

Vic helped Ernie get comfortable, then returned to the large living area. They swung out the casement windows that opened onto a wide balcony which wrapped around two sides of the house. A large pot-bellied, flat topped wood stove was positioned in the corner. A pile of split oak was stacked neatly nearby. Round, metal stovepipes ran through the ceiling from the top of the stove.

Pointing at the stove, Sam said, "That little booger'll keep this whole house warm on a cold winter's day, specially if I draw the drapes to keep out any drafts. I can cook on it and live up here like a man oughta live."

The groceries were put away and the four men made another trek back to the cruiser for the rest of the supplies.

"We need ice mostly," Sam said. "Without power, we have to use an icebox, and it's too far to carry in block ice. Ice chests are the best we can do."

They sipped their Dixies as they walked over the wooden walkway. Occasionally they would stop and listen to swamp sounds. A bullfrog bellowed a basso-buffo call from a dark place somewhere to the left and was answered by another nearby. Tiny birds peeped and flitted from twig to twig in the trees above. Far above, a hawk's screeing call warned all others that this was his territory.

"Don't get no better'n this," Sam said.

"Don't get no better'n this," Jack agreed, grinning his lopsided grin.

"You got a flashlight in yo' boat, Sam?" Nookie asked. "We gonna need it before we get back to de cabin. Sun goin' down fast."

"We got some. But we better hurry," Sam said. "Even with lights I don't like walkin' out there at night. You can step off that walk real easy in the dark and be in plenty trouble—specially from them snakes."

Sam's pace quickened and shortly they were at the cruiser.

As the group neared the dock, noises could be heard coming from the inside of Sam's boat. A figure darted from the cuddy cabin and jumped over the side into a small bateau in the bayou on the opposite side.

The men ran down the dock and reached the boat just as a small motor fired into life on the far side. The same man in the red cap full throttled his little boat, ran up on some cypress knees and nearly swamped before he gained control and sped away down the bayou.

"Son of a bitch!" Sam hollered.

"That was the same one," Jack said.

"I seen him too," Nookie said. "He followed us."

"They know where we are," Jester said.

"Nothin' we can do. Let's get this shit back to camp," Sam shrugged. "It's hard enough to negotiate that trail in the daytime. I don't want to at night unless I have to. It'll be dark in a minute, and if anybody wants to come in after dark, let'em."

They picked up the last of the supplies and hurried back down the path toward the camp as the night closed in around them.

༄

Sam announced, "Boys and lady, we're gonna have fresh seafood for dinner."

"Where are you going to get it?" Vic asked.

Sam swept his arm toward the lake behind the cabin in a grand gesture. "My little five acre farm. You catch the catfish, and we'll watch."

Vic asked, "How do I do that?"

"There's a nightcrawler worm bed down by the barbeque pit. Get a bunch and put 'em in the cans down there. Bring the rods and reels down from the porch, bait up, let your hook down to the bottom and see what happens. Plenty deep right behind the cabin."

The three men settled in the lawn chairs while Jack showed Vic how to bait the hook and spin-cast the wad of worms into the dark waters.

"If you feel something pulling on the line, jerk the pole up and hook it," he instructed.

The sun was gone, leaving only a smudge of orange low on the horizon. The stars sparkled in the velvet, moonless sky. Night came to the swamp. A million tiny frogs chorused in chanting waves from one side of the lake to the other. One side would become quiet while the other would start, then the other would blend until there was a roar of high-pitched chirps sundering the quiet. Then there would be a sudden, total silence except for a splash and a gurgle from somewhere in the darkness and a distant hoot owl answered by a closer one. Then the frogs would begin again, as if directed by some great frog conductor. The cool evening set in.

Jack sat back with a cigarette and beer, discussing the case with the other men, while Vic stood a few feet away, tensely holding the rod, waiting for something to happen.

Jack couldn't keep his eyes from the bouncing pony-tail tied in the red ribbon that highlighted the rest of the package and blended into the warm darkness. The three other men watched Jack watch Vic as they talked.

The tip of Vic's pole suddenly bent into to the water and she whooped excitedly. Jack leaped from his chair, and with his arms around her, helped her hold the rod.

"Hold on," Sam shouted, "you hooked somethin' big."

"Get de net! Get de gaff! Get de gun!" Nookie whooped, teasing Vic's vigorous efforts to land the big fish.

Nookie slid the bateau into the lake and grabbed the jerking, sweeping line. He couldn't hold the line and stop the plunging fish from sounding when the boat came near. "Play him some more till he wear hisself out," Nookie shouted. "I'll get de net."

Nookie pulled the landing net from under the seat and grabbed the line in the other hand. The fish surfaced enough for Nookie to slide the net beneath it.

The bearded snout of a slippery-skinned, wide-mouthed, bewhiskered monster catfish stared out from the murky waters, a hook firmly set in its jaw.

"Hoo boy," Nookie whooped as he twisted the hook free, "he gonna go five pound."

Vic's eyes bounced and gleamed. Breathless, she said, "I never. . .I mean, I didn't know what to do."

"You done damn good, Victoria," Jester said. "You held him, and if they hadn't messed with it, you woulda landed him by yourself."

"I want to catch another one," she said excitedly.

"Have at it," Sam said. "There's lots more catfish out there than there are worms in the worm bed. Looks like they're bitin' good tonight."

Jack and Nookie skinned the big cat and filleted the meat into thin strips while Sam started a fire in his propane burner. He put a deep skillet filled with peanut oil over the flame as Vic dropped another loaded hook into the dark water.

"Made a fisherman out of another one, Sam," Jack said, helping Sam skin and fillet the catfish.

"If I don't do nothin' good in this life but turn somebody on to fishin'," Sam said, "I think I'd done my job. If you love fishin', you got somethin' to live for."

"Hear, hear," Jester said.

Sam dumped seasoning and a delicate mixture of finely ground meal and flour in a large pan, then dipped the fillets in a big bowl of milk and spices. He then rolled them in the flour and dropped them into the sizzling skillet. A spicy aroma filled the air. When the fillets bobbed to the surface of the rolling grease, they were immediately removed and placed on paper towels to drain. French fries were cooked the same way, and just as everything was ready, Vic began squealing again, insisting that everyone leave her alone.

Her pole bent nearly double as she fought the tugging, underwater opponent. The men stood below, watching the bending pole and the line slicing back and forth through the water for a while.

Finally, Jack said, "Well, men, I want to watch this show, but I'm hungry." They loaded their paper plates and ate, sitting on the lawn chairs, while Vic whooped and yelled as she played the big fish.

꒦

Ernie ate a little of the fish and after dinner, he went into the living area and sat in an easy chair. Sam set up a small camcorder on a tripod pointed at Ernie, while Jack placed a cassette recorder on the table.

Jack dictated the location, date and time, then named the witnesses present. "Ernie, I am going to take your recorded statement, do I have you permission to record what you say?"

"Yes."

"What is your full name?"

"Ernest Myerson Hotchkiss, Jr."

"Profession?"

"Medical doctor, Board Certified in Psychiatry, employed at the New Orleans Mental Health Center."

"Do you know Dr. Rudi Bormann?"

"Yes."

"Tell us how you met him and what experiments he conducted while at New Orleans Mental Health Center."

"I met him at the University of Southern California. He was working with a doctor Jolly Westmert there who was giving LSD to elephants and other animals. Rudi said he wanted to do research and write a book, thinking traditional research methods didn't go deep enough. Too many social and legal restrictions. He regretted not having access to the prison population. He told me once that he wished he had access to Bergen Belsen or Auchwitz."

Jester snorted. Ernie paused and looked at Jack with uncertainty.

"That's okay, Ernie, continue." Jack turned and stared blandly at a contrite Jester for a moment. Turning back to Ernie, he said: "You were telling us about Dr. Bormann."

"Rudi wanted massive studies, and he was compulsively detailed. He experimented with electro-convulsive therapy, prefrontal lobotomies, drugs, and finally wanted to study sex, drugs and pain, and their relationship. He had no subjects, so he made arrangements with the deputies of the sheriff's office for young prisoners. The deputies, and others, had their pleasure while Rudi got his material."

Nookie made a sound and Jack glanced in his direction. The Cajun had nodded off and was snoring lightly. Jack remembered that they had been up all night.

"I think he enjoyed it, very much. He had the soundproof filming rooms built next to his 'labs,' as he called the bedrooms. I ran the camcorder so he could record and preserve the experiments and study them later."

Ernie began to sob. "I got in deeper and deeper. I knew more and more, and Rudi wouldn't let me stop. He threatened to leave me—to kick me out of the office, even murder me. The prisoners were being raped, and the rapes turned him on, and he became more and more obsessed. When he brought that little slut Ronnie over to my apartment, that was the last straw. I would have preferred him to kill me, he was doing it anyway!"

"Who else was involved?"

"There were some men in the city and state government. I'll try to remember their names—there were a lot. They'd select a young person from the streets or school grounds, and if the subject had no family with connections, charges would be filed. Then the subject would be picked up and put in detention long enough to conduct the experiments. When he didn't have the outside people, he used Parker and Destrehan, with members of the mob Sessums wanted to please, like Bosco."

"Nobody ever complained?" Jack asked incredulously.

"The subjects were chosen scrupulously. Nobody would believe the subject later. They were terribly poor, and usually the parents didn't care or felt helpless and did nothing if they did care.

Jack asked, "Is that the way they got Dawn Marie?"

"Yes. Mourier selected her. At the end, I learned Rudi was blackmailing them. He was making lots of extra money, and once when he was drunk, he said he was going to retire soon. Then Mourier showed up. I had never seen him before. When I asked Rudi who the man was, he just laughed and asked if I got any good pictures after it was all over. He put the video in a fake book in his bookcase. I took it after he committed suicide. It was in my pillowslip."

"We found it," Jack said.

"I had enough," Ernie continued. "Bringing Ronnie over did something to me. I guess I went crazy. You know what happened from there."

"Are there any more pictures, videos, documents?"

"Yes, in our filing cabinet-safe in our office. Everything is there."

Jack glanced at Vic and lifted his brows.

"Did you video the incident involving Dawn Marie Delacroix and Mourier on or about the eighth of September, 1995?"

"Yes. I videoed it and took photos."

"What kind of photos?"

"Just video on V.H.S. cassette with a Sony camcorder, and some thirty-five millimeter photos with high-speed film."

"Where are the photographs?"

"I don't know. Rudi took them, along with the video. When I found the film in his bookshelf, the photos weren't there. I didn't search more. He has other hiding places."

"Tell us what happened."

Ernie drew a ragged breath and paused, visibly struggling to control his emotions. "When that girl was picked up by the sheriff's deputies, she was given a strong sedative by injection. She was nearly unconscious when she was stripped of her clothing and strapped spread eagle on the bed. Then Rudi administered his serum intravenously. This particular combination of drugs has a strong effect. He strapped her down and she began having what we referred to as 'sexual seizures,' stimulating a compulsion to copulate. They were actually convulsions."

"Where was Bormann?"

"In an adjoining room watching through a two-way mirror. Rudi recorded it on the notes in the papers I gave to you that night when he brought that slut over to the pool."

"What happened then?"

"Parker entered the room, began coitus, immediately had an orgasm. He left the room. Destrehan had an enormous organ. He evidently ruptured something internally. She began to hemorrhage profusely, but that didn't reduce the effect of the drug, for she continued to have convulsions and spasms. The drug had an extraordinary effect on her."

"Then what happened?"

Ernie began to hyperventilate.

"Go on, tell us what happened?"

"Mourier came in. He was very calm. Very strange-looking man. Never changed expression. Looks dead. Big round face, like a moon."

Vic interrupted, "Small ears? No lips? Almost albino?"

Ernie nodded, evidently still thinking of an image in his mind that wouldn't go away.

Jack asked, "Hair almost white, cut close to his head?"

Ernie Nodded again.

Vic leaned forward and asked, "Eyes with no pupils. Like dead, black pools?"

Ernie finally turned and looked at her and said, "Yes. And like he had no nose, or at least it was turned up funny, making his nostrils look like little slits in his face."

"Jack," Vic said. "That's him. The one who has been following us."

"And," Ernie continued as if he had to tell it all or explode, "he got naked and inserted his tiny penis into her. She was bleeding profusely. After a few minutes, he pulled out a long, thin-bladed knife he had hidden under the pillow and shoved it to the hilt between her breasts. He had an orgasm as she went through the throes of death. Rudi told me later that Mourier said before the experiment that he wanted the ultimate experience. Even Rudi hadn't known what he meant by that."

"Is all of that on the video?"

Ernie nodded. "I've been involved in so many evil things because of Rudi. I never dreamed he would allow this to happen. It was like he didn't care if she was dead."

"Did Sessums know about the sex and using prisoners?"

"He didn't at first, but when he found out, he even encouraged it when he wanted political favors. Young innocent girls and boys were expendable, and they could be found anywhere. At first it involved only real offenders, but it got to where one could be chosen and arrested on trumped up charges. Then they were submitted for psychiatric evaluation and treatment, which involved the experiment. When released, they were, of course, destroyed emotionally and mentally, but that didn't matter to anyone—even me. I thought it was part of Rudi's dedicated quest to learn about the mind. I was wrong. He was just a very evil man."

I am showing and handing you a videocassette which I am marking EH, and putting the date on it alongside your initials. Do you recognize this videocassette?" Jack had Ernie hold the videocassette up to the camera.

"Yes, that is the videocassette of the video I took of the Delactroix girl's rape and murder."

"Did you run the video recorder that recorded this video?"

"Yes."

"And you recognize this videocassette as one and the same videocassette containing the video you made of the Delacroix rape and murder?"

"Yes."

"Okay," Jack said. "That's all for now, Ernie. We are going to end the interview. Have I had your permission to record this statement?"

"Yes."

Jack gave the date and ending time and then said, "Somebody should look at that video to verify if we have everything."

"Jester and I will," Vic said. "Jack, you couldn't handle it."

"I don't want to see it," Jack said.

Sam shook his head quickly. "Me either."

"Leave me out," Nookie said, holding his hands up as if to ward off attack.

Sam started the noisy generator while Jester set up the V.C.R. on the T.V. with the sound off. The two doctors watched the video while Ernie and Jack sorted through the pictures and reviewed the documents that accompanied them.

"Yes, these are the videos I took and the photographs, but I didn't know about the documentation in writing. Rudi did all of that; I never saw it."

"Ernie, if I can keep you alive and then protect you from prosecution after it's over, will you testify against all of these men, including Sessums and Mourier?"

"Yes," he whispered."

"We can't guarantee immunity, but we'll do what we can," Sam said. "Your testimony is the key to convicting all of those men, and I'm sure the D.A. will be willing to make some kind of a deal to get it."

"Then what would you do if you could get out of this, Ernie?" Jack asked.

"If I could retain my license, I would go into a family practice. I can't do Psychiatry any longer. For a long time, I've known it's a pseudo-science kept alive by federal money and drug companies. I hate myself for deceiving my patients for so long. They only got worse, usually as drug addicts or institutional cases. I had no idea how to help them. I could only guess and name the disorder given in books, and the books were written by men who knew no more than I, really. It was no help, just a good living for me. Many patients killed themselves."

There was a long silence as Ernie broke down sobbing.

"I must atone for my sins if I can," Ernie said.

They all stared dumbly at Ernie as he held his face in his hands and blubbered.

Jack brushed his palms together with satisfaction. "Well, Sam, we've got enough proof to send Mourier to the chair and Sessums to prison. And, of course, enough to get a money judgment for the those victims if it's collectable."

Sam and Nookie said nothing, still staring unsympathetically at Ernie, who continued to bawl.

Vic rewound the video and placed it back into its plastic case. She and Jester returned to the group, their faces drawn and pale after witnessing the unspeakable act of evil—now imbedded indelibly in their memories—recorded on that fragile plastic strip.

Jester stepped to the kitchen and brought back a fifth of Early Times, which he began slugging straight from the bottle. "Wish I had some of my white lightnin'. Numbs everything better and faster."

Sam took the videocassette gently from Jester and walked into the back of the cabin. In a moment, he returned without it, saying, "I hid it."

"I want to see Mourier dead. Everything Ernie said is there." Vic said. "It's all true. Too true. And more. I am sorry I had to see it. No, I want to see him die, horribly; he deserves the worst kind of death!"

"Vic, I'm sorry you had to go through that, maybe we can get him the chair," Jack said.

"That's too good for him," she said, barely able to control the pent up rage boiling inside. "I want to hurt him myself!"

"Yeah. In my years of dealin' with awful things, I never seen anything like that," Jester said.

Ernie returned to his little room and could be heard moaning and whimpering through the thin walls of the cabin. Jack said, "The D.A. had better cut a deal for Ernie, 'cause he might just walk off the pier. He has no future. They like little girls like that in Angola, and the baddest son-of-a-bitch there will claim him before he can sit down. Ernie's suicide material. Bein' dead's better'n what he's facin'. We better hide the guns."

"Done," Sam said. "Already thought of that. He can't even find a butcher-knife. All put away. Besides, I got a feelin' Ernie's a little smarter and cooler than ya'll think. He knows what to do to survive, and he's playin' it to th' hilt."

"Come on, Sam," Vic said, "he's really disturbed."

"Yeah, you're right. I'd be too, but that don't mean he ain't thinkin' of his own miserable hide."

Vic took a long straight pull from the fifth and tears brightened her eyes as the hot whisky scorched its way down her throat. She took a deep breath and hit it again, causing bubbles to rise in the bottle. She stared out onto the dark waters, while the men dealt with their own thoughts quietly. After a few minutes, she rose slowly and picked up the rod. "I want to catch another fish," she said, a grim look on her face.

"Boys and girl," Sam said, "I hate to tell you, but I gotta get back to town for a little hearing in City Court tomorrow. Won't be gone long. Just a few hours. I'll bring the other stuff we need."

"I'm comin' too. Gotta see to a little business of my own," Jester said. "Gotta FAX a little report on somethin' I did for the D.A. in Pensacola. Besides, I want to see if they found any of our stuff and the body."

Nookie cleared his throat. "Ahem, I gotta leave ya'll too. I didn' tole my l'il Pussy Beaucoup where I done got off to when we haul ass last night. She gon' think I done run out. I'll tend to that and come back with Sam and dem."

Vic's eyes caught more life. Finally she smiled and said, "And I can go fishing!"

"And we can go fishing," Jack added.

Jack shook his head in disbelief. "Sam, you made a fisherman out of her that fast! We got somethin' else to do together, Vic."

She turned slowly and pinned Jack with her eyes. "What is the other thing we can do together, Jack?"

The others seemed to go motionless at the quiet intensity of Vic's question. They all cut their eyes to Jack, waiting for his response. He stammered, "fishing."

Vic was given a bedroom across the wall from Ernie, so she could keep a watch on him.

Sam took to his king-sized bed in the back room. Nookie, Jack and Jester were given inflatable mattresses and sleeping bags. The three men elected to sleep on the porch under the stars.

The swamp sang, chirped, splashed, hooted, bellowed and screeched as the doctor, lawyer and Indian thief quietly talked the late moon up into the night sky and back down again.

Chapter 21

Jack woke to the rasping cries of a flock of white egrets passing over the cabin. He breathed in the coolness of the morning and watched the stars slowly fade as the sky changed from indigo to early morning gray. The swamp was still asleep. There was a splash as a big fish rolled in the far end of the lake and a frog urped in the grasses near the bank. Tiny birds flitted from limb to limb in the trees just outside the cabin, making almost imperceptible chirps like tiny bells.

Jack sat up, tip-toed to the kitchen, and turned on the gas burner under a small saucepan filled with water. He poured two heaping spoonfuls of Morning Call coffee with chicory that looked like ground up charcoal into a little white French pot and waited. He walked out on the porch and considered the events of the past week and what may be in store for the day.

Sessums knew exactly where they were. That was a given. The red-capped snitch surely would have made a report by now. To assume otherwise would be plain dumb.

With three men gone, that would leave only Vic, little helpless Ernie and himself to defend the fort against an attack.

What if they were attacked? What would they do? There were guns here, and maybe even a back door through the swamp in the other direction. Sam would know. Anyway, it's safer in the swamp than in the city.

Jack poured the boiling water over coffee grounds. The hot drops pecked on the bottom of the pot and he held his face over the rising steam. The aroma swirled up to him. He poured some milk into the still hot pan and boiled it. When the coffee was ready, he filled half his mug with boiling milk and the other half with coffee and two tablespoons of sugar.

Everyone awoke in the pre-dawn light and sat in the chairs on the balcony overlooking the lake. Vic baited up and started fishing immediately, dropping her line over the railing into the dark waters below.

Jack said, "Sessums knows where we are. There's no doubt about that."

"Of course," Sam said, "but this is St. James Parish, and it's outside his jurisdiction. I don't think he'd risk a raid by his Gestapo here. So you ain't got to worry about that."

"Even so, while you guys are gone, we could be left to defend ourselves. Jurisdiction don't mean shit to his boys. Is there a back door to this joint?"

Sam thought a moment, and said, "Afraid not. It's all pretty much swamp except this little piece of high ground we're sittin' on. Jack, you worry too much."

"Sam, you ain't experienced what I have in the last week. I know what them bastards can do; you saw my balcony. If they know about the video, they're comin'. You can count on it."

Sam went to the back and returned waving a videocassette.

"I'm takin' the Mourier video with me. Gonna make copies," Sam said. "And I'm gonna take half of the other videos with the documentation and pictures for safekeeping. Anyway, we ain't gonna be gone long, just a few hours. We'll be back just about dark. Besides, anybody'd be a fool to come in here after dark, not knowin' about the trail. You're half Injun anyway, Jack. Hard for anybody to slip up on you."

The swamp awoke slowly with morning birds peeping and squirrels racing along the mossy limbs of the pinoaks and beech along the banks of the lake. The shadows on the lake slowly disappeared, and soon the morning sun burst over the horizon, glazing the tops of the forest with gold. The group became quiet for a long time in a mutual devotional: an agreed upon moment to honor something they all felt together, unspoken, by being at the precise moment when the night gives way to morning with all of its large and small awakenings.

The tranquility was interrupted when Vic's pole suddenly bent and she squealed in delight. "It's so big. Such a big fish!"

Sam rushed to her side and said, "Don't try to pull him in all at once, let him run and play. He's too big to pull up to the balcony. He'll break your line unless you give him some slack. Loosen the drag!"

"What's the drag?"

Sam showed her how the reel could allow the line to pay out when the fish made a run. After a long time playing the fish until it was exhausted, she dragged a three foot long alligator gar to the bank, armored with scales and with a mouth full of needle-like teeth. Nookie ran downstairs and unhooked the vicious looking creature and pulled it high alongside the little boats.

"Good, eatin', garfish," Nookie exclaimed. "Gotta fix it right. Got too many bones to fry."

"We don't have time to cook him right. Besides, we got plenty other fish." Sam said. "Don't throw him back in."

Nookie shook his curls. "Too many gar in there already. I'll just kill him and get rid of him."

Vic was breathless and her eyes glistened. "Whew! That was fun. Coffee! Coffee!" She laid the rod down, and on her way to the kitchen she said, "Nobody touch that rod. I'm coming right back."

Ernie woke and looked over the rail at the group below. "I heard you talking about leaving. You're not going to leave us here alone, are you?" he asked the group generally, his eyes wide.

"We'll be right back. There's no way to avoid it. We need supplies and we all need to handle a little business," Sam said.

"As long as you won't be gone long," Ernie whimpered.

Sam drained his cup and looked impatiently at Ernie over his nose. "Just a few hours. Be back way before dark."

Sighing, Ernie walked to the balcony and, standing by Vic, looked over the edge."What's that?" Vic asked, pointing to a long, twenty foot net hanging on the outside of the balcony with lead weights along the bottom cord and balsa floats strung on the top.

"That's a seine," Nookie said, "you put a long stick on each end and drag him in the water. Them weight drag it to the bottom and the float keep the top of the net on the top of the water, and you pull him along and ketch them bait and things with him."

"You wade in the water and do it?" Vic asked.

"Fo' shore," Nookie said incredulously.

"But, if there are garfish. . ." She made a face at the evil teeth and eyes of the dead garfish on the ground below.

"Hoo! Them won't bother you none. I swum with them before and nutting happen."

"Well, you are not going to catch me swimming in that lake," Vic vowed.

Ernie relaxed a little, poured a cup of coffee, and retired to his room.

Sam made some biscuits and eggs for breakfast. Afterwards, they catalogued and studied the film and photographs. "This stuff'll go to Leone and some to Delahoussie, the D.A." Sam said.

"We'll need it all for the other suits we'll file for the other victims if they want representation," Jack said."

"You really want to help those poor bastards, don't you, Jack?" Sam said derisively. "You think that money will help 'em out? They'll just blow it and be worse off than ever. It don't do no good to give 'em money."

"Yeah, but it has a leveling effect, Sam. They'll know, even if they piss the money away, that somethin' can be done."

"Well, my lad," Sam said shaking his big head of gray curls, "I disagree. I see it as vindication. I want revenge, and money's a kind of revenge. When I got my clients money in cases they just blew it. Weak, but better'n nothin'."

"Call it what you want," Jester said. "It moves the victim from effect to cause point, even if just a little bit. It might tip the scales. Some of 'em might take charge o' their lives. What you boys do could be called 'social engineerin', maybe even 'social surgery'."

"Social surgery!" Jack said. "Scalpel, Dr. Leviathan. I need to remove these malignant growths: Mourier and Sessums."

"Malignant's puttin' it mildly," Jester said. "No tellin' how far their cancer's spread. I'm sure it ain't just in regards to them poor little children."

"It's gonna be like pullin' bad teeth," Jack said.

For two hours, they categorized the tapes, the documentation and photographs. "I'm splittin' half of this stuff. Divided, at least part is safe, and this damn video," he said shaking Dawn's video, "this damn video is enough to cut that cancer right out of New Orleans."

The rest of the morning Jack took Vic in the little bateau and taught her how to fish with a slender, whip-like cane pole, tight line, and a jig: a small hook with a lead weight on it covered with a sprig of colored hair. Soon she was pulling one big, fighting, slab-sided sac-au-lait perch after another from a submerged treetop. Jack had all he could do to remove the fish from her hook and hold the boat in place before she brought another in. He had no time to fish himself. Between landing them, Vic sat tensely, her lips pursed, tightly gripping the pole in her hands, waiting for the next bite.

Jack eyed Vic's perfect form in those white shorts, her turned up nose and tossing pony tail. She stuck her tongue out at him, and another big fish tugged at her line.

Jack gave up on trying to fish himself and he looked at Sam's serene little hidden lake. A big white heron waded the shallow, a string of turtles baked on a log in the noonday sun nearby, and a busy spider spun a big geometric web between low hanging cypress limbs on the tree they fished under. He pulled one of the green cypress balls from the tree, broke it apart and dropped it in the water and watched the oils spread a rainbow sheen on the water surface. *I am a happy man.*

Jack looked at his watch. "It's nearly noon; we gotta go."

Vic ignored Jack, and when he repeated his statement, she looked down her nose at him as if he had said the most stupid thing. Finally, at noon, the ice chest was nearly filled with the speckled panfish, but still Vic still insisted on staying. Jack paddled away from the treetop and Vic gave him a withering look.

I saw you out there, pullin' in these big slabs," Sam laughed. "I told Jester and Nookie it looked like we'd have more'n enough fish to feed a multitude. I'm gonna have to take some home and put 'em in the freezer. They won't keep here. You done good, Vic. Did ya have a good time?"

"Fantastic, Sam! I don't know why I never thought fishing would be this much fun. I can't believe how much fun I've missed."

"From the look of things, you ain't gon' miss it no more," Nookie laughed.

"I'll put a hitch on my pickup and get a boat!"

After lunch, Sam gave Jack a small set of keys and whispered, "Here's the keys to the cedar chest at the foot of my bed. There are two shotguns in there. The twelve gauge is loaded with Number I buckshot and the sixteen gauge has number six duck shot. There's more guns in the closet—some pistols and other pieces. I think you'll find enough for your protection if you need it."

Vic shushed Sam as he was talking about the guns, pointing to Ernie's bedroom.

Sam nodded, having forgotten about Ernie's suicidal tendencies, then added, "Best to stay in the cabin, pull the trap door up. Kinda like a castle with a drawbridge. Ya'll worry too much. We'll be back before dark."

After they left, Ernie came to the balcony and said, "You all please come up here. I heard Sam. He said to get up here. If you don't, I'm gonna pull the door up and lock it."

"Why don't you come down here for a little while, Ernie?"

"There is no way I would come down those steps. Those snakes, and that—that monster Vic caught. Where is it?"

"Buried. Stink up the place otherwise," Jack said, "and the snakes are way down there," he said, pointing to the trail.

"When I leave this place, I want either to go under sedation or for someone carry me out, preferably unconscious. I am not going to put a foot down on the earth around here. I loathe swamps and things like this."

"When we leave, I'll carry you on my back and I promise not to throw you into those alligators or snakes."

"Jack!" Vic whispered. "You said that like you would throw him in. He's terrified. Suppose you were in his shoes?"

"I'm not, and I'll carry him out and I promise I won't throw him in the snakes—okay?"

"You're not being funny," Vic whispered to Jack.

Ernie peered over the balcony and said, "Well, it looks as if you two would like to be left alone, so T.T.F.N., or ta ta for now."

Jack looked at his watch. "You know it's after four? The damned day has gone so fast."

"Well, here we are," Vic said. "A paradise except for the circumstances."

Jack held up his beer. "A jug of wine, a loaf of bread, and thou, singing beside me in the wilderness, ah wilderness were paradise enow."

Vic said, "I never thought I'd be included in a quote from the Rubiyat of Omar Kayhaam. Is this wilderness paradise enough?"

"Well, er, ah", Jack stumbled.

"What do you want to do now, Jack?" Vic asked, watching his expression.

"Maybe read a little. Play cards or chess, take a nap."

"I'll whip your ass in a game of chess."

"Wanna bet," Jack answered.

"Yeah, what?"

Jack looked into her eyes and met a challenge. *What is she saying with her eyes? I'm such a dumbass. I don't understand women at all. If I make a move, it could mean the end of our friendship. If I make a move and score, I know I'll be trapped by my own craziness. I can't risk that. This is different from just getting laid like I always do; get laid and hang around a little then leave. Dammit, why can't things be simple?*

Finally, Jack answered. "Dinner, wherever I want to go, or you want to go, for any amount."

"Done, pardner," Vic said, extending her hand for an agreement shake.

Jack took her warm, slender hand in his. Her fingers were soft, yet firm and pliable. He got a picture of those hands on his body, and he swallowed like a schoolboy.

WWL played songs from the sixties on the little battery operated radio. The Temptations sang "Ain't Too Proud To Beg," and Vic grabbed Jack's hand and made him stand and dance. Not being a dancer, he shuffled a bit while she moved in her white shorts in ways that made Jack miss the steps he did know.

"You're not a bad dancer, Jack," she said. "I could teach you some steps and you would be pretty good. But you must keep your mind on what you are doing."

"Yeah, right," Jack muttered, still thinking about the amazing way Vic could move, like her hips were built on a swivel.

"Where'd you learn to do that?" he asked.

"Do What?"

"Oh, I studied ballet and modern dance, and took gymnastics. Dad was stationed in the Caribbean when I was a teenager and my classmates could do some pretty wild voodoo dances."

It must be voodoo to make me feel like this.

When the music ended, Jack hurriedly lit a Picayune and sat down. They played "Nowhere Man," "Yellow Submarine," "Mellow Yellow," and "Tambourine Man."

They set the board up. Vic whipped Jack just like she said. The game took an hour. Several games took the rest of the day as Jack drank and smoked and Vic continued to fight him into long, drawn-out end games.

They dozed and read in Sam's big hammocks in the warm evening, lazily talking, dreamily drifting as the sun sank behind the trees. They made sandwiches and drank the last of the beer. Then they watched flocks of egrets and herons, black against the crimson horizon, silently winging their way to their roosts. The choruses of tree frogs sang their anthem to the night, the bullfrogs baroomed, and the catfish kerflopped in the still mirror of the lake.

Jack pumped the Coleman lantern into action. Its glowing white mantles seared away the darkness that swallowed the cabin as the sun dropped behind the trees.

Ernie was terrified and went to bed early.

Jack stretched out on the hammock big enough for two after dinner. He closed his eyes and relaxed, listening to the sounds of the swamp blend and merge into a single oneness, drifting slowly toward sleep. He felt the hammock shake as Vic crawled in beside him and lay her head on his arm.

Jack tensed for a moment as she snuggled her warm nose into the hollow of his neck and pressed her body against his. In that single instant, the juggernaut of Jack's pent-up emotions marched right over and crumbled the taboos of his lifetime. She trembled and melted in his arms as their lips met.

God, her lips are warm, he thought as her tongue sought his, finding it, played a rhapsody on his nerve endings that was broadcast to his very toes. *Another crossroads,* he mused, as he dived like a kamikaze straight into what portended to be an irreversible error, yet what he desired most of all.

His hand moved to gently encircle her breast, when the sounds of the swamp went totally silent. He heard a snuffling sound and a rumbling growl. Jack opened his eyes. There, just inches behind Vic's head, was the drooling, nightmare face of the most fiendish animal Jack had ever seen.

The face of Satan.

Chapter 22

Vic opened her eyes, puzzled at the sudden termination of Jack's ardor. His face was frozen in shock, staring at something just behind her head.

When she started to look, he said without moving his lips, "Don't move. There's a big Rottweiler behind you."

The figures of two men materialized from out of the shadows. Jack blinked, first seeing a man wearing camouflage fatigues, boots and gun belt. He thought it was a hunter or fisherman paying a late visit until he saw Sessums' face beneath the paramilitary cap. Behind Sessums appeared a short, pale-faced man in black. It only took a moment to recognize the weirdo from the quarter. The man who murdered Dawn: Mourier!

The big dog snuffled, his teeth snapping together involuntarily, as foaming slobber dripped from the loose folds of his drooping lips.

Vic stiffened, watching the direction of Jack's attention. "What is it, Jack? What is that sound?" she urgently whispered.

"Sessums and Mourier. And a bad dog. Don't move."

"Satan!" Mourier ordered.

The big dog flinched and lifted his baleful eyes to Mourier.

"Sit!"

Satan sat.

"Stay!"

Satan stayed.

"Satan won't bother you, Mr. Chandler, unless either of you make some unusual moves," Mourier said. "I must advise that any move can be considered unusual by

Satan. He will tear your throat out in less than a second. Get out of the hammock, both of you."

Mourier's gurgling whisper came from a small circle of a mouth that opened in a way that didn't seem to synchronize with the sounds that came out. He seemed to have no lips and chewed each word as if they all tasted bad. His flat black eyes had a darkness in them that spoke of things better left unsaid.

Jack rolled out easily, pulling Vic along behind. They stood facing Mourier and Sessums.

"Very cozy, Mr. Chandler," Mourier said in a dead monotone. "If you wish to live, give me the items you have stolen. We may spare your life."

Jack laughed and casually walked to the chairs just under the balcony and sat. Vic followed and stood by his side with her hand on his shoulder. He lit a cigarette and nonchalantly blew a smoke ring toward the lake. Maybe stalling them would give Sam's cavalry time to return.

Sessums gave Mourier an odd look and walked to where Jack sat. Standing directly in front of Chandler, he unsnapped the army forty-five from the holster and pointed the big gun right into Jack's face. Vic's fingernails dug into Jack's shoulder. He simply raised his hand and patted hers.

"Don't worry," Jack said, looking calmly into Sessums' blazing eyes, "these two buttholes think they're roosters, but they're just chickens with an attitude. They've had money and guns to cover their insanity, but that's all over now. They're history."

"I'm not insane," Mourier said abruptly.

"Oh, yes you are. You've done things like rape, and you murdered that little girl in cold blood. You were on candid camera, did you know that? Is that the act of a sane man?"

"Mourier's hole of a mouth began working as if he was sucking something. "Chandler, I am going to see to it you will never live to leave this place. Our sheriff's back-up is out by the boat, waiting for our signal. You'll be dead and there will be no witnesses to prove we didn't act in self defense when we call them." He held up his cell phone.

"You know somethin' Mourier, you are one ugly motherfucker. I guess the only way you could get any would be to buy it and then murder it. How many others did you do that to in your life? You need killin'. That's the best thing for you."

Taking advantage of the moment, Jack continued baiting and badgering. "And you, Sessums," Jack said, pointing his finger at Sessums. "Did you know your shrink friends filmed everything—your deputies, your political and mafioso buddies? A whole file drawer full."

"I'll burn this place to the ground with all of you in it," Sessums snarled. "I know that Hotchkiss is up in that cabin, and I want him down here."

"He won't come down," Jack said.

At that moment, the ladder stairway was pulled up and banged shut. The deadbolt securing it snapped in place.

Sessums' eyes glazed for a moment and he fired the forty five into floor of the cabin above. "Hotchkiss, if you don't come down, I'll burn you out," Sessums shouted.

"I'm tellin' you," Jack said, "he's more scared of snakes than he is of human snakes or fire."

"Give me the videos or I'll blow you away right here and now," Sessums demanded as he cocked the hammer on the .45 and pressed the big muzzle into Jack's cheekbone.

"Some of the videos are here, but Sam Leviathan took the film of Mourier killing Dawn and half of the other evidence with him. You'd get only part. He has enough to hang both of you, and he's making copies that'll be distributed all over the country. I tell you, you're both dead meat, regardless of what you do to me."

Mourier began making grunting noises, as he mouthed words with his little mouth.

Beads of sweat broke out on Sessums' upper lip. He looked at Mourier, who continued to stare vacantly, mouthing words about not being insane.

"Blow me away or just blow me. You'll never get a damned thing. This train's already on the track and runnin' with or without me."

Satan sat at Mourier's feet looking up at him, whining. Mourier said bleakly, "I'm OK."

"Okay, Malborn," Sessums said, shaking Mourier's arm, "so you're not insane. This is your party, get on with it."

Mourier stirred, looking about him as if waking in a new place. He hissed, "I should have never made you sheriff. Your incompetence brought us to this." His spitting words weren't just cold, they was lifeless and alien. "When we dispose of them and what they took, you will be replaced." Mourier turned his death mask face to Jack and said, "Give me what you have here, and then we are going to burn the house. I may not kill your girl if you do as I say."

Jack slowly raised his hand and gently pushed the barrel of the .45 away from his head and shouted, "Ernie. Can you hear me?"

A small voice came from the back of the cabin. "Yes."

"I want you to drop all of the videos, pictures and stuff down to us."

"No."

"Why not?"

"He'll shoot me."

"I promise not to shoot you," Sessums shouted.

There was a long pause, as if Ernie was thinking about it, followed by the sound of foot steps on the floor going back into the cabin. After a moment, the footsteps padded to the balcony.

Sessums raised his automatic and Jack yelled, "Ernie, get back!" There was a thump from above as Ernie ducked back into the cabin from the balcony.

"You rotten son-of-a-bitch," Jack snarled. "You were gonna shoot him."

Sessums slammed the barrel of the .45 down against the side of Jack's head, knocking him back into the chair. Blood spurted from his left temporal and cheek, drenching his face and chest with crimson.

Vic started toward Sessums, but he leveled the gun at her and snorted, "You can be dead in five seconds, girl. A belly wound with these loads take a lot longer."

Vic bent to help Jack. Blood streamed from a nasty gash above his eye. She stripped Jack's shirt from him and used it to staunch the bleeding.

"I need to get something to help him," she said. "I have a medical bag upstairs."

"Oh yes, I forgot you're a doctor. Let's not waste any more time," Sessums said.

Mourier said, "Let Satan help."

He pushed Satan up to Jack's face and the big dog began to lap at the flowing blood, lashing his tail with his ears pinned back, stimulated at the taste and smell of living blood, evidently readying to feast on Jack's head. Vic watched, her eyes wide at the spectacle of the dog licking Jack's wincing face and bleeding brow, the animal becoming more agitated by the second.

"Now. If Hotchkiss doesn't give us the film, I'm going to give Chandler to Satan for dinner. He loves human blood."

"Ernie!" Vic screamed. "Please throw down the stuff. They're going to kill Jack!"

A blizzard of photographs and papers flew over the balcony, accompanied by videocassettes in plastic boxes that bounced off the heads of the group below. The ground all around was littered with the evidence.

Sessums and Mourier stood in the middle of the material that had been pitched over the balcony and looked at the mess all over the ground. Satan stepped back and looked up.

Ernie let out a giggle as he released the seine that had been hung from the railing. The long net drifted down and settled onto Sessums, Mourier and Satan. Satan began biting and fighting the netting that had draped all around him, like a huge web, causing Mourier and Sessums to become entangled.

Jack opened his one good eye. "Run, Vic. Run."

Vic pulled Jack to his feet, who reeled for a moment before he regained his balance. He jerked out a big Bowie hunting knife that had been stuck in the piling beneath the house and they both sprinted down the trail toward the landing.

The night was dark, but there was enough illumination from the stars and moon to see the trail. When they came to the slough, they slowed to a careful walk and cautiously made their way over the uneven boards Sam called a bridge. Just as they reached the far end, Jack looked back. The big Rottweiler plunged through the darkness, followed closely by Mourier and Sessums.

Vic was ahead, and Jack shouted, "Go," but she hesitated as Jack turned around at the foot of the bridge and faced the dark form hurtling over the boards toward him.

A calm settled over Jack. Blood still ran down his face past the eye that had already swollen shut.

He crouched in the path, half naked, his face and chest glistening with blood. The hunting knife rested in his hand as if it were an extension of his own body.

Something shifted in Jack. His universe became still. A wide smile spread over his face.

Resting Lynx crouched in the path with the stolen blade singing in his hand. It had drunk blood before, absorbing the soul and essence of the enemy; with each kill, the blade was stronger. After this, the blade would be all powerful. It was coming, and he would kill. His long hair hung wet against his naked back and his heart filled in the ecstasy of combat. The paws of the devil hound beat on the bridge. The demon started its lunge, as Resting Lynx let out the blood curdling cry of the lion at the kill.

Satan stiffened and dug four trenches in the mud trying to come to a stop. Then he raised to his back legs, reversed direction, and crashed into Mourier, who was still on the bridge.

There was a grunt and a yip, and both Mourier and Satan splashed into the slough.

Sessums stopped short of the center of the bridge and played his light over the waters. Satan leaped about, howling and scrabbling over the bridge, dragging a dozen large cotton-mouths latched to his legs and haunches. He splashed down the muddy slough, picking up more snakes as he entered deeper water and a gathering of big alligators.

The water swirled and roiled where Mourier submerged. Reptiles attacked and thrashed around the figure rolling in three feet of mud and water. Sessums stood transfixed, his mouth open at the sight. He slowly backed off the bridge until he stood at the edge of the water. The beam of his flashlight showed a muddy figure slowly rising out of the water.

A human form slogged toward Sessums through the swirling waters, totally encased in a coil of writhing snakes. One was longer than Mourier was tall and as big around as his thigh. It had fastened its huge mouth to Mourier's jaw, encircling and spasming around his throat and head. Clamped onto Mourier were others ranging from as thick as a man's arm to as thin as a pencil. Every snake fang had sunk deep, and they whipped and slashed, wrapping themselves around each other and Mourier's body–a tangled mass of poisonous serpents, all squirting venom into their host.

Mourier spread his arms out on each side. Streamers of snakes twisted and hung from all parts of his head, neck and body, coiling around his arms and torso.

Sessums pointed his light into the face. The same expressionless eyes that had beheld Dawn while she shuddered her last breath in the coils of his own death grip now stared through a living, wriggling, curtain of reptiles.

Mourier took two slogging steps, toppled backward, and disappeared under the tumultuous, swirling waters.

Sessums stepped backward onto the muddy bank. He slipped, falling on his back, his right foot sliding into the muck. The flashlight beamed onto his feet. A dark form nosed up from the slough next to him.

Jack and Vic watched the scene from the other side of the bridge in the light of Sessums' flashlight. Satan continued howling for a while in the distance, then stopped suddenly right after a noisy splash was heard downstream.

When Sessums' light dropped to the ground, Jack and Vic cautiously crossed the bridge. They found him lying in the mud, an eight foot alligator tugging on his boot.

Jack noticed Sessums wasn't holding his gun and proceeded to kick the gator in the head several times. The gator held on. Jack grabbed Sessums' leg and pulled his foot out of his boot.

The sheriff didn't move.

"Get up!" Jack yelled. "That big son-of-a-bitch is gonna get you if you don't move!"

Jack pulled on Sessums' shoulders and dragged him several feet from the slough, then relieved him of the flashlight that was still tightly clinched in his hand. He put the light in Sessums' face. What he saw gave him a chill.

Sessums eyes bulged and he seemed to be gagging.

Vic quickly placed her fingers on Sessums' wrist and felt his pulse. She pointed the light into his staring eyes, pulled back his eyelid, and his hands flopped down lifelessly when she released them.

"Stroke," Vic said. "Massive embolism, I would think. Seems to be totally paralyzed. Lets get him back to the camp."

Jack retrieved the .45 Sessums had dropped in the mud, and ported him the hundred yards through the woods and laid him in the hammock.

"Ernie," Vic yelled.

"Yes," the voice came weakly.

"It's all over. Sessums had a massive stroke and I need your help. Will you come down?"

"No."

"We need to get Sessums to a hospital," Vic said to Jack. "He may just croak on us."

"So?" Jack said, looking at the helpless Sessums. "You know something sheriff, I oughta feel sorry for you, but somehow I just can't."

"My first duty as a doctor is to save his life," Vic said, "regardless of anything else. I am not his judge or jury, a higher authority should adjudicate."

"Sheriff, I ain't gonna judge you either," Jack said, "but I think you just got your reward."

Sessums attempted to speak, but he could only croak.

Ernie peered over the balcony and squeaked, "Are you sure it's safe?"

"It's safe, Ernie," Vic said. "You can come out. Mourier and his dog are gone and Sessums is, how do you say it, 'out of commission?'"

"I'm not coming down."

"Ernie," Jack ordered, "drop a fifth of Jack Daniels over the balcony. Check the kitchen cabinet."

Jack lit a cigarette and caught the fifth with one hand as Ernie dropped it over the edge. He unscrewed the cap and turned the bottle up. Big bubbles rose in the amber liquid until three inches out of the full bottle disappeared.

"Jack," Vic erupted while she watched him still sucking at the upturned fifth. "You'll die if you drink all of that. Leave some for me or I'll kill you."

Jack's one good eye watered. He belched, wiped his mouth with his unbloodied, naked arm, and handed the bottle to Vic. She turned the bottle up and slugged down about an inch, burped, and wiped her mouth on her sleeve. She grinned at Jack through her own tearing eyes and they both laughed.

"I think we better see what we can salvage of Mourier," Jack said. "The gators are probably at him by now, if they'll have him."

"Sessums isn't going anywhere, unless he has a miraculous recovery," Vic said. "And that's not likely."

"Now sheriff, you behave yourself and don't go wanderin' off anywhere. There's bad things out there," Jack said.

"Jack, don't torment him. You know he's helpless."

"Yeah, the sonofabitch was just about to kill us all just a few minutes ago and you want me to be sympathetic? I hope he stays that way."

As they started to walk away, Jack suddenly whispered, "Listen!"

The pounding sound of running came from the path leading from the slough. Jack and Vic backed into the shadows behind the cabin and waited. Jack wiped the mud from Sessums' .45 as they crouched in the darkness.

In a moment, Sam, Nookie and Jester panted into the camp, wild-eyed, followed by a squad of sheriff deputies carrying shotguns and pistols.

Sam yelled, "Jack, Vic, where are you?"

Jack stepped out into the light. His face and chest a mass of dried blood. His right eye was swollen shut.

A red faced Major wearing a gold oak cluster on his collar came trotting up, puffing, his service revolver drawn, pointing at Jack. "Drop it. Hands in the air," he commanded.

Jack dropped the gun. The Major spun him around, slammed him hard against one of the upright supports and brutally snapped cuffs on his wrists behind him. He screamed, "What have you done with Sheriff Sessums!"

The scene was filled with six deputies, weapons drawn, alert to every noise. One spotted Sessums lying quietly in the hammock and cautiously approached him. "Sheriff, you alright?"

Sessums struggled to speak, his breath jerking, but he was only able to loll his tongue out idiotically and make faces. It was apparent the right side of his face was drawing in paralysis.

"Major," the deputy shouted, "Somethin' wrong with the sheriff, come see."

The Major dragged Jack with him over to the hammock and leaned over, looking into Sessums' contorted face.

The Major frowned. "What's wrong, Sheriff?" Getting no answer but a gurgle from Sessums, he looked around in puzzlement, as if looking for an answer.

Jester introduced himself and Vic as doctors, and he as a coroner and asked the Major if he could examine Sessums. The Major reluctantly allowed Jester and Vic to go about their exam, and not totally convinced they knew what they were doing stood closely by, his service revolver held on both.

After a few moments, Jester straightened up and said, "Massive stroke. A bad one too. Completely paralyzed. Look at how the right side of his face is drawing on him. He understands everything we are saying and has all of his senses, but he has lost all motor control."

The major was a high ranking officer in the sheriff's department, the same rank as Parker. It takes years of dedication, service as well as intra office politics to survive that long in the harsh atmosphere of law enforcement to make that kind of rank and hold it. Jack thought he looked like a good man, whose senior was mysteriously disabled. He wanted answers and was entitled to them.

The Major frowned, concerned about the sheriff and perhaps his own job if the sheriff was disabled. "When will he be back to normal?"

"Hard to say. Maybe never," Jester said, looking sadly at Sessums, whose eyes blazed, still trying to talk but only gutteral sounds could be heard.

Nookie stuck his head through the crowd and stared at Sessums. "You mean the shariff done caught hisself a stroke?"

Vic and Jester nodded.

"I don't believe a damn word of it," the Major said. "Somethin's goin' on here and I intend to get to the bottom of it. One of you caused this!"

Sam asked Jack, "What the hell happened to you?"

Jack winked at Vic with his good eye and grinned. "We had some company. The good guys won. It was a dogfight. Sessums showed me how to use a .45, and then we all took a little jog to the slough."

The deputies listened, growing hostile at Jack's cavalier attitude. Vic interrupted and explained what happened from the time Satan found them in the hammock.

"This wild man attacked a Rottweiler," Vic laughed, pointing at Jack. "I couldn't believe it. He stood right in the path as that monster charged. Jack let out a scream like I have never heard anywhere, and the dog turned and ran the other way! It rammed into Mourier and both of them fell in the slough. Sessums had a stroke and nearly was eaten by an alligator."

"Whar's the dawg?" Nookie asked.

"Dunno," Jack said. "He had some cotton mouths on him when he ran down the slough. There was a splash and that's the last we heard of him. Name was Satan. Right name for that son-of-a-bitch."

"Gator got 'im," Nookie said sagely. "You know, gator do love dog."

The Major finally found his voice. "This is all horseshit. Chandler, you're a cop killer and I think you tried to kill the sheriff. You're under arrest for the attempted murder of sheriff Sessums. Where is Mr. Mourier?"

Vic pointed to the slough.

"Like I said, the Rottweiler knocked Mourier into the slough. He's still in there."

"You're gonna need somethin' to get Mourier out with," Jack said. "I ain't about to put a foot in there."

"You ain't about to put a foot anywhere, Chandler," the Major said, jerking up on Jack's cuffs causing Jack to grimace.

Vic headed toward the Major in anger and Sam grabbed her before she could get there, "Hold on Vic, this mess is just for a little while, till we get back. They may cause Jack a little pain and worry, but he's able to take care of himself, ain't you Jack?"

Jack winked, as the Major jerked his cuffs again, this time causing an obvious abrasion on his wrists where the cuffs were already too tight.

"Er, ah, Major," Jester said, "I am very concerned about your cutting off the circulation on Mr. Chandler's hands. It could cause him to lose his hands."

The Major glanced at Sessums, whose eyes were wide and bulbous, then back to Jack. "He ain't gonna need any hands where he's goin'.

Sam walked up to the Major and said, in almost a whisper, as he looked down on the stocky Major's burr cut, "You cause him any damage, and he's set free, you're gonna to be personally liable and you'll lose your job. I'll see to it. I know you are angry, upset and very concerned about the sheriff, and for good reason for none of this makes sense, but you'll get the truth later. So don't do anything rash, Major, it's not what you think."

The Major blustered a bit then roughly loosened the cuffs. Jack's hands had begun to turn purple. Jack rubbed his hands together to restore circulation.

The Major called for the local sheriff, paramedics and a coroner to meet him at Sam's dock. He was obviously baffled by the news about his boss, the high sheriff, and refused to accept what he heard. These people were clearly not the group of criminals Sessums and Mourier had painted them to be, but he had to do his duty and bring someone in. Jack was out on bond on charges of killing officers of the law, and now the high Sheriff of Orleans Parish had mysteriously suffered a stroke and the Sheriff's friend was dead. Jack looked guilty to him. His cynical mind, having dealt with the bottom feeders of the Big Easy all of his life, would not allow any room for doubt. One or more of these people was guilty of something. One of them was obviously Jack.

Sam thought for a moment and ran to the stair and told Ernie to drop the steps. He ran up into the house and returned with a large steel hook set into the end of a three foot staff.

"My gaff," he said. "Sometimes I catch a granddaddy cat and need this to get him in the boat. Mourier ain't gonna mind now."

Sam chopped a long limb from a cypress, stripped it of branches, lashed the gaff to the end and said, "Let's go fishin'"

The major released one of Jack's cuffs and then made him reach around one of the creosote supports, then reattached the cuff so that Jack was hugging around the post.

"You stay there," the Major ordered, scowling into Jack's face.

The slough still boiled where Mourier had fallen. In the light of several high intensity flashlights, occasionally a wink of white would surface and then be pulled back into the rolling, muddy waters. Dark forms thrashed about, stirring the snakes to a frenzy.

One of the deputies raised his pistol to shoot into the midst of the boiling waters.

"Don't nobody shoot into that," Sam yelled. "If we hit Mourier, it'll look like we killed him."

"Would you shut up!" The Major yelled at Sam.

Sam stood on the bridge and fished in the turbulence until he snagged something and pulled. The object appeared to be stuck in the mud until Nookie shouted, pointing to one side.

"Hey, Sam, the reason you ain't gettin' no place is a gator done got a mouthful o' Mourier."

Nookie then took a limb and beat the armored head of the big gator. The gator ignored Nookie's licks and continued holding a leg.

"Major," Nookie said, "I guess ya'll gotta shoot him. He ain't gonna let go. Shoot him in the gut, away from Mourier's body."

One of the deputies drew a bead with his sawed off shot gun and fired point blank into the gator's side. Fire leaped from the barrel and a roar thundered through the woods. The big gator thrashed and released the leg, flailing its six foot tail in pain. Snakes, along with mud and water, were hurled onto the bank, bridge and overhanging branches.

Vic screamed when a cottonmouth flipped out by the thrashing tail, hit her arm. She ran back several feet and beamed her light on the sinuous creature slithering back toward the water. The deputies scattered away from the slough.

Sam snagged something soft and pulled. The body sucked away from the muddy bottom and was dragged to the bank, still under attack by the snakes. It was swollen beyond recognition and the right leg was missing from the knee down. Most of the snakes released their hold, instinctively crawling back to the slough when the body was dragged onto the bank. Several crawled toward the lights.

Sam flailed them away with the gaff, knocking the rest from Mourier's body in the process.

"Lets get it away from here," Sam said, dragging the body with the gaff to higher ground.

The officers gathered around the body and the Major said, a worried look on his face, "that's Mr. Mourier alright."

The Major, not to appear as confused as he really was, took command and ordered everyone back under the porch. Jester, Nookie, Vic and Sam took long swigs from the fifth. Jack looked longingly at the bottle.

Vic and Jester were allowed to clean Jack and dress his wound. "Gonna take stitches, boy," Jester said. "I'll do it if Vic don't want to."

Vic got her medicine bag and found what she needed and Jester sutured a long, deep gash starting at Jack's hairline above his left eye ending at his cheek. "Knocked shit outta you boy. You probably got a concussion. Gotta take it easy."

While they were stitching and dressing his wound, Jack sneaked several long quaffs from the bottle.

The Major questioned Ernie, who verified everything Vic said was true, and allowed Jack to remove the cuffs long enough to put on a shirt.

"Ernie saved us," Vic said, "He dropped that net from up there on them. We ran while they got themselves loose."

"You're a hero, Ernie," Jack said. "If you hadn't dropped the seine, we woulda been a dog's breakfast. They were gonna feed me to Satan and there was nothing I could do about it."

"He was going to kill us all anyway," Ernie whimpered, "I had to do something."

They picked up the photos, videos and assorted evidence from the ground beneath the balcony, showing some of the stills to the awestruck Major.

"You're movin' in the right direction," Jack said to Ernie. "All you have to do is keep it up and maybe you'll make it. Your quick thinkin' gave me'n Vic the chance we needed to get away."

"Thank you," came a weak acknowledgment.

Everything was secured in the cabin. "I'll have to come back and get the other stuff," Sam said, pushing up the stair, closing the door over it and locking it. "Everything will be safe till I get back."

Vic, Jester and Nookie packed all of the evidence into the boxes, and persuaded the deputies to help carry things to the landing, including two igloo coolers filled with fish.

Two deputies carried Sessums on a makeshift stretcher and two carried Mourier wrapped in garbage bags on another devised litter.

Sam easily lifted Ernie to his shoulders.

"Sam, please be careful," Ernie whimpered.

"You be still up there, Hotchkiss. I'm not likin' you ridin' me any more'n you like ridin' me, so just shut the fuck up. I could make your pansy ass walk like you should."

"Oh God, please don't Sam!" Ernie rode Sam's big shoulders as if frozen with his eyes shut all the way to the dock.

The Major ordered everyone to get moving. He shoved Jack in the small of his back, toward the bridge. With his hands cuffed behind him, Jack teetered and Vic yelled, "Jack, be careful!"

The Major laughed as Jack nearly fell into the swirling snakes, obviously hoping he would fall in, but Jack straightened up and tripped on across, leaving the officer behind, nearly falling in himself.

Vic, Nookie, Sam and Jester caught up with the Major and Jack, walking alongside after they left the boardwalk over the swampy area.

"How'd they get here," Vic asked Sam.

"There's a fancy sixty foot cabin cruiser tied to my dock. Probably belongs to Sessums or Mourier."

"That's sho' nuff a peach of a boat," Nookie said. "Wish I had one like that."

Jack said, "When this is all over, Nookie, if there's any way, we'll get it for you with a legit title for all you've done to help."

"Mais non, Jack. You don' need to thank Nookie. He done pass hisself a good time, yeah!"

"How do you say, Naquin," Vic said, "Laissez le bon temps roulez?"

"Mais yeah, cher, let de good time roll. Hey Sam, if I'm gonna captain my l'il boat, I am ready to frappe' la rue."

"What'd he say?" Jester asked.

"Frappe' la rue. Hit the road," Jack said, his swollen face grimacing in an attempted grin.

"Eh bien, allons, cher," Nookie said, moving on out ahead of the group.

"Literally translated, Jack said, 'let's go, dear'," Jack said.

"He called us dear?" Jester said, making a face.

"Just an expression, meaning something like 'friend'. He really didn't call us 'dear.'"

Nookie stepped out and was soon a hundred yards ahead of the slow moving group.

Jester said, "You say that gator had a hold of Sessum's foot?"

"Yeah, Jack said, "damn gator don't care what he eats."

"Oh well," said Jester, "he'll be OK if we can get him to a hospital. He doesn't need my services as coroner....Yet."

Sessums' eyes blazed in fury as he listened to Jester's evaluation.

"I said you couldn't win," Jack said to Sessums, being carried just ahead of him. "I told you you didn't know what you were dealin' with."

The Major said, "shut up, all of you."

The group walked in silence the rest of the way to the dock.

Chapter 23

Just after midnight three sheriff's deputies from St. James Parish, two state police officers, two paramedics and a deputy coroner waited at the dock as the group arrived. Two cabin cruisers, marked St. James Parish Sheriff Flotilla, with lights strobing the night blue, were docked next to a huge sixty foot luxury yacht and a small runabout.

A long, and loud discussion took place between the law enforcement officers, and finally the Major from the New Orleans Sheriff's office spoke: "We're in St. James Parish jurisdiction. These officers will take over now." He stepped back and a squatty little deputy turned to Jack and Sam.

"The St. James sheriff's office is gonna assume jurisdiction over this matter. We're takin' all of ya'll in on suspicion of kidnappin' and murder. Anything ya'll say can be used against you in a court of law. Cuff all of 'em," he ordered.

His two deputies pushed forward and placed cuffs on everyone, including Ernie.

The deputy made everyone produce drivers licenses, which was difficult, for their hands were cuffed in front.

He studied the licenses one-by-one, and when he came to Jester, he asked, "Where you from?"

"Sunny South," Jester said.

"Don't get smart. I could book you for resistin'. Now answer the question."

"Okay, Jester said. "Selma, originally."

The deputy said, scowling, "You lyin'. This is a Alabama license!"

Jester said, "Selma's in Alabama."

The deputy didn't acknowledge, but said, "This license says you supposed to wear seein' eye glasses. I don't see no glasses on your face!"

"I have contacts, Officer."

The deputy stuck his face into Jester's and yelled, "I don't give a damn who you know, I'm bookin' you for resistin'!"

When he saw Jack's license, he actually spit on the dock near Jack's feet. "You're the cop-killer from New Orleans, ain't you?"

Jack didn't respond.

The little deputy snarled and swung his Billy club at Jack's head. Instinctively Jack bent his knees quickly into a squatting position and butted his head into the deputy's middle. The deputy, surprised and off balance, with the help of Jack's forward motion, stepped off the dock into muddy waters of the Little Mississippi. There was a tremendous splash.

"Man overboard!" Sam shouted.

Sam laughed and soon all of the cuffed ones were roaring.

The little deputy surfaced sputtering, "Shoot him. He tried to kill me!"

One of the state police officers pulled the dripping and furious deputy to the dock. "I lost my Billy," he screamed, scanning the dark waters below the dock.

Spinning toward Jack, the deputy grabbed for his pistol. The state trooper calmly laid his hand on the deputy's arm and drew him to the side.

He said quietly, but loud enough for Jack to hear, "Deputy, I think you should reconsider your actions here. This man was unarmed and cuffed, and you attempted to strike him. There are several witnesses. The subject was protecting himself and it seems you lost your balance and fell in. I'll write a report to that effect. And I'm going to check with my supervisor and see if you actually do have jurisdiction."

The radiophone crackled and the situation was explained to the voice at the other end. After a delay, the trooper said that the particular location was indeed in St. James Parish, and the deputy could assume control temporarily, but they would have to relinquish jurisdiction to the Livingston Parish sheriff's office when they reached the Blind River Landing.

"It seems, deputy," the trooper said, "that you have arrested two litigious lawyers, two prestigious doctors, and a psychiatrist. My supervisor suggests that you expedite your investigation and either charge them or release them as soon as possible."

"Hey! How 'bout me? You left me out," Nookie said, raising his shackled hands. "Ain't I liteejis an' presteejis enough?"

೪

The manacled crew was herded into Mourier's boat with the sopping deputy in charge. He ordered the other deputies to keep weapons trained on the dangerous group, particularly on Jack, the 'cop killer.' Sessums was laid in the elaborate bedroom, but Ernie refused to share the space with him and sat on the deck with the rest.

"Where's your boat?" Jack asked Sam.

"Somebody ripped out my distributor and stole my steerin' wheel."

"How'd you get here?"

Sam hooked his thumb in Nookie's direction, who held up both of his palms innocently with a silly look on his face. "I'm de hot wire king, dere ain' no doubt. Gonna have to leave somebody l'il speedboat at Sam's dock," he said, holding up his cuffed wrists indicating his inability to drive it back.

Sam grinned at Nookie. "When we got to the dock the Major said they were waitin' for a call if the Sheriff needed backup. So we all hauled out through the swamp in the dark. Seems we just missed the fun."

Sam smirked as he said, "Even smart criminals like Mourier and Sessums get caught."

"After a while," Vic said, "they can't tell the difference from right and wrong, even if they once knew it."

Ernie stared at the floor listening to the conversation over the drone of the big engines as the boat bumped gently over the glassy surface of the night river.

"And you," Vic said, bending to speak to Ernie, "you can make up a little of what you have done by testifying."

"Yeah," Jack said, "as long as these cases are unresolved, you're still not out of danger; there are many out there who would like to silence you so you couldn't identify the videos and pictures. A good defense attorney could make a big issue about the photographer not being there to identify the pictures."

Ernie clutched Vic's hand. "I wish I were dead," he whined.

Looking disgusted at Ernie's whimpering Jester said, "You came close, at your own hand, Ernie. Now live and try to make things right."

The St. James deputy screamed. "Shut up! I've heard enough of this bullshit! You're all going to jail until I get this matter settled—you 'specially," he said, jabbing a stubby finger just inches shy of Jack's eye."

Jack's eyelids narrowed to slits. A low growl gurgled deep in his throat. The deputy froze, gaping at the deadly smile on Jack's face.

Blind River Landing swarmed with local, state and sheriff's office law enforcement. Headlights illuminated the launch and dock like daylight. Red and blue lights flickered, and the radiophones sizzled on fifteen police units parked under the pines. A reporter from New Orleans WDSU TV stood by with her video photographer, busily filming the arrival of the boats.

An ambulance and a hearse waited among the cars for Sessums and what was left of Mourier.

"Hey," Jester whispered, "we got a reception. I feel honored with all this here attention."

"It's all for you," the deputy said. He jerked Jack up by his cuffs and dragged him over the side onto the dock.

Standing there to meet them was a tall, lean man whose weathered features were more those of a farmer than a lawman. He wore gleaming cowboy boots, neatly pressed western style pants and shirt, and a short brimmed Stetson. A gold star gleamed on his chest. He appraised the scene with calm detachment; a faint glint of humor gleamed in his pale blue eyes.

The soaking deputy dragged Jack up to him. "Look what I got here, Sheriff Hitchman. It's that killer we all been hearin' about, Jack Chandler. And look there," he pointed to Sessums lying on the stretcher in the boat. "It's Sheriff Sessums from Orleans Parish. He's paralyzed, looks like. They probably give him somethin'. They done somethin', look at 'em. You ever see such a bunch of suspicious lookin' perps?"

Two deputies lifted Sessums from of the boat on a stretcher and paused alongside Sheriff Hitchman.

"Sheriff?" Hitchman asked quietly, bending down to Sessums, whose jugular vein bulged as he tried to speak. "What happened to you?"

Getting no answer, Hitchman wrinkled his brow and turned back to the deputy, who stood dripping on the dock alongside. "And what happened to you?" Hitchman asked.

The deputy's eyes blazed as he jerked Jack up to his face and said, "This damned cop-killer tried to drown me. I'm bookin' him on attempted murder, assault and battery, resistin' arrest, an' attempt to escape."

Sheriff Hitchman didn't acknowledge the deputy. He beamed his light into Mourier's big cruiser and watched as two white-clad attendants lifted the grisly bag to the dock. He stared at the parade exiting the boat. First was a very shapely, dark skinned woman; then a rotund, bearded man; next a thin, pallid-faced young man who faltered when he stepped onto the dock; followed by a swarthy individual who could have been a pirate. A huge, white man was the last to disembark, and as he stepped from the boat, the vessel seemed to give a sigh of relief.

A tall brunette wedged her way into the crowd with her tape recorder. Behind her a young man with earrings holding a TV camera filmed the whole scene. "What's happening here and what has happened to Sheriff Sessums. Is this the cop killer Chandler? Who is in the body bag?"

The sheriff turned his back on the reporter and signaled two of his deputies to stand between he and the reporter and cameraman, who was videoing the offloading of the boat and particularly Jack.

The sheriff beamed the light directly into Sam's face and said, "Sam! I been waitin' for you. Maybe you can tell me what the hell's goin' on."

The wet deputy's eyes became very wide. He lowered the elevation of Jack's manacles.

"First thing you oughta do, Travis, is let 'em put Sessums on board the ambulance and that package there in the hearse." Sam said, pointing to the body bag and the long black vehicle. "Then I'm gonna tell you the wildest damn story you've heard in a spell."

Sheriff Hitchman directed the loading and then turned to the deputy still holding Jack's cuffs. "Let go!" he ordered. Jack's cuffed hands were dropped like they were hot brands.

"Okay, Sam, let's have it."

Sam held up his manacled wrists. Hitchman scowled and said to the deputy. "Take 'em off."

The deputy quickly unlocked the clinking bracelets as Sam rubbed the raw spots on his wrists.

"Now, release Jack, Nookie and these three doctors," Sam asked.

A peremptory wave of Sheriff Hitchman's hand produced a flurry of activity as the St. James deputies quickly removed cuffs from the others. The recently shackled crowd massaged their wrists and milled about on the end of the little dock jutting out into the river.

Finally, the commotion was over and Sheriff Hitchman, shaking his head, said, "Now, Cuz, what the hell's going on?"

Chapter 24

Sam introduced everyone to Travis Hitchman, the High Sheriff of Livingston Parish.

"Sessums suffered a massive stroke, Sheriff." Jester said. "He could have an infarction, er, a coronary if not given immediate care. He needs to get to a hospital soon as possible."

"Take him to the Seventh Ward Hospital in Hammond." The sheriff told the ambulance driver. "That's the closest, unless he wants to go somewhere else. Can he tell us?"

Vic put her head through the ambulance door. "Blink if you want to go to a New Orleans Hospital."

Sessums blinked.

"Now, as I name them, nod when I say the one you want. Baptist? Methodist? East Jefferson? Touro?"

Sessums blinked on Touro. Vic turned to the driver and said, "Touro. Hang on, I'll be right back."

Vic then walked back to Jack and said, "He may need help on the way. I am going to ride with him. Touro. I have my bag in case there is a problem."

"Well, I'll see you later," Jack said, as Vic paused and squeezed his hand, holding his gaze for a long moment.

"You are one crazy man, Jack Chandler. Take care. See you back home."

She walked briskly to the boat and retrieved her black bag. There was utter silence, except the crackling of the radios, while every man followed her shapely form as she trotted to the ambulance. The ambulance drove away, sirens squalling, followed by the hearse.

"Ya'll can go, too," the Sheriff told his lead deputy. One hard look was all it took from Sheriff Hitchman for the little St. James deputy to turn and leave quickly. Immediately, the parade of police units left in a cloud of dust through the pines to the main road, leaving the sheriff alone with Jack and his ragged looking crew. Fixing Jack with a level gaze, Sheriff Hitchman said, "The news is all about you, Chandler. You're like a one man army. You got the headlines last night and today. They said that you've been charged with murder and stealing a body from the morgue."

"Well, here I am, Sheriff. Take me in."

"No. I checked it out. You're out on bail. Right smart of news has been generated about you."

"I'll tell you the reason, Cuz," Sam said.

"Wait—before you start," Hitchman said. "let's get comfortable." He turned to a man standing by the door of the Blind River Landing Bar and asked, "Can we come in for a spell, Billy Roy?"

A little bald-headed man stood yawning at the door. He flipped on the lights to the bar and said, "Sheriff, ya'll come on in and make ya'll selves to home. I'll open the bar."

"I need a drink," Jester said, moving first toward the open door, followed by the rest of the troop.

The Sheriff turned to the reporter and cameraman who were trying to push their way in through the door. He said, with his gentle smile, just before closing the door and locking them out, "Sorry, police business."

The group settled around a table. Everyone ordered beer, and while Sam began telling the story from the beginning, the Sheriff slowly loaded his burned out pipe with an old dead cigar butt and began puffing an evil smelling smoke that made the group wince.

"Just so ya'll know, Travis saves his cigar butts for his pipe. He'll stink up a room quick."

"Waste not, want not," the Sheriff said dryly.

Sam began the story, and five minutes later, he said, "And that's when I saw you standin' at the dock. I didn't know you were gonna send a hot dog like that little shit that cuffed us."

"Not my hot dog. Belongs to Sheriff LaGarde over in St. James. Your camp's in St. James Parish, and they had to take initial jurisdiction. Didn't figure he would cause any trouble. I was gonna cut ya'll loose soon's ya'll got here."

"Thanks a lot, Cuz. We've seen too many of that kind, huh, Jack?"

"Damned straight!" Jack said, exhaling a cloud. "The law gave me a workin' over durin' the last week. Seems I ran into every rotten apple in the law barrel."

Hitchman looked thoughtful and said, "We do the best we can with them that we have."

Hitchman sucked on an unlit pipe, found a kitchen match in his shirt pocket, and finally got it going again as the others watched and waited.

"We got some rogue cops. But they get weeded out."

"We'd be in deep shit if they were all like that," Jack said.

"You bet, "Hitchman said. "Thank God they're not. When Sessums' bunch were heard on the radio, I figured I'd better take a look. I been knowin' him since he was Perez's boy down in Plaquemines. When his name came up involvin' my parish, I started listenin'."

Jack watched Hitchman take a long, slow draw on his reeking pipe and was glad this brand of lawman was the rule, not the exception.

"Now what?" Hitchman asked.

"I guess we go home," Jack said.

"No please," Ernie blurted in his high voice, on the edge of hysteria, "What about me? There's men out there who wish to dispose of me so I can't testify about what I know. I can't go back. They know where I live."

There was a long silence as the men thought of what to do about Ernie.

"We gotta keep this little guy safe 'til we can preserve his testimony," Sam said, pointing at Ernie. "Don't know what we're going to do with him."

"Sam's right," said Jack, "we can't let him go back to his apartment. He's the key to convicting the main defendants and I guarantee he wouldn't last on the street."

Hitchman drew on his pipe again and rested his quiet eyes on the shrinking Ernie for a long time. The others ordered more beer, some Planters salted peanuts and little cheese crackers, and waited while the sheriff contemplated. It was like waiting for water to boil while watching the pot.

Sam said, "Cousin Travis here–he's slow, but he's thorough. Sometimes you can go to supper and come back and he's still thinkin' about somethin'. But he'll get there. Just don't mess with him while he's at it."

Finally, Hitchman said, "This boy needs a safe place. From what you say, he's damned valuable. I could put him in lockdown, but it would take round the clock security. I don't have that kind of personnel. If it is like you say, even there somebody'd get to him and I don't want that on my hands in my parish."

"Freeze him," Nookie said, poking Jack in the ribs.

Ernie let out a little whimper, frowning at Nookie and Jack.

"That's your answer to everything, Nookie," Jack said, poking him back.

The sheriff's eyes twinkled at Nookie's bubbling ways, then became serious. "We got a family place in the woods north of Kentwood, up on the Mississippi line. Got T.V., runnin' water, inside plumbin', good enough kitchen, 'lectricity, attic fan, fireplace, butane gas heaters. There are a couple of air condition units that work sometimes. Even got a fishing' pond and some horses if he wants to ride. We can lay in supplies and he's safe for as long as you want him hid." "Thanks, Cuz," Sam said.

"Blood's thicker'n water, Sam. You'd do the same for me."

"Are there snakes, spiders and things like that?" Ernie asked.

"It's hill kind of country, Ernie," Sam said. "Nothin' like you just saw. Consider the human snakes first."

"Old man lives right up the road," the sheriff said. "He'll keep you company. He might be convinced to move in with you for a while. He's a crack shot, plays fiddle and can call a squirrel out of a tree right up to the mulligan stewpot. He'll keep you entertained in his way."

"As long as I'm not left alone," Ernie said.

"Alright, gentlemen," the Sheriff said, "I'll just relieve you of one witness-passenger, collect some tithes for supplies and we'll be on our way."

Jack and Sam emptied their pockets and came up with the total of fifty dollars between them, with a promise to send more when they got back to the city.

"I'll loan you a couple hundred," Jester said, peeling two bills from a fat roll.

"That oughta set us up. We'll need more as we go," the sheriff said, rising from his chair and indicating for Ernie to follow.

As they reached the door to the bar, the sheriff paused and said, "Naquin, I returned a van we found over there by Sam's boat shed. Joy riders probably hotwired it and took it for a spin?"

"That's a fack, Sheriff. You never know when them joy rider gon' steal you truck."

"And Sam," the Sheriff said, "my deputies brought back that little speed hull you two hot-wired to get back to your camp tonight. Nobody'll know any difference. I'll cover it with the owner if a problem comes up."

"That's the way justice is handled in Livingston Parish," Sam said, "Ain't no use in gettin' rough'. Travis keeps the peace like a gentleman, but he does what he has to do. Livingston's the home of the Klan and to be Sheriff, you gotta be lots of things to lots of people."

"I understand fully," Jester said, smiling at Sheriff Travis Hitchman with approval.

"Finally, boys," the sheriff said, "I don't think it's a good idea for my men to take you back to New Orleans, but I am sure my good friend Billy Roy here can find you a ride. Hows about it, Bill?"

"Sheriff, anything you say. I'll take'em myself. I been hauling cowshit in my old van—but if they ain't picky..."

The sheriff's features almost broke into a smile. "You ain't picky are you boys?"

The ride to the city was fragrant, actually enjoyed by Jack, Sam, Jester and Nookie, all originally country boys who thought the ride back was hilarious, comfortably reminiscent, and somehow fitting.

Nookie was dropped at Pussy Beaucoup's place and the others collapsed on the couch and chairs at Jack's apartment.

The three barely could keep their eyes open. Sam stretched, yawned, and said, "OK, Jack, where are we at in this deal?"

"Chapter two, Sam. We hooked the fish, but we still don't have him in the boat. Matter of fact, we don't even know what we got on the line. Maybe a damn shark, or just an old rubber boot."

Sam let out a long breath. "I been so busy doin' what we been doin' I haven't thought past gettin' you out alive and savin' the evidence. And you're still a target, Jack. Some may want you dead just out of spite."

"What else is new?"

Jester punched Jack on the shoulder, and Jack grinned, looking every bit like a pirate with his eye swollen shut and inflamed stitches running down the side of his head.

"You still ain't in the clear, Jack," Sam said. The charges are still on you, and no tellin' what the press is gonna do with this."

"Fuck 'em," Jack said, his head throbbing. It was nearly five. He closed his one good eye and drifted off.

Chapter 25

DAY NINE

V ic stumbled in at dawn, exhausted, and woke the three sleeping in their chairs. "Sheriff Sessums is not doing well at all," she said. "He has been so exasperated at his inability to talk that he had another stroke and now cannot move anything but his eyes. The difference is his blood pressure is out the roof. He's not going to make it."

Jack sniffed and shrugged. "You're not gonna get any sympathy out of me."

"The poor man is really miserable," Vic said. "I believe if he could speak, he would beg for someone to end his life."

"He ain't gonna recover, that's for sure," Jester said.

"He'll escape prosecution because of his condition," Jack said. "He allowed all of that to happen so he could keep the power and everything that went with it: the big house, the power, money, women. But how could he justify it? Maybe he finally realized it and called this down on himself. Still, I want him to know what he did, and understand. That'd be hell to live with if he has any humanity, but I bet he's blamin' everybody else for his problems."

Sam clicked on the six o'clock news and there, emblazoned on the screen was the exodus of them from the boat, giving each a closeup shot of their faces. It ended with and held on Jack's scarred and swollen face for several seconds while the anchor announced this was Jack Chandler, accused of several murders of law enforcement officers, now implicated in the mysterious death of Mourier and the paralysis of the high criminal Sheriff of Orleans parish. The whole message was that Jack was an outlaw murderer, still at large, continuing a killing rampage and the system was too cowardly or liberal to do anything about it.

"Jack, you gotta lay low." Jester said. "Some damn vigilante might just try to punch your ticket to make sure the law's carried out proper. I've felt that way myself when I saw some criminal get cut loose on a technicality."

"Me too," Jack said. "I want to get some sleep."

ᡄᢀ

They slept until noon on the chairs and sofa. When Jack opened his eyes, he was deluged with the pungent smell of chicory coffee and beignets in a snowstorm of confectioner sugar, all straight from the Cafe-du-Monde just down the street.

"I took a walk while you beauties were havin' your nap," Jester said.

Sam wiped the powdery sugar from his lips. "Okay, Jack, you ready to get to kickin' ass today? We got a lot to do and gotta keep you outta sight so some damn sniper don't decide to take the law in his own hands."

"Ya'll have enough to prove the murder," Jester said, "and the rapes of the other children, so what's next?

"Seems like we've done something," frowning as he gingerly touched the puffy side of his face with the tips of his fingers, "but all we've done is uncovered a pile of crap, and for what? Seems like our work has just begun if we intend to do something to help the victims, or even get the guilty bastards charged and tried. They're gonna fight us every step of the way. Maybe even try to remove or block us somehow. They might even make up some more shit about us and try to nail us."

"Jack, they already tried that on you, and nothing stuck. But you right, we have a long way to go. We gotta do asset checks on Sessums and Mourier. I know assholes like Destrehan and Parker didn't have a pot to piss in. We gotta find money. Surely Mourier has a paper trail we can follow to his assets."

"I'll help any way I can," Jester said. "If I can, I'll stay here and work with you all until they need me in Mobile and I'll hot foot back over there and back till we get ahold to something here. But first I gotta get back to Mobile for a couple days and then I'll be back. I'm part of this to the end."

"Thanks, Jestie," Vic said. "You can stay at my place when you get back."

Sam raised his hand. "He can stay with me. I have a couch."

Jack frowned at Sam. "Sam, your apartment is like your car and your boat. I don't think you've had it cleaned since I've known you. Jester deserves a better place to stay."

"Yeah, I guess you right. Need a bulldozer to get to the couch."

"Done. We're a team. The Four musketeers. Our job is just beginning. So lets get busy," Vic said.

"I'll do the asset check," Sam said. "We gotta learn everything we can about the enemy, dead or alive. I'll call my boy at Dun and Bradstreet. He can track a paper trail like a beagle tracks a rabbit."

DAY NINE

"I didn't believe that I could actually become inured to looking at all of that," Jack said. "Over the last two days, I actually got numb; and its been like an unreal horror show. Even a porno freak couldn't take two days of that."

"We got through it," Vic said. "We looked at every video from beginning to end, took digital stills of these criminals, and now we have documentation of over three year's worth of insanity."

"I don't know how you did it, Jack," Jester said, "It even gives me nightmares, and I deal with bad stuff all the time."

"Yeah, Jack said, stretching, pouring a finger of bourbon. "But you deal with death, not life violated to a point worse than death. The memory of rape and what it does to you is a constant you can never escape. That's what's in the minds of all those victims. A lifetime of mental pictures they can't live with but have to live with every moment. It affects every thought and everything they do. Can you imagine what such a violation does to you? I want to get redemption for them, not just money. Money'll redeem something, given enough of it."

He continued, "I'm gonna to blow up the stills to eight-by-tens, make a file on each individual victim, and a duplicate file on each individual defendant. We've identified nineteen defendants so far, ranging from Congressional Assistants down to Assistant D.A.'s. Bormann was buildin' himself a retirement based on blackmail. I wonder if there's any other stuff out there?"

Sam grunted, and shifted his big weight in the suffering chair. "Well, if there is, we ain't gonna have time to work any more cases than we have. This bunch is a career in itself.

"After we blow the pictures up, We're takin' it all to the D.A.," Jack said. "He's gotta prosecute. And we'll slam dunk'em with our civil action."

Sam stared into his cup as he quietly stirred his coffee. Jack said, "What's up, Sam. You're actin' funny."

"I got a report on Mourier," Sam said.

Jack said, "You don't look too happy about it."

"He had no wife, no children or living relatives that can be located. He possibly even fabricated his own identity for that matter. He was sole shareholder of a corporation called M.M., Ltd. He had a boathouse apartment, his boat, and an old car. There was a bank account with less than $10,000 in it. That's all anybody can find."

"What?" Jack said. "He was one of the most powerful men in the country. There has to be a whole set of corporate ownerships."

"My man at Dun and Bradstreet says he's never seen such a devious submersion of identity. Mourier simply disappeared in a complexity of interlocking corporate directorates, a damned cloud of legal ownerships. The ownership vests in his designees and proxy holders, whoever and wherever they are."

"But at least there are some available assets?" Vic asked.

"Almost nothin'," Sam said. "But we gotta get a judgment against his estate before any of his stuff is up for grabs. There must be somethin' else somewhere."

"What about the other defendants?" Vic asked. "Can they hide their assets and get away?"

"If they have anything that's subject to seizure, they can't," Jack said. "Their acts were intentional, and they can't escape through bankruptcy. They're like that big catfish you caught. They can run and they can try to twist the line around a root, but they're hooked. They're yours and can't ever own anything in their names. The only problem is that a slick lawyer can hide most anything, though. So I never get optimistic in collectin' judgments against somebody personally."

Vic smiled the smile of gratification. "I've seen enough horror in the last three days to harden me against any sympathy for any of them. I want to see them suffer. I wanted to see Mourier get it, and he really got it. I saw it with my own eyes. I am going to personally witness these men suffer in other ways, but suffer they will–some way, and I want to help make it happen."

Sam put his big paw on Vic's shoulder and said, "They will, Vic. I assure you, with me'n Jack on the case, they will. But there's more bad news."

Everyone waited. "Sessums owned nothing that isn't mortgaged to the hilt, including his businesses. Seems Mourier owned him body and soul. No telling what enterprises Mourier had that Sessums allowed. And the sheriff's office won't owe anything if their attorneys show he acted outside the authority of his office, and so did Parker and Destrehan. Could be the sheriff's office could skate as well. That's to be seen. That leaves Mourier's estate, whatever that is."

There was a long silence in the room. It seemed as if all of their efforts were for nothing except that of bringing the criminals to their just ends.

Sam had a humorous light in his eye the whole time he was telling of Mourier's and Sessums' properties. Jack said, "Sam, you're holdin' something' back. I know you. You got the very devil in your eye."

"Ahem. I saved it till last."

Vic and Jack both leaned forward to hear.

"M.M., Ltd. made one last investment in a very interesting property the day before Mourier went to his reward. He paid cash."

"C'mon Sam, dammit, spit it out."

"That particular piece of property is," Sam paused for effect, "the one and only, your very own apartment building right over your head, The Marquis de Mandeville Apartments."

Chapter 26

District Attorney Maurice Delahoussie, six foot six, ungainly, big hands, big feet, slackjawed, and lop-eyed, stared at Jack and Sam as if they were excrement walking into his office. He even wrinkled his nose in keeping with his diagnosis of the pair.

Jack's eye was still swollen shut, and the ridge of deep red stitches rode astride a yellow and purple bruise from his brow to his cheek. He wore jeans, tennis shoes and blue work shirt. Sam had on a wrinkled white linen suit that looked like he had slept in, scuffed white oxfords and a straw hat atop his mop of salt and pepper curls.

"Mr. Delahoussie," Jack said, trying a deferential route for a change, "we got enough evidence here to prosecute some of the biggest boys in our fair state for the foulest crimes on the books. It's your jurisdiction, not Charlie Leone's, because it happened here. It would behoove you to give it your immediate time and attention. We're working on the companion civil cases and intend to proceed immediately. You should have the opportunity to prosecute to avoid any embarrassment to you if I take my shot first."

Delahoussie called two harried-looking young lawyers into his office and told them to sit in. He laconically introduced them as his first and second assistants.

Delahoussie draped his long body over his leather office chair, peering down his nose at Sam and Jack, his jowls shaking slightly as he spoke. "Now what is it that you have to say?"

Jack wasn't sure who the D.A. was talking to because one of his eyes seemed to be staring off at an angle while the other would focus on him. Then the other eye would train on him while the previous eye would gaze off at an angle. *That's damned disconcerting,* Jack thought as he tried to keep track of which of Delahoussie's eyes was doing the looking.

Jack and Sam would occasionally both begin speaking at once, as each felt Delahoussie was addressing him. They laid the enlarged photographs and documents out on the big desk, all in neat, separate piles in chronological date order, as they explained the significance of each.

Delahoussie's jaw dropped and stayed slack as Sam and Jack recited the facts and evidence. His already bulging eyes popped even more as he held the gruesome photos up to the light as if the evidence he was seeing was somehow false.

"I can't believe it. I know some of these men!" he said.

"No matter," Jack replied. "We're goin' after 'em, and if you won't, the public is gonna wonder why. It's clear they're criminally accountable as well."

The Assistant D.A.'s fidgeted. Sam turned to them and said, "I know it's you on the front line to handle this. The boss here is gonna take some flack, but nothin' like you're gonna face. There'll be pressure to drop or reduce the charges and then the pressures of trial. There's lots of these bastards to prosecute. I think you should take some comfort in that you have no choice, since it's such a massive undertakin'. Hell, you might even make a name for yourselves."

The assistants shifted about in their chairs, glancing furtively at the scowling Delahoussie.

"And," Jack said to the assistants, "you ain't got nothing to do. We just laid your case out for you right there on the D.A.'s desk. We have the videos to back it up too. We'll get copies made for you."

A bright young assistant D.A. spoke up. "Without a witness, this evidence might not fly."

"Ahah," Jack said, "not to worry. We have the photographer of every one of these pictures."

"Who is it? And where is he?" Delahoussie demanded.

"Not so fast," Jack said. "We are gonna file our suits, get the defendants attorneys to answer, and as soon as everybody is in, I am going to take his video deposition with all attorneys present to preserve his testimony for you and for me."

Delahoussie and his assistants just watched as Jack walked about, pointing at photos and written evidence, and arguing his case to the prosecutor.

"The photographer-witness is in a safe house," Jack said, "and nobody's gonna know his whereabouts until the last minute, and not a minute before. There'd be a little temptation to put out his lights, don't you think?"

Delahoussie barked, "I'll order you to produce him before we take any action. And I'll enjoin your suits till the prosecution is completed, if we choose to prosecute.

"And I'll resist it until it is all in, for the safety of the witness."

"We can keep him safe."

"Yeah, like you and Sessums kept Bormann safe."

Delahoussie rose in his chair, standing tall enough to look over Jack's head directly into Sam's eye. "I hope you're not insinuating."

"No," Sam said, standing toe to toe with Delahoussie, staring him straight in the eye. "We ain't necessarily suggestin' you'd be lax in your supervision, we're just interested in keepin' our witness alive. Your track record's not so hot in keepin' vital witnesses alive."

Delahoussie puffed for a few minutes and sauntered about behind his desk, his thumbs hooked behind his suspenders.

"I'm to file charges in this case based on the evidence you've brought, but without a witness?"

"You did it for Sessums against me, didn't you?" Jack snarled.

"Well, er, that was. . ."

"Different? Is that what you were going to say? Different?" Jack said coldly, his fury mounting. "You didn't seem to think about witnesses then, just a couple of days ago. You didn't check a goddamn thing. You just slammed me with nothin' but a verbal from Sessums. What did he have on you, Delahoussie? Did he call in a big one?"

Delahoussie's face blanched and sweat popped out on his brow. "What? If you are suggesting. . ."

Jack had struck gold and so he kept it up, in spite of Sam's big frown at what he was doing. Jack knew that what a man thinks you know about him has infinite power. The unknown turns hidden fears into open terror.

"Yeah, I am suggesting. We got lots out of Sessums before he had his stroke," Jack lied. "I also know some things, but I'm not low enough to pull what Sessums pulled on you. You'll never hear it coming from my lips. But you got a job to do in this case, regardless of how you got jammed by Sessums.

Jack was on a roll. "You know, Delahoussie, I've had the best after me, and I've always landed on my feet. Set your dogs after this evidence and see how long it lasts. I'll see to it that Time, U.S. News, USA Today, all the media gets it. You've had enough bad press about land-based casinos and your ties to the mob."

Delahoussie sucked in his breath and started to protest. Jack continued his outraged tirade. He seemed to grow in stature as big as the room, his eye a blazing bloodshot orb peering through a swollen black and orange eyelid. "You set out to be President of the United States, and you finally settled for D.A. I know lots about you. Drop the charges against me, put the truth out about me, issue a press release about Mourier and Sessums in the Picayune–front page like I got–and I may work with you in this case. You could get lots of mileage out of this. Otherwise, I call the media, give them all I have, and you got nothin' but a pale hope you get re-elected to this miserable fuckin' office."

Delahoussie's face was pale when Jack finished. He nervously wiped his mouth with the back of his hand and unlimbered his tall, gawky form to stand over Jack again. Jack looked up at him, and then down at the feet of the ungainly man.

"You got on a pair of big-assed shoes, Delahoussie. What are they, size sixteens? Them are the shoes of a big man. Or they should be. Are you as big as your shoes, or you just got big feet?"

Delahoussie glanced down and frowned at his shoes and said nothing as Jack and Sam pulled the door closed behind them.

❧

SHERIFF IMPLICATED.
CHANDLER EXONERATED.
GRAND JURY RETURNS INDICTMENTS ON OFFICIALS.
DELAHOUSSIE PLANS FURTHER INVESTIGATION.

Sam read one headline after another from the Times Picayune, Baton Rouge Advocate, Shreveport Times, each telling of the investigation of corruption in the office of the Orleans Parish Criminal Sheriff and Orleans Mental Health, implicating state officials and assorted businessmen.

"You're famous," lad, "Sam said. "The whole story's covered in the magazine section and in USA Today."

"And he's got an invitation to appear on the Larry King show!" Vic exulted.

"You goin'?" Sam asked.

"Nah. Probably not. Too much publicity makes me nervous."

"You'd be a national figure," Sam said. "Maybe even work it into a movie part or somethin'. Maybe settle for Governor if you didn't want to move to Hollywood."

"Hey, man," Jack said, "I just want to be left alone and get to the end of this. Delahoussie's just tending to his business and that is his business now. But we still have lots of unfinished business. We got only part of what we set out to do, done. I don't need all that."

"Well, you got it, like it or not, Jack Chandler," Sam laughed, slapping Jack on the back. "Hey, how about that Delahoussie. I'm impressed."

"Delahoussie's a consummate politician," Jack said. "He's turnin' this into a political smorgasbord."

"Yeah, he didn't have a choice, did he?" Sam said.

"It was either go with us or stink with the rest of 'em," Jack said.

"I read in the paper today that two of the defendants committed suicide," Vic said slowly.

"That's just the beginnin'" Jack said, as if talking to himself. "When word got out we were filin' this, and that Sessums was in trouble, every victim came forward. Nobody was shy this time."

Sam took a hefty set of legal papers from his battered brief case and said, "A consolidated petition by all victims against all defendants. It's in final, all you gotta do is sign on the line. Give it a read and see if there are any corrections."

Jack scanned the petition, scratched his name on the bottom, and handed them back to Sam. "It lists all of the parties, and I guess the allegations in each case as to time and place are all correct?"

"I checked 'em myself," Sam said. "They all correspond with the evidence."

"You may file when ready, Gridley," Jack said, shaking Sam's big hand.

"Damn the torpedoes, filin' suit ahead!" Sam grinned as he leaned forward, lifted both elbows, picked up his right foot to the level of his left knee in the fashion of Jackie Gleason leaving the stage, and said, "And awaaaay we go," as he side-stepped from the room.

෴

Jack got back to work and was making a checklist of cycles to complete on each case, including credit and background checks, depositions, etc., when the phone rang.

"Hello, Mr. Chandler?"

"Yes."

"This is Robert Costanza. I met you at Charlie Leone's office when you brought Bormann in. I was his attorney."

"Oh, yeah. What's up?"

"Well, I have been asked to represent Mourier's estate by certain corporate interests. Were you aware that the Marquis de Mandeville is owned by his personal corporation, M. M., Ltd?"

"Yeah. We found that out."

There was a short pause as the implication sank in. "I guess it is a little late, and unusual, in view of what has happened since the previous manager evicted you, or tried to, but I am rescinding any eviction orders.

"What's the catch."

"I am authorized to offer you a year's free rent in exchange for releasing any claim for damages occasioned by your eviction.

I know you have a large suit against Mr. Mourier's estate, and that claim potentially encumbers certain of his personal properties, including the stock of MM, Ltd. You probably have done an extensive asset check by now?"

"Oh, yes, we're freezing his properties until we get judgment," Jack said airily, "But we haven't dug into his corporate holdings. That's going to be very interesting."

"Ah, ahem, that's part of what this call is about," Robert the lawyer said. "We would rather you not be motivated to pursue this particular avenue, as your case has a limited value, and we would be willing to make a substantial offer to settle."

Shades of Sessums, Jack thought. *When Sessums offered a 'reasonable settlement,' he and Mourier were still vertical and unpunished. Now both are horizontal and Dawn has as much earthly vengeance as she could ask. The rest of the story on those two will be resolved on a plane other than this earthly one. So what's left? There's no way Dawn can be brought back or Martin and Estelle be granted surcease of sorrow for the indescribable loss of their one and only child. It's reached the point where it does involve money. And lots of it.*

"Like what?"

"One hundred thousand dollars," Robert said grandly, as if he was announcing the sweepstakes winner.

"Robert, go fuck yourself." Jack said quietly.

"Er, Mr. Chandler. I didn't get what you said."

"I said, fuck you," Jack said with a bit more emphasis.

"Mr. Chandler, you don't mean you are willing to carry this thing all the way through trial?"

"Fuckin'-A, Robert. Fuckin'-A." Jack's felt a rush of rage at the smarmy tone from this smarmy little dweeb and what he represented. "I'm gonna get that Orleans Parish jury so pissed they'll give those folks ten million. I know we don't have punitive damages in Louisiana, but you know the court of appeal isn't supposed to disturb a jury verdict."

"Oh yeah, Robert. I got a witness and a movie of your client raping and murdering that little girl, and when I'm through with your client's estate, I'm gonna drain every rotten penny that son-of-a-bitch ever made."

"Well, ah, I'll convey your feelings to my people, but I feel sure we can improve the offer," Robert the lawyer said, but now there was a note of pleading in his voice.

"Okay, get after it. But you're wastin' your time, and mine. I was preparing for this case just as you called. I'm expediting this, and I could conceivably have it up for trial in a couple of months. Of course, I'm gonna to dig deep into who and what he owned in the meantime. Looks like he must have owned you."

"Well, ah. No. I mean, I have been counsel for some of his interests, but I have not been made privy to any of his business. I am just a messenger in this case."

"Well, Robert, tell your people we' are shootin' the moon in this case. If Delahoussie don't get everybody, I sure as hell am."

"But your target in this case is dead."

Jack paused as his rage became cold fire. "That's for sure, but his memory's not, Robert. And there's revenge, and there's justice. They haven't known revenge—just stuff I've told 'em and what they've read. Thin soup for what they've lost. I'm gonna give 'em a revenge feast in court. This is gonna be a nuclear event, and if my diggin' doesn't go deep enough, I'm sure he screwed enough people that somebody'll be very happy to spill the beans."

"Ah, Mr. Chandler. I have to get back with my principals, and if you don't mind, I will get back to you."

"You're pissin' on my leg now. Frankly, I don't want to hear from you again, 'cause you don't understand what I'm gonna do in court. I'm gonna make any lawyer representin' Mourier wish he never heard the name. That jury'll want to lynch him for just bein' there."

"Would you accept the offer on keeping the apartment?"

"Let me put it to you this way, Robert. I'm not signin' or agreein' to a damn thing. I never moved out and am stayin'. We'll get title to this building anyway as part of the judgment, so I'm wonderin' why you even bothered to call me about it. You must think I'm stupid."

"Ah, well, Mr. Chandler, then I will get back to you."

"No need," Jack said as he hung up, angry at something. Maybe just angry at everything.

Jack called Martin and told him of the offer, and Martin said, "If you say take it, we will, lawyer Jack. We leavin' it all up to you. You know it ain't just about the money We standin' ready for anything after the other night. We enjoyed that little ass trompin' more'n you know."

"I know it's not about the money. But I ain't takin' that," Jack said. "I don't know where we're headed, Martin, but I have a feelin' about this. Just hang with me, man."

"We all hangin' lawyer Jack. We all hangin'."

꩜

The Cathedral bells chimed five. Jack thought, *Quittin' time—been a tough day of sittin' around bullshittin'. Better knock off and have a toddy.* Just as he started to the kitchen to make a bourbon and water, the phone rang again.

"Hey, Jack, you 'ol son-of-a-bitch, what you been up to?"

Jack's eyelids narrowed and his lips curved up in a half smile. "Well if it ain't Fred Campbell," Jack said, acting pleased to hear from him.

Picking up on no hostility, Campbell kept to the 'good 'ol boy' track and said, "You're sumpthin' else, Jack. Damn if you ain't worked yourself into the catbird seat. You ain't done too bad for a country boy."

Jack was silent, waiting for the next volley.

"You still there?"

"Yeah. You called me, Fred. What you need?"

"Wa'al, Jack. Me'n you, we go way back, don't we?"

"Get to the point, Fred."

"Okay, if you insist. There's some boys come to me to see if I could talk to you about a little business proposition."

"What is it?"

Fred brightened at the aspect of being able to get through the wall that Jack was slowly building as the call proceeded.

"I think we better get off the phone to talk about it, Jack. You know how phones are. I'll meet you up at the Plimsoll Club at eight tonight."

"No."

There was a pause. "What'd you say?"

"I said no, Fred."

"You don't even know what I got to talk about. Opportunity like you never seen."

"Like Cabal. Like your deal with Paris? Yeah, I know you, and you got a rat in your pocket."

There was another long pause.

Jack's voice was even and deliberate. "What you want to talk to me about is cuttin' some slack for some of them sleaze clients of yours. I'll cut 'em some slack."

Relieved, Campbell said, "Alright. Jack, you always were one of the sharpest. You know which way the wind blows. I'm really glad you're willin' to work. There's a couple of 'em that's kinda mean–Carlo's boys. Wantin' to get rough. Now none of us want any more ugliness, Jack. Not good for bidness."

"Since you put it that way, and you're talkin' for the mob, and you're deliverin' a threat, then tell 'em I want their dicks."

"I don't think I got what you said."

"Dicks. Mount their dicks like little stuffed weenies. I'll hang 'em over my fireplace like trophies. They stuck their dicks into them kids, ruined their lives. So it's only fair to trade their dicks for lettin' 'em off. Parker already donated his. Wish I could have saved it."

After an even longer pause, Campbell said, "C'mon Jack, let's get serious."

"I'm dead serious."

"Come on, Jack, don't act so damn crazy."

"Dicks, Fred. Dicks. The whole thing; cut 'em high, back to the curlies. I don't wanna be cheated by just gettin' a nub. Tell your fuckin' clients they can get rough, like you say. They can kill me, but there'll be a hundred other lawyers in line behind me itchin' to handle this case. Gettin' me won't stop the motion. And when I'm through with 'em, I'll have their asses too, and they'll wish they'd never been born."

There was an expectant pause, when Jack continued. "Fred, this is one time you're on the wrong side. You better watch your own ass."

There was silence at the other end of the line.

"And, Fred?" Jack said.

"Yeah?"

"Fuck you."

Jack hung up and let out a gleeful whoop.

❦

"I filed it," Sam said. "Twenty copies to be served on twenty defendants. The clerk spent nearly an hour stampin' and cussin'."

"Did the judge approve they be filed as paupers without havin' to post court costs?"

"Piece of cake. He looked at all of the affidavits statin' our clients didn't have enough money to file, and when he saw where they lived and what it was about, he signed all of 'em without lookin' back. Looks like everybody is gettin' in line to be in on the kill. Now, we don't have to put any money up durin' th' whole case to get 'em served or anything. Gives you a feelin' of power, don't it Jack?"

Vic asked, "You mean that you didn't have to pay to file that huge set of suits?"

"Right," Jack said. "If you're too poor to post costs—and costs can be plenty—you can file free. Otherwise, only the rich would have access to the courts. If it's a good case, usually the lawyer puts up the money to file and all of the costs later as you go. Gets 'em back if he wins. In this case, we'd have to get a bank loan just to file it. Would have been several thousand dollars. The clerk's the only one pissed 'cause he didn't make any money on the filin'."

"Now that you're finished with this part, what next?" Vic asked.

Sam took a deep breath and sighed. Jack looked up at his mammoth form and said, "OK, lets have it Sam. You don't sigh like that unless there's bad news."

Sam handed Jack a report, shaking his head at the content.

"Asset report on the bastards who did this to the kids. Two suicides, four more have taken off for parts unknown, but they can't avoid the comin' show. None of 'em had anything of value. Two left widows and children. It's sad as hell. As to the rest, it's gonna be like chasin' a rabbit down a hole. Useless. Only one or two could pay a little bit of a judgment against 'em; they all look good, with their Cadillacs and big houses, but they're all mortgaged to the hilt. What liquid assets they have can be hidden. It's gonna be a dry haul."

Jack groaned. "You sure about the Sessums? We sued Sessums personally, maybe he has somethin'?"

"Nope," Sam said. "Big garden district house–three mortgages. A bunch of notes owed all over town. Wife's got money, but we can't touch that. He's a zero."

"Sessums is in I.C.U. at Touro," Vic said. "He's fully conscious, but all of his systems are failing. I think he is willing himself to die. Poor man."

"Poor man," Jack sniffed. "I'm sorry. But I ain't got any sympathy. Bein' Mourier's personal property was probably hell enough, but he was willin' to fry me–and use his power to ruin those kids' lives. Nah, I don't feel one drop of pity."

Vic looked at Jack and said, "I remember you saying that a person always finds a way to be punished, cause they're really good down deep. Do you still feel that way?"

"Sure. I think even Mourier may've had a whole world of goodness somewhere down under all that garbage. It's the garbage that made him do what he did. He was insane, and I think he was wantin' to punish himself. Most crooks get themselves caught red handed. He had a choice about goin' into that swamp to get us on his own. He was really takin' a chance, even with that big dog and the backup. He could have hired a damned army with all of his pull, and we wouldn't have had a chance. I think he knew he'd lose. There's a part of him that wanted to."

"Jack," Sam said, "every time I hear you pontificate philosophy, I know you're crazy!"

"I gotta try to figure it all out, Sam. Philosophy's just a word that means you're tryin' to make some genuine sense outta things. We gotta find a source of money. My philosophy now is to find a deep pocket to pay the damages."

"Unless the sheriff's got some, we're screwed," Sam said, and it looks like he's a zero.

Vic threw up her hands. "You mean that those children may not have any way to recover anything after all of this?"

Jack pulled his lips tight in a grim smile, took a deep breath and shook his head slowly, "unless somethin' turns up."

"Oh yeah," Jack said, ". "I have some news for you guys."

Vic and Sam perked up and looked at Jack with interest.

"First, a lawyer named Robert called and offered a hundred grand to settle."

"Did you take it?" Sam said quickly.

"Hell no. Told him to fuck off."

"Whew!" Sam whistled, I knew you hadn't, but for a moment there you had me worried."

"And, he told me I could move back in and offered me a bunch of free rent if I didn't sue the guy who kicked me out."

Vic sat bolt upright in her chair and said, "Well?"

"Well, what?" Jack said, enticingly.

"Are you moving back in?"

"I am not agreeing to anything. Since it belongs to Mourier, we'll get it in judgment anyway. So, I'm back!"

Vic squealed and flung her arms around Jack and kissed him full on the lips. The thing in Jack went crazy, blasting off like fireworks in a Fourth of July night sky. He pushed her away, his pulse thudding in his ears and his adrenalin pouring gasoline on the roman candles.

Sam beamed as Jack came up for air, breathless and shaking slightly. "I'm glad for you, boy. This is home to you. You got everything you need here."

"And more," Jack said, lightly squeezing Vic's hand and then withdrawing his.

"You had two calls?" Vic asked.

"Yeah. Fred Campbell called. Wanted to cut some deal on some of his neanderthal defendants."

"Which ones?" Sam asked.

"No matter."

"Let me guess," Vic said, "you told him to fuck off."

Jack's grinned. As a matter of fact," Jack said, scratching his head and looking as if he had a realization, "it seems that's what I have been tellin' people like that for most of my life!"

Vic was studying a colorful flyer promo advertising The Court of Two Sisters restaurant. "Somebody slipped this under the door. She handed it to Jack.

Inside was pasted a note: *Mr. Jack Chandler, you have won a free palm reading by Swami Ataturk.* Jack read it and handed it to Sam.

There was a rosy glow in the western sky over the rooftops as the trio walked up Chartres. The Quarter slowly changed her face from a slumbering, dreaming lady to a sultry, come-kiss-me Jezebel.

"Look's like th' redneck convention's in town," Sam pointed to three beefy, sweaty men, staggering as they approached them from the opposite direction on the sidewalk. They wore suits, with ties pulled loose, carrying the large, hourglass-shaped goblets from Pat O'Briens. They were singing, terribly off-key, what passed for the lyrics of "Born to Lose."

The sidewalk was wide enough for four to walk abreast. Jack and Sam moved aside to allow the three wallowing drunks to pass. As they drew abreast, the drunk trio stopped.

One looked at Jack and then at Vic, and with glazing eyes said to one of his buddies, "Looks like a white boy done got him a little chocolate pie."

Jack's hand shot out and grabbed the man's tie and jerked. Already unsteady, the drunk pitched forward and fell face down on the sidewalk at their feet.

Jack stepped over him and said to the two others, whose ruddy faces reflected astonishment at the sudden horizontalization of their confederate, "This is a civilized city. Leave your barbaric ways at the city limits if you should ever return."

Jack dusted his palms, put his arm around Vic's waist, and stepped on down the sidewalk with Sam in their wake.

"Now who is this barbarian, Jack?" Vic teased.

"Jack, them damn clothes you got on is the only thing that separates you from that wild man you said you had been in your alleged past life," Sam said.

"I knew there was somethin' missin' in today's menu," Jack said, his eyes gleaming. "I was havin' withdrawal symptoms—just needed a little action. Now I'm all better."

They walked through the plaza in front of the Cabildo and the St. Louis Cathedral. Artists had set up their easels along the wrought-iron fence bordering Jackson Square. Tourists milled about and the horse-drawn buggies clip-clopped around the square and down the Quarter streets.

They crossed over one block to Royal and entered a corridor filled with ferns and paintings. At the far end was a doorway that led into what appeared to be a jungle, and they headed toward it. The sound of a gypsy violin wafted down the hall from the open door at the end, riding on the fragrance of sweet olive.

The tuxedo clad maitre'd bowed slightly when he saw Jack. "Mr. Chandler! Do come in," he said in what sounded like an east European accent. "Do you have a place you prefer to sit?"

"I told you," Sam said. "You're famous."

The large courtyard was filled with candlelit tables under the low-hanging branches of a massive live oak. A splashing fountain lent a counterpoint to the strolling musician coaxing tears from his violin as he played "When a Gypsy Makes His Violin Cry."

Jack pointed to a table under an arbor of an ancient wisteria with a leg-sized trunk from which grew vines spreading fifty feet in every direction, even climbing up the three stories of balconies of apartments on each side.

"This place smells so sweet from the wisteria in the spring, you nearly pass out."

"Ah, yes," the maitre'd said, "it is lovely then."

They ordered drinks. "I'll just have a large order of oysters Rockefeller," Jack said. Sam ordered a steak and Vic a crabmeat salad.

Across the room sat a dark, thin-faced man with a sharp black goatee. He had a milky cast over his left eye and wore a turban with a large moonstone set in the front.

His eyes were soft, but alert, like a bird's. Somehow his appearance wasn't harsh, in spite of the trimmed black goatee and moustache.

After Jack's party ordered, he walked to their table and said, with an odd, knowing look, "Read your palm?"

Jack unfolded and showed the flyer to the swami. Are you Ataturk?"

A small smile played around the man's thin lips. "I am Swami Ataturk, Mr. Chandler."

"How'd you know my name?"

"Swami knows," the man said, placing two fingers on his forehead.

Jack cut his eyes at Vic, who widened her own eyes in return. Sam shrugged and said, "Swami knows, Jack."

Again there was the Swami's enigmatic smile. "Your hand, please." The swami extended his hand to receive Jack's.

"Which one?"

"The one you will give."

Jack gave him his right hand, and the swami turned it over in his own and examined the back, the fingers, and finally the palm. His eyes met Jack's.

"You have a most interesting hand."

Vic lifted her brows and grinned at Sam, who shrugged and lit a large, black cigar.

"What do you see?" Jack asked.

The Swami said, "Change. You are going through change. You are strong, but you have great doubts of yourself. It is as if you are evolving in some way. You are having a very difficult time in making a decision. I see a trip to faraway places, wealth, and adventure. You will never be without risk and danger, for it sustains you, gives you strength. You seek it. It has always been thus for you."

"So? I know that already," Jack said, drawing back his hand.

"Ah, but I also see in you something else, Mr. Chandler," the Swami said in a hushed voice. "Beware of what you may learn. You are moving into a higher circle, and new knowledge means danger for you, and for your friends. Tread lightly and be aware. This knowledge can be used to great advantage, but it portends peril. Listen to your inner voice when the knowledge comes, and use it wisely."

The swami stood and salaamed, touching his forehead with the tips of his long fingers, then backed away.

"Wait, how much do I owe you?" Jack said.

"Nothing. My payment will be your reward," he said, his robes whirling as he turned and glided past the fountain through a door at the back of the restaurant.

Jack frowned and looked quizzically at Vic and Sam. "What the hell do you think he meant by "my reward is his payment?"

"It all sounded like lots of hokum to me," Sam grunted, "but the price was right."

Jack raised his empty glass and the waiter bustled to their table.

"Who was that swami?" Jack asked. "I don't think I have seen him here before. He isn't the usual guy that hangs around here."

"Who are you speaking of, sir?"

"That Swami, with the robes and turban. The guy with the spiked beard that just left through the back way."

"I don't know, sir," the waiter said, glancing toward the rear of the restaurant. "The swami who works here is off tonight."

"Well, then, who. . ."

"I'm sorry. I didn't see him, sir. If someone is bothering you, I could call the manager."

"No, he wasn't bothering us," Jack said, shaking his head.

They re-ordered drinks, and Sam said, "Now that's downright weird. He looked and talked like the real McCoy."

"Eerie kind of guy," Vic said. "When I was in the east with my parents, we saw all kinds of fakirs and seers on the streets. This one looked even more real than those."

"Made my skin crawl," Jack said, picking up an open book of matches lying on the table to light his cigarette.

He glanced down at a flyer the swami had laid on the table. Something was written in elaborate script across its blank back side. Holding it up to the light of the candle, he read it aloud. "Mr. Chandler, knowledge is power. See p333, Voodoo in NO, Bouillabaisse Bookstore."

"Willya look at this?" Jack said, showing the inscription to Vic and Sam.

"He musta left it," Sam said.

Vic's eyes gleamed with excitement. "Lets go tonight," she said.

"Okay, but I gotta have my oysters first." Jack said. "This place makes the best in town. Bouillabaisse'll be open till nine. It's just a block away. We have nearly two hours."

CHAPTER 27

The strawberry incense was almost as powerful as the mustiness of the books that were stacked, piled and jumbled on the floor and shelves of the rambling old bookstore. A diminutive bald man was nested in a ratty easy chair behind a high, dusty glass showcase filled with old and rare volumes. He looked up from a book and peered over his wire-framed reading glasses at the interlopers who intruded into his domain.

There was a hush in the store, a sense of peace not unlike the feeling of serenity of the park, but with more of a motionlessness, as if time stood still. Jack's covetous eyes drifted over the disordered volumes that filled every inch of space from the floor to the ceiling.

The owner returned to his reading as the three stood in the narrow foyer and gazed in wonder at the seeming chaos surrounding them.

Jack asked quietly, "Ambrose, do you have *Voodoo in New Orleans?*"

The man lifted his eyes and tilted his head to see who had called him by name. He had the look of a man wakened from a dream, but still dreaming. Jack knew what that was like, reading and dreaming.

A bright smile lighted Ambrose's pale face and he said, "Oh, hey, Jack. Long time no see. Where ya been?"

"Here and there. Got a new smell here."

"Oh, that. Dead rat. Couldn't find him. Incense kills the smell."

"Don't know which is worse, Ambrose," Jack said, sniffing loudly while wrinkling his nose.

"Me either. No matter, both keep the tourists out. Ha Ha."

Jack introduced Vic and Sam to Ambrose Villiere. "Ambrose is the sole heir of the Villiere estate. He could stay on his plantation and collect his books, but he'd rather live in the Quarter with the rest of us weirdo's and sit in this dustbin and sneeze and read. Can't say I blame him."

"Beats being a lawyer," Ambrose said, frowning.

"You bet," Jack said, reaching over to rub Ambrose's bald head. "This little bastard and I went to law school together. His old man said he would cut him out of his will if he didn't go to law school. After Ambrose got in law, he learned that he couldn't be disinherited in Louisiana; we had forced heirship before his old man died, and as sole heir, Ambrose would get all of the estate he wanted, regardless of what his old man did."

"Didja get ya degree?" Sam asked.

"Oh yeah. To please the old man," Ambrose said. "I finished Order of the Coif, Cum Laude, and all that, but I was losing my hair anyway. Why should I lose my mind?"

"You got that right," Sam said. "It's a damned jungle out here in the trenches. More agony then glory for damned sure."

"From what I see of my old classmates," Ambrose said, "you either join a big firm and lose your soul, or lose it and your mind on your own. I'm lucky. I'm keeping mine, thanks to the laws of forced heirship and a crooked old great granddaddy who I am sure lost his soul runnin' gamblin' halls, whorehouses and a small loan business at the turn of the century."

They all laughed.

"Ambrose," Jack asked again, "do you have *Voodoo in New Orleans?*"

Ambrose lifted his arm, and with a hand motion, vaguely indicated the rear of the store. "At the end of the first aisle, turn left. Go to the end, turn right. Then to the very back of the store there's a doorway into another part of the building. There's a section in there on sorcery and witchcraft. It's in there somewhere. There's a little bit of everything here. There's another floor above this one and a loft above that—all filled with books. There's a light switch on the wall if you can't see in the dark." He smiled and returned to his book.

"Thanks," Jack said to the top of the little man's bald head.

"Okay," Vic said, leading the group, "left to the end, then right to the end."

The shelves sagged under the weight of thousands of heavy, leather-bound, gilt-edged antique volumes of every size and on every subject imaginable.

The farther they walked, the darker the aisles became until finally, Jack had to flick on his Zippo to light his way. They looked like spelunkers carrying a living torch, walking though a book lined cave.

They came to the end and found the door to the room Ambrose told them about. Sam flipped the switch and two low wattage bulbs revealed a huge brick walled room with eighteen foot bookshelves reaching to the ceiling. The walk space between the shelves barely accommodated Sam's bulk.

"How the hell did he get up there to put books in," Sam said.

Vic pointed to a step-ladder on wheels at the far end of the aisle, then turned and pointed to the floor. "Look, footprints in the dust. I bet Ambrose hasn't been back here in months. Somebody else has."

Jack held his lighted zippo low to the floor and there were what appeared to be fresh shoe prints in the dust. They followed the prints around the end of the aisle. Whoever had made the prints had stopped and moved about within a small area.

Jack and Vic were able to easily maneuver in the narrow space, but Sam gave up and said, "I'll wait out here."

"Here it is," Vic said excitedly.

She pulled a book from a tightly packed group and Jack said, "The dust has been cleaned from it. *Voodoo in New Orleans!*"

It fell open, revealing a folded sheet of onion skin paper in the center. Vic gingerly removed it and handed it to Jack. In the light of Jack's Zippo, he could make out a series of typed, numbered lines and sentences, but the details were too vague to read in the darkness. He could, however, read the name 'Mourier.'

"Bingo!" Jack said. "Lets get out of here. Over coffee au lait at Cafe Du Monde, the three hovered over the thin, crinkly sheet of paper.

Swiss Volkbank, Bern (FYM07a)
Banque Cantonale de Geneva, Geneva (GR0098)
Bank Hofmann, ag, Zuerich, Zurich (R0783)
Banco do Brasil, SA, Cayman (9743)

Inner Circle/Templars
Miquel Rameros, Bogata. (Poppy)
Joseph Rugerrio, Sicily (Hand)
Angelo Francesco, Las Vegas (Casino)
Josh Bosche, Hong Kong (99)
Yanni Onassis, Athens. (Barque)
Steephe Craagghe, JoBerg (Kraal)
Claude Cabal. US/Houston (Silk)
MA Smythe, London, (Whip)
Gil Bates, US, (Micro)
Mosler Nobbish, Tel Aviv (Data)
Donald Rockefeller, US/IMF. (cash)
Boutros Boutros-Ghali, UN, (pax)

Mordicai Mourier, US/NOLA (grave)
Ito Mitsui, Tokyo, (bank)
Helmut Kohl, West Berlin, (Heil)
Holdings: RCA, FIVE SISTERS, CIBA-GEIGY,
ELI LILLY, AT&T.

There is more. If you need, leave note where you found this, and more will be provided. This should be enough to accomplish your goal. This is dangerous information. Use sparingly if at all.

You will also profit by from checking this out:

PROBATE NUMBER 60-988, Crockett County, TX. Check Midland News. "What is this?" Vic asked.

"I can see one thing," Sam said, "the first section gives bank account numbers in Switzerland and in the Cayman Islands. Mourier's accounts!"

Jack leaned back, took a deep breath. Sam and Vic looked at him oddly. There was a long silence. The calliope on the Mississippi Queen, a big sternwheeler on a run from New Orleans to St. Louis, was tooting and wheezing 'Dixie' just across the levee. Tour groups began filling the tables around the trio.

"I think I know what the inner circle is," Jack said quietly.

"Tell us," Vic said, bending near.

"There's always been stories about the 'gnomes of Zurich,' and talk about the big conspiracy to control the world among a powerful few men. You know, the Illuminati and all that? The One Worlder's? Somebody's tellin' us that this is a list of these very boys, and I think we just erased one name from the list."

"Huh?" Sam said.

Vic frowned and looked closely at the names.

"Those are code names," Jack said. "Kraal, Poppy, Silk. If this is what my gut tells me it is, this is the list of the top rung, probably with one of them as kingpin. I don't know what to do with it, if it's true."

"If it's true," Vic said, "what can they do, even if they know you have it? You can't prove it, and if you could, so what?"

"But if you know one thing about a person with a guilty mind, and they know you know something on 'em, they always think you know a lot more," Sam said.

Jack smiled to himself, recalling the bluff he pulled on Delahoussie.

"Oh," Vic said, shrinking down into her chair. "If they know we know, they might think we know more than we know."

"Right," Jack said, folding the paper into a small square and holding it between two fingers. "That's what worries me. The swami was right. Just knowin' this could be dangerous, if it's not just the imaginin's of some paranoid nut. I'm not too sure I'm happy about having this little piece of paper."

Sam said, "you could be right. That is too much information. "Those Cayman and Swiss accounts will be hard to get, even with a judgment."

They quietly sipped coffee and stared at the paper. Jack rocked back and forth slightly, his features drawn tightly in thought. "We gotta get this probate pleading. I guess we could call and get it overnighted to us."

"Yeah," Sam said, "but what about this newspaper. Maybe it's linked. Has to be. That means somebody's gotta go read the microfiche for that period."

Jack nodded, looking off into the street, half aware of the bearded black man playing "Do you know what it means, to miss New Orleans," on the sidewalk just twenty feet away.

"Hell, I'll go," Sam said, banging his big fist down on the little marble topped table. "I'll leave tonight if there's a flight."

"Cool," said Jack, "I'll keep things on track here and start digging into these accounts while you find what you can. Maybe it'll be worthwhile."

They forgot the romance of the Quarter, and checked the flights to Midland on Sam's cell. He made reservation for a red-eye to the Dallas Fort-Worth Airport and a car rental.

Jack stared at the paper and his lips moved into a faint smile. Looking up at Sam and Vic, "This could be scarier than Sam's snake patrol."

Vic put her hand on Jack's arm and squeezed. "Be careful. I want you to win, but it shouldn't cost you your life—and this may."

"Not to worry, Mama, I can be subtle—believe it or not. I'm not always a sledgehammer."

"Yeah, right," Sam said. "I believe it when I see it!"

"Jack, what you think is subtle can etch glass," Vic said. "Just don't make them shoot up our building again."

Jack patted the pocket he had placed the paper in and said, "This is the bomb, and I won't let it go off. I just thought of somethin' that puts my finger on the trigger for a change.

❧

When they arrived back at the apartment, Martin's squad was busy moving Jack's furniture back into his office and apartment.

"Ho, Martin. I'm back in business again!"

"I hopes so, lawyer Jack. We been worryin' 'bout you not havin' you office back. Since you filed them lawsuits, I been holdin' back more people than you can count want to come see you 'bout all kinds of stuff. You number one to the people now!"

"Thanks, Martin. I can use all the help I can get. Money's bad short and we don't have time to work on anything but these cases. If we win, we all should be in good shape. If we don't, I'll be lookin' for anything that comes through the door."

"What's it look like, lawyer Jack?" Martin asked.

"Looks good, I think. We're optimistic."

Jack looked around his office and smiled. The hardwood floors had been waxed and the woodwork all given a complete polish.

The phone rang, just as Jack started to sit and light up a cigarette, it was Jester.

"Jack, they found the body. Whoever vandalized the lab abandoned their stolen vehicle in some woods outside of Meridian with the body in the trunk. The coroner had it in their morgue since then trying to make identification. Not too many loose bodies out there that already been autopsied. I identified it by phone and it's being shipped to Tharp-Sontheimer Funeral Home on Rampart as we speak."

Jack relayed Jester's message to Sam, Vic and Martin. He sat back with his eyes closed and took a long breath.

"Thank God!" Martin said. "I gotta tell Estelle!"

Martin raced up the stairs and in a moment a shriek came from upstairs, followed by loud sobbing. Jack shook his head and got around to lighting the cigarette he had been holding between his fingers.

"Thank God is right," Jack said. "They can finally put their baby to rest! She's travelled long enough."

Still on the phone, listening, Jester said, "I'll see ya'll tomorrow. I want to see the rest of this show. Any source of money for the victims?"

"Nope. Nothing much. Not near enough," Jack said grimly. "One kinda sorta lead. Sam's going to Midland, Texas to check out something that popped up."

"What popped?"

Jack told him about the little man with the cast-eye and the card. "It's worth a shot. Plane ticket. I'm paying, Sam's goin'."

"Wa'al, alright then. I'll see ya'll later this evenin'. After being with ya'll, livin' alone here is like a morgue."

"Hell, Jester, your house *is a* morgue most of the time."

"Guess you right about that. See you later."

✧

Martin and Estelle later came to Jack's apartment. Martin held Estelle around her shoulder with his big arm as they sat quietly on his sofa. Estelle's eyes were red and her cheeks were glistened with new tears. She was trying to be stalwart and make an announcement to Jack.

"Lawyer Jack. We decided. . ." Estelle began, her voice hollow and controlled. "We ain't gonna have no long wake. When we bury my baby. Will you walk with us?"

"It would be an honor for me to accept," Jack said, thinking of being chosen to march in the parade to the cemetery. He had seen funeral processions with jazz bands before, but never thought that he would serve an official position in one.

"What cemetery, Estelle?" Jack asked.

"St. Louis Number I on Basin." She cut her eyes oddly to Martin, and said, "Some of Dawn Marie's kinfolk been laid to rest there."

Martin smiled knowingly.

The oldest cemetery in New Orleans.

At noon the following day, Sam called.

"Hey, whatcha got?"

There was a long delay, Sam was laughing so hard he could hardly catch his breath.

"Hey Sam, what's happening?"

"You ain't gonna believe it. I checked the probate records, then the newspapers in Midland, and...."

"And what goddammit!"

"Bingo! Not just Bingo! Bing freakin' go!"

"Whaddya mean?"

"Jack, I just faxxed it to you. Don't hang up, just go to your fax machine and read, lad. It'll blow your mind!"

"Dammit Sam...."

At that moment, Rhonda sauntered in with a sheaf of papers. She frowned at Jack's purple and gold swollen face. "These just came." She handed the batch to Jack.

Jack pressed the speaker phone on, and put the receiver back on the hook. "I got it."

"Read, m'boy!"

He flipped past the transmittal page and opened to a document that said Succession of the ***Estate of Frederick Mourier Cabal***. Jack sucked in his breath. Several pages in he read, *"The Brothers Malborn Mourier Cabal and Claude Cabal shall each receive an undivided interest in all of the properties of Frederick Mourier Cabal, share and share alike."*

"Sam, this is incredible. Cabal is that man's brother?"

"Not only that, my boy, they were twins!"

"Jesus. Nature plays cruel tricks. What else did you find?"

"I'm bringing with me a whole raft of property ownerships, oil interests, school records, newspaper clippings of the goings on between these two boys. Seems they were always at odds with each other, suing each other and quarreling over the property until finally a big lawsuit partitioned the whole enchilada. After that they never had anything to do with each other again, or at least that's the scuttlebutt around Midland."

"Whoa! That means Cabal inherits all of Mourier's estate as the only heir, plus all of its debt. That means he's gotta pay Mourier's bills if he accepts the succession."

"You got it! Old man Cabal was quite a pirate. Started out with shallow well production in this whole section of Texas. Buyin' up royalties for nothin' from people who didn't know there was oil on their land. Got controlling interest in USA Royalties, Ltd, the big oil and gas company here. Controlled the Permian Basin area where twenty percent of the nation's gas reserves are stored here. He was a multimillionaire, maybe a billionaire, and when he kicked the bucket, his two sons got it all. Claude hated Mourier because he was a nasty little turd and Mourier hated Claude for his good looks and everything Mourier lacked."

"That's why Cabal tried to lure me out of town. Mourier called out some favor Cabal owed him."

"You got it, Jackson. We hit the damn jackpot."

"I'm calling Cabal this minute. He's on the spot. He owns now what Mourier owned, if he claims his estate and he's a fool not to. What we're going to get out of it is only a dribble of what there is. But I'm going for the gold."

Sam laughed again. "Get'em hepcat. I'll be there this evenin'.

"Make sure you get here in time, we're going to put on a big feed here in the lobby for Estelle and her family. You know how hard it is on a family when they're going through this."

"Set aside a whole table for me," Sam said.

❧

After going through a battery of interference from secretaries, a silky baritone voice came through the line.

"Mr. Chandler, how nice of you to call. What may I do for you?"

Jack could tell by the hollow resonance on the phone that Cabal was using a speaker phone and probably had someone listening with him in the room.

"Mr. "Silk" Cabal, lets cut the social bullshit and get to the meat of this matter. You and I know full well what happened a few days ago, so don't pretend. I'm sure you've received a complete report on your brother, Malborn Mourier Cabal."

There was no response for a few seconds. Cabal asked smoothly, "My, ah, brother?'"

"Yes. Your brother."

"I'm not sure what you're getting at."

"This call is probably bein' recorded on your end and it is on mine," Jack said, "and I can tell you have me on your speaker phone so whoever's there can hear. That don't bother me. In checkin' Mourier's assets, and usin' certain sources I have, certain information has reached me about his relationship with you, as well as I have a list of numbered Cayman and Swiss accounts. I might also mention both of your affiliation with an association where you are known as Silk and Grave. You know full well what that means. I also have a copy of your father, Frederick Mourier Cabal's succession in my hand as we speak. You want more details?"

"Mr. Chandler, can you hold on for a moment? Someone here was just leaving."

When Cabal came back, his voice was cold. "Now. What were you saying?"

"You are the sole heir of your very sick brother, Malborn Mourier Cabal. If you accept his succession, you will own everything he owned. You are the man to cough up the damages he caused, and while I am at it, since he also owned and directed Sheriff Sessums, who allowed all the horror to happen, I am going to collect it all from you for all the victims.

"Just what do you want?"

"I can get a big judgment against Mourier as it is, and have no trouble seizin' and sellin' these things here, and the Cayman and Accounts, but I want to make it easy, and fast. There's no other source to satisfy the other claimants."

Jack imagined Cabal's handsome face frowning, drumming his manicured nails on the exotic wood on some gleaming desktop.

"I'm just listening to you rant, Mr. Chandler."

"Oh I'm ranting all right. You haven't heard anything yet. There's quite a number of children whose lives have been destroyed, and he murdered young Dawn Delacroix in cold blood while having sex with her just to have "the ultimate experience." Jack could feel the blood beginning to pound in his temples at he let out his pent up hatred. "You liquidate Mourier's estate easily and work a settlement for all the claimants, not just limited to Dawn's parent's claim."

"I am not responsible for anything Malborn did in his life."

Jack's got control but his voice became as cold as steel. He could visualize Cabal as a coiled serpent on the other end of the line, every bit as evil and ruthless as his dead brother. "Ah but you are wrong. If you take one cent of his money in the succession, you take it subject to this claim. And there are millions in the Cayman and Swiss accounts, and I have the number of every one of them. Your name'll come up during the trial. I'll see to that, and I'll file a lien on the succession proceeds that'll stop any distribution until a judgment is satisfied. Hell, Cabal, you're a lawyer. You understand what I can do! And I'll do it. I owe you nothing."

Cabal sighed. Jack could hear him wilting.

"What do you want?"

Jack exulted as Cabal toppled his king in this short lived chess match.

"Alright. Here's the idea. The biggest claim is for Dawn's parents. I want two million for her. I get twenty-five percent as a well deserved fee; they get a mil and a half clear and I get the rest. Don't you think that's reasonable?"

"Go ahead. Let's hear it all."

"And for the other twenty, I can get them to take $250,000 each. And, of course, I get my regular fee of a quarter. Each will receive $50,000 cash, and the rest will be paid through a structured payment schedule over a twenty year period so they won't spend it all at once.

"Plus, for those who'll accept, I want a guaranteed college or trade school education set up through your best resources. You guarantee these people get a fair start in life without any hassle. It could be done as a tax break for somebody as a big time gratuity. I'm sure the bright boys on your payroll can figure a way to get some 'mileage' out of all of this, as your buddy Campbell puts it."

"Jack," Cabal changed to a more personal tone, "You are going to make a hefty fee when all is said and done."

Warning bells jangled in Jack's head as Cabal's demeanor switched from cold reservation to what seemed to be appreciation. Having sampled Cabal's silky weenie before, Jack felt the hair on the back of his neck rise in resentment and battle-readiness.

Jack said nothing and Cabal continued. "Jack, I reneged on our last agreement. You have every reason to distrust me. And I don't blame you. After seeing what you have managed to pull off here, I see you would have been the man for that job after all."

Disregarding the flowing warmth and flattery, Jack said, "Cabal, I accept your apology, if that's what you are doin'. Bein' the slick cat you are has its price. Your credibility with me is shit. Once bit, twice shy. The only thing that'll work here is the deal."

Cabal laughed. "The point is well taken. Your censure is accepted, Jack. With power, I must accept some responsibility, and I will. You have my word as a gentleman, if that means anything."

"We'll see." Jack said. "So, we got a deal?"

"Malborn's estate will be liquidated in keeping with your wishes. But I will handle this from my own funds immediately to get it out of the way, and his estate won't have any wrinkles to complete. He was quite wealthy. Is there anything else?"

"I don't want to seem greedy, but there are a couple of other things."

"Yes?"

"I want title to this apartment building and to Malborn's boat and a lifetime prepaid rental on the apartment at the Yacht Basin. I'm gonna give the boat to a friend who helped, and the boathouse apartment to my associate, Sam Leviathon. The apartment building will be put jointly in the name of myself, Victoria Keens-Dennison, Sam Leviathon, Dr. Jester McConothy of Mobile, whose help saved the day, and me."

"Done."

"There is a condition to all this," Cabal said.

"What?"

"That you buy me dinner when I come to New Orleans next. I wish I could be there to seal this deal with a handshake—so I guess it will have to be later. In Texas, all we need is a handshake."

Jack thought, *this guy is so damned oily. I don't think he can help it. I wonder what he's really like down inside. I'd be scared to look. His insides may look like Mourier's outsides.* Jack shuddered at the thought.

Thinking it better to be friendly, Jack said, "I look forward to it. But remember, we had a handshake once before. I want this to be done immediately."

"Yes, ah, you are entirely right. I am chastened thoroughly. I must tell you this, Jack. You probably think badly of me, and you have every right to do so. I was trying to protect my troubled brother and our family name by tempting you out of the case. That was wrong, but it was business. I loathed my brother. I must be candid. I treated him badly when we were young because of the way he looked and acted. He was never quite, well, ah, right. He despised me as well. So I am happy to somewhat redress at least one of the wrongs he did by this. Will tomorrow be soon enough?

"Fair enough. Who will I hear from?"

"My attorney is Lehmann Forbes. He will call first thing tomorrow."

Jack fell back in his chair. Cabal's voice echoed in his head, saying things Jack only dreamed of hearing from any man. Jack realized he felt weird, light, reeling, unreal. He let the moment carry him.

Jack's innate cynicism swept in and he thought of the first time Cabal had stiffed him. Cabal was another category of man completely, a category Jack simply didn't understand, reserved for those who had no moral boundaries and who could foul or play outside the rules and win. Good guys don't always win. Playing with someone like Cabal you lose, that's all there is to it. If and when it came through, Jack promised himself that he would allow himself the win. The money had to be distributed, and then there would only be one thing left to do… Bury Dawn.

Jester and Sam got back in town at the same time, and both came panting up the stairs, wide eyed and grinning.

"Sam tells me you found the pot of gold," Jester said, between puffs.

"Yep, and that ain't all," Jack's eyes glittered and danced.

Both big men flopped onto the sofa and chair and said nothing, waiting to hear Jack's next announcement.

"Well?" Sam said, impatiently.

"I ain't gonna tell you 'till Vic gets here. She's on her way."

Finally, Vic arrived.

Jack told them all to sit down and he would announce the verdict. They sat on the sofa and chair, while Jack held forth like a judge making pronouncement, describing the conversation with Cabal and the deal made, holding back the business with the boat, and the apartment building.

They all jumped up, did a high five. Sam and Jester did a little jig, looking like two hippos doing a do-see-do.

"Can't believe you pulled it off, Jack," Jester said.

"There's a little more. I got title to the boat for Nookie, Sam, you have lifetime rental of the Marina apartment, and the four of us get free and clear title to the Marquis de Mandeville Apartments. Sam you can move in, and Jester you got a place to stay anytime you want here. Twenty five apartments in the building and that's a neat little income for us. I just want my office and this apartment. Sam, we'll split the fee."

"Naah," said Sam. "I'll take 10%. Half's too much. You're the one who risked the most."

The additional information left them quiet, smiling at each other. They spontaneously reached across the coffee table and joined hands. Vic said, "pardners!" They all echoed, "pardners!"

"I've heard of Forbes," Sam said. "A cold blooded old scoundrel. Pushin' ninety and still going strong."

"Well, we get to meet him tomorrow," Jack said. "But I believe it when the cash is in my hand."

"What time is it? They should be arriving downstairs with the tables and food," Vic said. "I ordered everything you said, and told Estelle to get her family and all her people over this evening."

"Lets go help," Jack said, and they all went downstairs. Tables were being set up with tablecloths, refreshments, and then the food arrived.

Central Grocery, Felix's, and Frank's Italian Restaurant catered a huge meal in the lobby just outside Jack's office. Tables were loaded with Italian specialties, Muffeleto sandwiches, meats, pasta, and sweets—as well as shrimp and oysters, prepared every way possible. Martin and Estelle's family and friends flooded the place, and in an hour, the mountain of food was nearly leveled.

"Lawyer Jack," Estelle said, "this been very hard, but you made it easy as it could be with all you done. I don't know how to thank you, but whatever happens in the case, it'll be alright with me and Martin."

"We'll do what we can." Jack said. "You and Martin try to settle down. I know it'll be tough, but at least the worst will be over soon. I want to help you get as much money as I can. It won't bring her back, but it'll be something, and it'll buy you some things that'll make you feel better anyway."

"I don't care," Martin said. "If you git us nothin' that's alright. We know what you done done. Ain't many men'd do that."

"Thanks for the confidence. We oughta know somethin' by tomorrow."

Martin and Estelle looked at each other questioningly, and then Estelle said, "When you get it all together, me an' Martin got somethin' to tell you, but we can't tell you now."

Jack looked from one to the other. "What is it? Is it somethin' I need to know?"

"No," Martin said, "but we gonna tell you somethin' that you gonna find interestin' as soon as you git it all finished. We can't tell you now."

"Well, okay. Whatever you say. You got my curiosity up now."

Estelle's eyes gleamed and she smiled for the first time in weeks. "You gonna be surprised."

CHAPTER 28

DAY TEN

Jack listened to the early morning sounds of the Quarter: foghorns and river boats, a faraway dog barking, and a pair of drunks stumbling along Royal beneath his balcony. He fell back on the sofa and slept until ten when Sam banged on his door.

"Jack, ain't gonna believe this. Lehmann Price has been callin' all mornin'."

"Oh shit," Jack said. He thumbed through the big New Orleans phone directory, found a number and dialed.

"Mr. Forbes?" Jack said when a reedy voice answered. "Jack Chandler. You have been calling?"

"Yes, Mr. Chandler. Claude Cabal gave me certain instructions. I want to verify it so we can effect the transfer of real estate immediately and place the cash in the proper bank for you."

"Ah, yes," Jack stuttered. "Do you have a time schedule?"

"I want to complete the agreement today. You and the parties receiving the properties be here at one this afternoon. If Dr. McConothy cannot be present, one of you can act for him under power of attorney. I need the particulars of the property transferees."

Dr. McConothy will be there, so will Dr. Keens-Dennison." Jack gave the names, marital status, and addresses of all parties, then stipulated terms about insurance and taxes.

"I expect you at one," Lehmann Forbes said.

"Thank you, sir. We'll be there."

Jack slapped Sam on the back and hugged Vic.

Jack pressed his fingers against his lips in thought.

"We gotta get the names and birthdays of all of the plaintiffs, and for those who are still minors, we need to name their guardians or custodians. There's no rush to get the details straight, but we do need to get all of the money placed first."

They scrambled through the files and typed a list of the plaintiffs with their ages and guardians. It was nearly one when they finished and the foursome drove to the Baronne building to the venerable offices of Forbes and Levy.

The elevator took them to the twenty-second floor. A bespectacled, elderly receptionist regarded them without salutation as they approached her desk. She stiffly waited until Jack broke the silence.

"Ma'am, we're here for a one o'clock appointment to see Mr. Forbes."

She looked the group up and down cooly, lingering on Jack;s huge yellow and blue hematoma and puffy eye, and motioned for them to sit. There were only three worn armchairs in the reception area. Jack stood. On one wall hung a large map of the French Quarter. There were no foolish things like magazines, plants or decorations. Jack expected deep carpets and mahogany walls from such a reputedly prosperous firm rather than these spartan furnishings. On her desk was a small plastic name-plate with Frances Forbes etched on it.

The woman buzzed through and said, "Your one o'clock."

She then motioned to the door, and Jack led the way. "Thank you, Mrs. Forbes," he said graciously.

She lifted her eyebrows as they filed through the large mahogany door to the hallway on the other side.

At the far end of the long hall, a tall, rail-thin old man motioned for them to come his way. They looked into the offices to the right and left of the hall as they walked. There were busy lawyers, clerks and secretaries in every one—some sharing tiny cubby offices. Jack thought of a battalion of Bob Cratchits, all sitting on high stools, scribbling away through the night. Nobody smiled or talked. It was deadly silent except for the mill of computer keyboards clicking down the desolate hallways.

The crane-like man signed for them to sit. His office was on a corner of the building and had glass windows on two sides giving an unobstructed view of the quarter and the great sweep of the Mississippi forming its crescent curve.

The man eyed the four with the predatory look of an ancient hawk. "I'm Lehmann Forbes. Which one of you is Chandler?"

Jack nodded.

"Then you're Leviathon, and you Dennison? You McConothy?"

They nodded.

"Title to these properties will be transferred now. Will you look over the deeds?"

Forbes disappeared down the hall while Jack and Sam examined the papers. They lifted their heads in unison as they heard Forbes screeching to someone. His voice sounded like a snapping whip, "I told you I needed that research this morning. You'll stay all night if you have to. I want it done right or I will dock you again."

Then, they could hear his footsteps back up the hall, and he said, "You two, in here!"

Forbes returned with two hollow-eyed, middle aged men who were to act as witnesses. Each had the look of a prisoner of war and none spoke or seemed to have the will to.

Sam and Jack carefully studied the documents and the copies. They had been typed perfectly. The parties signed, then Forbes presented a power of attorney from M.M., Inc. He then signed for the corporate representative. Not a word was spoken as the papers were handed around for signing, witnessing and notarizing.

At a curt nod from Forbes, the witnesses left the room.

Forbes handed a signed, notarized title to the boat to Jack and then said, "Now, as to the money. Here is a set of releases and a cashier's check in the amount of seven million dollars, payable to you, Mr. Chandler. This represents the full amount of the settlements you stipulated. You can decide on how the money is to be disbursed. Mr. Cabal asks that you have your clients sign this release."

"He will give the money before the release is signed?"

The old man gave a wicked smile and said, "I wouldn't have, but this is his wish. He wants to show you how much he trusts you."

Then Jack said, "Hold on a minute, there's another thing. I didn't want all the money at once. We were going to buy structured settlements."

"Mr. Cabal said he trusts you to do what you wish."

Jack sat back in his chair as if struck.

"Hey, that's not the plan," Jack breathed. "We agreed to have a company set up the structure."

"Mr. Cabal wanted to complete it without delay."

"How am I to work out the structures?" Jack asked.

"That's your problem, Mr. Chandler. We have no further business, so there is no reason for you to stay. I have other more pressing things to attend to."

The tall man rose from his seat and looked down his beaked nose at Jack.

"I have some pressing things to attend to as well," Jack said as he started walking away.

Jack smiled brightly at the scowling old man and walked out of the door, followed by Vic and Sam.

Sam whispered, "Forbes didn't like you very much."

"And you didn't like him," Vic said.

"Fuck him."

"Your motto," Vic said, gripping the title to the Marquis de Mandeville in her fist.

Jack glanced into the library. Books were stacked everywhere, and several older man bent over their labors, squinting in the low light. A dark, thin-faced, balding man looked up furtively from his work and nodded, giving a knowing smile.

Jack nearly stumbled over Vic, but kept walking. He nearly laughed out loud. The little man had a milky cast on his left eye and wore a black, pointed beard.

Chapter 29

Jack deposited the check in an interest-bearing account at the Hibernia Bank, and then called all of the claimants. He scheduled two every hour the following morning with Sam taking one and he taking the other.

"This way, we can get 'em all on the line in one day without there being lots of time for rumors to fly and things to get bogged down."

"We should be able to clean it all up by tomorrow night," Sam said.

"We better get us a bunch of typists in here to complete the paper work. None of the claimants will release the sheriff or any of the defendants. If we can recover anything from them, it'll be lagniappe," Jack said as he picked up the phone and dialed his secretary's number.

That evening, Jack and Sam riffled through two tall stacks of documents, one for Jack to handle with specified clients and the other for Sam.

"I have an investment specialist coming in tomorrow morning to meet with all of us," Jack said. "He'll set it up for 'em, and they'll start gettin' somethin' every month. If they want an education of some kind, we can get that too. Tomorrow ought to be a helluva day. Nothin' good has ever happened to any of those poor bastards; this is gonna be a shock."

Jester helped put some of the papers in order and said, "Damn, I'm useless as tits on a boar hog around here. Maybe I should get on back to Mobile."

"Hang on, Jest," Sam said, "wait till the funeral, then go. You been a player this long."

"You got it, I'll hang, and stay outta ya'lls hair till ya'll get all ya'lls business done."

"Somebody's at the door," Sam said, hearing the buzzer.

Jack pressed the button that released the outer apartment door lock. They could hear the bolt slap open, followed by footsteps on the hard, cypress floorboards of the hall. The door was pushed open to Jack's office.

Nookie, dressed in a lime-green leisure suit, silk lime shirt with an open collar and a huge gold chain hanging around his neck, stood grinning in the doorway. Hanging on him was a tall blonde, bursting out of her very short, low cut dress that displayed extraordinary amounts of hide, high and low.

"Hey, you koo-yon, you know my l'il Pussy Beaucoup, Norma Jean. You done seen her dance at de Sudden Exposure."

Sam's appreciative eyes scanned the abundance before him and Pussy blew a kiss for his benefit. She was utterly accustomed to having horny men ogle her stripped nakedness, for which they paid a price to see, but not touch. Only Nookie could access those charms, though she was a walking preview of her main event at all times.

After the introductions, Nookie asked, "Whar's Vic?"

"She had to work this evenin'," Jack said. "I'm sure she would like to see you, though."

"What you want wit' Nookie? Puss off work tonight, an' we goin' out to Paradis whar dey got a big Parish Fair. Me'n Norma gonna see if we kin get stuck on top of de farris-wheel." He winked and poked Jack in the ribs.

"Here," Jack said, hiding some papers in his hand, "hold out your hand."

"Shoop," Nookie said, "What you hold in yo' hand? It ain't someting gon' bite ol' Nook, haih?"

Nookie held out his palm. Jack dropped the papers and keys into it.

"What's dis?"

"You said you wanted a certain boat? There's the title, keys, and keys to the boathouse at the Westend Harbor. All you got to do is to send the papers to the Wildlife and Fisheries to register it in your name. It's yours, with a freezer full of aged KC T-bones steaks."

"Mah poo yi yi!" Nookie whooped. "Mais yeah, mebbe we gon see how mah new boat float. Maybe we can see if she will rock," he said, leering wolfishly at Norma Jean a/k/a Pussy Beaucoup. "I bet dat boat ain't never been broke in good. Hey, whar de boat at—out at dat, howyacall, yacht place on de West End?"

"Yeah," Sam said. "Don't splash all the water out of the yacht basin."

Pussy stretched and pressed her chest out, causing her breasts to nearly leap out of their restraints, a tiny bit of brown showing the rim of a nipple. "You got a big boat now, Nook?"

"Uh huh."

"Got a bed in it, you say?"

"Uh huh."

"I suddenly feel sooo tired," she pressed her pelvis against him, blowing a little bubble in his ear. "You don't need to go to no fair. I'll give you a roller coaster ride."

"Coo! Dis woman makin' threats!" Nookie said, bunching his shoulders together and sticking his tongue out with a silly expression.

"C'mon, I'll show you which slip it's in," Sam said. "Jack gave me Mourier's apartment above your boat. I wanna take a look at my new digs. You know, Nookie, we gonna be kind of roommates."

"Hoo! De coonass an' de redneck, roommates! Ha Ha."

"You don't play loud music and I won't piss down into your boat," Sam said.

"We gonna git along, roommate," Nookie said as the three walked from the apartment. Norma Jean looked over her shoulder at Jack and gave him a little goodbye bump with her high-rise derriere, then blew a big pink bubble for him to boot.

Chapter 30

DAY ELEVEN

The next day Vic opened the door for Sam, who sported a new pair of gleaming cowboy boots, holding a six pack of Dixie and a box of contraband Havana cigars. "Time to celebrate, Jackson," he said to Jack who was sprawled on the sofa watching the news.

"Gotta get you a pair of these," Sam said, pointing to his boots while handing Jack a beer and the box of cigars.

"He's got six pair in the closet, but nothing like those," Vic said, looking at the tip of gold on the toes and the elaborate leather work.

"Always wanted a pair like that," Jack said, "and since we are such ass kickers these would be proof."

"They make a statement for sure," said Vic.

Jack slid a cigar from its cedar wrapper and sniffed. Shaking his head in pleasure he said, "where'd you get these, Sam? Black Market?"

"In the street man, in the street."

"Well, you boys deserve some good things after what you pulled off for all those kids," said Vic.

Sam and Jack lit up and beamed at each other in only the way men can when they have won a hard fought battle together.

"Thanks for letting me sit in on the distribution of the funds to those kids.," Vic said, touching Jack on the back of his hand, "it was a once in a lifetime experience." It was everything I could do to keep from crying every time a new set came in, scared and suspicious and hopeless, and leaving with a whole new life laid out for them."

"Yeah, Jack," Sam said, "your idea of making Cabal pay for their education through college, and monthly payments for twenty years, instead of lump sum was great. Now they can't blow it all at once and can make something of themselves."

"I take it back, I did cry." Vic said, "I had to leave the room when you met with Tyrone and little James. Tyrone is going to buy his mama a house out of the projects and you two are going to help James' auntie to find a house too, and James wants to go to school and learn to play the piano. I won't ever forget the look in his eyes when he knew he was going to get a piano."

"What time did we do the last one," Jack asked.

"Nearly midnight," Vic said.

"Yep, that was an experience of a lifetime," Sam said. "You don't get to make your clients happy too often, and we made a washtub full of it today."

"Several lifetimes, Sam," Jack said. "Money talks and bullshit walks, and it did a lot of talkin' yesterday."

The only thing left was the disbursement for Martin and Estelle. "I'll give it to 'em tomorrow at the funeral," Jack said, "I hope it will help lighten things a little."

∾

Jack, Vic, Sam and Jester and Vic went to the final wake. Dawn's coffin was visited by masses of people numbering in the thousands. Estelle and Martin asked to be permitted to open the coffin and see Dawn one more time. The morticians had done as good a job as possible, using a picture of her as a model, and the results were passable, but the sight caused Estelle to faint and Martin to cry out in agony.

The long days and waking nights had found Estelle and Martin hard by the closed, gleaming coffin, engulfed in wall-to-wall flowers, keeping vigil, hoping against all hope that a miracle would bring her back to them. Occasionally Estelle would rise, walk to the casket, and flutter her hands among the flowers as she moved and rearranged them over and over. Martin watched her, holding in his own grief for his daughter and his suffering Estelle.

The chapel overflowed with the largest outpouring of people in anyone's recollection. As the hundreds filed by the coffin, Jack noticed that many laid little mementoes and gifts at a small shrine that had been set up alongside. When he asked Martin about it, the short answer was, "she was special."

∾

Sam and Jester went out on the town after leaving the funeral home. On the way back to the apartment, neither Jack nor Vic spoke, both deep in their thoughts trying to reason through the whole affair. Jack finally broke the silence. "Damn its rough. I don't have a kid, but losing one, specially your only one, gotta be as bad as it gets."

"Did you notice how many people there were? There were lines of people a block long outside the chapel, waiting just to walk by the coffin, and they all touched the coffin as they passed it and said a prayer or something."

'Yeah, and all those flowers, and little things they placed all around. Incense, jars of stuff. I never been to a funeral here anyway, so they really make a big deal of it."

"This is more than usual, Jack. I'm black, and I've been to many black funerals. There's always lots of preaching and music and flowers and eulogies, but nothing like this."

⤜

Jack half-opened his eyes and realized he had fallen asleep on his sofa. The patio was silvered in the light of the full moon that had risen after midnight.

He went rigid at what he beheld.

The trim figure of a long-haired girl in a loose cotton dress was silhouetted against the open door, standing only a few feet away.

A chill ran through him as he heard her call his name in his mind.

"Jack?"

His fear was not from the presence of an unexpected visitor in the wee hours of the morning, for he had been awakened by women in the night before. It was something more. Something was wrong with this picture.

"Thank you for what you did for Mama and Papa, and for me."

"Dawn Marie?"

Jack's skin prickled and he felt an impulse to break and run. *This is a dream,* he thought, *and since it's a dream, I'll relax and let it carry me. But I seem to be awake. This is too damn real.*

"Mama and Papa know where I am. We talk. They don't worry any more."

"Is this a dream?"

"If you want it to be."

"How are you speaking?"

She laughed lightly. "There are many ways of talking."

"What do you want?"

"Just to thank you, and to let you know I am doing fine and I am happy."

Jack realized that he wasn't talking with his mouth. Instead, he was "sending" thoughts to her.

"Where did you go?"

"I will stay with my body until it is buried–the only right thing to do."

"What are you going to do?"

"I'll be around. I'll get another baby body; I'm in no hurry."

"You act like that's the way it's done."

"Everybody does it," she giggled. "What do you think happens? It's simple. Just pick a family, get in the baby when it's born. A brand new life, new name. Maybe a boy next time."

Jack said nothing, continuing to stare at the shapely silhouette against the doorway.

"Maybe even be *your* baby."

"My baby?"

"You'll have one someday. I can wait. You'll be a cool dad."

"Wait a minute now. What're you sayin'?"

"I think it's time for me to go," she said. "Thank you so much. I'm fine now that Mama and Papa will be taken care of."

"Did you want revenge?"

"No, not to hurt because I was hurt. I was angry at being treated like that, and I loved being Dawn. She was pretty and so happy. And loved Mama and Papa. But I don't hate—that's a human thing. I wanted justice, and you did that. That's my revenge."

"Will I see you again?"

"Do you want to?"

"Yes. I want to know more."

"I'll be around. You already know more than you remember. You just forgot—on purpose."

"What do you mean?'

"Gotta go. Bye!"

Jack blinked and she was gone. He knuckled his eyes and sat up, walked out on the balcony and looked about. Nobody was there.

"Damn!" Jack swore out loud. "I must have been dreamin'. Or else I'm goin' nuts."

Chapter 30

DAY TWELVE

The following morning was overcast with a drizzling rain. The Olympia Jazz band led the hearse bearing the coffin, following behind was a silent throng of well-dressed relatives and friends, all carrying umbrellas. The band—consisting of a tuba, two saxophones, clarinet, banjo, trombone, two trumpets, and a bass and snare drum—played doleful hymns as they slowly filed down Claiborne Avenue. Each sad-faced band member wore a black jacket and a black hard-billed cap with *Olympia* embossed in gold on the front.

Ahead of the band, a black man dressed in a white satin shirt and pants and short jacket led the entire parade. His huge pendulous paunch stuck out like a huge bass drum. He walked stiffly, holding a tasseled umbrella cover his head, and wore a "this is very serious business" look on his face.

Jack and Vic walked up front with Martin and Estelle. Jack's hand was held in Estelles tight grip as she stoically kept her eyes riveted on the coffin through the back window of the hearse.

By the time the procession reached and entered the cemetery, it had grown until the marchers filled both sides of the wide boulevard, blocking traffic in both directions. The tide of humanity swelled until traffic police were called to control the flow of mourners.

St. Louis Number I: a brick-walled city block of above ground tombs and vaults, large and small, some stacked six-crypts high, one on top of the other. Many had sunk into the earth. There were no underground burials in New Orleans. The city is below sea level and coffins would float and even travel underground if buried. All of the crypts in the cemetery were ancient and crumbling, some dating back two hundred years, their time-worn inscriptions barely legible.

The tombs were called ovens, with the remains decomposing rapidly in baking New Orleans summers. Over the centuries, the occupants were simply pushed back into the vaults and new tenants placed in. Many held a dozen sets of remains in one single vault.

He wondered about Dawn Marie, the child of a poor black family, being interred in such a historic cemetery.

The multitude massed around the rear of the hearse while the pallbearers lifted the coffin and carried it to the gravesite. They slowly played "Just A Closer Walk With Thee" as the coffin neared the crypt. The rain had slowed and then ceased completely. The air was close and muggy.

An old tomb had been re-opened to allow placement of Dawn's coffin. Jack didn't pay attention to which one. He stood, one hand gripped by Vic and the other by Estelle.

The crowd gathered around the coffin. Every hand that could reach and touch lifted the coffin high as the snare drummer beat a slow, dirge-like roll. The drummer abruptly stopped, and in the dead silence, a voice cried out, "Turn the body loose!"

In the quiet, the casket was lowered and slid into the narrow crypt. The warm morning sun suddenly broke through the clouds and bathed the scene in a shaft of golden light.

The only sound in the gripping silence was the drummer tightening his snares. The crowd held its breath. The drummer cut down with a terrific roll, then the band began exultantly playing "When the Saints Go Marching In." In jazz jargon, the band completed "the second line," symbolizing the reaffirmation of life's victory over death.

Then the crowd briskly marched through the cemetery gates and out onto Basin Street, where the short-legged leader in white stepped out and strutted, pumping his fringed umbrella into the air, sometimes standing in one place and shaking his huge belly up and down in time with the pulsating rhythm.

The throng began to jump and dance to the irresistible beat. Soon the streets were filled with prancing, dancing men and women who, minutes before, were glum and forlorn. Martin and Estelle didn't smile, but their relief was evident. The most wrenching moment of the ritual had been completed. They could finally try to reconstruct their shattered lives.

A crew quickly closed the crypt as they watched. Jack noticed the workers were very careful and kept their eyes averted as they sealed the tomb. The only sound was the trowel putting the face of the marble tomb back in place, and they finished quickly, gathered their tools, each mason touched the tomb with the palm of his hand and left.

The clouds gathered again, and the day darkened. A muted hush blanketed the ancient cemetery. It was more than a tranquil peacefulness, it was a total stillness, as if the grass itself wasn't growing. Jack felt as if he was in a time bubble of utter solitude.

Sam and Jester stood back at the cemetery entrance gate, allowing Jack to have some private time with Martin and Estelle.

He stepped over debris that had fallen from a crumbled tomb, daring to look inside at the pile of dirt and leaves that had accumulated on what once had been laid there, perhaps two centuries past.

Estelle knelt beside the crypt for a long time while Martin, Jack and Vic waited, with Sam and Jester standing back several feet away. Fresh flowers had been placed in twin urns alongside. Presently she stood, and brushed the dead leaves from her skirt, turned and said something to Martin. Both their faces were streaked with tears.

The smell of carnations filled the still air, and there was a faint scent of something else—some aromatic oils or incense.

The ancient marble vault containing Dawn's coffin was surrounded by urns, vases, jars, snuff bottles, and even soup cans filled with flowers—some fresh and some wilted. Over the years crude X's had been scratched and marked all over the two-tiered cement tomb. Jack knew what that meant—voodoo. Trinkets, beads and herbs were scattered all around. Jack recognized the ash residue in several small burners as incense. Similar but new things surrounded Dawn's crypt. Two or three new X's had already been scratched on the tomb. He then turned back to the couple who seemed a little nervous.

Jack leaned over and read the old inscription on the brass plate set in front of the tomb. He frowned and looked baffled. He asked, a question in his voice, "Marie Laveau?

Estelle looked inquiringly at Martin and he said, "Tell him."

Estelle swallowed hard and said, "Lawyer Jack. In that tomb are the bones of Marie Laveau. She was Dawn Marie's great, great, great grandmother. We named our baby Dawn 'cause she was the new light, born again, born as the sun rose. We gave her name back."

The hair on the back of Jack's neck bristled. Vic's grip tightened on his hand.

"Dawn had the power, Lawyer Jack," Martin said. "She already had clients. She would have been great again."

Marie Laveau! Jack thought. *The legendary voodoo queen of New Orleans! A virtual goddess; feared and revered during the early nineteenth century. Buried right here. In the same tomb with Dawn.*

"Marie Laveau reborn?" Jack asked.

Both nodded.

Jack's legs felt weak. So this was the surprise. He wished there was some place for him to sit and let all of this soak in. His dream of last night swam before his eyes. He remembered his own vision and said, "I understand. I've lived before."

"We know, Lawyer Jack." Martin said.

"And we know you know," Estelle said. "I knew and Marie, ah, Dawn knew, before you knew. She told me somethin' about you bein' like a big cat that hadn't woke up, but when you woke, you would be somethin' else! That's why I work for you. It's 'cause you understand."

Jack swallowed hard, looking at the tomb, Estelle and Martin, trying to get a grip on what he was being told.

"You got somethin' to tell us, Lawyer Jack? Martin asked.

Jack paused to change mental gears from the avalanche of these new thoughts cascading through his head.

"I got you a settlement. You still have your case against the Sheriff and Bormann's estate. This is Mourier's part."

"How much?" Martin asked incredulously, taking hold of Jack's arm.

"You take home, tax free, $1,500,000."

"Lordy!" Martin said. He turned to Estelle who hadn't said anything. "Mama, we got lots of money. We can get you a fine house in a fine place. Get you a housekeeper."

Estelle dreamily turned to the tombs and said. "Dawn Marie. I gonna put a nice fence around your tomb so's there won't be no more trompin' around and messin' with your restin' place. I know you gonna come back when you want to, but I got the money to make it all nice."

"You want it?" Jack asked.

"That's damn good money, Lawyer Jack," Martin said. "We accept."

Jack took the papers from his coat pocket. "Sign this release against Mourier's estate.

They laid the papers on the surface of a nearby tomb, signed them, and handed them back to Jack.

"Here." Jack said, handing them the cashier's check.

Martin extended a tremulous hand and drew it back, saying, "Here baby, you take it."

He then held Estelle's hand steady as she slowly took the check from Jack's hand. She held it up to the tomb and said, "Dawn Marie. Look what I got. It ain't gonna replace you. But it gonna help me and daddy stop hurtin' so bad."

She turned and embraced Jack and Vic. Martin joined in and put his huge arms around all of them. They clung to each other, trying to understand what had happened and why—trying to reconcile this reality with what they all knew it should have been. Hot tears coursed down Jack's face, and mingled with Estelle's and Vics, whose faces were pressed to his.

Estelle pulled away and said, "Martin, tell him now."

Martin nodded and walked to his truck and returned with a small cotton bag with a leather drawstring. He knelt by Marie Laveau's tomb and swept the leaves and dirt from the top of a flat marble marker. He took five little man-like figures out, one at a time, and laid them side by side on the dusty surface.

Each was five inches tall, carefully made of cotton ticking and moss. None had faces. Three had olive green, poplin pants sewn on them. One was wrapped in something, and the other was charred.

"What's that?" Jack asked.

"Don't you know?"

"Not really."

"Look," Estelle said.

She held up the three with the olive pants. One had a needle thrust through it's head, another was in shreds with the crotch torn out, and the other had been painted with something that made it as stiff as a board.

Jack resisted the thought that gradually sank in. A chill ran through him. The head on the doll with the needle through its head had been painted brown.

Destrehan!

Jack slowly lifted his eyes to Martin's and then Estelle's. They nodded gravely.

The green cloth was made of bits of sheriffs' uniforms that had been sewed on the dolls. There was Parker–ripped to shreds, and Sessums–paralyzed. Bosco–charred black. The wrapping on the final one was dried snake skin.

"Who did this?"

"I did," Estelle said.

"The morning we went to the morgue with you," Martin said. "We went to early mass–daybreak–an' we realize we needed more help than that. Much more. Estelle went into a trance and found Dawn Marie and she tole her what to do. She made 'em when we got back."

"That was before I met Destrehan!" Jack whispered to himself.

A few drops began to spatter on the tomb and the day turned suddenly dark. The street lights popped on out on Basin Street.

Martin picked the voodoo dolls up, gently placed them back into the cotton bag and pulled the drawstring tight.

Estelle placed her hand on Jack's arm and said, "Dawn's here, you know."

Jack didn't say anything, not daring to look around. Afraid he would see Dawn standing there. He nodded so slightly it was almost not noticed.

"You can't see or hear her 'less she wants you to."

Jack hesitated and then said, "Yeah, I know."

"She come see you last night, didn't she?" Estelle said, her eyes shining.

Jack smiled, and nodded, "Yeah."

"She say she would," Estelle said, as Martin unfurled their big umbrella.

"She say she sho' do like you. Said she gonna keep her eye on you, just in case."

Jack turned and asked, "Just in case what?"

"Just in case," Estelle said, unfurling their umbrellas in the sudden downpour. As Vic opened her umbrella, Jack noticed Martin and Estelle both were finally laughing, looking back at him, as they walked away.

Sam and Jester followed Estelle and Martin. Vic made a sign for Jack to follow, watching Jack stand in the pouring rain, apparently looking at nothing.

So many pictures swarmed in his head of the events of the past weeks, and what he had just been told. A feeling of warmth and peace flowed through him and he knew he had done the best he could, and that was plenty. He finally allowed himself the win he had denied himself for the past few days.

I won! Its been a hoot! Things are alright!

Jack found himself actually purring. He started to walk, and then thought, *All that's done, and behind me. What's next?*

He heard a familiar young girl's voice in his head, *Yeah, Jack. What's next?*

∽

Jack carried his Dixie out to the balcony, needing a little time to himself to sort things out. *I'm rich. Get some space. Go to Europe. Sam can handle everything when I'm gone. That's it. I'll just get out of Dodge for a while and figure out what to do about Vic.*

He sat on the balcony for a rollercoaster hour, killing three beers and several cigarettes, thinking of skiing the Alps, seeing the art of Florence and the Louvre, maybe even extending it to a trip around the world and visiting Russia and Singapore. Then he would fret about leaving Vic behind. Maybe losing her.

The door slammed open and Vic walked in. With her hands on her hips, she angrily snapped, "I took the liberty of answering your goddamn phone. It was ringing off the hook. It seems some Judy person is seeking your companionship. She said you gave her a long ride during the storm."

Jack shrugged. "I did give her a ride to her home in Montegut when her car got flooded out."

"From what she implied, you gave her a good ride alright. This Judy asked lots of questions about you. Says you are a real stud-muffin."

"Just a ride in Nookie's truck," Jack repeated lamely.

"I bet you did. I have no right to be jealous, but I am. I don't own you, you son of a bitch! I used the master key to get in here, and I shouldn't have. I won't do it again, and I won't answer you phone again for you!" Vic's voice picked up in intensity.

Holding his hands up as if to ward off an attack, Jack said, "You know I'm having a problem with this thing. I guess I'm just scared—and chicken. I gotta have time to think about it, and some space."

Vic's eyes brimmed with tears. She clinched her fists and held her breath, ready to launch a volley Jack wasn't ready to receive. He waited for the inevitable assault that would slam him headlong into a decision he had long failed to confront.

I am about to lose her, he thought. *This is a nightmare. This isn't happening.* His mind seemed to splinter into painful shards of uncertainty as he watched her begin the next level of offensive, and he knew each missile would land squarely in his heart and expose his contemptible soul.

"Space! You've had nothing but space and time. I had better rethink this 'thing' as you put it. If you can't do better than that, I can."

Jack watched himself and Vic as if from afar, detached, trying to withdraw from the wrenching pain in his gut as Vic let out a sob and glared at him through eyes that knew as much pain as he was feeling.

"What do you mean?"

"Just that. I might care for you, but I don't have to put up with your misgivings any longer. Maybe I need some space too! I have options. I won't bother you anymore."

Jack never had any hard decisions, but this was a big one. He was petrified. *I am hurting her. I can't lose her,* he heard himself saying to himself. *I just can't lose her. I am about to lose her right now.*

Jack's heart pounded and his brain seemed to be on the verge of meltdown. Why did he feel this way. In the South, his position was perfectly valid...or was it? *Where did this idea about black and white differences come from in the first place? Where did any idea come from?*

Time stood still as his mind flashed over the past, and he heard a high-pitched country voice saying, "You can make out with a colored gal, but you better not get caught if you figger to do good in business. It'll foller you the rest of your life."

That was the voice of his foreman at the sawmill where he worked when he got out of high school. Jack had valued this man's opinion. He had been his surrogate father. Those bigoted ideas had followed Jack all of his life, and he now knew he had made them his own. And it was all a lie!

Something within him gave way and seemed to break open, whiffing away in a sudden mental release that lifted him out of himself and he saw himself and Vic in a completely new light. The fetters of aberrated memory fell away, and he was free!

Hot tears of relief swelled in his eyes as the frustrations and fears of his life melted. A calm certainty filled him.

Vic continued her tirade. "I'm going to resume my life, and I am not going to sit idle while you chase after Judy and God knows who else while I am left here wondering. This is an all or nothing "thing," as you put it. As of now, it is nothing! Good-bye!"

She spun on her heels and headed toward the door. Jack stepped in front of her and blocked her way. He was filled to bursting with words he had refused to think, much less speak, but they were on his tongue and ready.

Vic stood rigid, obviously about to shove her way through to freedom from this man she could not understand and who was proving not to be the man she thought he was.

"I love you," Jack whispered.

Vic's breath was ragged and tears streamed down her amber cheeks. She stared unbelieving at Jack and ran the back of her hand under her nose.

"I've been such a damn fool," Jack said, his own eyes beginning to fill and glisten. The floodgate of his emotions broke, and his mind began to run wild with words he had wanted to say for so long but couldn't.

Vic sniffed and wiped the tears from her cheeks, staring at Jack as if he was totally insane.

"I just had a realization. I knew I was about to lose you, and I can't explain it, but I finally know how much you mean to me and you mean more to me than I can say."

"What are you saying, Jack Chandler?"

"I am saying I love you. I want to be with you. To be your man, to, ah…"

Vic's tears were beginning again, but this time not from anger. "To what, Jack?"

Jack let out a pent up breath and gently held her face in his hands, tenderly wiping away her tears. "If you'll have me, live with me for the rest of my life, have my babies, be my wife?"

A long moment lapsed as they looked into each other's eyes. Vic slowly pulled Jack's face down to hers, pressed her lips against his, then drew back and said, "I accept your proposal, you crazy bastard!"

Jack let out a whoop, swept her into his arms, lifted her as if she were a feather, and carried her to the bedroom.

On the street below, a crowd of tourists from Yokohama looked up at the balcony with the wrought iron Spanish lace. They nodded knowingly at each other at the laughter and love sounds spilling over the gallery above.

PROLOGUE

The trial was about to start. The courtroom was filled with the sort who go to hangings, hungry for blood. The circumstances of this case were just what the bottom feeders love. The military didn't like its adjudications exposed to the light of day, but there was standing room only, the crowd buzzing and speculating upon the atrocious charges against Sergeant Nolan. Scattered in the crowd were a half dozen reporters who feed on this kind of sorry business, and they all wanted to see Nolan swing.

Riggs McCall, lead attorney for the defendant and my co-counsel, looked like a coiled rattler. I was shocked at his transformation when he walked into the courtroom. He seemed taller, and deadly. I had never seen him like that, but I, too, had undergone changes since we'd met just five months before. It could easily have been years.

The counsel table faced a panel of officers sitting in padded swivel chairs behind a long table. In the middle was a full bird colonel, flanked by two light colonels, who in turn were flanked on each side by majors, who were flanked by captains at each end. Their expressions were as hard as stone.

To the left, the Law Officer, the senior ranking officer who acted as the judge over the proceedings sat behind a high enclosure.

Lambrusco, the prosecuting attorney, supported by his two assistants, like jackals hunched over a kill, had staked out the favorable position near the law officer and the witness box.

I was irrevocably deep in this whole mess, and it was anybody's guess what the next two or three days would bring.

My whole future was entangled with Riggs and this trial. My carefully planned rise to political power, perhaps a bid for the presidency itself, even my father's banking business relationship with the Defense Department was in danger of crumbling if the trial did not go well. Going well, to them meant a conviction. And I was helping defend this bastard. How did I get into this mess?

Chapter 1

When I first met Riggs McCall, he scared hell out of me, and I knew immediately I had to keep my distance. He was trouble simply because he was cocky, self assured, and would get in your face in a heartbeat, and that was the wrong attitude for a lieutenant in the U.S. Army. Acquaintances like that didn't fit my long term plans in using the Army as a stepping stone to my political future.

The fact that he didn't give a damn showed not only in the way he carried himself and how he wore his officer's hat at a jaunty slant over his brow like a World War II fighter pilot, but more the knowing smirk that tugged at the corners of his mouth and the faint light of mockery that somehow illuminated his pale blue eyes.

We met on the first day I reported for duty at Fort Lucky, Louisiana in late November, 1961. I had no idea then how involved our lives would become, nor for how long. I did know, however, we were very different, and I didn't want anything to do with him at all. It might rub off on me and I had plans other than being friends with a maverick.

Long before I got to Fort Lucky, I had learned that a second lieutenant, lawyer or not (and I was), is a soldier first and lawyer second. He keeps his mouth shut, his pants zipped, and he salutes nearly anything that moves. Basic training is not just hardening and training in survival and killing skills, but an education in proper military-political etiquette. Kiss ass, and when you're not doing that, be as invisible as possible, and keep your head down at all times.

Boot camp and basic training operate a food processor; it chops you up and pours you out in a nice blend. You look like everybody else and you had better act like everybody else whether you think like them or not. This is where Riggs's problems began, and why they continued. He was a country boy with little sophistication, and had no basic training when he came into the army, being brought in under an emergency program because of a shortage of army lawyers. He chose being an officer for three years rather than being drafted and being a private for two. He went almost straight to his post assignment from law school. He hadn't learned to blend in, even if he could have in the first place. He never kept his head down, and he was always getting hit.

I had been more fortunate, indoctrinated in lessons Riggs never had. Exclusive private schools in Dallas, Virginia Military Institute (VMI), and then cum laude from the University of Texas with a law degree. My father was president of the largest bank in Dallas, and my parents both made sure that I had the best and that I was the best.

I had reached my Dad's six foot two in the twelfth grade. He referred to us as "long tall Texans." On the day of my graduation from law school, as I stood outside the hall in my cap and gown, I finally felt as tall as he was. He shook my hand, beaming, and said, "Son, play the game. Rise and fall with the tide. You are part of a team you're going to learn about as you go. You've been groomed for greatness."

I never had any doubt about being the best and I never questioned who the team was and what game the team was playing. I should have.

෴

Fort Lucky sits in the big piney woods in the northeast quadrant of Louisiana. About twenty-five miles wide at the northern boundary and twenty miles on the eastern and western sides, the huge reservation contains thousands of acres of dry sandy hills, high pines, swamps, and miles of a thick, raspy-leaved, ground-hugging vine called kudzu. Lucky is twenty-four miles from the nearest off-post real beer, but that was the least of its problems. Rattlesnakes on the ground and red wasps in the bushes give the ground soldier trainee plenty to think about.

The Lucky Cantonment was built during the First World War and renovated as Fort Lucky during the Second. The buildings were still primitive—one and two-story temporary barracks—with some cinder-block structures, heated by steam from coal-burning furnaces. They shipped the coal in from Wyoming rather than tap one of the world's largest pools of natural gas, the Monroe Gas Rock, a few miles away.

Lucky was a particularly inappropriate name, subject to all manner of ribald humor. They borrowed it in a time of intense patriotism from a nearly forgotten Confederate general, Ananias Z. Lucky, a former Methodist bishop whose own luck ran out before the Union guns at Cold Harbor, Virginia.

Thus, right from the beginning, Lucky was the antithesis of its name, and those unlucky enough to get assigned there for more than temporary basic training all agreed that if God should give the world an enema, Lucky was the locus where the instrument would be inserted–*anus mundi*. I readily agreed with this conclusion when I first drove through its streets and reported in at post headquarters.

The billions in cold war appropriations for military build-up had just touched Lucky when I arrived. New billets for married officers and enlisted personnel were under construction, and a spanking new seven-story hospital stood gleaming just beyond the renovated post exchange and commissary. There was new equipment, and a sense of apathetic frenzy, if that makes sense. Every cloud on the horizon took on the shape of a mushroom. We knew war was inevitable, and this kind of war would be apocalyptic, leaving nobody untouched. None of my friends wanted to have children.

As for me, I didn't ask for or want to be at Lucky and had never expected this duty assignment. Right after law school in Austin, I passed the bar and they gave me my ticket to the courtroom. I framed the license issued by the Texas Supreme Court authorizing me to practice law. It was my passport to way beyond mediocrity, and like an icon ready to hang on the wall of my first office, it lay on the back seat of my ragtop Pontiac as I drove to my first assignment.

Every young man faced conscription into the army unless he joined the marines, navy, or air force or was deferred for some reason, as I had been while in school. With my engineering degree from VMI, I went straight into law school at UT, after which I had two choices: first, I could use my ROTC commission as an infantry second lieutenant, with six months in the reserve on active duty; second, the Judge Advocate General's Corps (JAG) the legal branch, held out a first lieutenant's commission as a carrot, but a three-year obligation went with it. If it had not been for these two options, I would have had a third choice, if you could call it that, because this was the Cold War when all young able-bodied men were eligible for the draft. The draftee served two years active duty as an enlisted man.

I chose the first. I wanted to get back home as soon as possible to start my life in politics. A six month tour would get me back quickly, and the amenities offered an officer were surely more pleasant than two years sharing barracks with a bunch of draftees or three as an army lawyer in some Staff Judge Advocate Office. I could do six months "standing on my head," and a favorable military record would help my future plans. I knew, with my family connections, I could easily be a state representative within three years and in three more a Texas congressman, with an eye toward U.S. Senator in ten. I knew where I was headed. My father and his friends had practically guaranteed me smooth sailing on the seas politicana. But the easy tides became a tidal wave at Fort Lucky, and I was swept away in the storm almost immediately.

For once my plans didn't work out exactly as anticipated. I was called to active duty during the Berlin crisis in June, 1961, the day after Kennedy said, "Ask not what your country can do for you—ask what you can do for your country." My big surprise was that my six-months obligation had been scrapped in favor of two years active duty and later was even extended to three years. If I hadn't exercised my option, my draft board would have sent its tidings instantly on graduation. As many of my buddies in law school soon realized, the ink wasn't dry on their certificates before their draft boards began to reel in the line that had been snagged for their seven years of undergraduate and law school. The breath of the world's mightiest fighting force was warm on our young necks.

My military schooling at VMI gave me a good understanding of the army way of life, and wearing the uniform was second nature. I finished my summer program at Fort Jackson, South Carolina and had completed the Basic Officers Orientation Course at Fort Benning, Georgia, before reporting to active duty. I went to Fort Belvoir, Virginia, for basic for engineers, then jump school at Fort Campbell, Kentucky where I was qualified as a paratrooper.

I was prepared for anything.

ॐ

Fort Lucky's two-story whitewashed headquarters sat in the center of a circular park, with streets, like spokes, extending out from the center of the hub. Manicured lawns surrounded the immaculate building, the delicate zoysia grass turned to a light brown by the frosts, and flags snapped in the cold November winds. Instantly I felt, and later grew to barely tolerate, what seemed to be the collective personality of the post, a pervasive sullen attitude that floated like a dismal shroud over the area. It came from the hard-eyed MP guards at the front gate, the infantry training areas, the helicopter and air training base at Louzon Field, and the rows of military barracks and parade grounds spotted throughout the base.

Places have collective personalities and Fort Lucky's ranges from a high of spitting antagonism to a chronic sulking apathy. There is a palpable, stifling resentment, and it is reflected in the cheerless faces of the men and women who serve and live there.

I parked my car in the paved lot near the Big House, the headquarters building. The little gold bar on my shoulders meant nothing much to anybody, particularly since I was not from West Point nor was my daddy RA, regular army. But I was an officer nonetheless, and now, after being in the army for just a few months, I was accustomed to enlisted men old enough to be my father, and far more experienced than I, saluting me and calling me "sir." One of these grizzled old sergeants passed me under the spreading oaks that led up to the Big House door. He snapped a brisk salute and barked, "Good morning, sir," with heavy emphasis on the sir, and kept walking. I returned his salute. The corporal on guard at the door also saluted me.

I was to sign in with the Officer of the Day at the front desk just inside the big double entrance doors, which was standard procedure upon arriving at any new post assignment. The OD would then dispatch you to your unit, noting the time of your arrival, and giving directions to your assignment. When the OD, an energetic captain named Daniels, saw my name tag and orders, he made a phone call—to check in with my unit, I thought, but instead, he ordered a young private to escort me to another office in the building.

Thinking there was some mistake, I said, "Captain, am I not to report to Company C?"

Captain Daniels smiled warmly. "Yes, you are, lieutenant—later."

I was baffled, and a bit worried, as I was hurried up two sets of stairs, through a series of offices and corridors, and finally into a neat little waiting room attended by a pert, middle-aged lady. She smiled at me over her reading glasses when I identified myself and told her I had just arrived on the post. She dialed a number on her rotary phone, said a few words, then led me to a door on the right.

The simple plate on the door read, "Major General Brandon Stewart." There were two silver stars mounted on the plate above his name.

I had not known I was to meet the Old Man, but when I entered I found myself in the presence of the Fort Lucky's commanding general himself.

Dad always told me to go to the top man first. The top at any military post was usually found at the officers club among wives and wanna-be generals, because that's where things really get done in the peacetime army. Intending to follow his advice, I knew it would be a cinch to cut through the country club butter of officer's clubs. I was raised in country clubs, and small talk was my item. But that would take strategic planning and tactical timing. This sudden short cut had not been included in my initial battle plans.

On the other hand, achieving a diplomatic faux pas for ignoring strict protocol on one's first day on post by not going directly to one's unit portended consequences not in keeping with well-laid plans to conquer Lucky on one's own terms. But here, during my first hour on duty at Lucky, I found myself facing a huge bear of a man behind an acre-wide desk across the broad expanse of a bare hardwood floor. This man commanded the lives of tens of thousands of men at any given time, including mine. Somehow I must have made a serious blunder by allowing myself to be escorted to this, the loftiest of chambers on this post.

Cigar smoke permeated the room, and had for a long time, judging by the depth of it. Windows had been closed for winter, cigars had been smoked, left smoldering in trays, chewed and half-smoked stubs forgotten and abandoned dead about the room, and now every pore in the leather chairs and every cell of the wood furniture, floor, and ceiling took on the acrid reek of smoke.

The heavy, dark-haired general behind the desk frowned over the unlighted cigar stub he wore between his thin lips. Two small brown eyes aimed at me like twin gun barrels as I was ushered through the door. He returned my best and snappiest salute with more a wave at his brow than a salute.

"Come on in, Lieutenant," he said, extending a hammy hand. I leaned forward and he enveloped mine in a crushing grip.

The smile froze on my face until he released my mangled fingers and waved me to a submissively low chair in front of his massive desk. His back was to double Westside windows, which made me squint to see his face in the dark silhouette. His already dominant persona was magnified intensely by this throne-like positioning.

I felt, and acted, appropriately impressed and obsequious enough. He, in turn, was obviously pleased at my crisp uniform and the gleaming crossed infantry rifles on my lapels. The winged silver parachute on my chest meant I had finished jump school, and the little pewter-hued medal of a cross within a laurel wreath, from which hung two tiny pewter plates, proved that I had qualified as expert, or superior, in firing the rifle and pistol. These decorations entitled me to share the rarified air breathed by men of war. As sacred symbols of the dedicated ground soldier, they said it all. The only thing missing was the Ranger patch, earned after going through the intense physical survival and combat schools for Rangers. I wanted that patch, and would get it. The Army would pay for it.

I had gone to jump school because it was fun, and the chance to do those things again in civilian life wouldn't appear. It took only a short time after my basic schools anyway, but there was method in my madness, for one thing was sure: being a certified paratrooper paved a golden four-lane highway through the quagmire of military socio-politics. The look on the faces of officers and enlisted men unequivocally proved that I possessed the key to the inner circle of military acceptance when they saw these small decorations. There was always a small smile and the flow of I-see-you-brother.

The expression on this big general's face was one of near love as he took in the cluster of miniature trophies on my chest. The holy triumvirate: crossed rifles, the winged parachute, and expert medals. Keys to the kingdom of military ease.

"You sure as hell don't look like a damned lawyer," the general snorted. He grinned and tried to light the black stub snagged between his big teeth.

I just grinned back, as if we both had some kind of secret. After a moment of silence he began to laugh, and opened a folder lying on his desk.

"Your personnel file, Madison."

I probably registered surprise, and I remember losing a bit of my studied aplomb as I stretched upward to see what he had in his hands. It was not logical that he, the commanding general of this largest of infantry training posts, should have my file, particularly at this time and place.

"You sure you don't want to forget that damned law bullshit and get a regular army commission?" Without waiting for an answer, he continued, "I'll recommend it, and you'll be let into the real Army, not that chickenshit reserve."

This was time to hold out the bait, so I answered, allowing a twinkle in my eye, as if lightly moving an evasive pawn in response to his bold gambit: "Well, I don't know for sure right now, sir. I haven't had much real army life yet, since my experience has mainly been schools. I want to see what's offered."

He eyed me through the flame of the match he held close to fire up the black stub in his mouth. Never taking his eyes from me, he chewed on the shredded end and swallowed the bits of tobacco leaf and juice, puffing to keep the stump of a cigar alive. After a moment, he snorted a laugh and said, "You got what it takes, Madison–as I can see right here in your record–to get my job."

The CO of the post doesn't interview every fresh second lieutenant who hits the post, and I sure as hell wasn't going to tell this man that the army was just a temporary inconvenience for me. Instead, I would throw out a lazy line and let my bait float on the water to see what happened.

"I am not going to rule it out, sir. The army offers lots of opportunity and I hope to decide while I'm here."

He pushed himself up from his chair, and looked down at me from at least six feet two. His bulk seemed to fill the space behind the desk.

"I know a little about you, Madison. You got politics in your blood. Remember, Ike was president, and a good military record can put a man where he wants to be. But you got to be mores' a prima donna."

I nodded as he walked around the desk to stand beside me. I stood, knowing that a junior should never sit while a senior was on his feet, even though there was nothing in the books about it. He stood near me and we were nearly the same height, so I was able to look him straight in the eyes. He smelled like the room.

Seeing he was testing me, and maybe trying to get under my skin, I deliberately stiffened–slightly. Further reaction on my part would have indicated defiance and any less would have suggested insecurity. I had been born to diplomacy, for I could swing easily to the precise body position, facial expression and tone of voice that would create any needed effect. I did it then.

"Sir, I plan to earn my keep, and more."

"Thought I'd get a rise outta you. Nah, you're no prima donna, boy. You got the Makin's of a damn good soldier, and from what I see, you can play the game."

"Thank you, sir," I said, not knowing what else to say. I was still somewhat baffled at the presence of my personnel file on his desk, but I wasn't going to blow anything by asking questions.

"What do you plan to do while you're at Lucky, Madison?"

It was no time to give lengthy speeches, like some candidate for office. His military mind wouldn't appreciate bullshit, but probably would appreciate stock, non-committal answers, for that was the ass-kissing way and he knew I knew it, and I was willing to do it. That was one of the tests. I answered with a quick "Be a good soldier, sir." I was still trolling my bait and he was taking a look.

Nodding knowingly, without taking his hard eyes from mine, his lips worked into a small smile around the cigar.

"Madison, you smart bastard, I know you already. I've seen your type. You want the best. You're like me. Don't hold out, thinking that you can get something you couldn't get otherwise. But I don't mind you playing the game. I'll be watching you."

He crushed my hand again, studying my discomfort at his close proximity and the fact that my fingers were being mauled.

"Before you go to your unit, you better get over to the Staff Judge Advocate's office and meet some of them lawyer buddies of yours. They could use some of your savvy."

He grinned, and I could feel him mentally dismissing me.

Quickly, I snapped to rigid attention, holding my salute stiffly, waiting for him to give his responding salute. The lower ranking personnel never releases the salute until the senior's salute is executed fully.

General Stewart paused, watching me as I held my joined fingers tensed by my right eyebrow, allowing my hand a slight tremor as the drill teams do to show they are hard at attention. He slowly raised his hand in salute, a calculating expression on his broad face.

"Thank you, and good day, sir."

"Good day to you, Lieutenant."

I about-faced and left the room, thinking the SOB knew exactly what I was doing. For a SOB like me, the thought was more than a little disconcerting.

NIMROD S PERIL

Nymphae, the insatiable queen of the Island Kingdom of Eros, has kept her irresistible beauty over hundreds of years by drawing the life from men. She thinks the essence of young Wanderer Nimrod Woodbine's spiritual purity will give her the immortality she craves. He must go to her of his free will. She kidnaps Musette, Nimrod's beautiful human-size mouse traveling companion, knowing Nimrod will try to rescue her. Nymphae's goal is to consume the essence of his very being, leaving him as a living husk in a tortured spiritual eternity as her helpless slave, joining the hundreds of other used-up lovers she keeps in standing coffins in her dungeon. His quest is filled with many dangers, but Nymphae, is the most perilous of all.

Chapter 1

Nimrod Woodbine slept beside a smoldering campfire as morning began to light the sky. Musette, his traveling companion, was rolled in a ball. Her light fur, jerkin and leather pants kept away the morning chill.

Dozens of tiny Ruby Cheepers flitted through the web of branches above them, welcoming the dawn with their bell-like peeps. A Chortler gargled in the nearby stream, and the huge blossoms of a burp bush suffused the encampment with a spicy fragrance. Nimrod rolled over, drew his cloak more tightly around him, and slipped into deeper sleep.

He was startled awake by a loud rustle that sent an eddy of leaves and dust swirling around the dying campfire. A winged man-like creature struggled into flight, its ragged wings so broad and near they almost blotted out the morning light. As it labored toward the treetops, Nim gasped to see Musette's limp form lying in its arms.

Nim raced frantically through the woods screaming Musette's name. He tripped and crashed over a boulder. The last thing he saw before smacking his head was the creature disappearing over the treetops.

He was awakened by the gibbering of three blue Farkles standing on his chest trying to give him lightwater from his waterskin. For a time he seemed to peer through a veil of gauze, until finally his eyes rested clearly on the jabbering Farkles perched just inches from his nose. Bickering noisily among themselves, they pulled and poked at his waterskin. In their bustle and excitement, one of them tumbled backwards off his chest. The raucous way it scolded the others for knocking it from its perch drew a grunt from Nim and made the quarrelsome Farkles aware he had regained consciousness. As they boisterously commended themselves for this development, the memory of the strange creature and Musette's limp form suddenly brought Nim to his feet. "The thing must have cast some spell on her," he cried. They looked quizzical and puzzled. "It's impossible to catch her napping--she sleeps with one eye open."

The Farkles broke into a pandemonium of excited jabbering. Nim learned from them that an emaciated, tortured-looking winged man had badgered them to tell where Nimrod was. When they refused, he had wheedled the information from Jugbutt Longtail, a grizzled old Possum still furious with Nim for chasing him away from Musette's warren two revolutions past.

The question was where to search for her. The Farkles fluttered onto his shoulders and tugged at his earlobes. "To the east, to the east!" they harmonized, pointing toward the sky. Nim thanked them, hurriedly gathered his belongings from around the campsite, and set out eastward at a run.

Many friends shared their fare with him and wished him well as he hurried along the roads and paths to the east. Prissy Lightfoot supplied him with waybread and lightwater before sending him on with a passionate kiss. Never before had she demonstrated her affection for him so clearly. Later his wandering cousin, Trotter Woodbine, gave him a fat, stuffed turnip baked with currents dulcetto as Nim hurried past his campfire in Wonderweald.

An Eldermeister Wanderer stopped him to admonish him against hastening east. "Haste makes waste," the old one said gravely, "and the waste of your time and training can scarcely produce the greatest good for our culture." Agonized by the loss of his best friend, he politely ignored the Eldermeister's warning and raced onward.

Although he was just 16 revolutions old, Nim was already tall, leg long, and strong. To his youthful stamina and vitality was now added the power of his compelling determination to find Musette.

His journey through the dismal forest known as Dreadweald robbed him of sunlight for three turns and forced him to camp twice in the grip of the forest's deep gloom. By the time he spied the sun glinting through a break in the trees ahead, the weald had secured a fearful grip on his soul and had nearly exhausted his ability to fend off the portending doom hanging over the place. But now, rejuvenated by the sunshine and the open landscape before him, he continued onward more cheerfully.

Just beyond a grassy knoll, an old stinkwadd squatted absently in the middle of the path. The beast picked its nose and belched as its leathery wings rasped in the morning breeze.

"A Stinkwadd." That's all I need right now!" Nim grumbled as he approached the repulsive creature. Its foul odor forced him to stop an arm's length from it.

"I must pass!" he said, almost reeling with nausea. The Stinkwadd grunted and glowered at him from under its sloping brow, but it remained motionless. They glared at each other.

The Stinkwadd dug deeper in his nose. "You may not pass," it grunted.

"But I must. I have to reach the rim before Stepshadow."

"Nobody crosses and lives. You're just a kid," it said, eyeing Nim from head to foot.

It shut its eyes, ignored Nim, straddled the path, and as if to punctuate the finality of his refusal, let go particularly musical flatulence that made Nim gag.

Nimrod knew what to do; Stinkwadds were utterly defenseless to the weapon in his rucksack. Nonchalantly he took a peanut butter sandwich from his rucksack and began eating it with an exaggerated display of pleasure. He smacked his lips, moaned with rapturous delight, and rolled his eyes ecstatically toward the lavender clouds scudding overhead. When the aroma of the peanut butter reached it, the Stinkwadd's bushy brows quivered and its tail began to twitch. A tear of intense longing welled up in the depths of one of its smoky eye sockets. The beast sniffed the air noisily and eyed Nim sidelong, first with one eye and then the other, all the while clawing at an itch on its scrawny backside.

Staring contemptuously at him, Nim took another slow, deliberate bite from the sandwich, then held it well away, as if to prevent the reeking creature from snatching it out of his hand. But he was wise to the heart of the Stinkwadd. He was certain that even the mere prospect of peanut butter would reduce this one to helplessness.

Overcome with unbearable desire and anticipation, the Stinkwadd collapsed tearfully. "I'll let you pass. Just a little taste. Please!" The words spilled shamelessly in a miasma of foul breath. Tremulous blue bubbles drifted out of its mouth and settled like grapes in the Gruttle bushes along the path.

"Oh, all right!" Nim muttered with deliberate disdain. "The rest is yours." Nim tossed the remainder of the peanut butter sandwich into a nearby shrub. With rasping wings and clattering claws, the stinkwadd fell awkwardly upon the sandwich with feverish intensity.

Nim seized the moment to resume his journey. Glancing over his shoulder a few moments later, he saw the beast lolling in ecstasy as its long, purple tongue snaked out of its mouth to lick his mustaches. "The afterglow of peanut butter, I suppose," Nim muttered as he continued on his way.

As Nim raced on toward the Lightbrink, the stillness gave way to little zephyrs that tugged at his cape, bearing sweet fragrances and birdsong. His heart lifted in the open spaces, freed from the pall of Dreadwood. He couldn't linger. He had to reach the edge before Moonflicker; otherwise it would be impossible to cross the Lightbrink today.

He had crossed a Lightbridge once before. But it had been a different one in a different place. Besides, Musette had been with him and had helped him negotiate the tenuous steps of the air stair. He recalled how she had bounded a few steps ahead to extend a helping hand to him. Still, their journey across that Lightbridge had been perilous and terrifying. Now anxiety welled up in him as he hurried toward another one, for this one he would have to cross alone.

The image of Musette suddenly loomed in his mind and stung his heart. She wore snug, gray leather pants, a dark jerkin, and a cocked hat sporting a little firefeather. She was a mouse, of course, and she was shorter than him by a head. Nimble and trim, with fine gray down on her face, and soft brown eyes set above an upturned nose and full pouty lips, she was as pretty as any girl in his eyes.

"If only she was human," he sighed. Then instantly he pinched off the thought for she was a mouse and they could only be friends.

Although Wanderers travel alone and need no one, Nim and Musette had wandered together for nearly two revolutions. She was good company, she made him laugh easily, and no better hunter or dodger could be found anywhere under the suns. But now she had been missing for four sleeps. Nim missed her and was worried about her, but he suppressed his fears and continued eastward.

He had been running fast for some time. The land rose and became rocky when suddenly he came to the meandering ridge that formed the lip of the void, a vast, deep chasm across which he knew a lightbridge had been thrown. Although no sign of the bridge could yet be seen, he knew it was the only way across the chasm to Eastover and Highharbor. And he knew that the bridge materialized only when the twinsuns touched the opposing horizons in their trajectories across the sky. Only then would the steps of the lightbridge be shadowed on the near and farside and then become visible.

It was legend that ancient Dreambuilders had built the Lightbridges out of mere dreams. That was why they existed only in the brief period of the day known as Stepshadow. At the first instant of Moonflicker and throughout the day, they not only disappeared from view; they became nonexistent. Only in stepshadow were they solid and real. Only then could one cross a Lightbridge, and then only by racing madly across it before its steps evaporated in the descending night. Those ancient builders must have been fleet indeed.

As he started toward the top of the ridge, Nim braced himself for the shock he knew he would experience when he gazed across the void. Yet the immense, silent panorama he saw from the top drew a cry of alarm from him. The breadth of the chasm was so great that even in the pristine sunlight he could make out only dimly the high, distant landfall he would have to reach before dark. Bordered by a broad sidewalk of velvety smoothstone, the void meandered snakelike across the landscape as far as the eye could see. It seemed to cut the world in half.

Momentarily overwhelmed by the sight, Nim sat down abruptly on the sidewalk away from the lip of the brink. Like a child who drops a rock into a well to see how deep it is, he absently lifted a fist sized stone and pushed it toward the void's edge.

The rock rolled across the smoothstone sidewalk and dropped over. He listened intently, but didn't hear it strike bottom. It vanished silently into the clouds below. His heart thudded at what he had to do.

Nim struggled to overcome the fear of crossing the immense chasm on a winding bridge of unconnected steps that might ultimately evaporate beneath his feet like shreds of fog fleeing the morning sun. He would plunge like that rock into the unfathomable depths of the void, his arms flailing the air and his screams of terror echoing down behind him. How long would he fall before he was dashed on the floor of the void? How many broken skeletons already lay there?

He dared not linger on the lip of the Void for even one full turn. The void was inhabited by nocturnal flying raptors called Void Kytes, which dined on flesh they ripped from the bones of those who elected to spend the night on the edge of the void. Besides, he simply had to find Musette, who by now was surely somewhere on the other side of the void. Faced with little choice but to cross the Lightbridge tonight, Nim heaved himself up and carefully walked the dozen steps down the ridge to the smoothstone sidewalk.

He stepped gingerly across the sidewalk and reeled slightly when he peered over the cold lip of the void. "One thousand long strides an ell makes," he murmured, recalling a verse from a didactic poem he had learned verbatim under a stern tutor when he was hardly more than a toddler. A wall sheer and as red as blood plunged many ells straight down from the toe of his boot to an immense bank of thick clouds roiling in the cold jaws of the void below. Looking across the void, Nim could see nothing except the sea of restless clouds and the hazy image of the promontory projecting over the void far to the east.

Nim sucked in his breath suddenly when he saw two Void Kytes circling lazily far away to his left. *If they see me, they can pick me right off the Lightbridge for dinner. Oh my!"*

Stepshadow was drawing near. The twinsuns, popularly called Mere and Pere, each of which was about to set where the other had risen that morning. At midday Nim had seen them appear to merge at the zenith, where it was believed that they kissed before beginning their descent to opposite horizons. The great, orange orbs approached horizontal equilibrium. Nim sprinted along the crimson rim, searching for a sign.

A deep, worn, grove in the stone led from a long disappeared path to the edge. It was set about on each side with circles symbolizing the twinsuns. This is it! Nim sat down quietly to prepare himself to spring onto the lightbridge the moment its first steps shimmered into existence.

He closed his eyes, summoned his developing powers of farsight and farhear, and imagined the bridge and the whereabouts of Musette.

He heard Musette's soft voice cry, "Be Careful!" The warmth of her unmistakable voice overwhelmed him with sudden sorrow. Within a few moments, he surrendered days of suppressed tension, grief and fatigue in a flood of hot tears. Then he settled quietly once more to await the appearance of the lightbridge. Exhausted from the days and nights on the road, and the overbearing life-sucking dreadweald, he dozed.

Moments later, Nim physically jumped as he snapped awake. For a few moments he had forgotten where he was and what he had to do. *Did I miss it?* Noting that the twinsuns were fearfully close to their horizons, he breathed a sigh of relief.

His question was answered when an obsidian cube the width of a span of arms shuddered into view just a step out from the edge of the sidewalk before him. He leaped to his feet and watched it pulse and waver feebly as it gained substance in the gathering twilight. Then step after step began to appear, the higher and more distant ones materializing as the twinsuns descended closer to the horizon. Finally an entire stairway materialized, extending upward and outward to the east as far as the eye could see.

Nim walked tentatively up the first several cubes. Persuading himself that he would remain safe so long as he concentrated on the next cube and ignored the chilling space around the cubes, he summoned deeper courage and stepped out. Terrified at first, he nearly lost his balance as he stepped to next higher cube. Then he started a rhythmic pace, and soon was sprinting cube to cube. Racing against time, he gathered speed until his stride had lengthened into a hard run.

He had no idea how the lightbridge would disappear when darkness arrived. After all, no luckless soul ever caught upon it at that moment had returned to tell. Would the bridge simply vanish like a pricked soap bubble?

His mouth burned with thirst, his lungs heaved for oxygen, and every sinew of his legs seemed to scream in protest. But it was too late to turn back or even to pause on one of the treacherous cubes for a little rest or food. The precipitous rim from which he had departed receded steadily behind him, while nothing but emptiness and the pulsing cubes lay shimmering ahead. He dared not glance down except to rivet his line of sight on the next several cubes he must scale as he pursued the fleeing daylight ever faster toward a destination as yet unknown to him.

Almost an hour later, after climbing ceaselessly to keep pace with the setting suns, he saw that the steps led to a rocky ledge shaped like a huge hand, its palm and fingers jutting over the void at a distance still far above him.

With the flaming crests of the twin suns about to slide behind the Edge and darkness rising fast from the ebony maw beneath him, Nim could no longer resist the compulsion to glance over his shoulder. He was horrified to see that the steps behind him were now melting into the encroaching dusk faster than he was scaling the ones still ahead of him. The great emptiness produced by the disappearing steps was catching up to him with terrifying speed.

Time and light was running out. Instead of receding behind him before disappearing, each step from which he leaped evaporated just as his foot sprang away from it. He was two strides from the rocky ledge when the final step before him suddenly shuddered like a stone seen beneath a ripple of water.

With an anguished cry, Nim lunged toward the ledge, catapulting himself high over the shuddering last step just as it faded and vanished. He plunged to a jarring stop between the index and middle fingers of the stony hand extending from the ledge.

For several minutes he lay exhausted and immobile in the huge palm. He heaved for breath as perspiration stung his eyes and his heart thudded wildly. Not until he had recovered his breath and became aware of the refreshing coolness of the stone on which he lay did he sit up and look behind him.

He sat with his back against the stone, panting, staring at the route he had taken from the west rim. Below him yawned the unfathomable emptiness of the great Lightbrink he had just crossed, its billowing clouds far below, now umber smudges in the profound darkness. Both horizons were aflame as mere and pere's blushing rims dropped from view. Darkness advanced from the northeast, where the distant Nimbus began shooting its radiant shafts of swirling silver and gold across heavens dotted with skydiamonds and streaked with meteor showers.

Soon the lavender moonlight of the quadmoons, the four purple moons now clustered to the west, shone brightly enough for Nim to continue his journey. He ate a meager meal from the store of waybread, vigorsnaps, lipsweets, and assorted nuts, berries, and grains in his rucksack. Tiny sparkles of lightwater flickered through his waterskin when he lifted it to his mouth, and he was glad to find it still comfortably full.

It suddenly turned very cold. Nim shuddered, drew his cloak closer about his neck, and buried his head well under its cowl. Turning then to the alien, sinister land lying ahead, he set off through the soft lavender moonlight, his breath ghostly shreds of white vapor trailing aimlessly in the frigid night air.

ABOUT THE AUTHOR

uthor L D Sledge served as a Captain in the U.S. Army Judge Advocate General Corps as trial and defense counsel, practiced law in New Orleans, and was a courtroom lawyer in the capital city of Baton Rouge for the remainder of his forty three year career. He is now living well and enjoying his lifelong desire to write in Clearwater, Florida as a novelist and ghostwriter. Other books by the author: *Command Influence*, a riveting military courtroom thriller set in the cold war of the sixties and *Nimrod's Peril*, a wild and dangerous quest to rescue Nimrod's kidnapped traveling companion. Visit http://ghostwritersforhire.org, leave your address and receive a free copy of *The Melting Pot, A Cajun Cookbook.* Read free chapters each and buy these books as paperback or ebooks at http://ldsledge.com, at Amazon,or order through your favorite bookseller. See him on Facebook.

Made in the USA
Columbia, SC
27 January 2018